WAYS AND MEANS

WAYS AND MEANS

A NOVEL

DANIEL LEFFERTS

THE OVERLOOK PRESS, NEW YORK

Library of Congress Control Number: 2023936453
ISBN: 978-1-4197-6819-4
eISBN: 979-8-88707-032-2

Printed and bound in the United States

2 4 6 8 10 9 7 5 3 1

This book is a work of fiction. As is true in many books of fiction, this
book was inspired by events that have appeared in the news. Nevertheless,
all of the actions in this book, as well as all of the characters and dialogue,
are products solely of the author's imagination. The names of some
real people and companies appear, but they are applied to the
events of this novel in a fictitious manner.

ABRAMS The Art of Books
195 Broadway, New York, NY 10007
abramsbooks.com

To my parents

"There is much to be said for giving up such grand ambitions and living the most ordinary life imaginable, a life without the old longings."

—Walker Percy, *The Moviegoer*

CONTENTS

PART ONE

THE BLUE LIGHT

THE FIRST THING Alistair thought about was the money. At seven that morning he'd left Palladium and marched to the Citibank ATM on Union Square. The total in his account was $600 and change, even less than he'd figured. If he'd known he'd have to flee the city and disappear he would have been more economical in his spending. But you couldn't give a poor student $10,000 a month and expect him to be entirely shrewd, even if he's a finance major who's spent four years learning how to be shrewd if nothing else. It seemed appropriate, in light of this, that he wouldn't even get his degree.

When he'd returned to his dorm, cash in back pocket, he'd stood dumbly in his room, wondering if he could overdraw his checking account (he knew he couldn't), wondering if his credit card had a cash-withdrawal option (he knew it didn't). Mostly he was buying time, another thing he couldn't afford, until he had no choice but to accept the obvious. Before he left the city he would have to pay a visit to Mark Landmesser and Elijah Pasternak, the couple whom he'd been sleeping with for the better part of a year and whose relationship he was all but certain he'd destroyed.

The night before, after cutting his ties with Nikolai and accepting his final payment from him, Alistair had met up with the couple, hoping to mark the end of his dark days with mind-voiding carnality. Mark and Elijah knew little about Alistair's job, but Elijah had proposed going out to honor the occasion—in Elijah's mind quitting a job was more of a reason to celebrate than getting one—and, given the unseasonably warm May air, Alistair had left his jacket, containing his last $10,000, on their couch. At dinner, though, rather than toasting him, Mark and Elijah fought, fought like they never had, and after the bill had been paid Alistair judged it too indelicate to return to their apartment for his cash. He figured he'd go back when the smoke had cleared. But when he returned to his dorm he found Nikolai on the street, waiting for him, walking back and forth beneath the NYU flag. He told Alistair that the groundskeeper was dead, that they were surely next, and that they needed to vanish immediately.

"Keep it on," Nikolai said, referring to Alistair's burner. "I will find you soon. I will come up with a plan. Oh—my friend!"

"Where am I supposed to go?" Alistair said.

"You ask me?" Nikolai said. "What do I know? This is your country! Your crazy fucking country!"

Before Alistair could think to ask him for anything, Nikolai turned and walked off down the street.

He still hadn't decided where he'd go. Their boss, Herve, had extended his operation far and wide, and he had people everywhere. Alistair's plan was to get on a Greyhound to California and get off at whatever place seemed halfway suitable for lying low. But no matter where he got off he would need, he was sure, more than $600 and change.

He paced his tiny bedroom in Palladium, five floors above Fourteenth Street. He checked the time—eight-thirty, too soon. He needed to head off any nosiness about his sudden departure, and if he called the men too early and asked after his jacket with undue desperation they would certainly nose. Plus, having worked barely a day in their lives, Mark and Elijah tended to sleep late.

He went to the window and looked up at the sky, into the windows of the office building across the street, down at the sidewalk. The day was bright, the century young, the city rich, the trees abloom. From below came the familiar indecipherable din of cars, cyclists, buses, workers careering their way east and west, each trailed or preceded by a morning-long shadow, each figure appearing from Alistair's vantage happy, unguilty, free. He looked at the old Consolidated Edison Building across the way, at its colonnade and its clockface. Every night the tower's electric blue glow shone through his blinds. For years, as he'd drifted off to sleep, Alistair had projected all manner of desires onto this light, had organized all manner of erstwhile cathexes around it. But the light was extinguished now, and, along with it, possibly, him.

He stood over his desk and composed a note to his roommate, who'd left already for their Financial Modeling seminar.

Vidi—

I'm going on a work trip. Can't-miss opportunity. Won't be back
for graduation. Good luck at Morgan Stanley (not).

Alistair prided himself on having lied not too outrageously. He really was
going on a work trip, insofar as he wouldn't need to go off the grid if it weren't
for the work he'd been unwittingly drawn into, and he really did have a can't-
miss opportunity to avoid being exterminated by Herve.

He began packing. He planned to leave behind enough of his possessions to
give credence to his work-trip story but not so many as to overburden whichever custodian had to clean his room. He'd leave behind most of his toiletries
and the majority of his clothes and shoes. He'd leave behind his textbooks.
Advanced Corporate Finance, Investments, Distressed Securities, Risk—these
would be of no help to him now.

He opened his JPMorgan Chase duffel and loaded it with clothes. He
wished he had a different bag to use. After he'd left his internship at the bank
the previous summer, in his offerless shame, he'd buried the duffel at the back
of his closet and pledged never to look at it again. But his only other piece of
luggage was a large suitcase his mother had given him as a high school graduation present, and he couldn't bear rolling around so cumbersome a reminder
of her, and he thought it best to pack lightly.

He had to call his mother, of course. But the task of heading off *her* nosiness, of navigating the laser maze of her skepticism and worry—of, maybe,
talking to her for the last time—was so daunting that he hadn't let himself
really contemplate it, not yet.

He laid in polo shirts, button-downs, chinos, half zips. He would have liked
a cruddier, more attention-deflecting getup, but all he had was his Patagonia,
his Brooks Brothers, his Club Monaco. He loved this wardrobe, had put himself
in debt to amass it, for the very reason he knew it would serve him poorly as
a fugitive: it made him bright, made him conspicuous, made him seem like a
someone (or rather like an everyone else, but in the most enviable way). He
needed clothes more nondescript, drab, unimposing, more befitting of his actual
economic station, of the lower-middle-class nothing he'd taken every step over
the past four years to leave behind. Instead, wherever he went, he would look

like the finance bro that he was, or that he'd wanted to be. Who he was really, who he wanted to be now: these were questions he would deal with later.

When he finished packing he sat at his desk and opened his laptop. He looked for a last time at his student loans: $100,325. (Alistair found it cruel that a mere three-hundred-odd dollars should mean the difference between his being five figures and six figures in debt. The distinction between these orders of magnitude was too psychologically enormous to be decided by so piddling a sum.) One incidental benefit of disappearing, he'd realized that morning, was that he would no longer be responsible for his loans. He was free of his debt, free of it! For how long had he dreamed of this day? Yet his reprieve brought him none of the joy he'd expected it would, and his impatience for it, his fixation on it, now seemed to him myopic and mean. Cancel your debt, lose your life: he seemed to be living out the definition of a Pyrrhic victory.

He checked his work email: connorblack@phakelos.com. (Alistair had come up with this alias by combining the names of his two favorite porn stars, Connor Maguire and Vadim Black, who, because the world was a cruel and godless place, had never been in a scene together.) He scrolled past emails from his likewise aliased confreres until he reached the last message the groundskeeper had sent. Next to the empty subject line ran a snippet of preview text: *Last warning. And if you think I'm making an empty threat, then you are so fucking sadly*

In a new tab he navigated to the groundskeeper's obituary. He realized for the first time how similar the man's name was to his own, and as he stared at the photograph, a formal Army portrait, he saw afresh their resemblance: blond hair, blue eyes, an expression of doomed Rust Belt naivete. He scanned the text:

. . . passed away unexpectedly . . . donations may be made to the Veterans Mental Health Crisis . . .

Utter bullshit.

All Alistair could remember right now was the groundskeeper's fidgety niceness. Yes the groundskeeper had blackmailed him, yes he'd gotten himself in deep shit and dragged Alistair and Nikolai into it too. But in the end he was just an upstate kid looking to save his life by taking money from people who had too much of it, and Alistair understood this. In truth there was nothing he understood more.

He was about to return to the groundskeeper's email, with its nightmarish images, when he stopped. He didn't know much about the technological prowess of Herve or his minions, but if they could hack into his computer and determine his whereabouts they would surely try to do so now. He leaned away from his desk, stiff-backed, and picked up his phone. He could wait no longer.

He called Mark. Elijah was all jokes, enthusiasms, curiosities: he would ask why Alistair needed his jacket so urgently and, after the blowup at dinner the night before, he would likely inveigh against Mark, trying to solicit Alistair's partisanship and affirmation, taking up precious time. Mark, by contrast, was all facts and short sentences: he would let Alistair into the apartment, he would give him his jacket, he would say goodbye. They were always like this with each other, Alistair and Mark. Their reticence was a measure of all the things they wanted to say to each other but didn't know how.

Mark and Elijah had introduced Alistair to Nikolai, an acquaintance of Elijah's old art school friend Jay, knowing only that Nikolai did something finance-adjacent and figuring that he could give their down-on-his-luck boy toy career advice. Since then the men had shown minimal curiosity about Alistair's job, retreating instead into their sundry petty dramas. If this had irked Alistair before, if it had struck him as evidence of their self-absorption, he was grateful for it now. The less the men knew the better, and they knew next to nothing.

Mark answered after two rings, short of breath.

"Sorry," Alistair said. "Are you busy?"

"Hold on," Mark said. He lowered the phone and made some shuffling sounds. "I'm packing."

"Packing?" Alistair said. "For what?"

Mark was still catching his breath. "I think last night settled things for me."

"Where are you going?"

"Home. New Jersey."

The Landmesser Palace, as Elijah called it. "For how long?"

"Not sure," Mark said. "But I'm not renewing."

During their fight the night before, Mark had threatened not to sign the June 1 renewal on their two-bedroom in the Eros Ananke, the blandly luxurious tower on Cooper Square where he and Elijah lived, entirely on Mark's dollar. But amid the hundred other ultimatums and aspersions Mark and Elijah had exchanged, while Alistair had bowed his head and tried to stopper his ears, no single one, and certainly not this one, had sounded particularly consequential. "You're not serious."

"I think I am," Mark said. "Maybe I'm not just a—how did Elijah put it—a suckling pig—something?"

Stuffed to death with his own money. When Elijah wanted to he could really draw blood. "Maybe you two just need a break."

"I guess we're about to find out."

Alistair imagined the men's apartment strewn with boxes, piles of clothes, the contents of disgorged dressers and shelves. He imagined his jacket, his envelope, his $10,000 in cash, getting lost amid so much upscale flotsam. "Is Elijah there?"

"Gone," Mark said. "Fled to Jay's. Naturally."

Jay Steigen: his center part, his braces, his imperious gaze, his adolescent laugh, his empty contradictory provocations—Alistair couldn't imagine anyone ever going to him for comfort. But then Elijah's inclinations, his perverse affections and fascinations, had always puzzled him. He tried to think of a delicate way to broach the subject of his jacket, but Mark saved him.

"I'm glad you called," he said to Alistair. "I was hoping to see you. Before I left."

Alistair felt an illogical parental worry on Mark's behalf. He was thirty and had seemingly limitless family money. Surely he could manage his own affairs or pay someone to manage them for him. Nevertheless Alistair wondered if he knew how to pack a box, hire a mover, terminate a lease. He'd offer to help if he weren't running for his life. "Can I come now?"

"I'm a little sweaty," Mark said.

"I've seen you sweaty," Alistair said.

Mark gave a laugh, a single rueful exhalation, more like a sigh. "I'll be here."

After he hung up Alistair brought his laptop to the bathroom, ran it under the faucet until its screen went black, then stowed it in his desk drawer. He shouldered his duffel and looked at his suite, said goodbye to its bare walls and specked-tile floor, and headed to the elevator.

Downstairs he rushed out of the lobby and turned left toward Broadway. Technically it would be faster to take Third Avenue, but his hours in the city were numbered, and he wanted to treat himself to a true thoroughfare.

On Broadway he found a sidewalk dense with workers in the final footrace of their commute. He held his duffel to his side snugly, weaving, jostling, squinting in the brilliant morning sun. He kept to the curb, dancing around Citi Bike docks and volcanic islands of black trash bags. For a moment he forgot himself, forgot his emergency, forgot his panic, and zeroed in, as he always did, on the most fuckable men. He noted a tan bearded guy in a trim navy suit, two gazelles wearing black workout tops and leggings, a beefcake staring red-facedly into his phone. He spotted a twink who caught his eye and smiled. After a moment, though, his panic returned, and as he passed more men he became more worried that any one of them might be a lackey in Herve's employ, a hired gun who'd been informed of his general movements and whereabouts and was now set on finding and disappearing him. He began to cruise with a new, terror-inflected purpose. He realized that keeping an eye out for potential assailants and seeking out biceps and succulent backsides were in effect identical activities: that he registered perusers and possible pursuers with the same hyperacute focus and the same libidinal force. It was as if his suspicion had, like a parasite, taken over the mechanism of his desire.

In his paranoia he shifted his attention to objects. He cataloged various instances of material splendor. He counted two Burberry jackets, two Moncler puffer vests, one pair of Persol sunglasses, three Goyard totes, and, on the street, four BMWs, two Range Rovers, and one Porsche. The buildings on either side gave to these objects a kind of vertically oriented velocity, a sense of accumulation and futurity, a climaxward charge. For years Alistair had subsisted on this charge, harnessed it to fuel his studying, working, fucking, fantasizing. But where in the end had all his dreaming led him? To a Greyhound. To nowhere at all.

He passed a woman wearing a Hillary pin and, a little later, a man wearing a STRONGER TOGETHER T-shirt and both times looked away. As much as this overearnest swag reassured Alistair—that Clinton was unstoppable, that she would squish Trump handily—it also rattled him. The last thing he wanted to think about right now was the election, increasingly the only thing on anyone's mind. Best to keep his eyes on the sky: an errant cloud, a wind-smudged contrail, the spire of Grace Church, with its tiny sun-spangled cross.

He put a hand to his forehead, realized he was sweating, marched on.

As he was turning left on Eighth Street he felt his phone vibrating. He reached for it, worrying that it was Mark calling to rescind his invitation. But the caller wasn't Mark. And before it occurred to Alistair that his phone as much as his laptop would offer up a digital breadcrumb for anyone tracing him, before it occurred to him that he hadn't yet prepared his lie, he answered.

"Hi, Mom," he said.

"There's Alli," his mother, Maura, said. "How's Alli doing today?"

"Good, busy, on my way to class." His mind worked furiously, but nothing plausible came to him. He'd been hoping to call his mother later, after he'd had a chance to construct a halfway believable explanation for why he wouldn't be able to see or talk to her for a period of time he couldn't specify. But who was he kidding? No such explanation existed, at least not one Maura would believe.

"Which class?" she asked.

"Futures and Options." In fact this class had started a half hour ago.

"I'm assuming those words don't mean what I think they mean," Maura said.

"They're types of derivatives contracts."

"So no."

Alistair heard the sounds of the SUNY Binghamton campus around her: trees shivering in the breeze, voices on the footpaths, possibly the pock of a serve on the nearby tennis courts. Maura worked as an administrative assistant at the university's admissions office. She took every opportunity to step outside, breathe unfiltered air, abandon her needling colleagues, and call him. For the last few months, though, their conversations had become strained, punctuated by silences. Maura didn't know what Alistair's job entailed, only that she hated his secrecy around it and the profligacy it inspired in him, and she didn't quite believe that he'd quit the job, as he'd told her he had, just as she was sure not to believe whatever fabrication he was soon to cook up for her.

"I guess you're in finals season," she said.

"Don't I know it," Alistair said. He made to cross Lafayette Street, in violation of the orange Stop hand, then jumped back at the blare of a truck horn.

"And how's the job hunt?" she asked. "Any leads?"

Alistair suspected this question was mainly a test of his assurance that he'd extricated himself from his previous mysterious employment. When it came to his future his mother didn't care whether he landed a good job or made good money: she cared only whether he was good. He crossed Lafayette, scurried around the Astor Place Cube, and set off down Cooper Square. He tried to suppress his heavy breathing. "I'm taking things one day at a time," he said.

"Well, I'm certainly on board with that."

Maura had never understood Alistair's ambition. She resisted his obsession with money, she resisted his interest in a profession that she fuzzily judged to be evil, she resisted most of all his insistence on doing well for himself so that he could do right by her. Alistair's father had died when he was six, and almost ever since then he'd exerted himself in the hope of one day supporting Maura, giving her a better life, rescuing her from her sad widowhood and all-but-poverty, whisking her away from the admissions office, away from Binghamton, for which she was much too smart, much too pretty, much too special. Now he'd failed, utterly and irreversibly.

"Are you OK?" she asked. "It sounds like you're running."

"I am running," Alistair said.

"Are you late?"

"I really hope not." Mark and Elijah's building rose before him, a bluish glass obelisk soaring frictionlessly into the sky.

"You sure you're OK?"

"Yes," Alistair said. He listened all the more keenly to the background sounds around her: a coach's whistle, cars cruising along campus roads at leisurely speeds, birds chattering in branches. As a rule Alistair thought of Binghamton as a postindustrial sinkhole that it had meant everything to him to escape. Yet there was no place he'd rather be right now than his hometown, three hours north and worlds away from New York City, no one he'd rather be with than Maura.

"I'll let you go," she said. "You'll call me later?"

"Yes," Alistair said.

"You promise?"

"Yes!"

"Love you."

He said he loved her too and hung up.

At the Eros Ananke he gazed up at the fourth floor and located, in a corner window, the silhouette of the other person he was about to lie to, the other person whose heart he was about to break. He could see Mark's broad shoulders, his tousled hair, his sturdy jaw, his endearingly rigid posture. He was waiting for Alistair, faithfully as always. After today he'd be waiting for a long time.

"I'm sorry," Alistair whispered to himself on the sidewalk.

He crossed the street, breezed into the lobby, and gave the doorman his name.

Mark stood at the window, looking down Bowery, waiting for the blond wonder, the improbable object of his desire, resplendent—Alistair McCabe.

He'd woken up shortly before seven, though to say he'd woken up would be to overstate seriously the depth of his sleep. Really he'd spent the night replaying his argument with Elijah. He'd run through Elijah's attacks on his impotence and passivity, he'd run through his counterattacks on Elijah's hypocrisy and sense of entitlement, he'd pictured Alistair's look of petrified embarrassment. He seemed to believe that if he stayed up long enough and went through the script enough times he could solve the mystery of his unhappiness. It didn't escape his attention, as he fought off dreams, that one of Elijah's more memorable charges against him was that he'd slept his life away.

After they'd returned from the restaurant Elijah had made clear, with quick imperious gestures, that he would be spending the night on the couch. When Mark had finally sat up in bed and looked at his phone he'd found a text from Elijah saying that he'd gone to Jay's and would be back that afternoon ("maybe"). In another era, one more suited to Mark's temperament, this message might have come in the form of a physical note and possessed the romance of longhand. Instead the text appeared between a news alert about a proposed monument to the gay rights movement and another about a body that had washed ashore in Brooklyn with its feet submerged in concrete. Mark had swiped away the alerts along with the text and decided to leave New York City.

In the three hours since then he'd frankly shocked himself by his resoluteness. Every step he took to realize his plan was a riposte to Elijah's contention that he was ineffectual and indecisive. He'd gone to the UPS store as soon as it opened and bought a dozen variously sized boxes. He'd hired movers, at a rush premium, to come for his things later that day. He'd called his mother,

Janet, and told her that he and Elijah needed a break and that he would be living at home "very briefly." He'd decided not to make much of the fact that she'd fielded this news matter-of-factly and without asking questions. Maybe it wasn't surprising that things between him and Elijah had gone south. Or maybe, for all her professed naivete on the subject of money, Janet suspected his reasons for giving up his apartment weren't strictly connubial.

He kept his gaze trained out the window, half in hope of spotting Alistair on the street and half in fear of facing the disordered room behind him. For all his adamancy he felt it hovering at the edges of his mind: a whimpering panic, a creeping regret, a weakening of his conviction. His life with Elijah had come to nothing, but this fact did little to shake his terrified sense that it was the only life he had any claim to.

Mark and Elijah had been together for eight years. They'd met in late fall 2008, when they were both twenty-three, at an East Village gay bar whose walls were painted Communist Party red. Elijah, having graduated with a degree in studio art from Vassar, was working as a graphic designer at a Midtown advertising firm. Mark—English, Hamilton College—was the oldest and least competent unpaid intern in the editorial department at the *New York Review of Books*. Some things Elijah and Mark bonded over that night were their enthusiasm about the newly elected Barack Obama, their inability to match quite the enthusiasm of their peers, their possession of jobs proximal to but in substance fatally remote from the careers (artist and writer respectively) they actually wished to pursue, their anxiety about the recession, their complete ignorance about its causes or the extent to which it would affect them, their tribe-betraying dislike of pop divas and drag queens, their fondness for gin, and their mutual gin-fueled opinion, which gathered force as the night progressed, that they'd just never met another person so fun and good-looking. In retrospect Elijah must have left the bar believing the boy he was going home with was a full-throated creative aspirant who shared his entry-level poverty. In fact, until Elijah's moony gaze had prompted an attempt to impress, Mark had never told anyone that he wanted to be a writer, and had given no thought to what a career as a writer, or any career, would even look like. And if Elijah wondered how an unpaid intern could afford the newly renovated West Village one-bedroom to which Mark brought him, he didn't ask questions.

For six months, there were very few questions. They accepted each other's circumstances and habits as only twentysomethings separated by a wide economic gulf can. Elijah spent fifty hours a week at his job and an additional ten hours airing grievances about it. He spent further hours complaining about having neither the time to paint nor money for a studio space. He sought refuge at Mark's apartment and availed himself of its comforts, its large liquor supply, the steady assembly line of fine takeout food that fed into it. Mark, after failing to receive a full-time offer at the *New York Review of Books*, tried to lend credence to his profession of writerly ambition by submitting to journals lightly revised creative writing assignments. He kept up with his dwindling supply of female friends from college and boarding school. He attended the noisy, energy-sapping, gastronomically repellent dinner parties that Elijah and his roommates hosted at their cramped, sticky Alphabet City apartment. He organized his weeks around every free, sexually exploitable hour in Elijah's schedule. Every chance he had to get his hands on Elijah's body, to bury his face in his ideally furred ass, to press his chest against his delicate back, he seized.

On the fucking front, they were certainly a match. What Mark didn't understand then, what he grasped only now, was that in the early days of their screwing they were fleshing out, quite literally, their future roles. Elijah knew the way to turn Mark on was to be sweet, reliant, impertinent, and pliable. Mark knew the way to turn Elijah on was to be sturdy, quiet, empty-headed if not quite dumb, and domineering. Evidently Elijah saw Mark as an all-American golden boy of mind-altering and will-demolishing virility. In certain heated moments he said as much. This surprised Mark, who'd never thought of himself this way, and who derived no personal meaning from his masculinity. His alpha male appearance was more like a costume in which he was shocked but largely content to find himself trapped. Something else Mark found surprising was the extent to which Elijah seemed to depend for his arousal on feelings of intimidation and even fear. He seemed, as he knelt, as he spread his legs, as he moaned, to be working himself into a state of awe, fascination, and worship. Mark suspected Elijah's desires and ideas about sex were more complicated and interesting than his own. He took this as a sign that for all his unproductivity Elijah was a genuine artist, or at least a more genuine one than he. And for all his surprise Mark fulfilled his assigned role, consented to be the power-wielder, the tab-payer, the pants-wearer: agreed to be, for lack of a better word, the man. He wanted Elijah, if for no other reason than he felt obligated to want something and knew of nothing else to want.

Rising from this strong foundation of sexual chemistry was their much flimsier shared identity as "artists." Mark told Elijah exactly nothing about what he wrote (a reflection as much of his shyness as of the fact that he wrote little), and the descriptions Elijah did offer Mark of the art he'd made in college tended to be too threaded with abstractions and defensive obfuscations to make much sense of. All Mark gathered was that Elijah had done a series of paintings at Vassar that had made him, for reasons they both agreed were dubious, into a pariah. The problem, he told Mark, was that he was still in the early phase of "building" his "practice," which involved "constructing" his "sensibility," which required large swaths of time. If he had a clearer grasp of his vision and purpose (and some studio space!) he could put his few free hours to better use. But to "construct" his "sensibility" he needed months, possibly a year, actually ideally a few years, of complete focus. Hobbling his progress, he said, was the fact that he had no real community. His one good friend from Vassar, Jay Steigen, had moved down to Richmond and in any case wasn't a "connection to brag about." His other artist acquaintances he mostly resented for having parental money enough to work part-time or not at all (this last point, Mark felt, was made with strained delicacy). Elijah's parents, both schoolteachers out on Long Island, could offer only their sincere, uncomprehending encouragement.

Mark listened and nodded and shook his head but couldn't sympathize: he shared neither Elijah's sense of urgency nor his financial pressures. And this made him feel guilty. He had an embarrassment of time but no genius, no afflatus, fueling him to take advantage of it. He had started a novel, based none too loosely on his years at boarding school, but on a typical writing day he spent the bulk of his time changing punctuation, auditioning different typefaces, and searching Thesaurus.com for simpler, less vampiric word choices. In sixteen weeks he wrote twenty pages. Mostly he read premodernist novels, went on walks, and lived in his head. He began to suspect that he'd designated himself a writer only because it was the most obvious occupation for someone who liked to read novels and who lived in his head—qualities that did not seem to him particularly unique and certainly not unique to professional writers. He began to suspect that he was an ordinary person who would be leading an ordinary life if he didn't have money and that Elijah was an extraordinary person who would be leading an extraordinary life if he weren't broke. He wondered if the least he could do, while he wasted his potential, was lend a helping hand to Elijah, who was certain to nurture his own. And so, one night, at the end of six months, he disclosed some information that Elijah had surely been trying to suss out. The information was that he, Mark, was rich, that he didn't work because he didn't have to, and that if he and Elijah, well, if Elijah was open to it—he shrugged, lowered his eyes, smiled with one side of his mouth and then snapped his lips flat—well, if Elijah was open to it, maybe he didn't have to work either?

That they didn't have to work at all was actually an overstatement, born largely of Mark's poor grasp of math. After Mark had graduated from Hamilton College, his father, Arty, had opened a trust fund for him in the amount of $995,000. Mark had known this money was coming to him. His older brother by two years, Eddie, had received the same sum upon graduating from Boston College. He'd also known the number was intentional, a lesson as well as a winning example of Arty's broad sense of humor. Arty himself had earned every dollar he had, and while he was happy to give his sons a lift he wanted them to be responsible, as he'd been, for crossing the million-dollar threshold themselves.

Arty was the founder and CEO of a chain of trailer parks ("manufactured housing communities," in industry parlance) called CommonWay. Mark knew little about the parks, only that the company had many of them, scattered across the country, and that despite the impecunious state of the people who lived in them they generated, in aggregate, a lot of money. According to guesstimates by Eddie, Arty brought home four million a year. The company itself appeared to be worth twenty times this. Mark was unsure, morally and logistically, why the meager lot rents paid by blue-collar workers and Social Security beneficiaries should make one family so very rich. Certainly, growing up in Ho-Ho-Kus, New Jersey, he'd been shielded from any unsavory details about the feudalist arrangements on which his comfort depended. Even after he'd gone to college, absorbed the progressive creed, and committed himself, if perfunctorily, to progressive ideals he found it hard to summon any serious opposition to his family's wealth. In part this was because all his life he'd been fed a saccharine and exploitation-excusing tale about a boy named Arthur Landmesser who'd grown up poor in Passaic, exercised shrewdness and discipline, and reaped the riches available to any hardworking American. In larger part it was because he very much wanted his trust fund. Leading up to graduation, as he wrote final papers on Henry James and Charles Bukowski, he worked through a maze of self-recriminations and defensive counterarguments that in time became so convoluted he could hardly make sense of it and that in any case led, when the day came, to his accepting his father's gift without reservation. After that, the only meaningful question was what to do with it.

For an instructive example of how to spend his $995,000 wisely, Mark could have looked to his older brother. Eddie was a private equity associate whose animating ambition was to achieve an equivalent level of success as his father and then, in oedipal fashion, surpass him. Upon graduating he'd sunk part of his own gift into a one-bedroom in Murray Hill and invested the rest aggressively. During the recession he'd taken a rather devastating loss on his positions, but in the time since his fortunes had risen along with the phoenix of the US economy. He was now the sort of mid-seven-figure millionaire who dated models and, when the spirit moved him, traveled by chartered plane. Being an investor with a proven track record as well as a supreme jerk, Eddie would have been glad to dispense condescending advice to his feckless little brother. But Mark hated Eddie, and he hated math and making plans, so instead he parked his $995,000 in his checking account and lived expensively without monitoring his funds.

Two years into dating, Mark and Elijah relocated to the Eros Ananke so that Mark could have a second bedroom in which to "write." In time this second bedroom became a mockery of his aspiration. He spent his days whipping up the courage to work, procrastinating, recovering from his guilt at having procrastinated, and running fifteen-minute errands for which he blocked off whole afternoons. Things weren't much different for Elijah. After quitting his job at the Midtown advertising firm he secured a small shared studio space in Gowanus, but he visited it infrequently and when he did he returned home with a dim, distracted expression that made Mark reluctant to ask about his progress. Elijah also set up a one-man, very part-time freelance graphic design business. Though he never asked how much money Mark had, and though Mark never told him, he appeared, by availing himself of this small income stream, to be hedging against the possibility that it wasn't illimitable.

Nevertheless, many of Elijah's daily expenses were charged to Mark's account. And though their outlays were substantial, and though he understood the basic principle of subtraction, Mark never agonized about the southward trajectory of his funds. On the semiannual occasions when he snuck a peek at them, the figure—$800,000-something, $700,000-something, $600,000-something—was always so large that it registered in his mind only as a hazy, nonnumerical muchness. And as the years went by and his and Elijah's problems mounted, this muchness came to feel like the one thing he could depend on, even as the figure hurtled inexorably toward zero. Amid all the things that troubled him—Elijah's failure to find his artistic footing, his own failure to do much of anything, the sputtering out of their sex life, the readiness and twisted logic with which they blamed each other for their unhappiness, the dawning realization that the roles they'd agreed to play were false and constricting and no longer sustainable, the steady existential drumbeat of time passing, years passing—this muchness was the one thing he didn't worry about.

Now, nearly a decade after they'd met, the fruits of this muchness lay in disarray around him.

So far he'd filled three boxes with clothes, four with books, and one with liquor. He considered the hand-cut crystal whiskey glasses but didn't feel like wrapping them. He considered the ebony-and-boxwood chess set he'd bought with the intention of learning to play but decided he didn't want to be taunted by reminders of his inertia (he suspected he would be taunted enough on this front at his parents' house already). He considered his various exorbitant kitchenware purchases but conceded that he hadn't actually used any of them—the exception was a sunset-colored Le Creuset Dutch oven that he'd once peed in when a diarrheal Elijah was camped out in the bathroom. He thought about the wall hangings but most of them had been Elijah purchases. He stared for a moment at the framed vintage poster of Leni Riefenstahl's *The Blue Light*, which for all the trouble it had caused him at Vassar remained Elijah's favorite film. Mark saw in Leni's expression an echo of the way Elijah had once looked at him: fearfully, with fascination, with awe.

He looked, for the hundredth time that morning, at Alistair's jacket on the couch. He went over to it and, for the tenth time that morning, raised it to his nose for a sniff. The jacket was a lesser Barbour but a recognizable Barbour nonetheless (olive quilting, gold press studs, brown corduroy collar), which may have explained why Alistair, who safe to say hadn't grown up with Barbour jackets, was still wearing it in May. Its scent was a rich olfactory concentration of the boy Mark had come to think about nonstop: he detected Old Spice, coconut shampoo, and sweat. He had the idea to bring the jacket with him to New Jersey, where he could raise it to his nose all he wanted. He brought it into the bedroom and stowed it in an open box of clothes, hoping Alistair wouldn't remember that he'd left it. When he returned to the living room he looked afresh at the havoc he'd wreaked and wondered what Alistair would make of it when he arrived, if he would be as surprised as he himself was by his resoluteness.

The sad fact, Mark knew, was that he and Elijah would have continued on in their way, spending and dithering and piling up resentments forever, were it not for three developments that occurred in quick succession and that altered irrevocably the delicate chemistry of their mutual hostility and dependence. The first was the arrival of Jay Steigen. Jay had come to New York the summer before on the dollar of Howie Gallion, a bashful North Dakota zillionaire whom Jay had met in Miami and who'd agreed to support Jay's art practice in exchange for some form of companionship that Mark tried not to think about. Everything Mark hated about Jay—his bloviating denouncement of the contemporary art world, his glib contrarianism, his merry insistence on ruffling feathers and bolt-stunning sacred cows—Elijah found perversely alluring. Elijah and Jay had begun to spend more and more time together and, despite Mark's repeated protestations, Jay had become a permanent, increasingly unbearable fixture in their lives.

The second development was Alistair, the bright-eyed wunderkind whom Mark and Elijah, feeling experimental, had invited home with them one night and then, in their sexless desperation, invited over again, and again. In time Alistair too had become a permanent fixture in their lives, but unlike Jay he'd found a way into Mark's heart: Mark had fallen hopelessly, relentlessly in love with the kid.

The third development was the inevitable but nevertheless staggering drying up of Mark's muchness. Some months before, the number in his checking account had finally dipped down into the five-figure range—had finally become, in other words, an actual graspable number—and presently he had only $50,000 left. At the rate he and Elijah were spending this was unlikely to last more than four months.

Mark was unsure which of these developments had provided the most fuel for his argument with Elijah the night before and was providing the strongest motivation for his decampment to New Jersey now. But he wanted to believe he wasn't leaving only because he was running out of money. He wanted to believe he was leaving too out of a refusal to brook Jay's provocations any longer. And he wanted to believe, even more, that he was dismantling his life with Elijah as a way of making room for Alistair. He wondered if he'd have the courage to tell Alistair this, to make so unprecedently bold a gesture, when he arrived.

He was laying the ebony-and-boxwood chess set in an empty box, having decided another taunting reminder of his inertia wouldn't be the worst thing, when the buzzer rang. He went to the intercom, pushed back his hair, and confirmed that his polo gave to his pecs a flattering if fictitious muscular slope. He tried to calm his heart.

When he opened the door he was surprised to find that Alistair was carrying a duffel, breathing hard, and sweating.

"Going somewhere?" Mark said as he let him inside.

Alistair lowered his bag to the floor. He nodded slowly before responding. "It's my mom's birthday."

Mark clocked the patches of sweat in Alistair's armpits, the dots of moisture along his shirtfront. It was warm out but not, he thought, that warm. "You won't miss class?"

Alistair's eyes passed over the living room, the couch, the boxes sitting at odd angles on the floor. "I'm done with everything," he said. His voice was soft, the edges of his sentences uncertain, as if he were choosing his words carefully or swallowing context. He wouldn't quite meet Mark's eyes.

"Done with Nikolai, done with school," Mark said. "New beginning."

Alistair considered this for a moment. "We'll see what's next."

"You'll find something soon," Mark said. "Any bank would be lucky to have you."

Alistair continued to dodge Mark's gaze. Ordinarily he was cocksure yet sweet, but now these characteristics seemed to have collapsed in on each other, canceling each other out. He was shy, distant. "I'll be OK," he said. "Thank you again. I really appreciate your help."

"Don't mention it."

Back in October, shortly after Mark and Elijah had met Alistair and ascertained that he was broke, they'd introduced him to Nikolai Daskalov. Nikolai was an employee of Howie's brother, Herve Gallion, whose fracking company, sold for some billions a few years back at the height of North Dakota's oil boom, was the source of Howie's wealth. Mark had never met Herve—he was reported to live modestly and reclusively back in Williston—and he wasn't sure what Nikolai's work for him entailed. It appeared to involve managing Herve's money and assorted oligarchic pet projects and, given that Nikolai lived in New York, keeping tabs on Herve's spendthrift, dissolutely homosexual little brother. Mark also wasn't sure how he felt about guiding Alistair toward a person associated even peripherally with Jay. But Nikolai seemed harmless, endearingly accented and antic: he and Mark often exchanged commiserating glances at Howie's dinners. And the job Alistair had ended up accepting from Nikolai seemed innocently administrative. If Mark wondered how Alistair felt about working for an earth-plundering plutocrat he resisted asking. When it came to taking money from the morally suspect he had his own compromised ethics to answer for. But he had divined some unease about the job when, the night before, he'd learned that Alistair had abruptly quit.

Alistair continued to scan the living room, the couch in particular. Clearly he remembered his jacket, but Mark found it doubtful that he'd come with the sole purpose of retrieving it. Maybe the room's disarray was making him nervous. "I'm thinking I might take a break from everything," he said to Mark. "Leave the city for a while. Check out."

Mark nodded at the boxes. "We're on the same page."

Alistair forced a laugh.

"Maybe it'll do us some good," Mark tried. If he was going to say anything to the effect of wanting to be with Alistair, or at least of wanting to entertain the possibility, he needed to move beyond pleasantries. "And maybe, when we come back, we can start fresh."

For the first time Alistair looked him in the eye. But all he did was nod.

Mark gestured for him to join him on the couch. Alistair sat primly, legs together and back straight, as he continued to scan the room. In his sweatiness, his odd shyness, his inexplicable anxiety he looked even better than he usually did, harder and softer at the same time. The light from the window caught his hair, gilding it, and made his eyes look like shallow swimming pools.

"So," Mark said, gesturing at the boxes.

"I guess you're really going through with it."

"You were there last night. You heard everything."

Alistair had heard it all. He'd heard Mark rail as never before against Jay, and he'd heard Elijah assert, with new conviction and hostility, that Mark hated Jay only because he envied him his "originality" and "daring." He'd heard Mark reply that Jay was neither "original" nor "daring" but merely a provocateur whose access to money gave his ideas a spurious heft and who in any case had nothing to show for those ideas. He'd heard Elijah reply in turn that if Mark wanted to throw stones at people who had access to money and nothing to show for it he should remember that he lived in a glass house. And he'd heard Mark answer, with withering scorn, that Elijah should know because he lived in the glass house with him. Alistair had heard it all, and as he'd squirmed in his chair and cast his eyes queasily around the restaurant he seemed to have registered that he himself was as much a subject of this argument as their artistic failures and their sick financial arrangement and Jay. Mark and Elijah competed for Alistair's desire, for his loyalty, his affection. They pawed at his body as a way of clawing at each other.

"Couples fight," Alistair said. "I'm sure you've had arguments before."

"Not like that," Mark said. "Simmering resentment is more our style."

"Well, so you were bound to boil over," Alistair said. An impatience had crept into his voice. He sounded not so much irritated as pleading. "Now you can reset."

"And start simmering again? For another eight years?"

Alistair shrugged weakly, with adolescent helplessness. Mark knew that Alistair's father had died when he was a child and that his mother had never remarried, and he sometimes wondered if Alistair's involvement with him and Elijah had been his most sustained exposure to a couple. "But you've put in so much time already."

"I'm aware of that," Mark said. "But I'm only thirty. I'm only half dead."

Alistair looked away, and Mark immediately regretted mentioning his age. For all the reasons he was attracted to Alistair's youth he was also intimidated by it. Alistair's vigor and ambition reminded him, with a titillating masochistic pang, of his own complacency. He also found his interest in Alistair's youth a touch creepy. Strictly speaking there was nothing illicit or even exceptional about his desire. But his fixation on Alistair's springtide suppleness seemed nevertheless to belong to the category of lust for which clueless johns and handsy gymnastics coaches went to prison.

"You're not dead," Alistair said. He was sounding more and more impatient, as if a bolus of feeling were rising in his throat. His eyes continued to dance from surface to surface, everywhere but Mark's face. "But what'll you do?"

Mark shook his head, seeing more clearly with every passing minute the foolishness, the futility, of his departure. "I'm hoping some time at home will give me an idea."

"Maybe you'll finally write."

"Maybe," Mark said. He loved how callowly oblivious Alistair was to how this *finally* sounded. "But I've been trying for a while now, and I've written barely anything."

Alistair couldn't resist a mocking smile. For all his youth he was formidably grown up when it came to work and money. Mark and Elijah had never made sense to his interest-calculating, internship-chasing, salary-negotiating brain. Another perverse aspect of Mark's attraction to Alistair was that if he reminded him of anyone it was Arty and Eddie. "And yet you don't do anything else," Alistair said.

"That's correct," Mark said.

Alistair continued to smile mockingly, and this heartened Mark. He was glad to be the butt of a joke if it meant Alistair could relax, stop scanning the room for his jacket, let down his guard, give him access to his deeper reaches. "I still can't wrap my head around it," he said to Mark.

"Around what?"

"Your life."

"It's simple," Mark said. "Imagine the last time you had a weekend when you didn't do any of the things you planned to. Now imagine that weekend lasting eight years."

Alistair's gaze softened. Despite the lower-middle-class chip on his shoulder he did seem to appreciate this about Mark: his unforgivable laziness. "What about Elijah?"

"What about him?" Mark said.

"What'll he do?"

"That's up to him."

"You're putting him on the street?"

"He's a grown boy."

Alistair seemed to gather more fully the direction of Mark's thought, and his forehead creased. "But you support him."

"I'll help him, while we figure things out, or don't," Mark said. He heard himself hedging: not quite making a break from Elijah, not quite committing himself to Alistair, not quite doing anything for fear of giving anything up. His life felt to him like a long series of not-quites. "But actually that's another complicating factor."

"What is?"

"The money."

"What's complicated about it?"

"It's gone."

Alistair was visibly startled by this—as Elijah would be, as Mark himself had been, however unreasonably. "Gone?"

"Going fast."

"How did that happen?"

"Apparently, if you keep spending and spending without earning any income, your money eventually disappears. This is something I've learned only recently."

Alistair spoke with a note of resentment. "Can't you just ask your dad for more?"

"I don't know if that offer's on the table," Mark said. "I think it would conflict with his views on personal responsibility. But I can ask."

"And if he says no?"

"Then I don't know."

"You'd get a job?"

"I guess that's the idea."

"What kind of job?"

"Haven't gotten there yet." Mark had gotten only as far as his arrival in New Jersey later that day. If he mooched off his parents he could keep his money at its current level while he plotted his next steps. He wasn't sure what capacity for planning or initiative-taking would present itself now that hadn't presented itself in the last eight years. All he was sure of was that he disliked these questions. They were the same questions, he knew, that Arty or Eddie would ask.

"I like the image of you working," Alistair said.

"Like as in find hilarious?"

Alistair smiled again, then looked away, and his pleading impatience returned. He seemed to want to leave. Mark worried that he'd divulged too many disorienting and unflattering details. He certainly wasn't making a very good case for himself as a potential suitor. He moved closer to Alistair and touched his knee to his.

"Don't worry about me," he said. "I'll be back soon. And you'll be back soon, right? And maybe, when we're back—" He trailed off. All the words available to him felt humiliating, dumb and sentimental distortions of the longing in his head.

"I think you and Elijah need to work things out," Alistair said. "I don't see a place for me in that."

"And if we don't work things out?"

"You will," Alistair said; and he seemed not entirely happy to say it.

"I'm not so sure," Mark said.

"You should try," Alistair said.

"Why?"

"Because you just should."

Mark hadn't expected Alistair to insist on his repairing things with Elijah, and his insistence didn't augur well for his diminishing fantasy of being with him. "I don't know if I want to," he said.

"Try," Alistair said. "And while you're doing that I think I should disappear." He tremored a bit, as if stumbling retroactively over his words.

"I don't want you to disappear."

Alistair tremored again. "I might anyway."

Mark took Alistair's hand. "Look," he said, "I know you and me and Elijah have our arrangement. He and I are one thing and you're—something else. I know we've all tried to be very careful about respecting boundaries. But I've known you for a while now, and feelings happen, and boundaries blur. And I've been thinking."

"Thinking?"

Mark trusted that what he was about to say wasn't surprising. He could as little hide his feelings as express them. "You have to know that I'm in love with you," he said.

Alistair stared at the hand Mark was holding.

"And I think you might love me too."

Alistair closed his eyes. When he opened them they were damp. Mark had never seen this emotion from Alistair, and he would have been glad of it if he didn't suspect, for reasons he couldn't pinpoint, that it had causes beyond the things they were saying.

"Have you ever thought?" he said. He felt himself moving his neck, as if testing the fit of a collar. "Have you ever considered?"

"Not now," Alistair said.

Mark nodded. "You're leaving. Checking out for a while."

"Maybe for a long while."

"How long?"

"Long enough."

They fell silent. Mark had an instinct to keep talking, explaining, preempting, convincing. But he felt he'd already said too much. In his effort to overcome his native shyness he'd taken on a gabbiness that was foreign to him and that he didn't much like. He felt embarrassed. He drew his thumbs over the back of Alistair's hand, he pushed at his palm with his fingers. The gentleness of this touch struck him as being worlds away from the tawdriness of their usual exertions, when they would pass Elijah back and forth as if he were a piece of gym equipment. Being intransigent tops they'd never been inside each other, had never forayed into each other's mucoid inner regions (regions as mysterious to themselves as to other people), had never summoned the will to let the other's will prevail, and as he explored Alistair's hand he felt that this touch, for all its timidity and for all the ribaldry of their past encounters, was the closest they'd ever come, really, to fucking.

Alistair took his hand from Mark's and resumed scanning the room.

"You're looking for your jacket," Mark said levelly, "aren't you."

Alistair widened his eyes and nodded uncertainly, as if he'd remembered only now that he'd left it. He was a terrible actor. "Where is it?"

"In the other room."

Alistair sprang up, but Mark stood and put out his hand. "I'll get it."

He went to the bedroom. In a delayed response to the utter failure of his proposal his heart began racing and his legs wobbling. He suspected he would be replaying this conversation weeks, months, years down the road, taunting himself with it on sleepless nights. He pulled Alistair's jacket from the box and raised it to his nose; its scent had already faded. As he was folding it and draping it over his arm his hand passed over an object, soft and bulky, in one of the pockets. He spent a moment in perilous, resentment-fueled consideration, then slid his hand inside. If Alistair refused him access to his deeper reaches then he would infringe on his privacy in whatever petty, irrelevant, meaningless way he could.

In the pocket was a creased, unsealed white envelope. Mark crept his fingers under the flap and pushed it up. Inside was a stack of green bills, all $100s. He estimated, with clumsy, lurching guesswork, that they added up to five, maybe ten, thousand. He could think of no other source for this money than Nikolai. But the work Alistair had been doing for Nikolai didn't strike him as the kind that paid in such large installments, or in cash—there was something dirty, déclassé, about this paper. He wondered if the cash explained, somehow, why Alistair had decided working for Nikolai wasn't his thing. But after a moment these thoughts subsided in the face of the signal one, the painful one. Alistair had come for his money. He'd come for no reason besides. While Mark had been making a fool of himself by professing his feelings Alistair had simply been biding his time.

He returned the envelope to the pocket. He went back to the living room. Alistair was standing by the front door, holding his duffel. He watched Mark approach as if he were a relay runner waiting for the baton.

"Here," Mark said. He made no effort to hide his indignation.

Alistair took the jacket. He moved his hand with attempted subtlety to the offending pocket and squeezed. "I think we both have a lot to think about," he said.

Mark gave no reply.

"If you don't hear from me for a while, it's because I'm thinking."

"I don't expect to hear from you."

Alistair's eyes were still damp. He moved his lips.

"Have a nice time at home."

Alistair looked at him fixedly, as if he were about to sketch him, and opened his mouth to say something. But then he dipped his head in goodbye, turned to the door, and left.

For the next hour Mark sat on the couch in silence. He distracted himself by making an intensive study of the sounds outside his windows: buses hissing, trucks gurgling phlegmily, planes keening as they crisscrossed through the air, carrying people and freight, facilitating exchange. When he grew too used to these sounds he turned on the TV. CNN was showing a clip of Trump speaking at a recent debate. Nothing could have suited Mark's masochistic purposes better, he felt, than the sound of this man's pitiless hectoring.

"Our country and our trade and our deals and most importantly our jobs are going to hell," Trump told the moderator.

Mark put his face in his hands. All his adult life he'd believed that deep down inside him lay the kernel of one greatness, one glorious offering, and that when he found it and formed it and brought it forth to the world it would make up for all his cowardliness, his paralysis, his passivity. For years he'd believed this gift was a book, and even as this belief had come to seem more and more delusional he'd held on to it for lack of any other object, any other bright light, to organize his life around. And then he'd met Alistair McCabe and decided he'd been wrong, his gift was plainer, his offering was his love. But Alistair didn't want this gift, and he had no one else to give it to, and he had nothing else to give. He'd been living in a fantasy, and now the fantasy was over.

"Our country is in serious, serious trouble," Trump said. "It's a bubble and it's going to explode, believe me."

Mark resumed packing. He waited with dread for Elijah's return. He did his best to push thoughts of Alistair away, but one kept nagging at him: not his disbelief at Alistair's hard-heartedness, not his undiminished yearning for him, but his sense, which rose like debris from his subconscious and emerged more fully as the minutes passed, that Alistair had been afraid of something.

———————

"You awake?"

Elijah opened his eyes. At the edge of consciousness he recalled a dream of the ocean. But what he'd taken for the sound of waves, he realized now, was actually the sound of Jay flipping pages. Jay was sitting up in bed, across the room, with some paperbacks and his gray five-subject notebook splayed before him. Elijah shut his eyes and pressed his face into the couch. He wanted to return to the ocean, to its salt, its sun, its cool uterine weightlessness.

"I'll get you coffee," Jay said, sliding off the bed. "With sugar! For my poor friend."

"Thank you."

Elijah sat up. He couldn't tell what time it was. Jay's studio, on the top floor of a Midtown walk-up, had only two windows and they both looked onto the air shaft. At all hours of the day it looked either very early or very late. "How long have I been asleep?"

"Since we graduated," Jay said. In the narrow kitchen off the living-room-bedroom, under the harsh white light of a naked bulb, he dumped sugar from a Domino cylinder into a mug. "You've had your beauty rest."

Elijah pieced together the preceding hours. He'd left his own couch at six a.m., taken a car to Jay's, spent some thirty minutes filling him in on his fight with Mark, and then, apparently, fallen asleep on another couch. He had a newly sharpened sense of himself as a vagabond, a supplicant feeding on others' hospitality, roaming in search of soft surfaces on which to lay his weary head.

Jay handed him the coffee and leaped back onto the bed. "The rest of us," he said, "can do with less sleep."

Elijah, in his grogginess, tried to smile reassuringly. Jay wasn't unattractive—in his way he was dashing, almost princely—but he wasn't exactly an ideal image to wake up to. He had penetrating blue eyes and a bony, angular frame;

he wore his sandy hair buzzed at the sides and floppy and center-parted on top, if only to give himself something to shake as he talked; and when his mouth wasn't hung open in boredom or arranged into an impish grin it was wrapped around his USB-chargeable vape. As of last summer he also had braces, though on this point he couldn't be blamed. During his childhood his parents had neglected to fix his mangled dentition and in his twenties he'd been too poor to do it himself. Only after he'd met Howie Gallion, a year earlier, and come into his patronage had Jay had enough money to see a dentist, but by then his teeth were too far gone for Invisalign—something about his incisors. He looked at Elijah now and smiled happily and metallically. He held up one of the paperbacks: Nietzsche.

"Your favorite," Elijah said.

"I don't have favorites," Jay said.

Jay returned to his notebook. He was always scribbling passages from things he read, jotting ideas, refining his strange worldview, more recently making notes toward his mysterious art project, which, like the braces, Howie had promised to pay for. Elijah was curious about the contents of the notebook— his curiosities were wide, impartial, varied—but he respected Jay's privacy, and he was somewhat scared to look at it.

"Listen to this," Jay said. He read a Nietzsche quote he'd transcribed. "*Untroubled, scornful, outrageous—that is how wisdom wants us to be: she is a woman and never loves anyone but a warrior.*"

"Very sweet," Elijah said.

"I think you misheard."

"Talking about the coffee."

"And this," Jay said. "*I am opposed to the pernicious modern effeminacy of feeling.*"

"I'm confused," Elijah said. "Wisdom is female—but female feeling is bad?"

Jay looked at the notebook with a crestfallen expression. He was thirty, he was fifteen: holing up in his room, flying out occasionally to impress and distress, balking at the unmoved faces of his listeners, racing back to his bed flustered and flushed. He pulled his vape from his pocket. A little blue light on the end of the pen glowed as he inhaled, then dimmed as he breathed out. "I see your point."

"I'm not smart enough," Elijah said. "You know this."

Jay flashed a silvery smile, half of pity, half of agreement. "You have other kinds of intelligence."

"Don't be so nice."

While Jay sank back into Nietzsche, whom he referred to as "the Neetch," Elijah sat forward and checked his reflection. He pushed back his dark hair, taking succor from its thickness. He reveled in his runner's leanness, the chiseled contours of his arms. He sat back and sipped his coffee. Who could begrudge him his vanity, he thought, when he had so little else going for him? Economically he was powerless, artistically he was a failure, intellectually he was a dim light: he knew this. But on this last point he felt a perverse pride, a limp and luxurious self-acceptance. He'd never had much interest in ideas. He liked colors, lines, feelings, sensations; ideas for him had a way of hardening these things, blanching them, drying them out. Why Jay, who pretended to intellectual distinction, had ever taken a liking to Elijah was a mystery, just as it was a mystery why Elijah had taken a liking to him. Half the ideas Jay spouted Elijah couldn't make sense of and the other half he urged him, with a hushing voice and flapping hands, to tone down. But he was content to let these mysteries be. He and Jay liked each other without quite understanding each other, and this seemed to him as good a foundation for a friendship as any.

He rested the mug on the floor (Jay had no tables) and went to the bathroom, which belonged on a blog about the horrors of Craigslist. Grouting black with dirt, irremovable rust stains on the toilet bowl, thin wooden shelves that looked to be held up by paint. He rinsed his face, ran a wet finger over his teeth, gargled and spat. He watched a cockroach scurry under the moisture-bubbled vanity. There was no logical explanation for why Jay lived in this apartment. Howie paid for Jay's life and as Elijah understood it the carte was blanche. Jay could easily ask for an upgrade; he could more easily live with Howie in Howie's penthouse a few blocks west. But Jay seemed to value his independence and he seemed to prefer his independence dingy, and Elijah both respected this and resented it (in Elijah's experience these feelings usually came as a pair). He sometimes wondered who he himself might have become, what he himself might have been motivated to accomplish, if he'd left Mark's plush nest and elected for a grubby monastic existence much like Jay's. If Mark followed through on his pledge to end their lease he would soon find out.

When he emerged from the bathroom Jay had put aside the Neetch and was waiting for him. He patted the bed but Elijah returned to the couch.

"Ready to talk when you are," Jay said brightly.

"There's nothing to talk about," Elijah said. "It's over. Even if he can't say it, even if he pretends all he wants is a break, it's over. And now I'm homeless."

"You really think he's serious about moving out?"

"He's very unhappy."

"Aren't you unhappy?"

"Of course," Elijah said. "But my unhappiness has no threat attached to it. My unhappiness has no consequences."

Jay sucked on his vape. He disliked Mark, if with much less fervor than Mark disliked him, and he clearly fantasized about a scenario in which he and Elijah palled around, free of commitments and attachments, like a gay Tom Sawyer and Huck Finn, as they had at Vassar. But he would never outright say this. He was delicate with Elijah if with no one or nothing else. "If Mark is as serious about ending the lease as he is about his writing," he said, "it'll take him two years to call a mover. And then another two years to book them."

Elijah had to concede that Jay had a point. But this depressed him as much as it reassured him. "So what, then? We stay together, making each other miserable forever?"

"Unless you decide your unhappiness does have consequences," Jay said. "If you're so unhappy you could leave, you know—of your own volition."

"I don't have any money," Elijah said. "And I love him."

"I'd encourage you," Jay said, "to consider the ordering of those sentences."

Elijah did love Mark, more than Jay knew, more than Mark knew, more than he himself cared to admit. But it was also true that the meagerness of his savings was a factor in his reluctance to end things. Every year his freelance graphic design work brought him somewhere in the vicinity of $20,000. Most of this, in an effort to shore up some sense of financial independence, he spent, and over the years he'd managed to set aside only $7,000. If Mark kept his word he'd be forced to find his own place, and between the security deposit he'd have to put down and the new furniture he'd have to buy and the cost of the movers he'd burn through his money in the first month, after which he'd have to ramp up his freelancing considerably just to keep a roof (he imagined a low, water-stained ceiling, bordered by nicked and overpainted crown molding, in some charmless corner of Brooklyn or, God help him, Queens) over his head. He resented the scant time he put into his job already. The thought of spending forty, fifty, sixty hours a week designing corporate slide decks, medical brochures, wedding invitations, personal websites, making sense of incoherent briefs and reliably grotesque "mood boards," fighting email wars of attrition with clients who knew everything about their "vision" except how to describe it, sitting in on meetings with skeletal marketing teams at poorly funded, badly conceived, nowhere-going startups: it made him want to drink bleach. He was content to do this work only as long as he didn't have to rely on it, only as long as it constituted a mere performance of self-sufficiency, only as long as it remained, in the time it occupied, secondary to his art, his failure to produce art notwithstanding. He was unhappy, to be sure, but he didn't trust himself to survive on his own.

"It just makes me sad," Jay said. "I think you're talented. I think you could be great. But I see you perched in Mark's apartment, like a parrot in a cage, and I wonder if he's holding you back."

"It's not his fault," Elijah said. "He's as supportive as anyone could be. If I couldn't make it as an artist with his support, I never will."

"I'm not convinced," Jay said. "He's a good guy, sure. I guess that matters to some people. But don't you think his support comes with stipulations?"

"Like faithfulness?" Elijah said. "Then how do you explain Alistair?"

"He wants you to be a good guy too," Jay said. "Clean and wholesome. When he brings you around his family he wants you in your polo shirt and khakis, commenting on the weather, complimenting his mother's canapés, clapping when his father taps the ball into the hole."

"Mark hates his family."

"He pretends to," Jay said. "All that queasiness about his father's trailer parks. You'll notice it didn't stop him from taking the money. I have no sympathy for people who pooh-pooh the supposedly evil enterprises that they're completely parasitic upon. Make your choice!"

When it came to Jay, here lay the rub: for every ten off-the-wall things he said, one stuck.

"And in any case he's just like them," Jay said. "Decent, decent."

"What's wrong with decent?"

Jay looked at Elijah questioningly, almost forlornly, and then shook his hair. "Has it ever occurred to you that Mark's support is dependent on your *not* succeeding?" he said. "That, if you made something brilliant, he'd resent you?"

"I seem to have made him resent me without making anything brilliant," Elijah said.

"That he wouldn't be able to stand it? The sight of you coming into your own?"

"I wouldn't know. I haven't come into my own."

"That's what I'm saying," Jay said. "I think you stay in your cage because you know if you leave you'll upset him. You think you'll lose everything. But what you'll lose isn't everything. I think you have much more to gain."

Elijah wasn't sure he found this line of reasoning persuasive. The more likely explanation for his failure was his terminal inertia. He'd dawdled, he'd dallied, he'd deluded himself with bedtime stories of artists who hadn't broken out until middle age. He hadn't shown in any group shows, not even crappy ones, he hadn't been strategic about making connections, he hadn't finished any of the projects he'd started. His only tenable path to success at this point was grad school. But he wasn't sure he could get into a reputable program, and he wasn't sure he could pay for it, and his memories of Vassar were still traumatic enough to make the prospect of returning to school repellent. Nevertheless he entertained Jay's logic for a moment. Undeniably there was something appealing about it. Maybe Mark was, in some subliminal way, responsible for his failure. And maybe this was why he clung to Jay: because Jay believed in him, maintained his faith in him, saw him in the light in which he most wished to be seen.

"Feel free to ignore me," Jay said.

"I always do."

"God knows it helps to have money behind you. And God knows Mark is nicer to look at than Howie."

Elijah had an instinct to check his phone. But he feared a string of messages from Mark, alternately hostile and repentant, or, worse, no messages at all. "Are you still—"

"Sleeping with Howie?" Jay said. "I only had to open sesame for him once. He prefers fresher fish. He's in Miami this week, baiting them."

Elijah raised his brow. Miami was where Jay had met Howie the previous spring, during one of Jay's annual impoverishing South Beach coke binges. Maybe he was a platonic beneficiary now, but before he'd impressed Howie and fulfilled his want of a poor artist to support he'd been merely another one of these fish too.

"He likes my *ideas*," Jay said, reading Elijah's skepticism. "He's excited about my project. He loves *the arts*. Terrible phrase—*the arts*."

Elijah had been reluctant to ask about Jay's project, even though he was curious, and even though Jay's leering interest in the upcoming election seemed to offer a strong enough hint. He liked Jay's eccentricities, his convictions, his effronteries. Jay loved spectacle, hated preciousness, enjoyed cruelty, disdained prudishness, pursued at every turn and at all costs every contradictory argument, even if it meant contradicting himself, prized interest over rightness, fascination over goodness, loved the world in all its nastiness, wouldn't want it to be any less nasty; and there was a freedom in this, Elijah thought, a perverse generosity. But he suspected his curiosity about Jay's project would shrivel at the moment he brought it to life. Elijah preferred to be tantalized, strung along, whetted but never satisfied. He preferred being curious to knowing. Every time he'd finally come to know something, know Mark, know Alistair, know himself, he'd been disappointed.

He couldn't resist any longer. He dug in his jacket and took out his phone. His screen showed just two alerts from the *New York Times*, his only news. He barely ever clicked on them.

Jay, seeing his wounded expression, slapped the bed. "Let's go to Howie's," he said. "The studio is all set up. I want to show you."

Elijah looked out at the dusky air shaft and, after a moment, shrugged in assent. At the very least, some sunlight would do him good.

Jay sprang from the bed and collected his phone from the floor. "I'll tell my dealer to meet us there."

"You have an *art* dealer?" Elijah said.

"Coke," Jay said. "Don't rush me."

They descended the six flights of stairs, edging around piles of mail and bicycles propped against the railing. Outside the sun was piercingly bright. They walked west, past Ninth Avenue, past Tenth. At every crossing the squat old blocks of Forty-eighth Street gave way to blazing height and modernity.

As they approached Eleventh they encountered a woman walking a German shepherd. Jay crouched down, looked to the woman for permission, and took the dog's jowls in his hands. "Pretty, pretty, pretty!" he said.

The woman looked at Jay warily, clocking his braces, his passé haircut, his disconcerting boldness. You could tell this about Jay without being able to attribute it to any one thing he did or said: he dismissed, while never quite breaking them, the laws of behavior that held society intact. In public Elijah took it upon himself to act as Jay's guardian. *I promise*, his smile to the woman said, *he's harmless*. They walked on.

"I love a dog that can kill," Jay said. "He sits, he stays, he waits for his treat. But his genes remember. Ancient aggressions course through him. It's a little like the gays"—he flicked Elijah's arm—"don't you think? They lie around listening to Diana Ross, drinking their vodka sodas. But they lift, they run. They have bodies made for war."

Elijah imagined how Mark would respond to this statement. Probably with the same bug-eyed inhalation with which he responded to all Jay's theses about gay men: that they were the cruelest human beings on earth, that this was the source of their beauty, that in their adoration of money and material objects they made for the ideal capitalistic subjects, that their instincts nevertheless went beyond this, that at bottom they were authoritarian, lovers of hierarchy and harsh rule, that in their irony and jollity they intuited the truth about the world—that it was unserious, all surface, all entertainment, all play. Such were the ideas that Elijah, flapping his hands, often urged Jay to tone down. He was sure Jay wasn't serious, per his own theory, sure he didn't understand the impact of his words. And such were the moments when he missed Mark's decency. When he was with Mark he longed for Jay's weirdness, his heterodox freedom, and when he was with Jay he longed for Mark's conformity, his humdrum goodness.

When they reached Eleventh they came to a stop. Jay ran his eyes up and down Howie's building, the Die Kinder, a forty-story dagger of shimmering blue glass, then looked beyond it, toward a shorter tower a few blocks south. "Should we pop in?" he said, pointing at the second building. "See your boy?"

The shorter tower was home to Nikolai Daskalov, Howie's brother's right-hand man. Herve had installed Nikolai nearby so that he could keep an eye on Howie, even though Howie never did anything reckless, except perhaps for enable Jay: he had the docility of a very old child. It was into this building that every few days Alistair had disappeared to toil at whatever work Nikolai gave him—every few days, that is, until now.

"Alistair quit," Elijah said. "He told us last night." He stared at the tower, admiring its small demure windows, its siding of homely cream and brick red. Unlike most new buildings in New York, unlike the Die Kinder certainly, it had no will to intimidate.

"That's a shame," Jay said. "I worry about Nikolai. I was glad he'd found a friend."

Alistair's work for Nikolai had been a mystery to Elijah, as much a mystery as Herve himself, the man behind the curtain back in North Dakota whose wealth floated here, like a majestic weather system, and rained money into Howie's pockets, into Nikolai's, Alistair's, Jay's. But Elijah had gotten the impression, the night before, that something had happened—a disagreement, a disappointment, a tedious business difficulty—that had prompted Alistair to make a clean break. What it could have been Elijah didn't know, and in truth didn't care to know. He had his own problems to worry about.

In the lobby they waited for the elevator next to a sitting area of Veblenian ostentation and inutility: Elijah suspected that whatever purpose these plush, ocher-colored couches were meant to serve the actual support of human butts wasn't it. On the wall above the couches was a rectangle of black-and-gold signage explaining the name of the building: THE CHILDREN (GERMAN).

"Whether you stay together or break up," Jay said as they stepped into the elevator, "don't you think you'll have to make a decision about Alistair? He seems to be—complicating things."

"We're past that point," Elijah said. "Mark is in love with him."

"As are you," Jay said.

Elijah watched the floor counter tick up with ferocious speed. For a moment he said nothing. He'd thought he loved Alistair, in the first months of their entanglement, but then he'd watched Mark fall in love with him and realized that whatever he felt for Alistair wasn't love. He'd made a fantasy of Alistair, a bright fearsome enchantment, but after the light of his desire had faded he'd been left with a college student whose emotions wearied him, whose anxieties irritated him, and whose preoccupations failed to hold his interest. Meanwhile Mark had swept in, laying himself at Alistair's feet, offering him a tender, unflappable devotion that depressed Elijah, not because he wasn't the object of it but because he didn't believe himself capable of offering it, not to Alistair, not to Mark, not to anyone. To watch Mark paw at Alistair, kiss him longingly, fall into a dreamy trance after he'd left for the night: it made Elijah feel broken. He answered Jay with a deflection. "Aren't we all a little in love with him?"

"Oh no," Jay said as they reached the top floor. "I don't fall in love with people. You have to be careful, if you're serious, about where you direct your libidinal energy. Always into the work, never into people."

In Howie's apartment Jay flicked on the lights, tiny recessed bulbs arranged in unintelligible asterisms. Beyond the double-height windows lay Midtown in all its late-morning splendor. Millions of people were hived out there, in conference rooms and open-office tracts at unnatural elevations, typing and clicking and meeting and chewing, but from this sanctified turret Elijah couldn't see or hear any of it.

Jay paraded around the vast room, affecting an air of easy authority and haute boredom. Elijah was amazed by how readily Jay had assumed the comportment of the ultrawealthy. His parents operated a T-shirt printing service in Delaware, he'd gone to Vassar on scholarship, as of a year ago he'd been living paycheck to paycheck in Richmond. It made Elijah wonder if all people, deep down, had a secret capacity to be rich, an inborn seed of ruling-class preferences and persuasions that at the first drop of real money bloomed and flourished, choking out all their former middle-class timidity. But as he walked farther into the room he registered his own lumbering comportment, his own stooped shoulders and lowered head, and he wondered in turn why in all his years of soaking up Mark's largesse no such seed had ever bloomed in him: why he'd never come to feel, as Jay had, secure in his privilege.

He followed Jay to the far windows and out onto the terrace. Up here the spring breeze was sharper and louder, and Elijah hoped for a moment of silence. But Jay's mind was still on his looming crisis.

"You know, there could be a bright side to all this," he said to Elijah. "If Mark wants a break, and Alistair is neither here nor there, then your path is clear. You have no other libidinal objects to distract you."

"When you put it that way," Elijah said.

"And don't pretend you're homeless. You can stay with me. Or here. Howie has spare bedrooms he doesn't even know about. I'll take care of you."

"I appreciate it."

"And I could use help with my project. Maybe you'll feel inspired."

"I'm sure I'll feel something."

"I have the money now to go big. Howie says he'll pay for a gallery space. He'll pay for PR."

"I'm sure."

"Point is, you're free now. You have an opportunity."

"To do what?"

Jay turned back to the windows. "You think about that," he said. "I'll get the studio ready." He stepped into the living room and shut the glass door behind him.

Elijah sat in a teak lounge chair, staring emptily at the city. As grateful as he was for Jay's loyalty and offer of lodging he resisted the power dynamic he seemed bent on constructing: he as the master and Elijah as the apprentice, he as the sensei and Elijah as the uchi-deshi. Maybe Jay had been "free" for eight years but it was unclear as yet what artistic fruits his freedom had borne him. After college he'd decided to move to Richmond, he'd said at the time, because of all American cities he believed it to be the most sin-ridden, the most bloodstained, the most evocative of the country's glorious, terrible past, and for these reasons the most conducive to the development of his "theme." At Vassar Jay had shown a preoccupying interest in American mythology and its happy susceptibility to campification and perversion. His senior thesis was a series of photographs reimagining the signing of the Declaration of Independence as a lurid gay orgy: wigged delegates rolling around on the floor and spanking one another with scrolls, the Adams brothers having their way with Thomas Jefferson as he composed, John Hancock sniffing poppers as he dipped his history-making quill. Elijah found Jay's interest in Americana trite, and he judged his photographs to be crass and gimmicky. But he sensed that, unlike most of their classmates, Jay had landed on an idée fixe, a distinguishing specialty, and he worried that when he moved to Richmond he would plow his conceptual furrow with persistence enough to find success.

He'd been relieved, then, to learn, via quarterly emails, that Jay was floundering as much as he was. (The strained boastfulness of these emails was the clearest proof of this floundering.) In Richmond Jay lived in a studio apartment in a former cigar factory that overlooked rusted train tracks and a muddy canal. To cover his rent he worked a series of dead-end jobs, the longest lasting of which was as a bartender at a cidery. The only paid artistic work he managed to secure, as far as Elijah knew, consisted of taking photographs and designing posters for an all-female, all-cancer-survivor bluegrass band called Nocturnal Remissions. But with what free time he had and what savings he was able to set aside he made a series of video artworks and short films, in which he cast various fringe characters whom he met at gay bars and whom he paid with cider purloined from his job.

The first of these films, made with a used DSLR (great lighting, terrible sound), was a thirty-minute erotic thriller about a young veteran who attends a meeting for gay male sex addicts under the mistaken impression that it's a support group for sufferers of PTSD. Its plot involved an orgy-turned-shootout at a VFW and its title was *Between Iraq and a Hard Place*. The second was a nearly feature-length work about a fictional town called 9/11ville where every year a group of Teamsters kidnaps and murders a fireman, policeman, or football player so as to keep alive the country's lugubrious idolatry of men in uniform. The third was a mock war documentary featuring men wearing Confederate uniforms and striking suggestive poses—several of the men unbuttoned their gray jackets to reveal leather harnesses underneath. There'd followed shorter, less narrative, and arguably more artistic offerings: a video in which a man wearing a plague doctor mask reads from the "lost" sex diaries of John C. Calhoun, a video in which a man with a swastika tattoo plays Fuck, Marry, Kill with various trios of American presidents, a video in which a drag queen recites the South Carolina Declaration of Secession, her voice autotuned à la late-'90s Cher.

Every time Jay finished a film he sent a link to Elijah, and every time Elijah watched with the same mixture of embarrassment, horror, and reluctant interest. Whatever else could be said or not said of Jay's films they were unlike anything Elijah had seen: bizarre, politically incendiary, gleefully assaultive. Elijah told himself that if he was drawn to Jay's work, if he sometimes watched his films twice and even three times, it was only because he was an uncompromising aesthetic connoisseur. He wouldn't be a good student of art, let alone a good artist, if he weren't always on the lookout for fresh images, provocative sensibilities, instincts that offended, as Jay's certainly did. He had his own streak of perversity, and though he'd committed himself to suppressing it, though he'd spent the years since his humiliation at Vassar playing nice guy with Mark and distrusting his aesthetic tendencies, he took vicarious pleasure in watching his friend let his own streak run free. He never said any of this to Jay, of course. He limited his responses to stingy monosyllables: *Yikes! Huh! Wild!* And he always ignored Jay's recurrent closing question: *So,* Jay would ask him, *what are you working on?*

Elijah had no good answer. The only differences between him and Jay were that he was wasting away in loftier style and that for all his free time and material security he was failing to produce even shoddy work. The real miracle was that as the years went by he held fast to his dream of becoming an artist. Against all evidence to the contrary he still believed he had it in him. But he didn't say this to Jay, because he knew it sounded lame and because he knew it wasn't an answer to his question.

Growing up in Brookhaven, Long Island, Elijah had been fed a heavy diet of artistic encouragement. His parents noticed early his adeptness with markers and crayons, the discernment with which he helped select wallpaper or arranged objects when making cyanotypes, and they did their best, with their limited means and their limited understanding of art, to foster his talent. They themselves often spent weekends stripping and staining salvaged furniture, making valances out of discount fabric, and daubing sunflowers onto gallon jars for iced tea. He was taking after them! Perhaps because his parents were schoolteachers practiced in indiscriminate reinforcement, and perhaps because questions of quality would expose them to doubts about the worthiness of their own Saturday creations, they met every artistic offering Elijah produced with the same cheerful, all-purpose appraisal: "amazing." Every drawing he made, every papier-mâché sculpture he built, every painting he presented at his school's art show: "amazing." Their approval was like a washing machine that turned everything you put into it the same pastel shade of "amazing." Elijah leaned on his parents' support and loved them for it. But once every month the family packed itself into its Pontiac and drove into the city to go museuming, and along the road to the Long Island Expressway, in a wooded section of Yaphank, were a fire academy, a police station, a probation office, and a jail: austere, forbidding buildings, set back from the curb and cloaked in shadows, that sent a titillating, reproaching chill down Elijah's spine. He came to sense that the path to great art was paved not with "amazing" but with something darker, more mysterious, more alien and more menacing, and he came to believe that all great art had to account for this fact.

In his first years of college, though, he failed to produce anything that did account for it. His specialty at Vassar was harmless, idealized paintings of beautiful men. He painted beautiful men on beautiful beaches, beautiful men in beautiful gardens, beautiful men standing on beautiful promontories looking with beautiful emptiness at beautiful vistas. Insofar as he was required to provide a theoretical justification for this work he invoked the pioneers of undisguised homoeroticism: Henry Scott Tuke, Ludwig von Hofmann, J. C. Leyendecker, David Hockney. But even as a stupid undergraduate he was smart enough to know that the societal constraints under which those artists had operated no longer held and that it was therefore no longer provocative simply to paint hot men in various stages of undress. His work wasn't interesting, let alone menacing or mysterious. It was merely skillful, pleasing, merely "amazing," and, in the view of his classmates, old hat. They mocked Elijah for attempting to carry forward the extinguished torch of figurative painting. They pointed out that ninety-nine percent of figurative painters were obscure hacks and that the other one percent (who admittedly tended to be the richest and best-known artists of all) were peddlers of what was ultimately just very expensive comfort food, their work all technically superior but aesthetically retrograde carbs and dairies, like gourmet macaroni and cheese.

Elijah's only real friend at Vassar was Jay, who mocked Elijah's work too but with noticeably less zeal than he mocked everyone else's. In his isolation and lack of inspiration Elijah began to fear that he wasn't as promising an artist as his parents' unceasing encouragement had led him to believe. He hedged his professional bets by taking workshops in graphic design.

Then, in senior year, inspiration finally struck. For a fall semester elective, a film class called Narratives of Depravity, Elijah was assigned the Josef von

Sternberg film *The Blue Angel*. But at the library he mistakenly rented the Leni Riefenstahl film *The Blue Light* instead. For Elijah, the clearest sign that he'd arrived at a moment of genius was that he'd come to it by way of a happy accident. He was of the democratic, ego-sparing belief that all acts of genius were the results of happy accidents.

On its surface, *The Blue Light* was about a woman named Junta who lurks at the top of a mountain on the outskirts of a remote village, like the Grinch. The villagers suspect Junta of being a witch and have reason to. One night every month the summit of Junta's mountain emits a brilliant blue light that produces an enchanting effect on all the young men below. Unable to resist the lure of this blue light, the men sneak out of their homes, scale the mountain's steep face in an attempt to reach it, and, invariably, fall to their deaths. The actual plot of the film hinges on the arrival of a traveler who falls in love with Junta and thereby gains access to her mountaintop lair. He discovers that what generates the blue light is a quarry of valuable crystals and, in spite of Junta's pleading, organizes an expedition to extract and sell them. Elijah couldn't bring himself to care about this plot. His gay heart was little moved by the vagaries of heterosexual romances, and he took no interest in whatever message about ruthless greed Riefenstahl was clearly promulgating. What he cared about were the young men's deaths. That these deaths were suggested more than explicitly depicted made him fixate on them all the more. He felt as bewitched by them as the men were by the blue light. Already he sensed that he was in the midst of the major aesthetic moment of his life.

Over the next few months he produced a series of paintings that showed the young men in the moment of their fall. He experimented with painting some crumpled and bloody on the ground, but gore made Elijah squeamish and he didn't see himself as an artist who traded in shock. In any case what interested him were the seconds preceding death. He worked assiduously to capture the men's late-dawning realization that their desire would lead to their doom. The admixture of horror and heedless fascination, as their foot failed to catch a ledge, as their fingers slipped: Elijah could think of nothing more beautiful, really beautiful, than this.

Because the film offered few actual scenes of men climbing and falling he had to extrapolate, and because he had to extrapolate he saw no reason not to make the material his own. In something of a recapitulation of his earlier work he painted the men shirtless and, for reasons he didn't feel the need to interrogate, he cast them as blonds. He did (Lucian) Freudian things with color splotches on their faces. He worked with a fervor that he'd never felt before, that reinforced his belief that he'd had a stroke of genius, and that was only to some extent performative. The heft of the mountain, the brightness of the light, the fitness of the men's bodies, the terrified awe in their faces: Elijah sensed these slowly but steadily becoming the cardinal points of his consciousness.

He encountered no difficulties, hardly even anticipated any, until he presented the paintings at his final pre–thesis show critique. During the critique one of his classmates, a lispy, studious boy named Gavin Gates, pointed out, in his lispy, studious way, that after making *The Blue Light* Leni Riefenstahl had gone on to become a propagandist for the Third Reich, that Adolf Hitler had in fact taken an interest in Riefenstahl after seeing *The Blue Light*, and that it was therefore reasonable to categorize *The Blue Light* as a work of fascist or at least protofascist art.

"That's very interesting," Elijah's professor said. "Elijah, what do you think about that?"

Elijah stood stiffly, with his neck drawn back and his chin lowered. He knew nothing about history or politics and was, therefore, deeply afraid of them. "I didn't know Riefenstahl was associated with Hitler," he muttered, truthfully. "And I didn't see any Nazi stuff in the film."

"The point I'm making is subtler," Gavin lisped. "You can see overlap between this film and *Triumph of the Will*. The eroticization of the male physique, the glorification of death, the submission of the individual to a magnetic higher power. All features of the fascist aesthetic."

Elijah muttered, again truthfully, that he had never heard of *Triumph of the Will*.

"You might find it helpful to watch it," Gavin said. By now Elijah's classmates were regarding him with a collective hostile stare.

"This is all very interesting," the professor said. "Elijah has a lot to think about."

Elijah did think about what Gavin Gates had said. He thought about it for roughly an hour. He skimmed the Wikipedia pages for Leni Riefenstahl, *The Blue Light*, Adolf Hitler, Joseph Goebbels, someone named Ernst Röhm, and *Triumph of the Will*. He shrugged. It appeared to be true that Riefenstahl had shilled for the Third Reich, and it appeared to be true that *The Blue Light* had served as a retroactive audition for her role in Hitler's circle. But these facts, Elijah felt, bore no relation to his work. The paintings had been made without knowledge of this historical context and deserved to be judged on their own merit and without reference to it. Also, he himself was half-Jewish, on his father's side. Didn't that mean he was, by dint of his heritage, incapable of celebrating Nazism? Even as he mounted this defense, though, he set little store by it. He suspected no smart person, and certainly no seriously Jewish person, would believe it put the matter to rest. He turned over in his mind the possibility that Gavin Gates was jealous. As he turned it over and over this possibility became a likelihood, then a fact. He waited out the weeks until the thesis show, worried that Gavin would antagonize him further but hopeful that at least some viewers (perhaps those likewise unstudied in the history of fascism) would find his paintings to be as brilliant as he felt them to be.

Then, four days before installation, his professor summoned him to his office, where he informed Elijah, with apparently sincere regret, that the department had judged it best for him not to exhibit his work. His classmates had lodged complaints. They'd spread word of Elijah's paintings to other students, who'd lodged further complaints. A petition had been written and had attracted seventeen signatures. An associate professor in the Jewish Studies program had sent a letter.

"I do not personally believe the work is without merit," the professor said. "I think the work has . . . a quality. And this will not affect your grade. You will pass. You should be proud of yourself for completing your studies."

"But I didn't know!" Elijah said. "About any of that stuff. I just thought the film was interesting!"

"Why did you find the film interesting?" the professor asked.

"I thought it was beautiful," Elijah said.

"Well," the professor said, "perhaps the work before you now—and this is work we must all do—involves asking yourself what you find beautiful, and why."

The one person Elijah felt comfortable turning to was Jay, and Jay didn't disappoint. Though he wasn't in Elijah's critique class Jay had seen the *Blue Light* paintings. He also knew Gavin Gates and had spent considerable energy cultivating contempt for the brand of moral vigilantism he practiced. "This is the tragedy of living among small minds," he said to Elijah. "Including one who can't even pronounce his own last name. The paintings are genius. If you want me to withdraw my work from the show, I will. Just say the word."

Jay himself had received high compliments on his Declaration of Independence series. Apparently Gavin Gates had praised him for "mounting a queer subversion of America's foundational lie." Jay had scoffed and said he hadn't mounted anything other than the sophomore who'd volunteered to pose as Benjamin Franklin.

"I don't want you to withdraw your work," Elijah said.

"Well," Jay said, "thank you."

Elijah spent the night of the thesis show at home, in a vortex of self-pity to which he felt entitled and from which he therefore made no effort to extricate himself. Intellectually he grasped why his classmates had deemed his work offensive, but emotionally he railed against what he considered to be their failure of understanding. When he looked inside himself he saw a wonderland of colors and textures and tensions, all of them well-meaning, none of them evil or even political. He couldn't reconcile what his classmates had said about his work with the idyllic interior landscape whence it had sprung. He felt misjudged and instrumentalized. He felt that his classmates had scored a point that was minor and fleeting at the expense of his subjectivity, which was immense and timeless. The worst of it was that in scoring their point they hadn't generated any meaning or beauty of their own. All they had done was destroy his.

He moved to New York that summer intent on continuing his art practice but conflicted about how to proceed. He was determined to avoid ruffling any more feathers, even if he remained confused as to the precise reasons for this rufflement. Yet he felt an unmitigated allegiance to his paintings. He continued to think about the young men in the film. He pictured them lusting, climbing, struggling, slipping, staring up with fervor at the unreachable blue light even as they plunged to their deaths. He felt there was something beautifully, undeniably *there*. He did worry that his interest in such images, reflective as they apparently were of a quasi-fascist sensibility, betokened something unsavory about his aesthetic imagination. He took it as a bad sign that the one person who'd expressed respect for the paintings was the ever-unsavory Jay.

But where would he be, what integrity would he have, if he simply consented to let his fixation go?

He tried, at first in his little bedroom in Alphabet City, and later in his little shared studio in Gowanus, to channel his inspiration into new subjects. For a while he painted from Abercrombie & Fitch advertisements, attempting to imbue the models' expressions with terror but succeeding only in making them look like zombies. He painted stills from preclimactic moments in porn videos. He downloaded JPEGs of Hardy Boys covers, inverted their colors in Photoshop, and painted the results. All of this work struck him as quite bad. He felt none of the urgency, none of the compulsion, none of the divine erotic thrill that he'd felt when making the *Blue Light* paintings.

Part of the problem was that he was getting his erotic thrill elsewhere. He didn't think it was coincidental that the person he'd fallen in love with provoked in him the very awe and terror that he was trying to depict in his work. In his height and brawn and ungodly handsomeness Mark Landmesser was certainly a steep mountain. In his wealth and kindness and offer of security he certainly emitted an enchanting light. And in his willingness to be a killer in the bedroom, to yank and spank at Elijah's request, he certainly gave Elijah a frisson of blissful destruction. Laying his face against the mattress and raising his ass in the air, getting up on Mark's lap and digging his nails into his back, swallowing Mark's shaft until tears welled in his eyes and his diaphragm throbbed in preregurgitative convulsions, Elijah felt that he was getting as close as he ever had to the mysterious essence of the *Blue Light* paintings, whatever that essence was. It troubled him, it affronted his sense of his destiny, that he was so able and willing to locate this essence in everyday, immaterial sexual relations, rather than painting. He began to worry that art for him was not an innate calling but a kind of arbitrary heuristic, one of several possible strategies for fulfilling his hunger that, in the face of a superior strategy, had lost its utility.

When Mark began to lose some of his luster, some of his alpine formidability, Elijah recognized it as an opportunity to direct his hunger back into his art. Instead, he persuaded Mark to help him find another person, Alistair McCabe, with whom to satisfy his craving. Now that Alistair's luster had worn off too he knew he had another such opportunity. But he'd let so much time pass, he'd clocked so many failures, he felt hopelessly unequal to the task. His

destiny had come to nothing. That, finally, was the only answer he could give
to Jay's question about what'd been working on: nothing.

After twenty minutes Jay returned to the terrace and beckoned him inside.
Whatever minimal curiosity Elijah had about Jay's project had vanished. He felt
depressed, with every passing minute more so, and the cause of his depression
happened also to be its only alleviant: he wanted to go home, back into the
humid warmth of Mark's arms. Mark made him unhappy, but he kept him
safe. With Jay he would be free, free to be as unsavory as he might want to
be, and this frightened him.

He followed Jay through the living room and down the hall, past the dining
room hung with Bruce Weber prints, tribal masks of unknown and probably
criminal provenance, and a lurid red Anish Kapoor mirror. Only when they'd
reached the end of the hall did Elijah realize where they were going.

"You turned Howie's bedroom into your studio?" he asked.

"It was his suggestion," Jay said. He stepped into the room and spread his
arms, gesturing at the makings of a film shoot: camera equipment and lighting
equipment, laptops and monitors, loose cables and stacked hard drives, open-
mouthed Pelican cases, and, at the far end of the room, a black backdrop with
a single stool standing before it. "It's big enough. The light is good. Frankly,
though, I think he just likes the idea of the models being in the same room
where he sleeps."

Aside from the equipment and the backdrop the room was bare. Howie's
furnishings had been removed without a trace. The only other object Elijah
saw was a black duffel bag by the opposite wall. "Models?" he said.

"I'll start recruiting them next week."

"How will you find them?"

"Grindr," Jay said. "It's as much a classifieds as a sex app. I'll offer them a
good day rate. But not too good. I don't want professionals, if you know what
I mean."

"Don't know if I do."

"It's not the look," Jay said. "They need to be—" He raised his eyes to the
ceiling. "Well, let's say they need to need the money."

Every response Jay gave raised a new question. But Elijah had lost interest
in probing further. He took a half step toward the door, laying the groundwork

for his goodbye. His mind was all on Mark. He couldn't bear the thought of staying with him but he couldn't even conceive of leaving him. It wasn't over, not even possible.

"Can I show you?" Jay said. "I thought we could do a test shoot. It'll be fun."

"I don't know."

Jay walked toward the black duffel bag. Elijah looked again at the equipment, all doubtlessly top-line. He watched Jay cross the room with his new million-dollar assurance. Suddenly, strange as it was, he felt bad for Jay. In Richmond he'd been a prankster, broke and endearing, scribbling futilely in his notebook, making his dead-end films. Now he had new wealth, new ambition, new seriousness. He'd availed himself of bigger possibilities and, if his interest in the election was any indication, a bigger canvas; and Elijah wondered, with a shiver, how Jay's outré inclinations would play out on a grand scale. When he'd been poor he'd had nothing to worry about, nothing to fear and nothing to lose. But the money had changed that.

Jay knelt over the duffel and unzipped it slowly, with a showman's instinct for suspense.

"I have to go home," Elijah said, more loudly than he'd intended. He glanced at the half-open mouth of the bag and glanced away. He thought he saw something red. "I have to talk to Mark."

For a moment Jay was naked in his disappointment. Then he nodded and stood.

"You can show me next time."

Jay only nodded again. He seemed to be seeing the hours of aloneness before him.

"Save some coke for me?"

"No promises," Jay said.

Downstairs, an Uber pulled up to the curb in less than a minute. The driver was a South Asian kid wearing a barcode T-shirt who greeted Elijah by saying, "Yo." As they sped down the West Side Highway Elijah looked at the passing menagerie of ever-taller, ever-stranger new-construction buildings, all trapezoidal asymmetries and curvilinear sashays. It was if the wealth of the city, in pushing west, in squeezing into this last strip of land, had been forced to take on increasingly contorted shapes to express itself. The sun blazed.

He had every reason, he knew, to dread his return. There were exchanges to rehash, insults to retract, hollow pledges to make, rickety solutions to draw up. But for now he narrowed his thoughts to the discrete moment of his homecoming. He imagined walking in and seeing Mark's wounded, expectant face. He imagined them embracing in piteous apologies. He envisioned nothing beyond that and he refused to try, even as he understood that this was the cause of both their misery and their precarious complacence: this shared myopia. All the same he felt that this embrace might just possibly be the seed of something, a modulated understanding, an adjustment of expectations, a rejiggered mutual respect that would make their life together more endurable. He had little reason to hope for this, but he had nothing else to hope for.

The car pulled up to the Eros Ananke. In the elevator he tried to perfect an expression that would communicate his contriteness and vague hope. But when he stepped into the hallway he realized this performance was futile. There was no point in pretending; Mark knew him better than anyone. With him as with no one else Elijah was allowed to be his deficient self. He approached the door, smiling resignedly, and turned the key.

———————

After he left Mark's apartment Alistair took a cab to Port Authority. As the car lurched up Eighth Avenue he put his face to the window and took in every souvenir of city life, every umbrellaed produce stand and ornate stone facade and foppishly dressed gay he could lay eyes on. How much of this could he expect to find in whatever place he ended up hiding out in? He was reminded of a ritual he'd performed as a little boy whenever Maura had taken him camping in Ithaca. Before they left for the weekend he'd skip through the house, running his hands under hot water, cooling his face at the open refrigerator, pressing his butt down on soft couches and beds, savoring every last shred of civilization before he abandoned it all for a tent.

His observations did little to distract him from his dread of his forthcoming departure, his fear that he would be tracked down by Herve's men before he made it out of the city, his deep remorse at breaking Mark's heart. He'd been surprised by Mark's audacity; something in Mark's wobbling voice had told Alistair he'd surprised himself. He wasn't sure how he would have responded to Mark under different circumstances. It pained him even to imagine. And it pained him to imagine how Mark would feel, what further heartbreak he would sustain, when he tried to reach out to Alistair, as he inevitably would, and got only the silent wall of his voicemail. Standing at the door of Mark's apartment, clutching his jacket to his chest, Alistair had had the wild, fleeting idea to tell Mark everything. He knew Mark would have been shocked, he knew he would have been clueless and frightened. But he also knew he would have tried to help.

At Port Authority he stepped out into a cacophonous, malodorous sensorium: squeaking bus brakes, mephitic diesel fumes, shrill touristic chatter. Across the way the New York Times Building stood in the sunlight, looking down on the bus terminal impassively and a little huffily, as if it had been seated next to an unruly guest at a wedding.

The inside of the terminal had the look and feel of a sports stadium being evacuated after a bomb threat. Of the hundreds of people massed in the concourse Alistair appeared to be the only one moving inward. He glanced at the sign pointing to gates 1–56. These were the basement gates, to which he descended every few months to catch a ShortLine to Binghamton. He followed in his mind the long road upstate, through Jersey and Stroudsburg, Tannersville and Scranton, past rolling hills and blighted farms, all the way to the squat Binghamton depot, where his mother would always be waiting for him, standing apart from the crowd and its nicotine fog, huddling in her coat against the chill. He craned his neck, searching the crowd for suspect gazes. He ducked into a Greyhound ticket office.

He counted ten people in line and four ticket agents. According to the mysterious laws of bus station ticket offices this would take anywhere between twenty minutes and two hours. A customer at one window counted out his fare in crumpled $1s. A ticket agent completed a transaction and put up a sign reading NEXT WINDOW. A family of five, carrying yellow bags from M&M's World, crammed themselves into the middle of the line, either resuming their place or outright cutting. Another ticket agent put up a NEXT WINDOW sign. A child commenced screaming. Alistair fastened his grip on his duffel. He bounced his feet, pursed his lips, took shallow, furious breaths. Then, for reasons unclear to him, he abandoned the line and went outside.

A little more time, he needed a little more time, a few more minutes of fresh air and freedom before he consigned himself to whatever fate lay at the other end of his Greyhound journey: this is what he told himself as he turned west on Forty-first Street and made his way toward the river. He walked in the shadow of a long warehouse into whose grooved siding people had stuffed coffee cups, empty cigarette packs, soda bottles containing yellow-orange liquid. In the distance he could see the Die Kinder, brutal and sparkling. He looked for Nikolai's building, but couldn't see it. How he hated Nikolai. How much he missed him already.

He walked on. He hunched his shoulders and avoided faces. It occurred to him that the least he could have done was buy a face-shielding baseball hat at one of the souvenir kiosks in Port Authority. But as he crossed the West Side Highway he felt that some part of him actually *wanted* to be caught. Anything, capture even, seemed preferable to his dread.

He found a bench overlooking the water and sat. The river shone with diamonds of sunlight. To his right loomed the gray hulk of the *Intrepid*. Visitors traversed its deck, shuffling and inspecting, like ants looting the carcass of a whale.

He breathed heavily. Sweat trickled down his spine. His duffel, on his lap, made a convection oven of his groin. He watched a barge move stoically along the river, toward the bay, assured of the wide ocean that awaited it. He breathed in the marine air. He heard or imagined seagulls. Tears surfaced in his eyes, then retreated. He took out his phone: the last item on his to-do list.

Alistair hadn't given much thought to what he'd say during this call, so it would be wrong to say that it went differently than he'd expected. But he was nevertheless surprised by what he said and by what was said to him. He asked a question that he'd never intended to ask, that he knew he shouldn't ask, and he received an answer that he knew he didn't deserve. And all the while tears kept surfacing in his eyes and then retreating, and the barge continued its stoic passage toward the bay, and the gulls, imagined or otherwise, squawked at one another overhead.

He called his mother.

———————

Some eight hours after he'd left, Elijah found himself back at the Die Kinder. Jay had set a glass of vodka in front of him and gone for something in another room, and for a moment Elijah was alone. Beyond the double-height windows of Howie's living room the sky glowed with the last flush of sunset.

Jay reemerged with a not very small baggie of cocaine. He sat on the couch opposite, inclined his head at the baggie, and put out his hands as if to say it was there if Elijah needed it.

"Can I stay over?" Elijah asked.

"At my place? Of course."

Elijah looked at Jay with narrowed eyes, lifting one corner of his mouth.

"Right," Jay said. "We'll sleep here. It'll be like a slumber party. We'll tell each other scary stories."

"No need for more of those," Elijah said. "Just one night."

"As long as you need," Jay said. He sucked on his vape. The plume he emitted briefly engulfed Elijah's face, fogging his view—as was, Elijah felt sure, Jay's intention.

That afternoon, upon his return to the Eros Ananke, Elijah had walked into a scene so disorienting to him, so without precedent in his experience or even prefiguration in his mind, that at first he'd struggled to piece it together. The scene consisted of Mark, sweaty at the armpits, standing amid a dozen cardboard boxes. It consisted of shelves emptied of books, drawers of clothes, the liquor cart of its bottles, the picture table of its few Landmesser family photographs. For a moment the scene was silent. Elijah looked at the nervous expression on Mark's face and waited for him to relent, apologize, see the absurdity of his gesture and backtrack. But though Mark obviously had an instinct to do these things, though he moved his lips in a kind of prefatory whistle-wetting, he let the opportunity for such an about-face pass. And more than anything it was this, Mark's steadfast silence, that told Elijah a critical change had taken place. More than anything it was this that told him they were over.

Mark, breaking the silence, asked Elijah to sit and asserted the opposite. They weren't over, he said. He wasn't ready to consider that possibility. But he thought they both needed some time. He said something about this being a "chance to reflect," an "opportunity to regroup." He said something about

Elijah being welcome to stay in the apartment through the end of the month. He said something about his being happy to loan Elijah money until he found his footing.

Elijah, staring at the boxes, struggled to follow. He gave no replies, shed no tears, made no movements of his head. But after a while of listening to Mark—he felt he could hear in Mark's voice, in its lightness and breathiness, the fresh air of his new independence—he began waving his hands and saying, "Fuck you! Fuck you!" until Mark stood from the couch. A few minutes later the movers Mark had hired came to the door, and amid the commotion of their labor Mark and Elijah said nothing to each other, and rather than hang back for an extended goodbye Mark left with them after their final run, and then Elijah was alone.

The apartment looked strange to him, like a duplicate on another floor. Everything was the same except for the absence of an ineffable something, an extrasensory essence that he registered only now that it was gone. Without this essence the apartment was mere materiality: textiles, fixtures, doorjambs, walls. He sat on the floor in the middle of the living room for he couldn't even guess how long. And then he called the only person he felt he could count on.

"Like I told you before," Jay said to him now. "I'll take care of you. You can live with me. And don't even think about money."

Elijah reached for his vodka. He realized with surprise how little money had figured into his thinking over the past few hours. His inattention to this matter made him wonder if he was purer at heart than he gave himself credit for. But now, having been reminded of it, he felt the loss of Mark's support carving out a new depth in his misery. His stomach jumped and his center of gravity shifted, as if he'd stepped into empty space expecting a stair.

Jay leaned forward and opened the baggie of coke. He pulled a large art book, a Taschen of Frida Kahlo, from the far end of the coffee table and shook a mound of powder onto Frida's face. With a rolled bill from his wallet he vacuumed up a thick line. Incredibly, he seemed to try to do this quietly. "Your turn."

Elijah shook his head.

Jay rubbed his nose. "I have something better."

Elijah caught his drift and rolled his eyes.

"It'll give you something else to think about."

Elijah rolled his eyes again, but stood. No point in fending off his curiosity, he figured, when he had nothing else to look forward to.

He followed Jay to Howie's bedroom. All the lights in the apartment had been dimmed, and as he progressed down the hall he felt darkness closing in on him.

In Howie's bedroom Jay switched on a spotlight. He went to the stool in front of the backdrop and centered it. He turned to Elijah. "Take off your shirt."

"I am not posing nude," Elijah said.

"I didn't say nude."

Elijah stared at Jay sullenly for a moment, then took off his T-shirt and let it fall to the floor.

"Now your socks. And your pants."

"What did I just say?"

"You can keep your underwear on. I want you to get the full effect."

Elijah was sure that nothing good could come of this. But he was tipsy, desperate for a distraction, and despite himself intrigued; and so he let his curiosity override his uneasiness and complied.

"Perfect," Jay said, glancing at Elijah's briefs.

Jay instructed him to sit on the stool and close his eyes. "I'm going to put something on your head. Don't try to look at it, don't even try to touch it. Open your eyes only when I tell you."

Elijah winced as his skin met the cold stool. "Why?"

"I don't you want your experience to be spoiled," Jay said.

"By what?"

"Moral trembling."

Elijah heard Jay cross the room and unzip the black duffel. He felt him put something light and snug on his head.

"Now," Jay said after he'd taken his place behind the camera, "look at me."

Elijah couldn't see what was on his head. Jay had positioned it so that it lay outside his field of vision.

Jay stared into the camera's monitor and spoke with jittery deliberation. "I want you to imagine something," he said.

"Fine."

"You're on a lake," Jay said. "You're rowing from the dock to the center. It's a big lake. It's the first time you've gone out so far. The lake is surrounded on all sides by large hills. Until this moment you've assumed these hills are the highest things around you. But now, as you row farther and farther out, you see that past the hills are mountains, much bigger than the hills, craggy and steep. You're surprised, you're bewildered, you're amazed. You have no category for what you're looking at, and you can't stop looking."

Elijah was unaware of doing anything with his face. He was merely imagining the scene Jay described. But he must have made an expression that satisfied Jay, because a small red light on the camera's side told him Jay had begun recording. Jay tilted the camera toward Elijah's dangling feet and, very slowly, panned up, until the lens was fixed directly on Elijah's eyes. After a moment Jay smiled to himself, ended the recording, and beckoned Elijah to stand and come closer. As Elijah approached Jay turned the monitor toward him and played the footage.

It would be wrong to say that Elijah was surprised by what he saw on the screen; deep down a part of him had known. He watched as the camera traveled up his torso, showing his pale body luminous and tensed. He watched as it took in his face, his expression of perplexity, the glimmer in his eyes of reverence and fear. And he watched as it came to a stop and revealed, atop his head, a bright red MAKE AMERICA GREAT AGAIN baseball hat.

Elijah wasn't a news reader, but he was a student of images. He knew this hat, this badge of Trumpian loyalty, this totem of feverish jubilant cynicism. Already the hat had burned itself into the national consciousness and he suspected it would remain there indelibly. He felt a throb of repulsion. At the same time, he couldn't look away. He should have known then what kind of territory he was entering when he kept looking, trying and failing to resolve the contrast between his face and the hat, the familiar and the strange, the unsuspecting and the sinister. He should have known then when he gave up trying to resolve this contrast and accepted that its inability to be resolved was the very thing that furnished the image with its interest. He was frightened of what he saw on the screen and he was frightened of his fascination with it.

Jay caught Elijah's eye. He laughed, and when Elijah said nothing he laughed more nervously. Maybe he sensed for the first time that he'd misread, misjudged, gone in over his head; but if he did he smiled this warning away. "Don't be so *serious*," he said to Elijah. "It's fun. Have a little fun with me."

Elijah returned to the stool and wobbled tipsily. He felt himself falling, putting his arms out and finding no ledges, putting his legs out and finding no footholds, plummeting into a bottomless yet oddly inviting abyss. As he looked vacantly across the room Jay filmed him again. And in this shot, on close inspection, you could see tears.

————

Mark arrived at the Ho-Ho-Kus train station a little after three. In an Uber on the way to his parents' house he looked out at the passing landscape of his childhood, all shaded hollows and gentle hills, winding lanes devoid of utility poles, bright boxy houses veiled by springtime growth, in the trees yellow bursts of afternoon sun. He felt a sleepiness settling over him, a kind of narcotic withdrawal. But when the car pulled up at his parents' gate his pulse quickened.

The movers had beat him. As he trudged toward the house he passed their truck easing down the long driveway. He found his mother standing by the garage. She wore a cream cashmere sweater and black trousers with darted ankles. When Mark hugged her he detected vanilla, orange blossom, and possibly vetiver. She blinked at him.

"Did you tip them?" she asked.

"Shit," Mark said.

"I tipped them," she said.

Mark gave a flat smile. "Where are the boxes?"

"In the pool house. I assume that's where you'll be staying."

"In the pool house?"

"If you're going to be living here—"

"I'm not living here."

"—I figure you'll want some privacy, no?"

Mark looked over the freshly cut lawn to the little pond on the far side of the property, where a submerged aerator generated a small, violent geyser. "Can I come into the main house now?" he said. "Am I allowed?"

Janet shook her head. "That's our Markie," she said. "Never knows when people are just trying to be nice."

The Landmesser house was a sprawling stone complex on two acres. The only thing saving it from indefensible ostentation was the fact that its second story was all dormers and gables. Mark's father, who had a lifelong Passaic-shaped chip on his shoulder, took pride in the fact that he lived in "humble" Ho-Ho-Kus rather than "hoity-toity" Saddle River, to the north. But in fact the Landmesser property ran to the border with Saddle River, and their house was by far the largest in the borough.

Mark followed Janet through the front door and into the kitchen, where she put on a kettle. He waited for her to ask about his falling-out with Elijah, though he wasn't surprised when no questions came. Janet was socially oblivious to the point of pathology.

"Eddie and I have been playing Words With Friends," she said, taking out her phone. "He beats me *every time.*"

"He probably cheats," Mark said, swiveling on his stool.

"He just played 'vulva.' Thirty-four points. I had no idea he had such a large vocabulary."

"Are you going to ask me about Elijah?"

"Yes," Janet said. "How is he?"

Mark looked at the counter and scratched his head. "I mean this," he said, gesturing aimlessly. "Me, here."

Janet was moving tiles around on her screen. "Living with someone can be very hard," she said. "Eddie, you know, has never lived with a girlfriend."

"Eddie has never dated someone for more than six months."

"Well, every relationship is a lesson. So I guess he's learned a lot."

"And I've learned nothing, because I've been with the same person for eight years."

"Sometimes the first one isn't the one."

"It was for you and Dad."

Janet smiled as though she heard in this only the sincerest of compliments. "Sometimes people are just lucky."

Mark slid off his stool, said he would back for dinner, and made his way across the great room. As he stepped out onto the back patio the kettle screamed.

The pool house was actually an in-law guesthouse with a bedroom, spacious living room, and full kitchen. But traces of its preexpansion identity lingered. The walls were adorned with captain's wheels, glass buoys, and other nautical tchotchkes, the rooms smelled faintly of chlorine, the closets were crammed with old skimmer nets and foam noodles, and the pool itself, which Mark's parents kept heated and open nine months out of the year, cast a shimmery, euphotic glow on the ceilings.

He went to his boxes, opened the one on which he'd scrawled LIQUOR, took out a lesser whiskey, and poured some into a glass over ice. He made his way to the bathroom, which was outfitted with a small sauna, and stripped. He set the temperature to 170 and planted himself on the cedar bench. Within five minutes of sweating and sipping he felt drunk and near death. He was hoping to vacate his mind, but the more he tried not to think the more he felt the pang of the wound he'd received from Alistair and the wound he'd inflicted on Elijah. He saw that in this regard his escape was futile. He wouldn't be able to stop working over his humiliation and remorse. If anything, by clearing his mental docket of other concerns, he'd given himself unlimited time to fixate. He was stupid, stupid.

He went to the bedroom and napped. He woke a while later to the sound of the garage opening and a car door being slammed with masculine ardor: his father was home. He pulled the duvet over his head. In his luminous white cocoon, evocative of the forts he'd built out of blankets and chairs as a kid, he looked at his phone, navigated to Alistair's contact page, held his thumb over the Call button, then let the phone fall asleep. He himself tried to fall back asleep, but then he heard his mother yell from the patio: "Dinner!"

Given what he'd been through that day, Mark had expected Janet to make a home-cooked meal. Instead what he found on the dining table were left-overs from the Ridgefall Country Club: soggy Caesar salad, greasy charred Brussels sprouts, portions of strip steak, veal Milanese—his parents were not educated eaters. For freshness or perhaps color Janet had added a bowl of raw baby carrots. She'd poured wine.

Arty was already sitting at the table, wearing a red-and-tan checkered shirt that stretched over his broad belly. His hair, dull brown with streaks of gray, flowed back from his forehead and around his ears in a thick mane. He smiled at Mark ebulliently, and his dimples and rounded ruddy cheeks made Mark smile involuntarily in return.

"Markie, I understand you haven't come to us under the best of circum-stances," he said. "But take a seat, grab some grub. You'll be feeling better in no time."

"In no time," Janet said into her phone.

"As you can see," Arty said, "we did a little tasting at the club. Your mother's turning sixty this summer, as I'm sure you know."

Now I know, Mark thought.

"She wants it at the club. I say let's have it here, at the house. I say, if you really want to go somewhere, let's fly everyone to Hawaii. But your mother loves the club."

"I love the club," Janet said.

Arty heaved a portion of strip steak onto his plate. "And the pool house," he said to Mark. "You happy there? You comfortable?"

Mark sipped his wine. He slid some Brussels sprouts onto his plate. He decided he preferred his mother's obtuseness to his father's bullying solicitations. He suspected this was how Arty dealt with his employees: with a vehement kindness bordering on coercion, with a bear hug bordering on strangulation. "It's fine."

Janet plucked a baby carrot from the bowl and snapped it in half with her teeth. It sounded like she was eating ice.

"I can tell you," Arty said, cutting into his steak, "Eddie won't be very happy. That's where he stays on the weekends."

"Eddie comes on the weekends?" Mark said.

"Every weekend," Arty said. "New tradition."

Janet glanced up, then looked back at her screen. Mark sensed that he was missing context, news of some recent turn in the family dynamics. How easy it was, from the safety of his apartment, to forget that his parents and brother were real, that they moved through space and time every day just as he did. And how wearying, his belated realization that he would now have a front-row seat to their lives.

"We love seeing our Eddie," Arty said. "And now we get to see more of our Markie. Really, we're just over the moon. And I'm sure Eddie won't mind loaning his little den to you."

Mark thought of the sauna, of Eddie planting his hammy butt on the very bench where he'd planted his own hours before. "He can have it if he wants it."

Arty forklifted a piece of steak to his mouth. "I guess that depends on how long you're staying," he said. He looked at Mark as he chewed, his eyes crinkled and bright.

"Eddie is *annihilating* me," Janet said. "He just played 'scrotum.' Sixty points!"

Mark held the stem of his wineglass tightly. "Has it ever occurred to you that Eddie likes playing dirty words against you?" he said to Janet. "That he gets a kind of gross satisfaction out of that?"

"You don't choose your letters," Janet said.

"I understand the concept. I've played Scrabble."

"This is Words With Friends."

"Markie," Arty said. "I just want to say, I am so sorry about Elijah. That is terrible. I don't know what's going on with the two of you, but I love that boy like a son. So kind, so funny, so *handsome*. I mean, if I were a woman." He inclined his head at Mark. "Or."

Mark believed these words about as much as any other kind words that came out of Arty's mouth. His father's whole persona consisted of a booming, blustering sympathy for people ensnared by problems he felt himself superior to. He was all widened eyes and furrowed brows, shakes of the head and slaps of the knee. His real self, Mark suspected, he saved for his hours alone in his study. There he shed his goofy demeanor, felt his real feelings, aired his soul. "I'll be OK," Mark said.

"Of course you will," Arty said. "And we're very happy to have you here while the two of you work things out." He dug a piece of meat from between his teeth. "But!" he said. "But. I have my fatherly intuitions. You're my son, I've known you since you were a screaming little gob of goo. And I have a fatherly intuition that there's another reason you've come home. And so I have one question for you."

Mark closed his eyes and raised his glass to his lips.

"'Thrust'!" Janet said.

"Very simple question. No wrong answers. Can't get anywhere without honesty."

"Forty-five points! He's *demolishing* me."

"Tell me," Arty said. "Tell me honestly. Exactly how much money do you have left?"

Mark drained his wine, thanked no one in particular for dinner, and left the room.

He knew it was a win that he'd managed to escape without answering Arty's question. But as he headed back to the pool house he saw before him numberless hours in which the question would hang, and in which the answer, by remaining withheld, would take shape in Arty's mind more or less accurately, and in which Arty would either ridicule him for his irresponsibility or try to help him recoup his losses: Mark suspected the distinction between the ridicule and the help would be one without much difference.

In the pool house he put the whiskey bottle on the nightstand and drank in bed, staring out the window at the twilit backyard. He was thirty miles from New York, no closer or farther than he'd been when he'd arrived, but now the thick trees and deep suburban silence seemed to close in on him, separating him from the city, foreclosing possibilities. As he refilled his glass and refilled it again his longing for Alistair morphed into something like panic. He called him, but got only voicemail. He called again; voicemail. He registered, under rationalizing explanations, a vague but insistent fear. With every passing minute Alistair's story about going home for his mother's birthday seemed less credible. But he had little else out of which to build a working theory. For now all he knew was that the last light had left the sky and that some diffuse sublime dread seemed to be lurking in the trees. It was getting chilly out there, in the lush backyard, and it was getting dark.

PART TWO

LUMPENPROLETARIAT

ALISTAIR MCCABE'S INVOLVEMENT with Nikolai Daskalov and Herve Gallion had begun eight months earlier, after he'd emerged from his internship at JPMorgan Chase without an offer and hence, to his mind, without a future. It had also begun, in the way of such things, long before.

If Alistair hadn't been his father's son, he probably wouldn't have taken it upon himself to support his mother, her protestations that she didn't need his support notwithstanding. And if he hadn't been his mother's son, he probably wouldn't have flunked the career path he'd pursued in the hope of one day being able to support her. For all his foaming-at-the-mouth ambition Alistair had his mother's moral stubbornness, and in time this stubbornness had led him into spectacular failure. Unfortunately, it hadn't prevented him from thereafter agreeing to work for Herve, on a project that he'd sensed from day one was suspect. Now he was inextricably deep in shit, as implicated as Herve and Nikolai were, and he'd been forced to disappear from the world under mysterious circumstances. In this last regard he was most certainly his father's son.

Alistair's parents met at SUNY Binghamton in the late '80s. His father, Sean McCabe, was a Binghamton native from a large Irish family that had been in the city for generations and that made up a significant portion of its working-class substratum. Ever since Sean's death Maura had taken care to keep herself and Alistair at a fair distance from the McCabes—and for good reason—but it was nearly impossible to run an errand downtown without crossing paths with a McCabe janitor or a McCabe mechanic or a McCabe bar owner or a McCabe cop. A typical day in the life of a McCabe might involve taking off early from your custodial job at the Metrocenter, getting your oil changed for free at your cousin's auto repair shop on Front Street, rewarding yourself for your hard work with six rounds of Jameson, also for free, at your other cousin's pub on Main Street, and driving home tanked and happy in the knowledge that the cop who flashed his lights and pulled you over would be either another one of your cousins or someone who knew him. Sean, proud of his family though he was, wanted more for himself. His ambition was to follow in the footsteps of his cousin Cillian, a local landowner, real estate developer, and self-styled panjandrum who was the only McCabe to have struck it rich and for whom, after graduation, Sean promptly began working. Sean probably didn't need to study business to secure a job with Cillian, but one demonstration of his ambition, Maura had told Alistair, was his insistence on being the first in his immediate family to get a four-year degree.

Maura's own roots were less plebeian. She'd grown up in Ithaca, the daughter of a general practitioner father and homemaker mother. Her father was a descendant of WASPs who'd been in the country for centuries and whose wealth had dissipated long before he'd been born. The only things he'd inherited from his once-patrician forebears were some unscientific genealogical trees, two Duncan Phyfe chairs that no one ever sat in, an abiding if largely performative political progressivism, a susceptibility to depression, and a catastrophic love of drink. Her mother was from poor but self-regarding German stock. She'd married a doctor in the hope of escaping the austerities and humble pieties of her childhood, but even into adulthood she remained a champion of swept floors, crisp linens, airtight checkbooks, and bright-eyed community-spiritedness. Their marriage was a disaster. Maura's father didn't actually earn a very remarkable salary, and he militated fiercely against her mother's efforts to penetrate the country club crowd in Cayuga Heights, and what discretionary income he didn't set aside for Maura's college tuition (he was responsible and forward-looking only when it came to Maura) he sank into expensive neckties, first editions of T. S. Eliot and P. G. Wodehouse, his prized and breakdown-prone 1966 Cadillac Fleetwood, and the gradual demolishment of his liver.

For all this Maura greatly preferred her father. She found his drunken antics amusing. She inherited his hauteur, his disregard for pragmatism, his introversion, his wit. She rebuffed her mother's pleas to pick her face out of her book and go out and make some friends. Her mother bounded through their big, old, dark Queen Anne house, opening windows, arranging fresh flowers, scheduling double dates and tennis matches, smiling in besotted admiration at Ronald Reagan whenever his prosperous suntanned visage appeared on the TV. She was like a golden retriever trapped in a house with two cats. When

Maura's father finally succeeded in drinking himself to death, at age sixty, Maura's mother put in her mandatory month of grieving and then absconded to Sarasota, where one of her sisters lived, and there cultivated a new life organized around daybreak tee times, lunch in St. Armands Circle, and clambakes at her gated community's clubhouse. She never did form a relationship with Maura. If Maura preferred her father when he was alive, she preferred him even more after he was dead and forever wreathed in a hagiographic glow.

Alistair understood easily enough what his father saw in Maura. Photographs of them on the SUNY Binghamton campus showed a strapping, muscular, beer-thick Sean, his locks auburn and wavy, his cheeks freckled and pink, staring with mystified devotion at an arrestingly pretty Maura whose straight blond hair fell down past her shoulders and whose expression suggested that though she was content to be photographed she looked forward, after the picture had been taken, to being left alone. Alistair felt Sean must have been fascinated, intimidated by Maura, a doctor's daughter who'd grown up in moody, high-ceilinged rooms lined with bookshelves and dimmed by toile curtains. He must have felt that in order to touch her he had to keep back all his rowdy Hibernianism and concentrate in his fingertips only the tenderest and most delicate parts of himself, and he must have felt that in order to keep her he had to be better, someone deserving of her—someone else. He'd had ambition, but now he had a standard, a high summit, to aim for.

Less clear was what Maura saw in Sean. On this point, she'd admitted to Alistair, she herself was confused. It mattered that he was strapping, that he respected (in his intimidated way) the boundaries of her interior world, and that he doted on her, even if she wasn't convinced that she was the rara avis Sean made her out to be. But it also mattered that he possessed capabilities she lacked and even felt superior to. She pursued her English degree without giving any thought to how she'd support herself after college. She paid tribute to her father by rejecting the sort of dull, practical, upwardly mobile go-getterism she associated with her mother. She felt no particular desire to attain "success"; in her mind the word "success" had the shrillness of her mother's voice and the cheap, hard glint of her gold bracelets. But as she neared the end of senior year she spent more and more nights staring with terror into the void beyond graduation. And the only thing that made her fear abate was Sean, who as early as their junior year had pledged to support her. She sensed, as she put her arms around his big meaty back, that she was affixing herself to a part of human experience she had no affinity for, the part that consisted in pragmatism and concrete reality, and thereby achieving a kind of completeness. She forgave Sean his evident flaws, such as the fact that the aspiration that so consumed him—to be a real estate developer—bored her, or that he loved Ronald Reagan even more than her mother did, or that for every birthday, every one, he gave her a dozen roses and box of Russell Stover chocolates and took her to dinner at the AOH. In truth she loved him all the more for these flaws. She felt she'd found a person who would take care of her, who in his brawny simplemindedness would never supplant her father, and who in his kindness would never hurt her.

They married the summer after graduation and moved into a house on Carey Street, on the west side of the city, that Cillian owned and that he sold to them for a song. Cillian had lived in the house at one time, in some distant premillionaire past, and had held on to it and kept it in good order, he told them vaguely, for "sentimental reasons." The house was old and narrow, with white clapboard siding, a deep front porch, banging radiators, and three small bedrooms on the second floor that Maura and Sean planned to fill with children whose number was a source of cheerful contention with them.

"This'll be enough for the first two," Sean said, "and then we'll need to upgrade."

"The *first* two?" Maura said.

"I want little Seans," he said, kissing her forehead. "I want a million little Mauras."

Cillian put Sean to work so quickly and for such long hours that Maura was left to paint the walls and arrange their new furniture and wrestle the front garden into submission herself. She lived on buttered toast and frozen vegetables for three days before realizing she might need to learn to cook. Nevertheless she was happy. She had a husband she loved and a house that was hers and numberless hours of uninterrupted privacy. Her days were bracketed on the morning end by the stinging scent of Sean's aftershave and on the evening end by her yearning—it surprised her how unfailingly, how suddenly, it came on—for his return. She was perturbed only by how much Sean worked and by how little she knew about his job, and then only mildly.

But her worries started soon enough. One day, she went down to the unfinished basement, put her hand in a spirit of renovational curiosity to a segment of pink fiberglass, and felt the hard backing behind the fiberglass give. She spent some time inspecting, trying to snake her finger through the fiberglass's cotton candy tangles. She felt a sliver-wide gap running along one edge; she felt, she thought, an air current. She took a hammer, stuck its claw into the sliver, and pried. When Maura told this story to Alistair she maintained that she was concerned only about a possible structural issue, an opening in the foundation or a cavity eaten out by termites; she had no reason yet to entertain wilder suspicions. But after a minute of struggle she heard a small metallic pop, and then watched as the hard backing behind the fiberglass swung toward her, revealing itself to be a door and revealing, beyond it, an empty room, ten by ten feet, with concrete walls and a concrete floor, shelving on three sides, a small air vent, no windows, and a single operative light with a pull switch.

She did nothing for the rest of the day until Sean came home.

"What is this?" she said when she brought him to the basement.

Sean, still in his work clothes, had dark crescents under his eyes and seemed, in his forced chipperness and affectedly squared posture, to be drawing on depleted reserves of good humor. In the three months he'd been working for Cillian he'd taken only a handful of Sundays off, and a novel anxiety had begun to steal over him. He ducked his head obligingly and entered. "Secret room?" he said.

"Cillian's?"

At first Sean examined the room with open curiosity, like a Boy Scout who'd stumbled on a cave. But after a moment his expression changed, as if falling heavily into place, and his gaze turned inward. He was silent for a while, and when he spoke he deflected. "I know he put up the fiberglass" was all he said.

Maura tried to hide her agitation. She didn't know where it came from, and she knew even less what it might point to, and already something deep in her mind—a misstruck note, a fleeting shadow—told her she might not want to know. She asked hesitantly: "Why would Cillian need a secret room?"

Sean's gaze turned further inward, and he replied absently. "Valuables, maybe."

"Valuables go in a safe."

"Maybe he needed a bigger safe."

Maura told him to come out. "I don't like you in there," she said.

The fear in her voice roused Sean, and he seized on the opportunity, with a quickness that unnerved Maura, to assuage her. He forced a laugh and put up his hands in mock horror.

"Come out of there," Maura said. "Please."

They never talked about the secret room again, let alone entered it. But over the next few months Maura did gather, little by little, more information about Cillian and Sean's work. By Sean's account Cillian owned and collected rents on some three dozen properties in Binghamton and was at various stages in the development of untold more. Over time he'd progressed from modest assets (houses for young families or communes of university students, small buildings occupied by travel agents, dry cleaners, hardware stores, nail salons) to larger enterprises: office parks, strip malls, hospital annexes, nursing homes. Years before, he'd moved himself, his wife, and their twin boys from the west side of the city to South Mountain, where Binghamton's rather few rich families lived. There he resided in a seven-bedroom house with a home theater and walk-in cigar humidor.

Sean's job for Cillian was joyless and often unseemly. It consisted mainly of knocking on doors of tenants who were in arrears and then, when the generosity clock ran out, initiating the process of evicting them. He was also sometimes tasked with paying visits to people who owed Cillian mysterious debts. He passed his days consoling panicked lessees or weathering abuses from them or both. In the evenings he let off steam by going for long runs along Court Street. He ran through downtown, past the car dealerships, past the strip clubs, until there were only trees and the occasional speeding car and the river. The happy beer fat of his college days disappeared.

"Maybe you have enough experience now," Maura said to him one night, "to find a job with someone else?"

Sean was sitting at the kitchen breakfast nook, wearing an old Binghamton Colonials T-shirt that as an undergraduate he'd filled out easily. Despite the routine praise he'd heaped on Maura's cooking he was struggling to finish his dinner. From certain angles he was still the jocular, freckled striver she'd known since her freshman year. From other angles he was a stranger entirely. "Who?" he said. "He's exactly where I want to be. He's my only way of getting there."

Maura looked into his eyes, probing for depths that seemed every day more unreachable to her, and she thought of the hidden room under her feet. "Well," she said, "but by the time you *get there*—"

"It'll have been worth it," Sean said.

Every chance he got Sean laid out his grand plan. He expected that in five years he would have savings enough (complemented, he hoped, by financial backing from Cillian) to begin acquiring his own properties and start his own real estate empire. He expected that in ten years he would move his own family to South Mountain, where he'd have an even bigger and better house than Cillian's. He expected that in a not-too-distant future *he* would be the McCabe his scrappy younger cousins looked up to, and he expected that Cillian would be proud of him, would accept his encroachment and eventual victory in a spirit of fraternal good humor.

"Did you say 'empire'?" Maura asked.

Sean smiled in unembarrassed philistinic defeat. "My word person," he said. "I'll call it whatever you want."

Maura smiled back at him. She knew that Binghamton had once been a prosperous manufacturing hub, but mostly all she saw when she ran her errands were desiccated husks of former factories, hideous Brutalist structures dating from the last period of civic optimism, and sad storefronts flanked by shuttered brethren. To her it seemed that every year Binghamton took on more of the character of the depressed rural communities surrounding it, as if all those decaying houses and disgruntled rednecks just outside the city limits were creeping inward, in a kind of reversal of urban sprawl. "I just struggle to see it," she said. "I feel like there's a very small pie here, and all the slices have already been taken. More than a few by your cousin."

Love for Maura and quiet indignation—on behalf of his hometown, on behalf of the job with Cillian that he'd entrusted all his hopes to—were competing in Sean's face. "It's fallen on hard times," he said. "But there's action in the medical sector, there's action in the higher education sector. You have to try to picture it. You can't just look at what's in front of you."

"Maybe I like looking at what's in front of me," Maura said to him. "Maybe that's all I need."

Sean brightened. It seemed a continuing miracle to him that Maura had chosen him. Yet he insisted. He needed her to believe in the sunlit expanse that lay on the other side of the shadowland he was trapped in. "Try to picture it," he said.

She said she would. She wouldn't deny Sean his fantasies. His ambition, however pie-in-the-sky, was a major part of why she loved him—part of his tenderness, part of his simplicity. She encouraged his ambition even as it came to remind her, more sharply as time went on, that she had no specific ambition of her own. The $40,000 or so Sean brought home annually obviated the need for her to work, provided they practiced frugality (which Maura had a motivated genius for), and she was more than content not to seek out whatever low-level pedagogical or secretarial position might exist at the nexus of her unremunerative credentials and Binghamton's anemic job market. She did, that first year, turn one of the upstairs bedrooms into a study, and there did begin some applications to English PhD programs, but she never finished them. She had intelligence but no urgent desire to use it, to maximize it, to impress people with it. She possessed the unusual quality of not feeling the need to prove herself. And this unsettled her. She felt vacant, like she was missing something, something human, and maybe specially American.

She found an occupation or something like it in the spring of 1994, when she gave birth to Alistair. She saw immediately, staring into his pink squishy face, petting his whorl of white-blond hair, that she was in trouble. Her love for this strange not-quite-human was an abyss she suspected would swallow her whole if she let it. She'd thought she could never love anyone as much as she loved Sean or her father before him, but her love for Alistair was more involving, more *interesting*, than her love for either of them. It was so consuming and volatile and precognitively chemical that the word "love" didn't even capture it.

She stood guard, as he grew, against her inclination to smother him. A human being was not an artwork, not a project, not a receptacle. More than anything she wanted Alistair to be self-determining and free. But she nevertheless felt she'd found an opportunity to leave her mark on the world, to extend and permanentize herself in an act of concrete addition, just as Sean aspired to extend and permanentize himself by erecting shopping complexes downtown. She would form this little boy. She would make him kind, curious, and intelligent. She would make him into an expression of everything she valued. She took him to Recreation Park and lay with him in the sun, she set him down in the garden while she planted her herbs, she read to him from books of age-inappropriate complexity in preparation for the strict literary training she planned to subject him to. They passed whole days in what it felt beside the point to call happiness.

Sean was an active father and, not surprisingly, a good one. On his few days off he played with Alistair in the backyard, hoisting him onto his shoulders and running around and yelling, "Duck!" whenever they neared a tree branch. He helped Alistair glue plastic glow-in-the-dark stars to his bedroom ceiling, taught him the constellations, instilled in him his own boyhood love of astronomy. He hugged and kissed Alistair as few fathers Maura knew hugged and kissed their sons. And every summer, with such savings as he could set aside, he took the family on a weeklong vacation to the Finger Lakes, and by the time Alistair was six they'd done the full lacustrine hand.

But he did not, as Maura had hoped, cut back on his work. If anything he pursued his ambition all the more zealously now that he had a son to support. He wanted to send Alistair to St. Francis, the city's all-boys Catholic school, rather than the public schools that he himself had attended and that had a good record of sending kids to the University of Prison. He wanted to be able to throw Alistair around an even bigger backyard and to take him to more thrilling places than the Finger Lakes. Some years before, Sean had framed and hung on the living room wall a photograph of Rio de Janeiro, Brazil: the kind of random thing you happen to see in a *National Geographic* at the dentist's office and then latch on to and overidealize and elect as the object of all your otherwise formless longing. He wanted to take Alistair *there*, he said, pointing at the photograph of Rio's coastline, *there*.

Maura admired Sean's dedication to Alistair's well-being. But she couldn't help hearing, in his breathless descriptions of the life he wanted to give his son, echoes of her materialistic and status-obsessed mother. And she couldn't help feeling hurt by his implicit suggestion that the life they already had, a life she loved, wasn't enough. And she couldn't help wondering if Sean was displacing his own desires onto Alistair, running after them under the altruistic pretext of fatherhood. She knew that if she was alert to this possibility it was because she herself still felt every compulsion to smother Alistair, still continued to funnel her best self into him, had privately pledged never to have another child, lest Alistair have to share her with others or, worse, she have to share him. She knew that her love for Alistair was ultimately no less vain than Sean's, and she wondered if she bridled at his self-interested devotion only because it reminded her, in crasser and more flagrant fashion, of her own.

She got a clear picture of the life Sean wanted to give Alistair when, once every summer, she agreed to spend a day swimming at Cillian's house on South Mountain. Maura's goal during these visits was to compliment the house in such a way as to give covert expression to her repugnance ("So many living rooms!" "Does every bathroom have a ceiling mural?") and to keep Alistair away from Cillian's twin boys, whose idea of fun was to throw baby shrimp in the pool and spray the gardener with the hose. She endured stilted conversations with Cillian's wife, a prematurely aged, large-hipped woman who made her own game of paying repugnance-tinged compliments to Maura ("I wish I could pull off plain little dresses like that"). Standing in the vast immaculate backyard, watching as Alistair absorbed with amazement the alien plentifulness and splendor around him, Maura felt nagged again by her own vacancy. Why didn't she want this? And if she didn't want this what did she want? What did she gain, really, by her snobbery, her sanctimonious modesty? She studied Cillian, flabby and suntanned, as he lay in a white cabana chair and pulled on his cigar with quick, wet, puckering inhalations. She thought of all his properties, all the tenants who killed themselves scrounging together their rents, all the debtors who lived in fear of him, the secret room in her basement. She imagined suitcases of cash, stashed evidence, scenes of interrogation and abuse. She wondered if the Irish mafia was still a thing. She watched as Cillian stared with unaccountable fixedness at Sean, who stood in the shallow end of the pool bobbing a puddle-jumpered Alistair up and down.

"He stays trim," Cillian said to Maura.

"It's all that running," Maura said.

"Well," Cillian said, pinching his cigar's soaked end, "don't let him run too far."

It remained in Cillian's power, though, to decide how far Sean could run, and as the years wore on he did his best to keep him leashed. Sean assumed that after a brief period of drudge work he'd progress from bullying cash-strapped tenants to scoping out commercial properties and devising strategies for new acquisitions. But Cillian kept him in a holding pattern, increasing his salary only as much and as frequently as was necessary to keep Sean loyal and whetted. Maura gathered that the only side of the business Sean ever dealt with was its dark underbelly. He told her stories of tenants who made threats against him, of debtors so hopelessly deep in the red that he feared they would hurt themselves or others. Maura recalled one night in particular, in the summer of 2000, when Sean came home, put his head on her shoulder, and said simply, "I think you were right."

That ended up being the last conversation they ever had about his work.

From this point on, Alistair didn't need to rely as much on his mother's recollections. Though he was only six at the time he remembered well enough the day when his family's little world on Carey Street imploded. The facts were few and, as presented in the small article that ran in the Binghamton *Press & Sun-Bulletin* the next day, infuriatingly simple. One night in October, after an especially grueling week, Sean went for an especially long nighttime jog along Court Street. He'd been gone for two hours when a truck driver happened to see, in the cone of his headlights, a person's legs splayed on the side of the road. It took another hour for the police to arrive, identify the body, and break the news to Maura. They called it a hit-and-run. They had no reason not to. They pledged to do everything they could to identify the driver and put him away. But Maura, standing in the kitchen, holding the phone at a sound-muffling distance from her face, as a confused Alistair looked on from the living room, had no interest in what they were saying. Their talk of investigation and retribution implied a future, a forward continuation of days, and at that moment Maura could imagine no future, she felt that this day was the one she would live in forever, and they never found the driver anyway.

She wasn't so catatonic, in the weeks that followed—as her mother came up from Florida to look after Alistair and a train of McCabes delivered shepherd's pies to her door—as not to discern a few mysteries. How, for example, had Sean, who was fastidious about running against traffic, not seen the car swerving into his path? And why did the police find no skid marks, not even faint ones? Even the fastest-thinking absconder, they told her, would have at first hit his brakes. And why, a month after Sean's death, did Cillian call and tell her, in a theatrically ponderous voice, that he had opened an educational trust for Alistair in the amount of $120,000? This was a lot of money even by Cillian's standards; he was rich but not that rich. Maura doubted that he was directly responsible for Sean's death (he was terrible but not that terrible) but every likely explanation she followed in her mind—an evictee taking revenge, a debtor lashing out, a competitor sending a warning, a victim of an exploitative or scuttled deal evening the score, a business associate eliminating a person in possession of damning kompromat—led, however meanderingly, back to Cillian. His gift, she thought, expressed as much.

Alistair remembered with dismal clarity the winter that followed. To this day he attributed his frantic love of holidays, his insistence that these be singularly joyous events, to the misery of the Thanksgiving and Christmas he shared with his mother that year. Meanwhile, in adult spheres beyond him, Maura cashed in Sean's $50,000 life insurance policy, paid his outstanding credit card bills, did some math, and began looking for a job. She held Alistair to her chest, read to him, talked aimlessly with him. Many nights she slept with him in his bed. She pledged to give him a happiness she now believed was beyond her. She pledged to protect him from the kind of people and, more important, the kind of gnawing ambition that Sean had dirtied his hands and endured no shortage of humiliation in serving. She pledged to nurture in him something else.

Needless to say, Alistair had more than frustrated Maura's plans for him. He'd turned out to be more like his father than even in her worst nightmares she could have feared. And on the day in early May 2016, when he showed up at their house—after a three-hour ShortLine journey spent crouching in his seat, after a cab ride from the bus station to the end of Carey Street, after a sprint through the neighboring backyards to the patio door, where Maura stood waiting for him—he understood at once that by coming home and unloading himself on her he'd brought her full circle, had dragged her back into the muck that had swallowed his father whole, had exposed her again to the very sort of ruinous rapacity she'd done everything to shield him and herself against. And of all the things he'd done in the preceding months this to him felt like the worst.

———————

On the first of June Alistair woke to slivers of sunlight edging around the blackout shade over his window. He sat up in bed, pulled the shade back an inch, took in the yard, brilliant and dewy, then let the shade fall back. Since his arrival on Carey Street almost a month earlier he and Maura had lived by one rule, and it was a simple one: let no one, not a neighbor, not even a postal worker, see him. All day they kept the shades down and the house dark.

He checked the burner phone he'd used to communicate with Nikolai, which he left on and plugged in next to his bed at all times, the only risk he allowed himself to take. For the twenty-ninth day in a row: nothing.

He made his way downstairs, passing through the shaded living room toward the likewise shaded kitchen. He saw no purpose in peeking around the shades at the front of the house to check for the black SUV, the one that had appeared down the block shortly after his arrival and that rematerialized every day. He knew it would be there; he knew there was nothing he could do about it. All he could do was wait and hope, and he wasn't sure how much longer he could do even that.

In the kitchen he made himself a small breakfast and then went down to the basement, where he rolled out a yoga mat and did a hundred push-ups. After he finished he lay back, soaking up the sunlight from the tiny frosted windows at the top of the basement wall, the only ones he and Maura had decided they could leave uncovered. He avoided looking at the far end of the room, where Maura kept all the overpriced furniture he'd bought her at Christmas with his earnings from Nikolai. Maura had refused to make use of the furniture but had also refused to return it, maybe to spare his feelings, maybe to preserve it as a warning against any future acts of coercive generosity. To maximize space she could have stored it in the secret room behind the panels of pink fiberglass, but as far as Alistair knew Maura hadn't been in the room, had hardly even acknowledged it, since she'd first stumbled on it some twenty-five years ago.

He went back up to kitchen, sat at the breakfast nook, and opened the *New York Times* that Maura had left for him on the table. The regular meals, the regular exercise, the hour a day minimum of reading: all were done at Maura's insistence. Though she never invoked the word it was plain to her that Alistair was depressed, and she felt the least he could do, while he languished in this purgatory, was keep his body in good order, his blood moving, his brain active.

But the news, being consumed by the election, provided no antidote to Alistair's depression. His deteriorating mind found no refuge in a deteriorating world. Even when he flipped to less daunting pages, the business section, the real estate section, his thoughts sputtered. His eyes trudged from subject to verb to object in an uncomprehending slog. He felt every day more vacant inside, less capable of taking in new information, as if his mind were voiding itself, cleaning itself, making room for something—but what?

He thought of the wooden cross upstairs, in his desk drawer.

At eleven-thirty he stationed himself at the counter and began prepping. Every weekday Alistair made his mother lunch. At first Maura had fended him off, telling him, as she unfailingly did, that it wasn't his responsibility to take care of her. But Alistair had insisted. He owed Maura an unrepayable debt, he owed her his life, he felt it was the least he could do.

On the afternoon in early May when Alistair had run out of Port Authority and collapsed on a bench in the shadow of the *Intrepid*, he'd thought of his aimless cross-country journey and caved. He'd called Maura, laid everything out in all its grisly detail, and begged for shelter. She'd not only told him he could come home but demanded he do so. The only thing scarier to her than the danger facing him was the prospect of losing contact with him, of living in ignorance about where he was and whether he was safe. She maintained that they'd made the right decision. In truth she seemed to get a perverse joy out of having him back under her roof. But every day Alistair regretted burdening her more and more. He'd made her life miserable, a slow march of days spent in darkness and secrecy, and he'd put that life, however diminished, at risk.

They neither pretended this life was sustainable nor talked much about when or in what way it might change. Alistair still checked the burner every day for a message from Nikolai (after three days of having it on and receiving no assassinatory visits he'd been left to believe Nikolai's claim that it was untraceable) and he still trusted that Nikolai would, as soon as he came up with a plan, reach out to him. He knew Nikolai cared about him, he knew he felt guilty for ensnaring him in a plot beyond his ken. But as time passed Alistair's hope faded, because he also knew Nikolai was weak, shrewd in many ways but stupid in many others, and ultimately as powerless against Herve as he was. (Among the possibilities he half entertained, crammed into a lightless corner of his mind, was that Nikolai was no longer alive.)

He held out dimmer hope that Herve's scheme would fall apart on its own, that he'd make a misstep and expose himself and be brought to justice by the authorities. But in his daily scan of the *New York Times* Alistair saw no sign of such a misstep, no inquiries into the various properties Herve had bought up, no hints that any part of his project had come to light, and in the local paper no follow-up about the twenty-four-year-old groundskeeper who abruptly and for no evident reason had committed "suicide." Alistair suspected that even if journalists or law enforcement agencies began poking around in the right places Herve would remain clear of their prodding fingers, and he suspected too that even if the scheme fell apart Herve would still pursue his goal of offing the two people, himself and Nikolai, who might try to bring him down.

Going to the authorities himself seemed unwise. Given that he was too spooked to log on to Nikolai's server and access his work email—and given that Herve's tech hounds had probably wiped everything anyway—his only evidence was his testimony, which he couldn't count on anyone believing or being able to substantiate. And he worried that any attempt to destroy Herve, however feeble and futile, would, if discovered, redouble Herve's determination to vaporize him. Nikolai's words echoed in his head near constantly: *You have seen what he is willing to do. Now he is coming for us.*

Occasionally he and Maura discussed the nuclear option: they could obtain false identities and leave the country. But Alistair wasn't sure he had the wherewithal to secure fake papers, and Maura most certainly didn't. And so they passed their days in fruitless waiting, fruitless wondering, and more than anything it was this—the persistent interminable ticking of the doom clock, the lack of any endpoint or object to live toward—that depressed him. Without something to aim for he didn't know quite how to be.

Maura impressed him by her ability to hold up her end of their secret. When neighbors asked why she'd installed shades in every window and left them down at all hours she explained that she was trying to cool the house without employing the AC. She kept her few friends at a distance, she made excuses when it came time for her to host book club, and when anyone (a colleague, a St. Francis parent, a McCabe whose beckoning wave she failed to avoid in the grocery store) asked about Alistair she gave them the admittedly shoddy story they'd agreed on: after graduation Alistair had decided to hike the Appalachian Trail, she had no idea where he was on any given day but it sounded like he was having fun, she would let him know they'd asked after him.

With his access to the outside world filtered entirely through Maura, Alistair had no way of keeping tabs on Mark and Elijah, and this pained him. He thought daily of Mark's pitiful profession of love. He wondered where Elijah had landed after Mark had terminated their lease. On the few nights when the mood struck, he lowered his briefs, took the bottle of lotion from his night-stand, and got himself off to hazy images of their faces and bodies. He could never quite separate out from his fantasies the hurt he'd surely caused them, the shock and confusion they surely felt at his mysterious departure and still more mysterious unreachability, his anxiety about their anxiety about him. But oddly enough these worries only intensified his desire, hastened his stroking, drove him to an orgasm that felt as much as anything like heartsickness. He wanted to see them again, couldn't, needed to, couldn't. He'd lost the closest thing he'd ever had to love.

His mother arrived home at noon. She came into the kitchen, looked at the meal he'd laid out—sandwiches of tomato and mayonnaise, a salad dressed with olive oil and lemon juice (Alistair made no claims to culinary inventiveness)— and gave him a long hug.

"Productive morning?" she said as they sat. Her voice was at once shared joke and humorless parental concern.

"I exercised," Alistair said. "I tried to read."

"How's that going?"

"Still having trouble concentrating."

Maura pushed some salad onto her plate. "You're getting back into the habit," she said. "Remember all that Dickens you used to read?"

"That you made me read."

"Now all you read is those case studies. I remember you having a freak-out about a project on—was it Home Depot?"

Alistair swallowed a bite of sandwich and shrugged. "Home Depot's quarterly results are a leading indicator of housing market trends. They're a vital metric."

"I'm sure."

He watched Maura as she ate. She was still as pretty as she'd ever been. Her skin was tauter, her body trimmer, her hair more golden than given her forty-six years they had any right to be. But her cheeks looked more drawn than Alistair remembered, her wardrobe more drably suburban. (At Christmas Alistair had also used his earnings to shower Maura with new clothes, but as with the furniture she'd refused to make use of them.) During his brief visits over the past four years Alistair had never picked up on any signs of deterioration in his mother. He now suspected that whenever he'd come home she'd put on a show for him, had dressed and comported herself in such a way as to give the impression that she was happy, occupied, unchanged. Only now that he was living with her did he see how tedious her life could be, how little by little her loneliness and compulsory modesty had fatigued her. Maybe he hadn't noticed this before because he'd lived in the blinding assurance that one day soon he would be able to give her a better life, and maybe he noticed it now only because he knew he wouldn't, not soon, not ever.

"Speaking of school," Maura said. "NYU emailed me again. They keep reminding me they're taking 'extraordinary measures' by contacting a parent."

"What did they say?"

"If you don't take your finals by the end of the summer, you'll have to do the semester over again."

"And you said?"

"'He's hiking the Appalachian Trail, I can't speak for him, I'm sure he'll sort it out soon.'"

Alistair looked at the window, at the margins of sunlight streaming in around the shade. "A hundred thousand dollars of debt for nothing."

"If it makes you feel any better," Maura said, "a lot of people say that even after they graduate."

They ate in silence for a while. Birds made complicated conversation in the trees outside. The grandfather clock in the living room, a vestige of Maura's moth-eaten WASP heritage, struck twelve-thirty. Alistair asked Maura about the admissions office. It was her least favorite topic of conversation, but these days they didn't have many.

"We finalized the class of 2020," she said. "Now I'm spending my days putting together welcome packets. Maybe this will be the year I don't smear one with papercut blood."

"They give you such grunt work," Alistair said. "You need to ask for a raise."

"When I started my salary was twenty thousand. I'm at almost double that now."

And in the same time frame, Alistair wanted to say, the rich have increased their wealth by untold orders of magnitude. But if he said this to his mother he'd only insult her. To make peace with her life she had to believe that she had everything she could ever want, that she suffered no happiness-precluding privations or deficiencies. To countenance her exploitation would be to invite in a disgruntlement that her exploitation had rendered her powerless to do anything about. Alistair had observed this same dynamic, this same self-deluding, self-sparing contentment, in practically every middle-class person he'd ever met. But to observe it in his mother, the most intelligent person he knew, was particularly painful.

He shifted to a different though no less unfavorable topic. "Is it there?" he asked.

Maura looked at him with performative confusion.

"The SUV."

She only nodded. Alistair stared at his plate.

"Should I help you clean up?"

"I can do it," Alistair said. "I have the time."

"Try reading more. Or exercising again."

"I'll see you at five."

Alistair walked her to the door and then, awkwardly, walked back down the hall and stepped out of view before she opened it. He listened to the sound of her driving away. He imagined her in her car, cruising past Recreation Park, past St. Francis, down Riverside Drive and across the bridge to campus, availing herself with a free person's insouciance of all the landmarks of his childhood. He envisioned years of living in this crazy-making, spirit-killing darkness. And here it came again: the nagging vacancy, the feeling that his mind was emptying itself, that he was falling apart.

He went up to his room, where the wooden cross awaited him.

———————

In the spring of 2001, after she'd secured a job in the admissions office at SUNY Binghamton and cleared away the tangliest cobwebs of her grief, Maura turned her mind to the trust Cillian McCabe had opened for Alistair. She decided she couldn't stand to let it sit untouched. It felt like a weight, like a white elephant, like blood money: 120,000 cruel reminders of Sean, 120,000 disingenuous apologies, 120,000 invitations to renounce her anger in exchange for a reward she'd never desired in the first place. Cillian had spoken to her in money, a language Maura hated, and she felt that to let this $120,000 occupy space in her mind, let alone to express gratitude for it, would be to suggest that she heard and accepted his message, that she spoke this language too. She felt this even though Cillian made no inquiries into how she was spending the money. After he'd called to notify her of the gift he'd broken off contact with her, as she'd predicted he would, and beyond a few accidental run-ins over the following years they never spoke again.

At the end of the summer she pulled Alistair out of public school and enrolled him in St. Francis. Unlike many St. Francis parents, whom Maura would soon meet and then spend more than a decade strenuously avoiding, she had no religious motivations. She herself was an atheist and Sean had been only a Chreaster Catholic. But Sean had longed to send Alistair to St. Francis, and she wanted to pay tribute to his wishes. And the tuition, at $7,000 a year, was attractively extortive. Over the course of Alistair's education she would blow through more than half of Cillian's gift, and she was certain the remainder would be safely gobbled up by college. She could give her son the best education Binghamton had to offer (not a particularly high standard) and at the same time accomplish her goal of disappearing Cillian's money, of unburdening her mind of it.

It was ironic that Maura sent Alistair to St. Francis in order not to think about money, though, because the end result of his time there was that he came to think about not much else. Probably Maura should have understood, on that first day in September, when she walked him to the campus overlooking Recreation Park, that she was sending her son to a place where more than anything else he would learn the language that Cillian spoke. Alistair himself understood this, albeit in his seven-year-old's, not-really-understanding way. Upon arriving at the long, low tan brick building he stood at a distance from the other boys, holding himself erect, clutching his mother's familiar clammy hand, as he watched the younger kids play prebell tag in their white polos and blue slacks while the juniors and seniors held court, ties flung over their shoulders, on the hoods of their Audis and BMWs. He marveled at the crispness and cleanliness of his new classmates, at the neatness of their haircuts and the confidence of their gestures, squinting amid so many gleaming dark dress shoes. Though St. Francis was only up a short hill from his old school, Alistair felt as if he were breathing different air. He looked down at his own white polo and blue slacks and detected, with newly clear eyes, a few wrinkles and specks of lint.

By national standards the boys at St. Francis weren't tremendously rich. Most were the sons of doctors, lawyers, business owners, or executives at Lockheed Martin or BAE Systems, the only major manufacturing enterprises to have maintained a presence in the region. By Alistair's standards, though, they lived in a separate universe. They seemed to have been hiding from him all this time, living in a different Binghamton, up in the hills, behind stone facades and double-height windows, behind the services and industries that in his naivete he'd taken to be authorless and self-operating. And before he had the sense to abstract from their superior possessions and superior comportments the cash required to fund them, before he understood his classmates' superiority to be simply a matter of their having more of a liquid and potentially gettable thing, he imputed to them a kind of alien holiness. Cars with leather seats, parents who wore suits, the polos with the crocodile on the breast, baseball hats from Floridian lotuslands and ski sanctuaries out west: such were the indicia of a world that, because it was so different from the world of his house on Carey Street, because it appeared so impenetrable, so phenomenologically bizarre, it seemed silly to feel bad about being excluded from.

Except Alistair did, eventually, start to feel bad. As the years went by he became wise to the fact that for all their affluence his peers were not so alien, and not so holy. Down the halls they paraded, a stream of freckled and hormonally disproportioned boys, Ryans and Colins, FitzThises and O'Thats, unimpressive of intellect, uncreative in their bullying, unremarkable in sports:

and yet undeniably rich. It made his little heart ache to watch them behave like jackals—to etch breasts into desks, leave shits in toilets, throw one another against the lockers, bomb quizzes, skip class—and then, at the end of each day, to load themselves into their parental Lincolns and Benzes and return to lives that were assuredly better than his.

He himself was an exemplar of good behavior. He had Maura remove all scuff marks from his shoes, asked her to teach him how to mousse his hair and articulate a side part in roughly the ten o'clock position, was scrupulous about the neatness of a sheet of loose-leaf paper: he considered it unconscionable to submit a handwritten assignment from which every shred of perforated offcut had not been shorn. He was also quiet when he needed to be and outspoken when it served him. He raised his hand, elbow barely bent, whenever he knew the answer to a teacher's question, which practically speaking was all the time.

He seemed to have in mind, as he strove to perfect himself, a sort of imaginary rich kid, a cartoon version of his classmates—cartoonishly good-looking, cartoonishly proper, cartoonishly smart—that, when it came down to it, none of his classmates looked or acted anything like. And the closer he got to his ideal of a rich kid, and the further the actual rich kids deviated from it, the more resentful he became. He might be more like a "rich kid" than the rich kids themselves but he was still factually poor and they factually rich: his efforts at self-invention were powerless against this stubborn material truth. And he suspected this truth was ultimately what mattered. For all their mediocrity his classmates nevertheless lived in huge houses on South Mountain, and in the eyes of the world these houses surely redeemed their behavioral and academic failures, just as his own small house on Carey Street surely spoiled his victories.

That increasingly he felt his house, and his life with his mother, to be a site of despoilment: this made his little heart ache all the more. Maura's job was criminally low-paying, but by further perfecting her talent for thrift and drawing whenever necessary on the life insurance money Sean had left her she managed to establish a semblance of middle-class security. And, objectively speaking, there was nothing shameful about their life. Nothing shameful about their yard-sale and hand-me-down furniture. Nothing shameful about their food, even if Alistair was quick to disabuse himself of the notion that French toast for dinner was merely a "fun" alternative to chicken parm or beef stew, especially considering that this and other breakfast-for-dinners tended to coincide with the ends of Maura's pay cycles. Nothing shameful about their 1996 Ford Taurus, even if it broke down regularly and was princess-and-pea-sensitive to rumble strips. Nothing shameful about their "vacations" to camping grounds near Ithaca, which always included a drive by Maura's comparatively well-appointed childhood home and which therefore reinforced rather than provided temporary relief from the fact that they were pretty near to being poor.

Objectively speaking, there was nothing shameful about their life: this Alistair would assert to himself, again and again, when he got older. But middle-school Alistair did find it to be shameful, and occasionally he threw out obtuse suggestions for making it less so. He once told Maura he thought she'd make a good lawyer, for example.

"That would require my going to law school," Maura said.

"So go to law school," Alistair said. "You'd be great at it!"

"That would require my being ten years younger," Maura said. "Also my having many thousands of dollars. Give me a time machine and many thousands of dollars and I'll go to law school."

Another time he suggested they go on vacation to Hilton Head, where his one sort-of-friend, Jess Flanagan, went every summer with his family.

"I thought you liked camping," Maura said.

"We can try it this summer," Alistair said. "If we don't like it, we can go back to camping."

Maura pursed her lips and cocked her head, at once protective of Alistair's economic obliviousness and resentful of it. "Why don't you ask Jess if you can go with his family?"

"I'd want you to come too."

"I'm not Jess's friend, though," Maura said. "My only friend is you."

Another time he suggested they buy a house on South Mountain. "All the kids in my class live there," he said.

"All the kids in your class," Maura said. "The kids that, as you never neglect to mention, you dislike."

"It just seems like a nice place to live."

"Strange that it doesn't produce nice kids."

"We'd make it nice."

"How about this," Maura said. "After you go off to college and get rich, you can buy us a house wherever you like. How does that sound to you?"

In retrospect these suggestions were not only obtuse but surely hurtful. Maura must have felt bad enough about their straitened circumstances without Alistair rubbing her nose in them. And she must have been dismayed to find that her efforts not to care about money, to create a little world in which the ampleness of their love would render irrelevant the limitedness of their means, had been in vain. Alistair, in his class-consciousness, in his materialism and striving, must have reminded her of the worst parts of Sean, as well as the worst parts of her mother. For as much as she tried to prevent the assertion of these instincts in her son she was helpless against this genetic pincer movement: this was how she must have felt.

To atone for the hurt he'd unconsciously caused her, Alistair assumed the role of his mother's defender. He was ashamed of his life, but he was also ashamed of his shame, because he loved his mother and for all intents and purposes she *was* his life; and the more acute his shame became the more acute became his love, until the two feelings coalesced into one, weird and unwieldy. The anger he might feel about having a cruddy winter coat presented itself, weirdly, as an angry love for his mother. *My coat is just fine! My mother is just fine!* This was what he sought to communicate to the other boys: with his seriousness, his aloofness, his pool-stick-straight posture, his habit of totally annihilating them on tests. Never mind that the other boys never made fun of his coat. Never mind that they never said anything about Maura, except, on occasion, that she was a MILF.

Alistair's love for his mother: it was weird and angry and deep, associable less with flowers and sunlight than with earthquakes, hurricanes, lava.

By high school he'd resolved to take her suggestion, however nonliteral it may have been: he would go off to college, get rich, and vindicate them. He excelled in most of his classes, including English, which naturally made Maura happy, but eventually he decided economics would serve his purposes best. His aptitude in the subject gave him what felt like a weapon against his peers. The superiority of his classmates obtained on the level of the phenomenal: you could see their superiority, you could hear it, if you went to their houses and sat on their plush leather couches you could feel it. Economics, by contrast, was abstract: you couldn't see the law of supply and demand, you couldn't hear the distinction between real and nominal value, you couldn't feel the efficient market hypothesis. But such principles enabled Alistair to understand the phenomenal world, to penetrate it and, by and by, to feel a power over it, as if being able to gauge the price of something offset the pain of not being able to buy it. He could use this way of thinking to desacralize the phenomenal world, to wrestle it into logical submission, to strip his classmates of their superiority and to deprive their possessions—the stuff you saw and heard and felt—of their seeming immanent nobility. Plus, he was pretty sure that if he made a career out of this abstract thinking he'd be able to buy himself and his mother all the splendiferous stuff you actually could see, hear, and feel.

By tenth grade he was taking advanced economics, advanced statistics, and advanced calculus; and the same year he founded the St. Francis Investment Club, which admittedly was a failure (its one other member was Jess Flanagan, and the school limited its support to giving them an unoccupied classroom in which to hold their "strategy meetings") but which Alistair knew would nevertheless make for a bright spot on his future college applications; and in eleventh grade he began taking undergraduate finance courses through SUNY Binghamton's Bridges to the Baccalaureate program; and the same year he used the money he earned as a cashier at Target to buy subscriptions to the *Wall Street Journal*, the *Financial Times*, and the *Economist*.

He understood the principle of portfolio diversification, of availing yourself of gains across multiple markets, of being broadly rather than narrowly successful, so he also joined the tennis team. He turned out to be fast and, unlike his teammates, foresightful. His favorite tactic in practice was to hit the ball into no-man's-land, force his teammate to take the net position, and then vanquish him with an almost impudently gentle lob. His approach to tennis was of a piece with his approach to economics. Maybe his teammates had an inborn affinity for the sport, maybe they had better whites, but he could outwit them. By way of sheer shrewdness he could make them pant, make them feel neglectful and thickheaded, and he relished this. He spent his varsity years floating between third and second singles and, in his junior-year season, had the team's winningest match record.

"I'm the winningest!" he said to Maura.

"I'm proud of you," Maura said. "Except you don't need to be the winningest. I'd still love you if you were the losingest."

"Sure," Alistair said. "But I'm the winningest!"

The one time Alistair did not feel like the winningest was in Friday Mass, which took place at St. Francis Church, a Gothic Revival building across the street from and at stark architectural odds with the school. Every week, under the church's endoskeletal stone arches, Alistair sensed new criteria for success asserting themselves. For the duration of that hour he felt his muscles going slack, his eyelids drooping, his horse-at-the-bit champing giving way to a passivity, a kind of exhaustion, that radiated outward and cast unflattering light on all his annihilating, his shrewd lobbing and slicing, his questing after splendiferous stuff. It was the moral equivalent of the moment when, after his prepractice jog, he finally started to sweat: only after he'd stopped for breath did he begin to suffer the consequences of his exertions. Standing at the ambo, wisp-haired Father Fitzpatrick espoused kindness, guilt, humility, self-abnegation, the paltriness of the material world in comparison to the world to come, et cetera. All but the meek, he was fond of making clear, would be written out of the eschatological will. Never but during that hour did Alistair wonder if perhaps his thinking was wrongheaded. Nowhere but in those polyurethane-varnished pews did a program for living as compelling as his own, and perhaps more compelling, present itself. Maura, in her atheism, cautioned Alistair to take these theological teachings lightly. But the mood of that church nevertheless bore into him. He nevertheless occasionally mumbled along with the choir as they proposed he *Seek ye first the kingdom of God / And His righteousness / And all these things shall be added unto you* . . .

One area in which Alistair did take these theological teachings lightly was sex, which he numbered among the splendiferous things he would at the first opportunity pursue. He'd tested the flexibility of his desires, found them to be intransigent, concluded that if God had meant for him to like girls He would have engineered his senses accordingly. As it happened his senses wanted nothing to do with girls. At the coed dances held in the St. Francis gym he hardly noticed them. Instead, while he sat with Jess Flanagan on the floor, against a stack of retracted bleachers, he monitored the clench and release of male buttocks, the straining of torsos against snug-fitting tees, the passage of sweat beads down bristly napes, followed with his nose the olfactory heaven of near-passing seniors doused in Axe Body Spray or colognes from Hollister or Abercrombie & Fitch, while above him there thundered sundry early-'10s anthems, candies by Ke$ha and David Guetta, symphonies of whoops and dubstep wobbles, echolocative reverbs suggestive of infinite space—and it was all he could do at these moments not to lose his cool, not to stare for too long at any one wondrous bicep, not to let his smirk turn into a gape, not to slide to the floor in terrible agony-ecstasy.

Meanwhile, Jess: "I hate these things."

"Same," Alistair managed. "Terrible!"

Curiously, the boys Alistair most lusted after tended to be the very ones he most wanted to annihilate, whether in class or on the court. He had a thing for handsome jerks who drove Range Rovers and had two-point-something GPAs. The handsomer and meaner they were, the richer and dumber, the more likely they were to serve his onanist needs. Toward each of these boys he felt the same tripartite craving: wanted to be him, wanted to best him, wanted to bury his face in his crotch. It wasn't clear at any one moment, in his writhing and stroking and frantic reaching for more lotion, whether he was getting off on a fantasy of emulation or domination or, most fantastical of all, sheer tenderness. Wasn't clear, once his cravings had been dispatched and the result of his efforts lay globbily on his chest, whether he was feeling the satisfaction of a joiner or victor or lover. He panted with his efforts and with his confusion; then, twenty minutes later, he reached for the lotion again, selected a new boy, and started the process over, with no clearer idea of what particular hankering was driving him to strangulate his dick. Weird.

One thing very clear in Alistair's mind was this: he needed to go to college in a place where he could exorcise these cravings. Join the alphas, quash them, and in his free time bed all the boys he pleased. He needed a place, in other words, that was commensurate with his desires, a place where he could feast without having to apologize for his voraciousness or, in the case of sexual conquests, for his outré choice of meal. Life in Binghamton felt like one ongoing apology. He was sorry to be poor, sorry not to be the modest, contented son Maura clearly wanted him to be, sorry to have to contravene every available belief system by harboring a strong preference for dick. He was keen not to feel sorry anymore, was keen to find out who he'd be and what he'd do without the yoke of this sorriness.

His guidance counselor, a sweet-voiced deacon's wife named Mrs. Truitt, was alert to his good grades and his extensive catalog of extracurriculars, but she clearly mistook him for another vanilla-flavored high-achiever. She showed him packets from Bates and Colby, Middlebury and Wesleyan, Hamilton and Bucknell. To judge by their information packets these colleges were for kids who'd grown up rich, who had no reason to believe they would ever not be rich, and who therefore could afford to forgo his brand of ambition in exchange for twee humanitarianism, aimless athleticism, and inane creative endeavors. The Bucknell packet featured an article about a student who'd started a "shelter" for lost gloves. Perhaps decades from now, after he'd amassed his millions, Alistair could relax enough to send his own kids to schools like these. But for him, for his purposes, for the stage of transgenerational wealth accumulation at which he found himself (i.e., stage one): no. He didn't foresee being able to sate his appetite in such places. Based on the schools' miniscule student bodies and their middle-of-nowhere settings he didn't foresee being able to bed many boys either.

After he'd taken a day to peruse the packets he returned to Mrs. Truitt's office and plopped them on her desk and said, "How about Columbia. Or NYU. Someplace down there."

"Oh," Mrs. Truitt said. "Oh, *well*."

Of all the colleges Alistair applied to he sweated most over his application to NYU Stern. He appreciated that Stern did nothing to disguise the number of its alumni who'd become billionaires. His application essay was essentially a screed against Black-Scholes ("The unwisdom of outsourcing investment strategy to quants has, I think we can agree, been amply established"). Meanwhile, on the twelve-pound laptop Maura's mother had given him for his sixteenth birthday, he researched "gay bars in NYC," of which there appeared to be an infinite quantity.

He thought, *Yes.* He thought, *Yes, yes, yes.*

The one person who raised an objection to his college plans was, unluckily for him, the one person whose opinion mattered.

"NYU is extremely expensive," Maura said to him. "You have less in your trust now than it costs to go there for one year. And, because we have the trust, we're in that lovely not-quite-poor-enough bracket, so I'm not sure you'll get full financial aid. And, lovely bracket that we're in, I can't actually pay the rest."

"I'll get a merit scholarship," Alistair said.

"It still may not cover everything."

Alistair smiled diplomatically. "I can take out loans. I'll be making serious money. First-year I-banking salary is a hundred twenty thou. That's the *floor*. This is a riskless investment."

Maura stared at the little boy who somewhere along the way had begun shortening *thousand* to *thou* and speaking of salary *floors*. She wasn't even sure what the *I* in *I-banking* stood for. *I, thou*: these words meant different things to her. "See, I question that logic," she said. "Pay a lot to make a lot. To justify the debt you have to make enough to pay it back. You force yourself into a career you may not even like."

"I'll like it," Alistair said. "Trust me."

"You make money in order not to think about money. But the more you make the more you want. The money becomes only about itself. It's like an echo chamber."

Alistair estimated that at least seventy-five percent of this comment was directed not at him but at Sean and her mother. Echo chamber was right. "Even if I had to pay nothing for college I'd still study finance," he said. "It's what I'm good at. It's what I'm interested in."

"You used to be such a reader," Maura said. "You used to love astronomy. Those stars you and your father put on your ceiling? You loved those. You used to be able to point at the sky and say, 'Mom, that's Cassiopeia.'"

"The stars are still on my ceiling," Alistair said. "And I still love them. But I don't want to be an astronomer."

"I just want you to know you're allowed to do whatever you want to do," Maura said. "Even if it's not lucrative. Especially if it's not lucrative. It's important to me that you know that."

"I know," Alistair said.

But he knew also that it was too late. By now Charles Dickens had been replaced by Niall Ferguson and Nassim Nicholas Taleb. By now the stars on his ceiling had come to represent not their astral counterparts but other points of stellular yearning: Goldman Sachs, Morgan Stanley, JPMorgan Chase. He had a vision of himself rising and excelling and accruing until such time as he really would, with all due respect to his mother, not have to think about money, or least not think about it the way he had up to now. What Maura failed to see was the poetic thrust of this trajectory. Put in your years of striving and struggling until you found yourself in a twenty-foot-ceiling PH and could once again feel as light and carefree as a little kid. The grueling hours and furious competition and relentless jockeying, the bitterness of all this, was a means to an end that actually was quite sweet.

The good news from NYU, when it came in April, equipped Alistair with a kind of armor against his classmates. No longer did the other boys, the bulk of whom bound for midtier Jesuit schools, intimidate him. He was certain high school would soon turn out to have been the best period of their lives, that within ten years they would all be insurance brokers or pharmaceutical reps earning unremarkable salaries and feeling nostalgic about the superiority they'd enjoyed in Binghamton. If they were companies he would have recommended shorting them. And, perhaps because they no longer intimidated him, they no longer did it for him physically. He'd been to New York City just once, for a daylong museum marathon with his AP European History class, but if the men he'd seen there were any indication of what the city had to offer he was in for a reeducation of his senses.

Maura continued to fret, however. One evening in July, arriving home after a shift at Target, Alistair found her at the breakfast nook, perusing the NYU course catalog he'd left open on his laptop. "I want you to take one of these English classes," she said. "You can help me brush up."

Alistair sat across from her and turned the laptop toward him. Every course title mentioned a century that wasn't the twenty-first. "Maybe for an elective," he said.

"And if you don't like finance, or whatever it is you're studying, I want you to change your major."

"Never had trouble following my heart."

"And I want you to make friends."

"Hope to have less trouble doing that."

"And to date," Maura said. "I want to hear about the boyfriends." (Alistair's egress from the closet, at sixteen, had been an unremarkable event. Apparently for Maura it had been a closet with a glass door.)

"If there's any news on that front, you'll be the first to hear it," Alistair said.

Maura stared at him. "I see this sweetness in you," she said, but she trailed off, and then came the tears. This was the summer of tears. She said she would miss him, that he was all she had, but that he shouldn't worry about her, that it wasn't his fault he was all she had. She said she was sorry for objecting to his career plans and then, in her meandering way, proceeded to issue further objections to those plans. By the time she was done the sun had set. "Don't listen to me."

Alistair would have liked not to. He begrudged her the pity she elicited from him: this young, pretty, lonely person who'd lost her husband to restless ambition and was now afraid she would lose her son to it too. He felt sorry for her. He felt sorry not to be her intellectual companion, aesthetically inclined, gentle of temperament. He felt sorry that he cared most about the one thing, money, that she was determined not to care about at all. He wanted to get rich in large part so that he could come back and rescue her, and not least he felt sorry that she couldn't see that. All this: more sorriness he was keen to get free of.

"Just promise me," she said.

"Promise you what?"

She smiled through her tears. "I don't know."

He shut the laptop and took her hand. "I promise," he said, and then in September he went off to NYU.

———

Behind the shaded windows on Carey Street, the march of empty days to which Alistair's life had been reduced proceeded. He did his exercises, he made Maura lunch. He searched the *New York Times* unavailingly for any word of Herve. Every day Maura confirmed the presence of the SUV; every day Alistair checked the idle burner phone. The first week of June passed, then the second, then the third. Summer had arrived, but Alistair couldn't see its bounty.

He would have wondered how long this could go on if he could stomach the question. He feared he was already living the rest of his days.

Then, one afternoon, while he was busying himself staring at a wall in advance of Maura's homecoming, he heard a sound. The sound was one he'd so anticipated, so longed for and so feared, that at first he wondered if he was only imagining it—if his head had simply decided to do something about its own waiting. But the sound persisted, a repeating buzz, a vibration of plastic against wood, from upstairs.

He charged to his bedroom. He nearly tripped on his rug. He grabbed the burner from the bedside table.

"Oh!" Nikolai said when he answered. "Oh, my friend!"

Nikolai's Bulgarian accent seemed likewise to come from Alistair's head. He'd pined for so long to hear from him that he couldn't quite accept the object of his pining as real. He felt his cheeks flame and his heart thump. A surge of misplaced affection, of loving worry, coursed through him. "Where are you?" he said. "What's happening?"

"I have been everywhere," Nikolai said. "All up and down the coast. I am in Florida now. It is like being in hell."

In the background Alistair could hear a whirr of multilane traffic and, possibly, a low plane.

"The question is where are you," Nikolai said. "I have what we need. I have a plan."

Alistair was slow in responding, and when he answered he spoke in an embarrassed rush.

"You what!" Nikolai said. "You are stupid, my friend. Stupid, stupid!"

"They're here," Alistair said. "His men. They're watching the house." He explained about the black SUV, its undying presence down the street. "I don't know what to do. What's your plan?"

"My plan will not work," Nikolai said, "as long as they are on your ass. You need to get rid of them."

"How?"

"I cannot think of everything myself," Nikolai said. "It has been hard enough to put together this plan. Once they are off your ass, you will contact me. Then I will come for you."

"And then what?" Alistair said. "Are we going to the authorities? Have you been putting together evidence?"

Nikolai barked. "My friend, I must say, you have gotten very stupid. Do you want to end up like that kid?"

Alistair pictured the groundskeeper's face, as he did several times each day. Even as it grew fuzzier in his mind it continued to intrude on his thoughts, to send him to the couch in weak-kneed anguish. He thought of Herve's project, his deranged ambition, and, weak-kneed, sat on his bed. "We can't let him go on with it," he said. "We have to do something. It's the only way."

"Yes," Nikolai said. "The only way to get killed."

Alistair stared at the desk drawer that had lately become so familiar to him. The last time he'd opened it he hadn't shut it all the way, and he could see the edge of the wooden cross inside it. The cross seemed to be listening to him, just as he, however clumsily, however tentatively, had begun listening to it. "What if we just wait a little longer," he said. "Let Herve quit his search. And then we can see what evidence we have. We can think about who to talk to."

"You do not understand," Nikolai said. "There is no us gathering 'evidence.' There is no us 'talking' to anyone. There is only us trying not to get killed! You think Herve will quit? He will never quit. From what I have seen, he is only getting more desperate."

Alistair held himself erect. "What have you seen?"

Nikolai let out a long breath. "A while back Howie had me install a camera in his living room. He was convinced one of his housekeepers was stealing from him. I still have access to the stream."

Alistair asked again: "What have you seen?"

"Herve is in New York," Nikolai said. "He goes to Howie's every few days. I guess he thinks he can get information about us out of them. Howie, Jay, Elijah."

From elsewhere in Alistair's body came another surge of loving worry. "Elijah?"

"He must really be losing hope, if he is questioning them," Nikolai said. "He will not get anywhere with them. They do not know anything. They are too busy. Too consumed in their—I do not even know what it is."

"Consumed?" Alistair said. "What what is?"

"My friend," Nikolai said. "Jay has outdone himself. And he has dragged your Elijah into it too. He is living there now, with Jay and Howie. And the things I am seeing, with my little camera? There are crazy things happening in that apartment, crazy! But it is nothing we need to worry about."

Nikolai may not have seen cause to worry, but Alistair did. What antics had Elijah let himself get caught up in? With his thirst for adventure, his perverse fascinations, his eight years of pent-up frustration, he might let himself get caught up in anything. And Jay was certainly capable of crazy things.

"I must go," Nikolai said. He'd gotten closer to the whirr of the traffic, the whine of the low plane. "You will let me know when you have taken care of things there."

"Nikolai, wait."

"And then I will take care of everything else," Nikolai said. "I have got you covered, my friend. I am sorry. I am sorry you are stuck with me. I know I have not been such a good friend."

He hadn't been a good friend, not in the least. But as Alistair sat with the phone pressed to his ear it came home to him, as never before, that he was the only real friend he'd ever had.

"Goodbye," Nikolai said and hung up.

Alistair chucked the phone onto the bed and put his face in his hands. He sat breathing heavily, focusing on the womb-like light between his fingers. After a while he stood and went to the desk drawer.

Weeks earlier, while cleaning out his room, if only to give himself something to do, Alistair had stumbled on the small wooden cross every St. Francis senior had received at graduation. He'd stared at the cross for an unexpectedly long while; he'd felt an unexpected desire to touch it. And ever since then, at least once a day, he'd opened the drawer and checked in on it, as if it were a small animal he'd rescued and hidden away for safekeeping. He'd never before placed any value on the cross, and he didn't know why it was calling out to him now. All he knew was that in the frenetic aimlessness of his days his brief moment with the cross was the one time his head cleared and his vision focused. Up to this point he'd had other things to feel clearheaded about, to focus his vision on. But now those things were gone, and this one had remained, patient in its neglect, as if waiting for him, as if trying to tell him something. And what it told him now was that Nikolai's plan—merely to escape, merely to survive, merely to get away from Herve and forget about what'd he done, what he might yet do—wasn't good enough.

He went downstairs. As he sat on the couch, staring emptily at his father's framed photograph of Rio de Janeiro, he fixed his mind on the signal detail Nikolai had relayed. Herve was in New York—newly real, newly accessible, if only by daunting degrees of separation. Also he was getting desperate. Also he was losing hope. Alistair had long suspected this about Herve: that his wealth had grown up around him without ever transforming him, that at bottom he was still a boy, lonely and scared.

And Alistair was scared himself. He didn't know how to get out from under the watch of the men in the SUV, and, even if he managed to, he didn't know how to proceed. But the cross seemed to be telling him to proceed boldly—crazily, as Nikolai would put it. He stood from the couch and the old floor beneath him creaked. And, improbably, it was this sound that gave him his idea. All at once, as he rocked his foot on the floor and stared at the token of his father on the wall, he knew what he would do.

───────────

Alistair's first day at NYU, in the fall of 2012, offered every confirmation that he'd made the right decision. He felt the cloud of sorriness he'd lived under in Binghamton dissipating minute by minute. His dormitory, Third North, was situated on a hectic avenue crowded by confirmingly well-dressed and fast-walking pedestrians. The other students in the dormitory's courtyard were confirmingly attractive and arrogant. His room, on the tenth floor, had excellent views of lower Midtown, the towers of which were confirmingly hefty and hard. There would be no apologizing here, he saw. All around him lay an inorganic landscape rich with opportunities to exorcise his cravings.

"How will you sleep at night?" Maura asked, after the fifth or hundredth ambulance had screamed by. She stood in the four-foot passageway between the beds, glancing at the white walls and dimpled linoleum floor.

"Sleeping is not the point," Alistair said.

Outside, by the Ford Taurus, he and Maura hugged for a full three minutes. Twice Alistair tried to pull away and twice she clutched him closer. From over her shoulder he watched other students bidding their parents goodbye. He noticed that none of them were so indiscreetly affectionate. He avoided looking at the Taurus, hoping it wasn't obvious he was affiliated with it.

"Don't be afraid to come home," Maura said, after he'd managed to extricate himself. "If you miss me, if you're overwhelmed, whatever, come home."

"You can come here too," Alistair said. "We'll go to Times Square. We'll go to Rockefeller Center."

Another ambulance screamed by.

"Or I'll just come home," Alistair said.

Maura nodded and, before she walked off, pulled him into one last interminable embrace.

By the time Alistair returned to his dorm his roommate had arrived. After Alistair had received his housing assignment over the summer he'd practiced saying the roommate's name, Vidyadhar, a few dozen times. But when he greeted Alistair now he told him, mercifully, that he could just call him Vidi.

"Do you want to go clubbing tonight?" Vidi asked as he unpacked. His accent had a way of augmenting consonants, opening them up, exposing their quiddities. Alistair looked at his spread of possessions. Nothing in particular, aside from a shiny blue gown in a dry-cleaning bag, evoked his home country of India. Most of his clothes were from Ralph Lauren or Lacoste. He could have been from Binghamton.

"What club?" Alistair asked, trying to affect a cool skepticism.

"Pacha," Vidi said flatly. "The kids from back home are going to Pacha."

Alistair had hoped, with the fake ID he'd bought from a fellow Target cashier back in Binghamton, to check off some of the gay bars on his to-do list. But he figured he could get drunk with Vidi, satisfy his pledge to make friends, then peel away once he was sufficiently buzzed and horny. He was aiming to lose his virginity *tonight*. "OK," he said. "But we need to pregame." Alistair had drunk alcohol exactly once, the previous Christmas, when Maura had permitted him a single glass of wine, and he'd learned this word for preparatory imbibing only by eavesdropping on his St. Francis classmates.

Vidi dug through a Nautica duffel and brought forth a bottle of Smirnoff. "I'm ahead of you, man," he said. "You're slow."

Before they left for Hayden, the dormitory on Washington Square Park where Vidi's friend Arjun lived, they had to sit through a meeting with their floormates and RA. The RA was a French major named Abigail who kept winking while she listed everything they couldn't do. "There is no drinking," she winked. "There is no smoking," she winked. She was only twenty-two but already she had an old person's desperation to ingratiate herself with the young.

Alistair looked around at his thirty or so floormates. He counted twelve East Asians, six Indians, five Black kids, and eight white kids, of whom he was far and away the whitest-looking. He'd expected to profit by his conventional good looks, but now he felt conspicuously blond and blue-eyed, as though he were a UVA student whose GPS had sent him to New York City rather than Charlottesville. He also counted five quite evidently gay boys, identifiable by their princely posture or the feline angle at which they held their heads or, in the case of two, their freshly bleached hair. He also counted an array of exquisite shoes, bags, and oddly cut T-shirts that either bore logos he didn't recognize or, more formidably, *bore no logos at all*. He sensed the wealth evinced by such objects was such that it required no brazen proof. He sensed, in other words, that he was once again a poor kid surrounded by rich kids. But he felt protected, rendered immune to categorization and condescension, by his anonymity. The difference between St. Francis and NYU, he saw, was that no one here had to know that he'd grown up in a little house or that his mother was a glorified secretary. No one had to see him climbing in and out of the Ford Taurus. *Incredible!* was his realization. *No one here has to know I'm poor!*

After the meeting he and Vidi made their way to Hayden. At Alistair's request they crossed over to Fifth Avenue so that they could walk directly toward the Washington Square Arch. The sky was pale blue and the clouds overhead looked like wisps of pink cotton candy. Within ten minutes Alistair had laid eyes on more stunning men than he'd laid eyes on in all his years at home. He saw short beefy men whose athleisure apparel revealed disproportionately muscular thighs. He saw corporate types of arboreal height and stature. He saw asses straining against tight-fitting jeans or jiggling around in gym shorts. He also saw shopping bags from Club Monaco and Bergdorf Goodman that, to his overstimulated mind, seemed like extensions of the asses: like commercial iterations of the flesh.

"The women in New York are quite beautiful," Vidi said.

Alistair stretched himself taller. "So, something I should mention," he said. "I'm actually paying attention to the dudes."

Vidi looked at him with widened eyes and nodded vigorously. "Absolutely, man. That is absolutely cool."

Alistair judged Hayden, when they arrived, to be inferior to Third North by every metric except location. Arjun's room had ugly green carpet and ugly old smoke-yellowed walls. Assembled therein were about ten kids from Mumbai and, at a desk in the corner, Arjun's roommate, a hairy boy from New Jersey named David, who had taken command of the music. He alternated between hip-hop tracks studded with gunshots and sirens and house music numbers as ethereal as the inside of an infant's brain.

Alistair sat down next to a girl who introduced herself as Saritha. "How do you like Vidi?" she asked with odd ebullience. She was wearing a sheer black dress, silver high heels, bangles that covered each of her arms from wrist to elbow, and perfume that might have smelled good if there were less of it.

"I like him so far," Alistair said.

"Back home, we call him the automaton. If you ask him when he wants to meet he'll say 'ten-thirty-five.' If you ask him how far away the restaurant is he'll say 'one-point-three kilometers.'"

"I admire that precision," Alistair said.

"Try this." She proffered a plastic cup containing bright blue liquid. "It's Hpnotiq."

The drink tasted to Alistair like melted-down candy that had been spiked with Tilex. "Is there, uh, anything clearer?"

Saritha nodded and retrieved a bottle of Georgi vodka and another plastic cup from the floor. She poured him what appeared to be four shots' worth. The Georgi, it turned out, was merely Tilex without the candy. But the more Alistair drank of it the less awful it tasted. By the time his cup was empty he was experiencing sensations for which the word "drunk" felt like an unjust designation. Certain facts that might otherwise have seemed plain now took on exclamatory significance. He was eighteen! He was surrounded by kids from the other side of the world! In the course of a day he'd gone from living in the country's most forgettable city to living in its most spectacular one! Also possessed of new significance were the boys in the room. Why had he not noticed, for example, that Vidi's friend Kirit looked uncannily like Cary Grant? Why had he not noticed the thicket of black chest hair sprouting up out of David's tee? He looked at his phone and saw that it was 9:26. When he checked a minute later it was 10:41. He asked the room when they were leaving for Pacha, in a manner that to his ears sounded sufficiently cogent. But everyone in the room laughed, and Kirit slapped him on the shoulder. "Dude," he said, "you are *wasted*."

Transport to Pacha required four cabs. Alistair, hoping to affect financial ease, offered to pay for his and Vidi's and David's. The fare came to $18 plus tip. When he presented his ID at the doors of Pacha the bouncer rolled his eyes and demanded a cover of $35.

"You charged the guy in front of me twenty," Alistair said.

"Yeah," the bouncer said. "His ID was real."

Alistair paid the cover and, because Vidi didn't yet have American cash, paid his cover as well. Inside he waited fifteen minutes for a spot at the bar. The club, he decided, would have made for a good case study in price gouging. His vodka soda came to $22. Saritha asked if he would be so kind as to get "this one," and Alistair smiled and complied. She then asked if he would be so kind as to get "this one" for Kirit too, and he smiled and complied again.

The group found a corner of the dance floor and stood together under the blinding strobes. Occasionally one or two of them (most often David, who declared the DJ to be a genius) ventured into the crowd and returned sweaty and breathless. At one point Kirit went to the bathroom in search of ecstasy. He returned with a New School student named Eugenia. Very quickly Eugenia shifted her attention to Alistair. "I like your eyes," she told him.

"Thank you," Alistair said, stepping backward. "I like them too."

Kirit's flirtational approach consisted of biting Eugenia's ears and clutching her chest aggressively. Alistair found this repulsive, until he realized he would have few compunctions about applying the same maneuvers to a dude.

It was obvious, though, that he would find no dudes at Pacha. The leering and osculating and grinding he observed were all vexingly heterosexual. Eventually he scored a stool at the bar where, thanks to his increasing sobriety, he found the clarity of mind to do a quick and rather depressing self-audit. In his first hours of college he'd blown through more than $170. The funds he'd set aside for spending—the money he'd saved working at Target, plus the graduation gift he'd received from Maura's mother—amounted to $3,500. He'd figured this would get him through freshman year at the very least. If he continued spending at this rate he'd be broke by October. Saritha sidled up next to him and ordered six drinks. When she asked him if he wanted one he shook his head no, mainly for fear that if he said yes he'd volunteer himself as the bill-footer. Once the drinks had been delivered Saritha handed the bartender an American Express Gold Card that she apparently had and that apparently worked just fine. The bill, when it arrived, came to $144, to which Saritha added a $36 tip. "Come join us!" she said. Alistair's mood was plummeting, the specter of scarcity was rearing its head, he felt again shamefully poor and Binghamtonian. Yet he was determined to rescue the evening. "I'm getting out of here," he said.

He left the club and headed east toward Ninth Avenue. According to his research this stretch of Midtown was a gay paradise. He quickly located one of the spots on his list, a bar called the Rail, on Forty-sixth Street. To Alistair it seemed like a Pacha made palatable by its near exclusion of straight people. The strobes proved less offensive now that they were illuminating entangled male bodies. Prominent among these were those of the two go-go boys on the dance floor, who were taking turns rubbing on each other's backsides. $1s and $5s and errant $10s protruded from their neon-colored briefs. Alistair went to the bar and ordered a vodka soda that came to a more reasonable $12. He drank this down and ordered another. As he surveyed the crowd he observed that many of the men were gawking at him. He estimated (and this felt like an honest, empirical estimate) that he was one of the five or ten most attractive people in the bar. He caught the eye of a tall brown-haired guy who, his drunkenness notwithstanding, seemed handsome. All it took was a half nod to summon him over.

"Are you sixteen?" the guy asked, laughing.

"I have an ID saying I'm twenty-one," Alistair said.

"Do you have another ID saying you're sixteen?"

"I'll be nineteen in March."

Without further delay they began to make out. This was Alistair's first kiss. He hadn't expected the inside of another person's mouth to feel so substanceless. He felt he'd left the world of walls and floors and entered a zero-gravity world of wet flesh. He pulled away to get his bearings. He looked at the guy and saw pores he hadn't noticed before. He caught new whiffs of BO and garlic. He hadn't expected that such imperfections, such unflattering assertions of the flesh, would make him more rather than less turned on. He hadn't expected a body to taste and smell like just that, a body, and he hadn't expected to like it.

"I live over on Fifty-second," the guy said.

"OK."

Upon leaving the bar they exchanged first names. The ordering of this sequence, first tonguing then introductions, made Alistair feel as if he were in a rom-com that was being rewound. The guy, Lloyd, was a twenty-eight-year-old from Silver Spring, Maryland. He'd studied musical theater at Wagner College and for the past three years had been working as a manager at the Herald Square H&M. He was planning to return to school to get a master's in theater directing. He was going to apply *this winter*, he said. The canned and defensive manner in which he relayed this information suggested he made the same speech to everyone he met.

Alistair gave his school and major. Then, for reasons not abundantly clear to him, he said that he was from Boston, and that his parents were corporate lawyers.

"Very fancy," Lloyd said.

Lloyd lived in a microscopic studio on the top floor of a divvied-up brownstone. Alistair found it hard, upon entering the apartment, to discern where the kitchen ended and the bedroom began. The stove had been repurposed as a side table. Lurking on shelves and spots of unoccupied floor were Buddha statues, candles, packs of tarot cards, astrological charts, and books about creativity and meditation. Above the door to the bathroom Lloyd had mounted a framed quote by Thich Nhat Hanh that read, "My actions are my only true belongings." To Alistair he fit the mold of a person who, lacking fulfillment in work, has shored up his sense of worth by way of spirituality and other spurious forms of "meaning."

The advantage of the studio was that it contained no room that might serve as a presex antechamber. They were in the sex room already. They removed, in keeping with the evening's skewed sequencing, first their pants, then their underwear, then their shirts, then their socks. Every gesture and point of contact was a minor revelation. Alistair came into knowledge for which his years of watching porn had not prepared him. He was surprised, for example, that when he put Lloyd's dick in his mouth he felt no dick sensations himself. He'd only experienced dick-wetting from the perspective of the person whose dick was getting wet. In his mouth, though, this foreign dick was just insensate tough meat.

He was also surprised by Lloyd's eagerness to be fucked. To Alistair bottoming seemed like a joyless duty that happened to afford its practitioners collateral
pleasure. The argument that homosexuality was unnatural sounded silly until
you considered that the anus wasn't meant to have things put in it: that it was
more or less an improvised pudendum. Lloyd seemed to see the matter differently. He gave Alistair a condom and a bottle of Astroglide and got on his
hands and knees. He said, "Take me." He said, "Put it in me." He said, "Do it!"

Unlike the pleasures of bottoming, at least as Alistair imagined them, the
pleasures of topping were uncomplicated. He put his chest against Lloyd's
back and grabbed his shoulders for leverage. He reared back and for every
ten thrusts gave Lloyd a soft spank. He watched his dick push and pull at the
hairs around Lloyd's anus. The image called to mind the strip curtains at a
car wash. Lloyd gave every sign of enjoying himself. He punched the bed in
delight. He turned around and nodded encouragingly. He reached back and
pulled apart his cheeks. But Alistair remained skeptical.

"Does this actually feel good?" he asked.

"Yes!" Lloyd said.

"Do you want me to go harder?"

"Yes! Yes!"

Afterward, by the door, Lloyd moved in for a kiss. "I'd love to do this
again," he said.

Alistair smiled foggily, like a traveler pretending to understand the native
language. Part of him, too, would have loved to do this again. But another part
of him, and regrettably the greater part, balked at the prospect of sustained
intimacy with this stranger. Even as he presented his lips for the kiss he felt
the dawning of a mysterious deficiency. "I had fun too," he said and left.

His feeling, as he rode in a cab back to his dorm ($21 plus tip), was not one
of unalloyed celebration. He'd seen too much and done too much, had spent
too much money and traversed too much sexual territory, to regard his first
night in New York with one-note satisfaction. He felt in every sense of the
word profligate. Yet when he woke the next day at one p.m., to the sound of
Vidi phone-ordering three egg-and-cheese sandwiches, he felt that his real
life had finally begun. And when Maura texted him to ask, *How was your first
night?* he texted back the honest truth: *It was !!!!*

Further confirmation that his life had begun came the following week, during the first section of his Fundamentals of Finance class. The lecture hall, with its cedar-paneled walls and elaborate AV, bespoke inequities in departmental funding: most of the other NYU buildings Alistair had seen were a century old and looked every year of it. The professor, Luca Montagna, was a managing director of private equity at UBS. He told the students that every year the incoming class at UBS got stupider and that he'd come on as a lecturer to nip this stupidity in the bud. "You get these kids who think 'negative beta' just means bad," he said. "You get these kids who try to use the Sharpe ratio on leptokurtic distributions." He was every bit the brilliant jerk Alistair had hoped his first professor would be.

The lecture hall contained roughly a hundred and twenty students. Of these roughly eighty were dudes. Of these roughly sixty were either East Asian or Indian. Alistair recognized Kirit and Arjun sitting together four rows down. Alistair appeared to be the only one not to have gotten the memo that laptops were allowed. All he'd brought with him was a five-subject notebook and his TI BA II Plus. With few exceptions his fellow students wore cartoonishly serious expressions and made theatrical shows of typing every word Montagna uttered. Alistair was too far back in the lecture hall to make eye contact with him, but he nonetheless tried, by scribbling in his notebook with visible fervor, to draw his notice. Certainly Montagna seemed to be speaking directly to him when, in the course of overviewing the portfolio-management portion of their syllabus, he said the following:

"Many of you, upon graduating, will be earning more money than you can reasonably spend. It's imperative you learn now how to manage your own wealth."

Alistair wrote this down in his notebook verbatim. He then underlined it. He then flanked it with stars. It was just the bit of succor, the reviving tincture, that he needed. Over the past week he'd continued to subject himself to dispiriting audits. Half his tuition and room and board were being covered by merit scholarships and financial aid, which meant the remaining money in his educational trust would last him until the middle of his sophomore year. He was planning to pay for the rest, about $70,000, through loans. His meal plan, which at $5,500 a year should have gained him entry to Michelin-starred restaurants, was being taken care of by Maura's mother. Maura had also volunteered to send him $100 a month, but Alistair had pledged to use this only for necessities. Those dollars were too pitiable, too tied up with his teary affection for her, to spend on indulgences. The problem was that he lived in a city of indulgences, was determined to take advantage of them, and lacked the funds to do so. He considered getting a work-study job in the vein of his Target cashiership, but he worried grunt work would cut into the studying by which he hoped to leave grunt work behind. He'd forgotten, though, in his hand-wringing, that his poverty was temporary, that in four years he'd be a junior investment banking analyst and would have more money than he'd know what to do with. He was grateful to the man at the front of the room for reminding him of this.

After class he crossed West Fourth Street and entered the Office of the Bursar. He approached a woman sitting behind a glass partition. It struck Alistair as odd that the Office of the Bursar had seen the need to install partitions. "I'd like to take out a loan," he said.

The woman had the expression of someone who's been alive for hundreds of years. She clearly hated her job and Alistair didn't blame her. "NetID?"

Alistair gave it to her. After what sounded like a hundred keystrokes she peered at the computer screen and said, "Says your tuition is already covered for this year."

"My tuition, yes," Alistair said. "But I need spending money."

"Ah," the woman said. She hit the keys another hundred times and said, "How much do you want to take out?"

"How much am I allowed to?"

"You're approved to take out another twenty thousand for the year."

Alistair wished the woman hadn't told him this. "Let's make it ten."

"You need to do loan counseling."

"I already did it. I'm already taking out loans for tuition later."

Here the woman raised her chin and delivered a line that had clearly been drilled into her. "We advise students to do loan counseling for each and every loan they take out."

"I get it," Alistair said. "Interest rates, subsidized versus unsubsidized, I get it."

"I'm talking also about repayment."

"I assure you I get it."

Three days later, Alistair was $10,000 richer. He tempered his relief by promising never to do this again. He'd make the money last as long as he could and then, when it was gone, figure out something else. In fact he would end up performing this same transaction the next September and the September after that.

One benefit of this windfall was that it enabled him to pursue, without the distraction of being broke, his ambition of becoming a star student. Unfortunately, pursuing this ambition led him to renege on his promise to make friends. He tried not to roll his eyes whenever someone in his Calculus I class gave a ludicrously wrong answer, but his eyes possessed their own will and rolled anyway. He tried not to raise his hand too much in his Global Finance class, but his hand possessed its own will and kept floating upward, like a birthday balloon that's been cut from its bouquet. He tried not to commandeer his Global Finance group project, about microfinance in Bolivia, but his partners were two jocks from Southern California who kept bonding over their disappointment at the "unchill" East Coast and who kept screwing up the no-brainer tasks Alistair assigned them. He confirmed that BancoSud had been established in 1992 not 1892 (as Jock One had written), and that its average loan was $3,000 not $30,000 (as Jock Two had written), and in the end he did basically the whole thing himself.

As at St. Francis Alistair enjoyed correcting his peers, flaunting his intelligence, showing them up. The machete he'd used to bushwhack his way out of Binghamton was still in his hand, and every day he discovered new nettles and brambles against which to use it. But even as he swung and slashed and lopped he wondered if his bushwhacking might one day outlive its original purpose, might become an exercise born of habit rather than a survival strategy born of need. He wondered if his defenses, which he'd always assumed would be temporary, might in fact never come down.

The problem was that the kids at Stern were even richer, in many cases worlds richer, than the kids at St. Francis. His envy of his peers, his desire to quash them, and his determination to shield his economic shame from them increased tenfold. Nearly everyone he met had grown up in wealthier towns and gone to correspondingly better high schools. Nearly everyone had parents possessing interesting and lucrative jobs and second homes in Florida or Colorado or Maine. Nearly everyone traipsed across the wide Stern plaza with the carefree gait and congenial ignorance of need that Alistair knew he would never, no matter how rich he became, possess himself. And nearly everyone he spoke to asked where he'd come from and what his parents did in the happy assumption that he would be able to answer them with their same happy ease.

Instead he replied with curt evasions. He said he was from "upstate," letting his listeners assume that he meant Westchester. He said his parents were in "higher education," letting his listeners assume that he meant his parents were professors or senior administrators and also that he had parents plural. He knew he was hardly the only scholarship student at Stern. He knew his richer peers would never actually shrink from him in disgust. He suspected, in fact, that they would meet his divulgence with guilt-inflected admiration and pity. But he also suspected that they would withdraw from him ever so slightly, that some wattage of interest would leave their eyes, that they'd see in his alien background an unfortunate obstacle to relatability, and that his shame, feeding off these cues, would redouble. He didn't want to be seen as a person deserving of pity. He wanted to be seen as a force to be reckoned with. And so he preserved his anonymity, kept his machete in hand, remained curt.

His guardedness did not go unremarked upon. One night he joined Kirit and Arjun at the Hungry Pig, a bar on Second Avenue known for being lenient about IDs, where Kirit staged a kind of intervention.

"You need to loosen up," Kirit said as he filled their glasses from a pitcher of pilsner. The beer had the color and probably the alcoholic content of lemon Gatorade. "You're smart as fuck, but you need to loosen up."

"There are no women in this bar," Arjun complained.

"There's one right there," Alistair said. He gestured at a middle-aged woman wearing light jeans and a roomy blouse.

"That particular person does not satisfy my definition of 'women,'" Arjun said.

"Don't be a jerk," Alistair said.

"That's what I'm telling *you*," Kirit said. "Before I came to New York, do you know what my father told me? He told me, 'Kirit, above all else, this is a networking opportunity.' He said making connections was the most important thing."

Alistair trained his eyes on Kirit's watch, a Breitling with a royal blue face and three subdials. He wondered what it would have been like to grow up with a parent literate in finance, literate in "networking," to grow up in a cozy world of money and to trust, in consequence, that success consisted primarily in forging this same coziness with the right people. He sipped his beer and said nothing.

"You're shy," Kirit said, warmly, cozily. "That can read as rude."

"I'm not shy, or rude," Alistair said. "I'm focused. And I don't see why it matters. If I walk out of here with a four-oh and an offer from a bulge-bracket bank I don't imagine I'll have any problems."

"But these are your peers," Kirit said. "These are the people you'll be working with. And do you think the bulge-brackets want to hire shy people? Or rude people?"

"Between the engineers and the analysts I think they hire no one else."

"You know what I mean," Kirit said.

"This is the speech I'll make to girls from now on," Arjun said. "Connecting is the most important thing."

For all his obstinacy Alistair did know what Kirit meant. Already he had the premonition that some of his less smart but more socially graceful classmates would have no trouble glad-handing their way into jobs: that affability was a bigger factor than he gave it credit for. But the idea of being affable for affability's sake ran counter to the grain of his purity. He prized his intelligence, clung to it as his ticket to a better life, and he felt that to entrust his success to mere schmoozing would be to insult his own talents. He'd gotten this far on his own and he was determined to thrive on his own. So he took Kirit's suggestion and recast it as a challenge. He doubled down. He became a machine.

Most days he got up at six and stayed up until midnight. He read textbook chapters his professors assumed no one would read. He did the nonrequired supplemental problem sets they put on CourseWorks. He highlighted and underlined and highlighted and underlined. He emailed his professors with follow-up questions and news links pertaining to class discussions. He was only mildly deterred by the fact that they only emailed him back half the time. When his brain needed a rest he went to the gym, where with archaeological fervor he uncovered the lineaments of his pecs, his biceps, his triceps, his abs. He also kept up with his *Economist*, his *Wall Street Journal*, his *New York Times* Business Day. He followed the first stirrings of the 2014 midterms. He called his mother.

"Weather says a strong change of bloodshed next year," Maura said, referring to the elections. "Red upon red upon red."

Alistair offered a commiserating sigh. His mother had been hammering the progressive creed into his head for so long that he felt neurologically incapable of voting otherwise. In his short time at Stern, though, he'd come to see that thriving in finance as a Democrat would mean rooting for the party's social agenda while quietly working around its economic one. Luckily he'd come of age at a time when Democrats were as much in thrall to free markets as their Republican colleagues. He could honor his mother's liberalism and selfishly pursue riches at the same time without incurring any damage to his integrity. Perhaps, if he'd paid closer attention to the ongoing Tea Party antics, he might have sensed that this era of stability was nearing an end: that the fury of the class he'd escaped, spurred by resentment of the class he was angling to enter, would reach a breaking point. He might have sensed that this fury, for so long powerless against elite consensus, would soon enough, as it were, trump it. But for now all he sensed was that Maura needed confirmation of his sympathies.

"You won't find many allies in the Stern building," he said. "I wouldn't be surprised if some of these kids had Reagan tattoos."

"I trust *you* don't have a Reagan tattoo," Maura said.

"I would never get a tattoo."

He asked her how home was, and immediately regretted asking. The dishwasher, she told him, had broken and cost $300 to be repaired. Her property taxes were increasing, despite the fact that owing to the city's depressed real estate market the value of their house hadn't at all appreciated. The house's foundation was also starting to list, and the plumbing, which was galvanized, was beginning to erode. "Not that any of this is your concern," she said.

With every hardship she enumerated Alistair sank further into his chair. He considered sending her a few hundred dollars out of the living loans he'd taken out. But then he'd have to explain where the money had come from, and he could take a guess as to how she'd receive the news that he was paying for his life with borrowed funds. "Once I start working you'll have less to worry about," he said.

"I wouldn't want you to do that," Maura said.

"It's why I'm here."

"You need to live your own life. There are millions of reasons to go to college. Helping your mother should be the last on that list."

Alistair, staring at the pile of textbooks on his desk, thinking ahead to an all-nighter of problem sets and short essays, was surprised to feel a throb of anger. He felt that if Maura really loved him and wanted to support him the least she could do was accept his generosity. If she refused his generosity his sense of motivation would vanish. Even if he did have other reasons for being in New York they weren't the primary one and they certainly didn't number in the millions. Now Maura was threatening to take away the bright endpoint toward which all his striving was aimed, by which he justified his single-mindedness and urgency. His present existed only in terms of the future he planned to give her. If this future didn't matter to her he was left with only hollowness. "Agree to disagree," he said.

In the background he could hear the faraway roar of a motorcycle, which in its audibility and singularity betokened an otherwise soundless Binghamton evening. On Carey Street the sky would be almost dark, the first stars materializing, lamps going on across the way.

"Are you having fun?" Maura asked, by way of goodbye.

"I'm having fun," Alistair said, and then they hung up.

Admittedly Alistair was having some fun. He might have been a machine but he wasn't a monk. He rewarded himself for his studiousness by treating himself to New York City. He went out to dinner with the kids from Mumbai and, occasionally, so as to avoid becoming a complete social isolate, went barhopping with his fellow Sternies. But for the most part he spent his living-loan money on solo lunches, better clothes (he was relieved to find that the de rigueur uniform at Stern—Patagonia, Barbour, Charles Tyrwhitt—was more familiar to him from his time at St. Francis than the haute grunge worn by other NYU students), and gay bars. He selected the bar based on his mood.

If he wanted to find a guy with whom he could make minimal conversation he went to Phoenix or Barracuda or G Lounge. If he wanted to get wasted and have sex with whomever he went to Boxers or Industry or, with some nostalgia, the Rail.

He spent sweaty hours in Columbia dorms, New School dorms, and Hunter dorms. When he had no inclination to leave his own dorm, or when he returned from his excursions empty-handed, he went on Grindr. There were so many gay kids living in Third North that his app couldn't pick up anyone outside its walls. By night he dispensed with his condescension toward performing arts kids. There was no doubting the acrobatic talents of actors and dancers, no doubting the flatness of their abdomens or the firmness of their behinds. They also amazed him by their adventurousness. They rode him cowboy and then, without dislodging his dick, swiveled around and rode him reverse. They put their heads on the floor and their asses in the air and told him to go at them à la "dipstick." They told him he wasn't going hard enough. They told him he wasn't going fast enough. They took his come in their mouths and spit it onto his chest. Alistair was more of an away-game player, but every so often he had to kick Vidi out and use the home field. When Vidi would return, after biding his time in the basement common area, he'd say, "I don't know what it smells like in here, but I know I don't like it."

Because Alistair spent the bulk of his time either studying or chasing boys it was only natural that he should occasionally conflate the two, that his daytime exertions should become mixed up in his head with his nighttime ones. He once read the abbreviation for the London Interbank Bid Rate not as LIBID but as LIBIDO. The term "fat tail" called to mind his favored variety of tush. He defended his preference for one-night stands as a way of limiting his exposure to emotional risk. It was like the sexual equivalent of investing in T-Bills.

In truth, though, he felt his twin preoccupations to be of a piece. Both were sources of recurrent victories. An A in Financial Accounting was the bedding of a Columbia rower was a long note of praise on his final project for Executive Management was a three-way with two Northwestern kids on spring break. He was a top dog in the classroom and a top dog in the bedroom. He felt there was no test he couldn't ace, no professor he couldn't impress, no job he couldn't effortlessly land, and he felt there was no boy he couldn't charm, no coital maneuver he couldn't master, no gay bar he couldn't for the duration of his visit be the star of.

When he returned home after his freshman year he declined to ask Target for summer work. His successes, he believed, were such that ringing up bath towels was now beneath him. He spent his days sitting in a plastic Adirondack chair in the backyard getting a head start on the next semester's reading. On weekends Maura joined him and made her way, for the second time, through the early novels of Henry James. Occasionally she'd peer over the top of *The Portrait of a Lady* and smirk at whatever textbook he'd buried his face in.

"What are you reading about?" she asked.

"How to hedge against exogenous shocks," Alistair said. "You?"

"The opposite, I think."

On Sundays they listened to the distant bells of St. Francis. Throughout June and July the sky remained un-Binghamtonianally blue. Except for when he received an envy-inducing dispatch from the Mumbai kids, who were "backpacking" through Europe (Alistair saw no "backpacks," only plates of exquisitely arranged food and infinity pools at high-end hotels), he experienced nary a disruption in his good mood. The beautiful weather was like the beautiful weather in his head. Given the victories he'd secured thus far, he reasoned, how could he expect not to secure more victories, in larger quantities and at accelerated rates? Given how far he'd come, in so short a time, how could he expect his trajectory not to follow an exponentially upward curve?

Given how wonderfully things were going, in other words, how could he have predicted the disappointments that soon followed?

The first of these came the next summer, when he interned for a downtown financial-technology startup called Almsly. The company, which had something like $50 million in seed funding, operated an app that allowed users to request microloans from their friends. Borrowers set their own interest rates and loan durations and Almsly wasn't party to loan agreements, which meant lenders had no guarantee of being repaid. This concept struck Alistair as absurd—if only his student loan creditors were so magnanimous!—but all the kids in his class were jonesing to hop aboard the fintech train, and none of the bulge-brackets would grant internships to rising juniors, and Almsly had offered him a stipend large enough to cover the cost of summer housing.

The disappointment was this: Alistair had been hired to assist with "strategy," but in the mind of his boss, a porky Greek guy named Yannis, this equated to diddling around on social media.

"You'll be in charge of our Facebook page," Yannis told him on his first day. He was standing over Alistair's desk, one of about sixty in the company's open-plan office on Eighteenth Street, eating caramel popcorn from a large Christmas tin. The tin featured a Thomas Kinkade–style rendering of the Nativity. It was June.

"That's it?" Alistair said. "The Facebook page?"

"That's it," Yannis said.

"Nothing else?"

Yannis chewed. "Maybe Instagram. We've been very neglectful of our Instagram."

After securing the internship Alistair had spent several weeks researching Almsly and the growing peer-to-peer lending space and conceptualizing strategies. He thought Almsly should build its own payment platform rather than let its third-party payment facilitator lop 0.5% off its transactions. If Almsly insisted on being so borrower-friendly he thought it might as well allow users to set different interests rates and loan durations for different lenders. He thought it should test debit cards for international users without US bank accounts into which to transfer their funds. But every time he shared these ideas Yannis just said, "Focus on Facebook."

Alistair didn't have Facebook. He felt alienated enough without cobbling together an online persona that in its fakery would only further his alienation. In order to manage the Almsly account, then, to which he posted links to press releases and sunny articles about "P2P," he had to create a dummy account for himself. Once, when he left this dummy account up on his screen, another intern leaned over and gaped in astonishment. "You have no Friends!"

Nor, in his time at Almsly, did Alistair make any. He understood this was an opportunity to show that he could flourish in the corporate workplace. He knew it was a chance to heed Kirit's recommendation that he "network" and "loosen up." But given how sour his days at Almsly made him, and given how irrelevant this internship seemed to his larger investment banking ambitions, he didn't try very hard to succeed. Instead, in his sourness, he failed utterly.

Once a week at five p.m. the Almsly staff convened around a conference table laid with wines and cheeses that had been handpicked by the
ever-epicurean Yannis. But Alistair always gave these gatherings a miss. He
felt that to hobnob with his Almsly colleagues would be to forgive them,
in effect, for underutilizing his talents. Whenever older employees asked
him, with a nostalgic glimmer in their eyes, about his undergraduate life
he disappointed them with stuffy pleasantries. Whenever a meeting with
the other interns devolved into shit-shooting he returned them, with frigid
equanimity, to the topic at hand. And, every chance he got, he bombarded
Yannis with unwanted suggestions for how to turbocharge the company's
performance.

Given all this he was little surprised when, at the end of the summer, Yannis
beckoned him into his office with a stony expression.

"We can only bring back five interns next summer, and right now we have
six," he said. "So."

"So," Alistair said.

"We really appreciate the work you did for us."

Alistair had neither expected nor desired to be invited back to Almsly.
But he felt compelled to take a stand for himself on principle. "I am the most
ambitious and competent intern here," he said.

Yannis was making his way through the first of three takeout sushi rolls.
"Ambitious, yes," he said, tearing open a soy sauce packet. "Competent, no."

"How am I not competent?"

"We're like a family here," Yannis said. "We like good vibes. Success for us
is measured by how well you work with the team."

Alistair suspected that Yannis's emphasis on "good vibes," on such a frivolous
soft metric, had something to do with the fact that he was sitting on a bed of
easy VC money. When you were on such a bed you wanted happy lapdogs,
overgroomed Pomeranians, not hounds.

"You're not a team player," Yannis said. "You're a you player. And the only
time I hear from you is when you come to me with your *suggestions*."

"They're good suggestions!"

"You need to learn to know your place," Yannis said. "But hey, here, we like
to give goodbye presents." He wheeled his chair to one corner of his office,

where he kept a stack of Christmas popcorn tins, and wheeled one back. "Do you like cheddar?"

Alistair might have left Almsly that day feeling relieved, might have bundled his memory of his time there and buried it in his subconscious, if he didn't suspect that it contained a lesson. He worried that what was true at Almsly would be true as well even in the gilded preserves of investment banking: that even as a first-year analyst at a bulge-bracket he'd be charged with only menial tasks, chained to a boss too busy to mentor him, forced nevertheless to swear fealty to this boss and show him all manner of sticky-sweet obeisance, and judged not by his acumen or his adrenalized initiative-taking but by his ability to fit in, to "know his place," to be *cozy*. He was confirmed in this suspicion a few days before the start of his junior year when, at a Stern happy hour, he spoke to an alumnus named Cliff Warnung who was in his first year at JPMorgan Chase.

"Literally, my job is to spell-check my MD's pitchbook," Cliff said. The department had provided wine for those with name tags denoting faculty or alumni status, and Cliff had clearly availed himself of several cups of it. "The guy can't spell to save his fucking life. He spells 'telecommunication' as 'telecommunism.' He spells Capgemini with a *j*. I'm at the office spell-checking and fact-checking until three a.m. *regularly*."

"Terrible," Alistair said, sincerely. "But that's just first-year stuff, right?"

"Oh, sure," Cliff said, dripping wine on the floor. "Because I'm just dying to write my own pitchbooks. Dying!" He grabbed Alistair's cheek and stared at him. "Dude, *I am dying*."

Alistair offered, speaking less to Cliff than to himself, that perhaps the salary made it worth it.

"One twenty-five is nada, dude," Cliff said. "Even with the bonus. Half of which goes straight into Obama's welfare piggy bank."

Alistair detected in Cliff's blasé dismissal of this figure the same sense of security, the same cushy privilege, that he observed in so many of his peers. A number that would have meant everything to him, a new life, a new world, meant nothing to this loud drunk person.

"Anyway," Cliff said. He took out his phone, opened a blank email to himself, and proffered it. "Write down your deets. If you apply, I'll make sure your resume floats to the top."

Alistair considered the phone. This was precisely the type of networking Kirit had enjoined him to prioritize, precisely the type of "good vibe"–spreading that Yannis had held up as a criterion for success. But as before Alistair felt immovable, felt positively *calcified*, in his resistance. He remained firm in his belief that there was something unsavory, something immoral, about this route to success, and he remained firm in his refusal to take it. "I'm OK," he said.

"Yeah, fuck it," Cliff said. "Get out while you can. Go to South America. That's what I'd fucking do. You know anything about South America?"

"Nada," Alistair said, and he went home, and he went into his junior year racked by doubts and reservations such as he'd never before experienced. Everything he was learning about the path ahead was flying in the face of his ideal. Success, he saw, would require more than mere talent. It would require him to depend on others, crawl out of his shell, sully himself in intangible, immaterial fraternizing. But his shame and resentment had made him unreachable, had made him alien, and he'd clung to them stubbornly, self-lovingly, all the same. He'd believed them to be his greatest asset, his greatest motivator, his greatest fuel. But his greatest asset was beginning to look like his greatest liability. His self-love was beginning to look like self-defeat. Yet to recognize this was not the same as to rectify it. He feared the stubbornness lay too deep.

He nevertheless continued to go through the motions. He finished the fall semester with a 4.0. At the beginning of the spring semester he submitted internship applications to all eight bulge-bracket banks. He scheduled so many mock interviews at the career center that the head administrator there had to ask him to stop coming ("We feel we've done everything we can for you at this point," she wrote in her email). But the disappointments kept coming, and Alistair found himself less and less surprised by them. He wasn't surprised, for example, that he failed to score an internship at Goldman Sachs. He'd researched and prepared, he'd sailed through the perfunctory first-round interview ably enough, but when he sat down for the second-round interview, before a committee of dauntingly, expensively bright faces, his worst self-defeating instincts prevailed. He spoke formally, even coldly. He betrayed all the emotional expressiveness of an ice sculpture. When asked softball questions that were clearly invitations to chumminess, to slickness and clubbiness, he replied with terse monosyllables. He bungled, somehow, the conclusionary shaking of hands. He saw that he was screwing up and proceeded to screw up. Only when he'd returned to his dorm did he see the stupidity and irreversibility of his self-sabotage.

"I bombed it," he said to Maura on the phone, confused nearly to the point of tears.

"That seems impossible," Maura said. "I feel like your entire life has been an interview."

"Well, then it's been a wasted life, hasn't it!"

"Hey, no," Maura said. "Door closes, window opens."

"It's all doors, Mom! No windows, all doors. And they're all closing!"

"Not true," Maura said. "Not remotely true."

Alistair wished, at this moment, that Vidi were at hand. By this time they were living in Palladium, in a suite with separate bedrooms. Alistair enjoyed the privacy, and Vidi was the least consoling person in the world, but even his robotic intonations would be a comfort now. Probably he'd cite some Greenwich Associates report in which Goldman had been ranked low in global portfolio trading.

"I don't know what's happening to me," he said to Maura. "I think I'm having a crisis."

"Maybe you are," Maura said. "But maybe it's also an opportunity."

"An opportunity to do what?"

"To reflect."

"Reflect on what!"

"What you want," Maura said. "What you thought you wanted. What a part of you may be trying to tell you it no longer wants."

"I don't have time to reflect!" Alistair said. "It's too late!"

"You're twenty-one, Alli."

"I'm in debt up to my ears, I can't change my major, I can't drop out, I'm fucked. I chose this path and now I'm stuck on it. And you want me to *reflect*? Maybe that's what *you* do all day, reflect, but it won't do *me* any good." He saw at once that he'd gone too far, further than he'd ever gone. He said nothing for a moment, but he couldn't bear the silence on the other end of the line. "I'm sorry, Mom. I'm so sorry."

"It's OK," Maura said. "To be honest, it hasn't done me much good either."

There came some relief when he received a summer internship offer from JPMorgan Chase. He'd been as stilted in that interview as he'd been in his interview with Goldman, but clearly the committee there had been able to look past his demeanor to his straight As, his rhapsodic recommendations from professors, and the fact that he was already Bloomberg-trained. The relief, though, was soon followed by another disappointment. In the last week of May he received a call from someone in human resources who informed him that, contrary to what had been stated in his offer letter, he'd be interning not in investment banking but in trading. At the repo desk, of all things!

"The repo desk?" Alistair nearly wailed.

"We had to do some shuffling," the HR guy said. "But don't worry. The fifteen thousand is still yours. Trading interns normally make ten. Consider this a five-thousand-dollar apology."

"I don't care about the money." (Mark this day: for once in his life Alistair really did not care about the money.) "I didn't apply for an internship in trading. Still less in repo. What happened?"

"Just some unfortunate but unavoidable shuffling," the HR guy said.

Alistair had an instinct to ask if he had been, in fact, too stilted in his interview: if the hiring team, belatedly deciding they were unimpressed, had struck a compromise by punting him to a lesser post. But he was afraid of the answer he might get.

"You'll learn a lot," the HR guy said. "And I think you'll like the repo guys. They're real characters."

The guys at the repo desk, Alistair discovered that June, turned out to be characters from a Sunday cartoon about finance. He felt as if he'd been teleported back to the 1980s, when there were still men in color-coded jackets yelling and fist-bumping in trading pits. Suffice it to say these were not the gilded preserves of investment banking. His managers were all middle-aged, overweight, and unhappily married. They commuted from Long Island or Staten Island or Fort Lee. The other interns were all beer-bellied frat boys from state schools, and they seemed to enjoy being paid $10,000 to do busywork. Many mornings they arrived with stories of drinking binges that seemed always to culminate in some homosexual hilarity. They got so trashed they took off their clothes and danced naked. They got so trashed they fell asleep in one another's beds. They got so trashed they all piled on the drunkest of them and demanded he fellate them. Alistair had heard tell of the rampant homophobia in finance. He refused to pay it any mind. Aside from his excellent grooming he gave off no sign of being gay and he had no interest in playing the victim. But he could have done without everyone calling one another faggots. He could have done without the likening of aggressive gains to acts of sodomy. The kissing of cheeks, the slapping of asses, the assaultive fingering of peri-anus vicinities: he could have done without these.

Needless to say he made no effort to fit in. He told himself the fault lay with his crass and clownish colleagues. He told himself he couldn't be blamed for not being excited about a desk whose raison d'être was to broker unexciting trades. But the truth was that the wind had gone out of his sails, and he felt powerless to bring it back. And so he floated, directionless, in the sea of his self-alienation. He refused every drinking invitation the frat boys extended. He was as responsive to his bosses' fulminations about the Yankees as he would have been to someone speaking to him in Mandarin. He showed up early, routinely stayed late, completed every task assigned to him to satisfac-tion. He worked as hard and well as he always had, as if his old trusty tool kit were suited to the larger problem facing him, as if the local success of a report scrupulously fact-checked or a memo flawlessly composed could make up for his more general failure.

In week eight, one of his bosses, Paddy, gestured for him to join him in a conference room. Over a mountain range of squished Uline boxes Alistair could see the East River and, at the center of it, a ferryboat leaving a long, rippling wake.

"How are you liking things so far?" Paddy asked.

Paddy's defining feature was his nose. It was so alcoholically red it was hard to notice anything else about him. When he wasn't around the other interns called him Pinocchio. Alistair was pretty sure that they were thinking of Rudolph, that in their Busch-soaked brains there'd occurred an iconic-nose mix-up, but he never corrected them. "I'm learning a lot," he said.

Paddy leaned back in his chair. He crept a finger into the space between two shirt buttons and scratched. "That's the most I've heard you say all sum-mer," he said.

"I'm learning," Alistair said again. "Just really focused on learning." He understood that he was in the midst of a critical conversation, a potentially life-altering one, the offer conversation, and he knew that if he'd heeded his better instincts he would have prepared for it extensively and would now be doing everything he could to make it go well: would be sweating, talking too much, getting down on his hands and knees. But he was calm, imperturbably calm.

"Is this really the kind of work you want to do?" Paddy asked.

"Oh, absolutely," Alistair said in the voice of a choirboy.

Paddy put his hands behind his head, revealing two improbably large pit stains. He shifted in his chair in a manner recognizable to any male: he was unsticking his scrotum from his thigh. "I ask," he said, "because you don't seem to be enjoying your time here."

"I'm just very focused on learning," Alistair said.

Paddy smiled. "I've been in finance for a long time, and I've seen a lot of guys like you."

Alistair struggled to meet his eyes. "What kind of guy is that?"

"Smart as a whip, got ambition up the wazoo, but they keep getting in their own way."

It added insult to Alistair's injury that he was apparently a "type." Paddy was denying him the consolatory privilege of being at least unique in his failure.

"These guys can do the work," Paddy said. "They can handle the stress, they can see the patterns, they can be creative. But they can't do the long haul, or at least not yet, because they don't yet understand what it takes."

Paddy had preemptively nuked Alistair's sole objection: that he could do the work, and do it well. He also didn't need to ask Paddy what it took. He knew what it was, and he knew he didn't have it.

"If I hired you," Paddy said. "I know you'd be a good worker. I *know* that. But you can't just be a good worker in a silo. That's not all it takes. If I brought you on I'd have to look after you. I'd have to worry about you. And I have enough to worry about as it is."

For a moment the only sound in the room was the low hum of the air-conditioning. Alistair looked out the window for the ferryboat he'd spotted earlier, but it had passed behind a building. "I'm not getting an offer," he said, "am I."

"Afraid not," Paddy said. He leaned forward, benignly, trying and failing to draw Alistair's gaze. "Do some thinking about what I've said. About what you really want. Reach out when you have more clarity. We can talk about a rec."

Alistair looked at his hands. He studied the creases on his fingers, the pink mottling on his palms. He took comfort in the reliability of his body, its persistent sameness amid all the confusion in his head. He raised his eyes to Paddy. "Does that mean I can stop coming?"

Paddy laughed. He laughed rather hard. "No, kid," he said. "Your contract has a clawback. If you quit now, you'll owe us everything we've paid you so far. No."

It was a testament to Alistair's misery—to the sting of his rejection, to his desolate sense of futility—that he actually did quit. Between the living-loan money he had left over and the stipend installments he'd received from the bank he had $14,000 in his account. He left early that day and the next day mailed JPMorgan a check for $12,000. He trusted the remaining $2,000 would hold him over until September, when he could take out another $10,000 in living loans.

He spent the final weeks of summer testing the limits of his despair. He watched more TV in three days than he'd watched in three years. He ordered every lunch and dinner from a Thai restaurant that was a block and a half away. When he'd accumulated enough plastic Thai iced tea cups he began peeing in them so as to avoid leaving his room. He watched so much porn, and got so tired of the pop-ups, that he purchased subscriptions to all his favorite sites at a combined cost of $375. The total would have been higher, but there was a Labor Day sale.

He was not, he understood, without options. Banks occasionally took kids who hadn't interned for them, and he could honestly tell them his experience at the repo desk had taught him many things, first among them that he wasn't cut out for trading. But for now the problem of his future employment seemed distant, obscured by a larger, more ambiguous, more pressing problem. If he was going to live in the world, let alone thrive in it, he needed to untangle the knot of his pride and resentment, his debilitating alienation, his self-loving self-defeat. There was something wrong with him, deeply wrong, and he needed to fix it.

On the Friday before the start of his senior year he went to a student-organized happy hour at a Lower East Side bar called the Million Friedman. He framed this to himself as an exercise in crawling out of his shell, but he knew it was just as much an exercise in masochism. Surely everyone there would be discussing who'd received offers from whom. It was as if he had a wound and were in search of salt to pour on it.

At the Million Friedman he did indeed find salt to pour. His peers greeted one another like soldiers returning from combat, spewing the names of their future employers without being asked. Credit Suisse, Barclays, UBS, Citigroup, Goldman Sachs, Goldman Sachs, Goldman Sachs. Kirit, Arjun, Vidi, and Saritha, it transpired, would be reuniting at Morgan Stanley. Someone standing near them made the stupid joke, as they laughed insufferably and cheersed: "More like *Mumbai* Stanley!"

"Congrats," Alistair said when Kirit joined him in a booth. "I'm happy for you."

"Congrats to you too," Kirit said, delirious with euphoria. "You'll be a veep in no time. Word is JPMorgan has serious title inflation."

Alistair twirled his vodka soda, his fourth. He looked Kirit in his handsome, beaming face. "Not so."

Kirit knitted his brow. "No way," he said.

"Yes way."

"Dude, I'm so sorry."

"Don't be."

They sipped their drinks in silence while the room around them thundered with elation. Kirit put his arm around Alistair's shoulder and pulled him close. "Maybe you should go to work for the SEC," he said. "Take your revenge."

"Fuck you."

Kirit laughed. He turned his eyes to the crowd but kept his arm around Alistair. Some dark, delicious, depthy cologne radiated from his neck. "You'll be OK," he said. "I have faith in you. To be honest, I admire you."

"How's that?" Alistair said.

"You're smarter than the rest of us. And you don't tolerate bullshit."

Alistair gestured around the room. "Aren't I tolerating it? I'm sitting here."

"With a very grumpy face."

Alistair had been tensing himself against Kirit's embrace, but now he willed himself to relax into it, to enjoy the warmth of his arm. He took a gulp from his drink. He wanted to find some way to crack open his shell, to speak as he never had from his heart. But the only thing he could think of to talk about in this way was, inevitably, his mother. It gladdened him, it pained him, it made him want to cry: how inevitable this was.

"I think I get it from my mom," he said to Kirit. "She doesn't tolerate bullshit either." He heard himself talking in a new voice—soft, experimental. "She's a really good person."

Kirit pinched Alistair's cheek. "I bet she is," he said. "And I bet she's hot too." He shook the ice in his drink. "Let me buy you another one."

Alistair, moving gently, freed himself from Kirit's grip. "Maybe another time," he said.

He headed uptown toward Palladium. He planned to obliterate his memory of the evening, the assault of his peers' happiness, with ten hours of death-adjacent sleep. But Kirit's arm had left a ghostly warmth on his shoulders, and the cracking of his shell, however minimal and brief, had quickened his blood, activated a tingling in his groin, and instead of continuing up First Avenue he found himself turning on Thirteenth, toward Phoenix, one of the few bars where he could expect to be asked his name before being fed a tongue. He wasn't opposed to being fed a tongue, but mostly what he wanted was a benevolent soul with whom to practice cracking open his shell a little more. He entered the bar, ordered a drink, approached a corner table, and got double what he was seeking, and ultimately far more than he'd bargained for: not one but two benevolent souls, and in short order two tongues. It was there, in a darkened corner of the bar, that he met Elijah Pasternak and Mark Landmesser.

After his phone call with Nikolai, Alistair waited two days before approaching Maura about what he'd learned and the plan he'd devised. He knew she'd be dismayed, he knew she'd try to dissuade him, and he felt he needed to bolster himself beforehand, lest she succeed. But the march of days, until now cruelly slow and largely meaningless, had taken on a new urgency. He couldn't be sure how long his window of opportunity would remain open. And so, on the last Friday of June, he decided he could wait no longer.

Maura was in the kitchen. Alistair left his bedroom, where he'd been settling his nerves, and made his way downstairs, following the scent of lemon.

Maura slid a skillet into the oven. "This'll be ready in a few minutes."

"Come sit," Alistair said.

He led her to the living room. Maura waited patiently, almost amusedly, for him to begin speaking. But as the silence went on her face went slack, and some partial understanding, some partial dread, came over her.

He told her everything Nikolai had told him. He told her the plan he'd hatched—though not all of it, not yet.

Half a minute passed before Maura spoke. "You want to lay a trap for the men outside," she said, in cool disbelief. "You want to draw them into our house."

His plan, if such a thing were possible, sounded even more crackbrained coming from her. "It's the only way."

"We've spent almost two months avoiding every possible risk," Maura said. "Now you want to take the most horrible risk of all."

From the kitchen came the sound of sizzling. "They're watching for me," Alistair said. "They think I might be here, and they're waiting for any sign. I can't do anything until they're gone. If we do this, they'll think I'm not here, and they'll go away."

"And then you'll go away, by the sounds of it," Maura said.

She was veering into the part of the plan Alistair wasn't yet ready to tell her. One crackbrained step at a time. "Maybe," he said. "Maybe for a while. I don't know what Nikolai has in mind. But I have no other choice." The sizzling in the kitchen grew louder, and he gestured with his finger. "Is that burning?"

Maura's gaze was unwavering. "When do you plan to do this?"

"Monday," Alistair said. "When you're at work."

"And how will you draw them in?"

"I have some ideas."

"And let's say they come in. What then?"

"They'll look for me, but they won't find me," Alistair said. "I'll be hiding."

Maura seemed to be taking great pains to steady herself. "And where do you plan to hide?"

Alistair had dreaded saying this, however much he marveled at its fortu-
itousness. He was sitting above the very floor whose creak had given him the
idea. "Cillian has one more gift for us," he said. He inclined his head at the
floor, at the secret room below.

Maura turned away. She moved her eyes around the room, as if looking for
a place to rest her gaze, as if looking, maybe, for another person to consult.
But whom? They'd always been alone with each other. Their purgatory had
only clarified this fact. She breathed in slowly, and tears came into her eyes.
"How will I know what's happening?"

"I'll contact you on the burner," Alistair said. "You'll buy a prepaid phone.
They won't be able to trace us. I'll let you know when it's clear. And then I'll
talk to Nikolai."

Maura breathed in again, trying to hold back her tears. The sizzling from
the kitchen drew her attention for a moment, and then she returned her eyes
to the room; and it was as if the sizzling broke her, the futility of a wrecked
or rescued meal, because now she let the tears flow.

"We can't do this forever," Alistair said. "It's selfish of me to make you live
this way. I know that, you know that. What else am I supposed to do?"

Maura bowed her head. "I know," she said. "But now I get to be selfish."

"You?" Alistair said. "*You*, selfish?"

"I do know we can't do this forever," she said. "I do hate seeing you waste
away."

"But you never actually imagined me leaving," Alistair said.

Maura nodded dismally.

"Part of you wants me to stay here forever."

She nodded again.

"I'm all you have."

She didn't so much nod as let her head fall forward.

"Does it make it better if I tell you it's the same for me?"

"No," Maura said. "That just makes it worse."

By the time they'd finished talking whatever was in the oven was ruined.
They sat in the living room eating a dinner of crackers and cheese. Every so
often Alistair glanced at the photograph of Rio de Janeiro on the wall, at the
swooping shoreline and spectacular mountains his father had never lived to see.
He and Maura broached the subject a few more times but hazily, and with an

unspoken dread of all the questions they didn't have answers to. What would he do, where would he go, when would they next speak? How would either of them live, who would either of them be, without the only person who mattered?

After a few hours they said good night. In his bedroom Alistair went to the desk drawer. He pulled out the cross, lay it on his bed, hesitated, then lowered himself to his knees. He'd listened to what the cross had been telling him, he'd hatched his plan, but he still needed bolstering. And though he hadn't said the Our Father in a good four years he remembered every word.

———————

Alistair's first weeks with Mark and Elijah would later strike him as some of the happiest of his life, though he would never have called himself happy at the time. He was still humiliated at being rejected by JPMorgan Chase, distraught by the self-sabotage that had led to his being rejected, and racked by persistent, low-level panic about the sudden curtailment of his career possibilities. Nor would he have called Mark and Elijah happy. It was clear that he'd come into their lives at a moment of decline, that they were bored by each other, dried up, enervated. They seemed to him like a nation in the last stages of empire, impelled by decadence and wasting ennui to incite a revolution simply for the novelty of it, as a kind of test of the staying power of its institutions. But he liked the men more than he'd ever liked any man and, incidentally or otherwise, the sex was sublime.

That first night in early September, they sat at the corner table at Phoenix until the bar had largely cleared out. Mark and Elijah seemed nervous, tentative and self-conscious, keen to deflect attention from themselves and from the embarrassing sexual experiment they'd embarked on, so they asked Alistair about himself, and Alistair, drunk and consumed by self-pity, obliged. He told them about his summer at the bank, the mess he'd made of his opportunity, the unbearable joy of his fellow Sternies. He made them laugh. He realized for the first time that he was a none too terrible storyteller, and he realized it only then, probably, because he'd never before been so forthcoming. He showed Mark and Elijah more of his self than he'd ever shown anyone, absent Maura, and to judge by the charmed flush in their faces they liked this self very much.

"And what do you two do?" he asked them.

Mark and Elijah inched back from the table and flitted their eyes toward the space between them. They wore nice clothes, Mark in casual prep gear and Elijah in formfitting, muscle-accentuating black, and by this point Mark had spent, by Alistair's estimate, some $150 on drinks for all three of them. Their silence persisted.

"I want to hear more about the Stern boys," Elijah said. "I run past there all the time. My curiosity is boundless."

"Elijah is a graphic designer," Mark answered for him.

Alistair heard well-seasoned irony in Mark's voice. "Where?"

"He's a solo operator," Mark said.

"When I operate," Elijah said gallantly.

The facts were quickly coming into focus. "And you?" he said to Mark.

"Mark writes," Elijah said.

"What do you write," Alistair said.

Elijah turned to Mark, grinning impishly, enjoying himself, keen to share his humiliation. "Yes, Mark," he said, "what *do* you write?"

Alistair smiled. He envisioned inheritances, monthly parental subsidies, calls to wills and trusts attorneys in tony hometowns. But though he felt the spark of his old resentment it died out quickly. The plenitude of people of plentiful means had ceased to gall him. And he even appreciated, given his own recent failure, that Mark and Elijah had no obvious accomplishments to their credit.

Mark changed the subject. "I'm sorry you feel doomed," he said to Alistair. He had a curious way of looking at him both intently and obliquely. He seemed, in his shyness, in his almost sorrowfulness, to be drawn to Alistair's pain. "But you don't seem doomed to me."

Elijah shook his head, as if both to agree with Mark's assessment and to clear the air of Mark's dolefulness. He seemed to be drawn to other things about Alistair: his rancor, his daunting youth, his hard edges. "You'll be fine," he said to Alistair. "For now you should just have fun. That's why Mark and I came out tonight. To have fun." He eyed Mark entreatingly. "Isn't that right."

They spent the next few minutes wordlessly finishing their drinks, studying one another's movements, trafficking in one another's pheromones. By telepathic consensus they agreed to stand up all at once, and by the same unspoken consensus they agreed that Alistair would go home with them.

This wasn't Alistair's first threesome, but it was probably the most orderly. After they'd arrived at the Eros Ananke and gulped down another drink Elijah made clear, by sliding off the couch and getting on his knees, that he would be catching and they pitching. Elijah was a formidably expert fellator, but Alistair found it hard to focus on his gratification. He scanned the apartment, noting the sleek surfaces and upscale appliances, the characterless good taste of the furnishings and decorations, the everywhere bland magazine luxury. If he was overwhelmed by anything at that moment it wasn't Elijah's mouth but the handsome fragrance and expensive coolness of the air. He put his hand plaintively to Mark's neck.

As at a dinner party the guest served himself first. In the bedroom Alistair laid Elijah across the mattress and burrowed into him, heeding Elijah's commands to go harder and faster. Mark knelt at the head of the bed, moving forward every so often to deposit his (exceptionally large) member into Elijah's mouth or, less frequently but with more tentative intensity, to kiss Alistair. When he and Mark switched places Alistair noticed that Mark went much more slowly and gently than he had. Eventually Mark seemed to become aware of his comparative leisureliness and tried to accelerate but then, after a moment, gave up—Alistair sensed a delicate, collective embarrassment at this abortive effort. The only obviously awkward moment, though, came at the end, when Elijah asked Mark to give Alistair another turn in him. By way of explanation Elijah said he wanted to come.

Afterward, while Elijah used the bathroom, Alistair asked Mark how often they invited home a third.

Mark, pulling a T-shirt from a dresser, looked at him in something like wounded surprise. "Oh," he said, "we're not like that."

Alistair reached for his underwear on the floor. He heard a discriminating decency in Mark's voice, a private system of judgments and ideals, and he felt a compulsion to fashion his own image in accordance with it. "Oh, I'm not either."

Mark didn't look at him, but a smile of boyish gladness, of subdued excitation and confirmation, appeared on his face. "Good."

When Alistair finally left the Eros Ananke, at four a.m., he felt sure he would never see the men again, even though they'd each taken his number. The impression he'd gotten from Mark was that his and Elijah's adventure had been a one-off, and for all their evident romantic dissatisfaction they seemed too firmly ensconced in their coupledom, too married, to risk the emotional peril of a repeat. He was happy to let his night with them be simply the first taste of something: a new way of talking, fucking, feeling. He was content with that.

He was surprised, then, the following Tuesday, when he emerged from his Bankruptcy and Restructuring class, to find a sweaty, red-faced Elijah sitting on a bench in the Stern plaza.

"I promise I'm not stalking you," Elijah said.

Alistair took off his backpack, which seemed to him suddenly juvenile, and sat down. "I think you kind of are," he said. "But that's OK."

"I was on my run. I thought maybe I'd catch you. Pure luck."

"It's good to see you."

They looked together at the streams of tightly wound, breathlessly jabbering undergrads, at the clusters of side-parted and thick-watched MBAs. Though the temperature was high some sharpness in the breeze and harvest-time fragrance from the park augured fall. At moments like these NYU felt almost like a real campus.

"So this is your world," Elijah said, as he watched three men in identical blue button-downs bump fists.

Alistair felt strange sitting in the plaza with Elijah, as though two sides of himself were meeting for the first time. He felt exposed in his Sterniness and exposed in his creaturehood, the needy naked animal self he'd been with Elijah and Mark the Friday before. "It's your world too," he said. "You're looking at tomorrow's masters of the universe."

"Fascinating," Elijah said.

An MBA with a preposterously large Tumi backpack strode by, holding a headphone cord to his mouth and shouting. "I'll tell you one thing," he shouted, "I'll tell you one fucking thing, I'm not going back to *fucking commodities*."

Elijah followed the MBA with widened eyes and turned to Alistair. He lifted his brow, drew back his head, and moved his shoulders in mock indignation. And it may have been this more than anything that made Alistair fall a little bit in love with him, and by extension Mark. Elijah beheld the spectacle of frenzied capitalistic ambition that had consumed Alistair for the better part of his life and laughed at it. He didn't understand it, so he could see through it. He might have sensed this thought gathering in Alistair's mind, because he leaned forward and got to what was apparently his point. "When are you coming over again?"

"You really want me to?" Alistair asked.

Elijah leaned farther and pecked Alistair on the lips. "Do you not?"

Alistair felt a flush come to his cheeks. He was unsure how he felt about kissing a man in this most heterosexual of campus spaces, and he was unsure how he felt about kissing this man in particular: this pretty, facetious, impractical person who so clearly belonged to a different species. "What about Mark?" he said. "Does he want me to?"

A shadow of annoyance crossed Elijah's face. "For better or worse, we come as a pair," he said. "And yes he wants you to. You made an impression on him."

"Really? Did he say something?"

"Not a word. That's how I know."

Alistair pictured Mark's kind puppyish eyes, the broad hairy expanse of his chest, and tried not to smile. "I have homework tonight."

"I thought you said you were done for career-wise."

"I still have to graduate."

"I'm loving these reminders of our age difference."

"Sorry."

"Just come over after your homework," Elijah said. "Mark usually goes to bed early. But I'm sure he'll wait up for you."

Alistair did go to the Eros Ananke that night, and then again on Friday, and three times the following week, and four times the week after that. He went to class, he went to the gym, he went to the dining hall with Vidi and Arjun and Kirit, but by the end of September Mark and Elijah had become more or less the locus of his life. Only when he was with them could he stop thinking about his failures, or at least laugh at them, and so he spent as much time with them as seemed appropriate.

Not that any of them cared to establish what was or wasn't appropriate. Most of the rules they formulated they did so tacitly, if only because they seemed self-evident. Alistair would never meet up with either of the men alone, he would never accompany them to social gatherings (which the men didn't appear to partake of frequently anyway), he would never expect from them nor they from him anything other than sex and whatever might be construed as sex-adjacent. But the boundaries of what was appropriate kept expanding. He ate dinner with them beforehand and drank with them afterward. He went with them on chaste walks around the neighborhood, taking advantage of the last late sunsets of summer. Sometimes they fucked, it seemed to him, only so as to lend the rest of the evening a sense of carnal pertinence.

He learned more about them and the myriad reasons for their unhappiness. He learned about Mark's family, and he began to see how Mark judged his own life in terms of theirs: his chimeric "creativity" in terms of their practicality, his wastefulness in terms of their industriousness, his failures in terms of their stunning successes. He learned about Elijah's own chimeric creativity and his own likewise ample failures. He struggled, even amid his deepening affection, not to see the two of them as pathetic. Up to now he hadn't thought it possible to be at once so comfortable and so miserable, to possess so much wherewithal and so little will to use it. But his disdain for them was checked by the odd, unavoidable fact that they reminded him of his mother, who also spent her days in aimless ruminating, who also had talents she'd never put to much use. The only real difference between the men and Maura, Alistair decided, was money. Their abundance of it lent their aimlessness a kind of charming glamour, whereas her lack of it just made her aimlessness seem sad.

However pathetic, the men certainly never bored him. He spent his hours at the Eros Ananke in a state of suspense. He understood every day more clearly that they'd approached a decision point in their relationship, and that they'd invited him into their lives, if only unconsciously, as a way of determining its course, precipitating either its renewal or dissolution. He felt like an object through which they negotiated their differences, staged their disagreements, explored various postmarital possibilities. The sex was messy, protracted, strenuous: it left bruises. Elijah liked it hard and Mark liked it soft. Elijah liked his Alistair domineering and cocky and Mark liked his sweet and vulnerable. Elijah seemed for all his disappointment to be frantically optimistic, to believe that some opportunity, for artistic success or at least adventure, lay open to him, on the other side of his suffocating relationship. Mark seemed more resigned to his disappointment. He'd given up hope of adventure, if adventure had ever interested him, and if he was optimistic his optimism was more modest:

he was content to crawl into a narrow cave of love, provided the person he was with was content to be in it too and loved him back unconditionally. He seemed to live in the suppressed and dreary knowledge that Elijah met neither of these criteria: that the future co-occupant of this future cave would likely be someone else.

As the weeks went on Mark made his affection for Alistair clearer, though in ways that Alistair came to understand were distinctly Mark-like. He kept himself at a remove from Alistair but watched him studiously, quietly; for every twenty words Alistair and Elijah uttered he said two. When he mounted Elijah he focused his gaze and directed his thrusts in such a way as to suggest that Alistair was the one he wanted to be inside of, that he was using Elijah as a proxy anus, but he never forced himself on Alistair, never tackled him with the violent desire that Alistair suspected he struggled mightily to disguise. He showed his ardor by his timidity, his restraint, his good behavior. Occasionally, when Mark used the bathroom or went out to buy alcohol, Elijah would climb onto Alistair's lap and perform little acts of frenzied rule-breaking. But whenever Mark and Alistair found themselves alone Mark would sit with his hands folded honorably in his lap. And it was this difference between the men, the moral one, that struck Alistair as the most crucial. Mark strove to be a good person whereas Elijah strove to be, if not a bad person, something else. What vexed Alistair was that each man was allowed to be only one person, to occupy only his one defined self, while he, in order to satisfy both men's desires, had to be two people—upstanding or degraded, kind or cruel, gentle or hard-charging as the moment demanded—without any clear idea of which person he really was.

For the most part the conflicts between the men went unspoken. Mark and Elijah argued only occasionally and really only about one source of contention. Every so often, during that first month, Alistair heard about a man, a friend of Elijah's named Jay, who'd moved to New York earlier in the summer. Over time, as Elijah relayed incendiary remarks Jay had made or recounted raucous outings with him, Alistair put together a picture. He envisioned someone flamboyant, upsetting, risqué: the kind of person Elijah was made to love and Mark was made to hate. Alistair suspected that Jay occupied a position in their lives similar to his own, that he clarified their differences, exacerbated them, threatened to bring them to a head.

These spats always subsided quickly and Alistair was always glad when peace returned. For all the complexity of his entanglement with the men he liked it, lived for it, wanted to draw it out. Mark and Elijah made him forget about his troubles, and he wanted to dwell for as long as he could in this forgetting. But Alistair was terminally numerate, clear-eyed about dollar signs if nothing else. He should have known this forgetting would come to an end soon, and for all his anguish he wasn't much surprised when it did.

One night at Palladium, in the first week of October, he summoned the courage to peek at his Citibank accounts. Between the takeout and porn he'd nursed himself with in the weeks after his internship he'd blown through more than $1,200, and his fall-semester textbooks, which for all his professional fatalism he'd nonetheless felt compelled to buy, had set him back $500. His checking account was down to $250. There was no world in which this money would last him until the end of senior year, and even if by some miracle it did there was no relief awaiting him. In May he'd be exiled from Palladium and set down in the wilds of New York real estate, with its extortive rents and broker's fees, and after graduation he'd have to endure however many potentially ruinous weeks before he received his first paycheck at whatever job he managed to land, which job he couldn't be sure would be well-paying, which job he couldn't be sure he'd land at all.

How could he be so stupid?

He considered taking out another $10,000 in living loans, but the page he next navigated to, his Great Lakes account, sent a discouraging chill up his spine. As of the beginning of the school year, when his final tuition loans had gone through, his debt load had passed the six-figure mark. If he had an offer from JPMorgan Chase in hand $100,325 might have seemed manageable. But without such an offer, without any assured income at all, the number seemed like a death warrant.

He called his mother. All he would do was ask her to resume the $100 monthly allowances he'd put a stop to. As the phone rang he scripted his torturously apologetic request. Nothing clarified his debasement more than the fact that he, who'd gone to NYU with the purpose of rescuing her, was now asking her to rescue him. But when she answered she gave him a piece of news that deterred him.

"The Taurus finally gave out today," she said. "It's begun its transition to the next life."

"My condolences," Alistair said. In fact he'd been willing that car off the face of the planet for years. "What happened?"

"Who knows," Maura said. "It started smoking on my way to work. The tow truck guy gave it one look and said it wasn't even worth having serviced. I had to call my coworker and ask for a ride, and then I had to take a city bus home. I'm all for public transportation, believe me, but the Binghamton city bus—Dante could do something with that."

"Christ," Alistair said.

"One of the neighbors is lending me her car for now. And I'm steeling myself to make a call to Grandma."

"Why?"

"Because her forty-five-year-old daughter needs a new car."

"You really need to ask Grandma for a car?" Alistair said.

"I really do," Maura said.

"Go to Overman Ford. Every time I'm home I see their commercials. It's always something about zero down, zero interest for the first year."

"I should do that," Maura said. "And I would. If I could."

Alistair hesitated. He worried the answer to his next question might fell him. "Why can't you?" he said.

"Well," Maura said, and then she embarked on a long, meandering story about her finances, which appeared to be in about as bad a shape as his. Apparently, earlier in the summer, the house on Carey Street had finally begun to implode. Foundation and plumbing repairs Maura had long put off had become unavoidable, and to pay for them she'd had to take out a home equity loan in the amount of $25,000. The loan had turned out to be insufficient, and so for the past two months most of her discretionary income had gone toward making up the difference, with the result that she'd had to pay for a significant portion of her daily expenses on credit. Auto loan payments, however miniscule, were beyond her. Currently she was paying off the home equity loan and her credit card bill at the same time, and the monthly outlay was all she could manage. "I never use my credit card," she said. "I hate debt. Hate it."

"As you well should," Alistair said. "Why didn't you tell me about this?"

"I didn't want to burden you," Maura said. "I knew it was a big summer for you, with your internship and all. And what could you have done about it?"

Alistair hadn't told Maura that he'd blown his internship at JPMorgan, so he couldn't very well tell her that one thing he could have done was not quit and throw $12,000 away. "You still should have told me."

"I'm embarrassed," Maura said. "That's all it is. Mushy-brained, head-in-the-clouds Maura. She thought she could go her whole life not caring about money, not planning, not 'investing,' not looking for better jobs. But now her chickens have come home to roost. That's an idea, actually. I should get chickens. I wouldn't have to pay for eggs."

"You're not mushy-brained," Alistair said. "You work hard. You raised me all by yourself. It's not your fault that house is a hundred years old."

"If I'd thought about it for even five minutes, I would have seen that this day was coming. I saw the cracks in the foundation, I saw the water stains on the ceiling. But I just kept putting it off, putting it off, hoping for I don't even know what. Some stroke of luck? Some savior? Who, God?"

"You should have told me," Alistair said. "I would have found a way to help."

"This isn't your problem," Maura said. "I shouldn't even be telling you now. I don't want you to worry about me."

Alistair moved from his desk to his bed, where he lay with his cheek against the pillow. He felt that every bone in his body had turned to lead.

"I will admit, though," Maura said, "I did think about that. Your obsession with helping me. I thought, you know, if this had happened a few years from now, after Alli had started working, I might have buried my pride and asked. I thought you might like hearing that."

"I will help you," Alistair said. "I promise. Soon."

"I'm sure this house isn't through with me yet. Maybe by that time you'll be at the bank, swimming in bonuses."

The muscles of Alistair's face were so contorted that all he could do was puff air through his nose.

"But until then, really, don't think about this," Maura said. "Please forget I even mentioned it."

Alistair had barely hung up the phone before he mashed his face against the pillow and began to cry. He couldn't remember the last time he'd shed tears. Years of feeling seemed to be leaving his system. For a moment he felt newly calm, more alive to his surroundings, to the breeze from the window, the texture of the pillowcase, the smell of dining hall pizza on his breath: all these things seemed nearer. But his crisis soon returned, realer and more terrible for its brief abeyance. And more present in his mind than his shriveled savings, his engorged debt, his diminished prospects—all the ways he was failing himself—were all the ways he was failing his mother too.

He had no desire to tell Mark and Elijah about his newly discovered poverty, but as he trotted to the Eros Ananke the following night he felt it would be impossible to hide his distress. The fact of his destitution was too immediate, the number $250 impressed too deeply on his nerves, to keep it out of his voice, his body, his eyes. He resigned himself to spilling it, with no clear idea of how they'd respond. Maybe they'd be turned off. Maybe they wouldn't care. Or maybe they'd take pity on him and—well, it was enough to acknowledge this possibility without exactly formulating it.

"You look like you need a drink," Elijah said as he let him in.

"Please and thank you," Alistair said.

He gulped down three gin-and-tonics in rapid succession. His body went limp and his mind slowed, but the wound of his pennilessness throbbed unabated. He and Elijah sat at a chaste distance on the couch, Mark sat in the armchair, and something in the slackness of their postures suggested this might be the first night they forwent sex, which oddly enough seemed like a transgression in its own right. Was it already happening, five weeks in? Was he being sucked already into their sexless tedium?

"OK," Elijah said. "What's up. You look like someone died."

"Sorry," Alistair said. "Little stressed."

"School?" Mark asked.

"School. Other things."

"A boy?" Elijah said.

At the mention of this prospect Mark stiffened.

"Not a boy," Alistair said.

Mark leaned forward. "Tell us."

Alistair put his elbows to his sides and brought his knees together. When he spoke he felt as if he were kicking a rock off a cliff, just to see what would happen. "I'm broke."

He listened for the sound of the rock hitting the ground, but heard nothing. Mark and Elijah were silent. He understood at once that this word was foreign to their ears, and that it lit up realities and feelings they preferred to keep at bay.

"I thought you just spent the whole summer working at a bank," Elijah said.

"I did," Alistair said. "But I wasn't getting an offer, and when I found that out I quit, and because I quit early I had to give all the money back."

"And you still quit early?"

"I had to give back twelve grand." Though his eyes were on the floor he could sense Elijah rearing his head.

"That sounds like something we would do," Elijah said. "I don't mean that as a compliment."

Mark looked at Alistair in all genuine concern. "Do you have a scholar-ship?" he asked.

Alistair didn't doubt Mark's intelligence, but this was a hopelessly stupid question, the kind of question only a person who'd never needed a scholarship would have the ignorance to ask. All Alistair could do by way of response was smirk and try to keep the resentment out of his face.

Elijah offered his own hollow consolation. He took Alistair's glass, went to the bar cart, and topped him up. After he'd given Alistair his drink and sat back down he looked at Mark. Alistair watched through bleary eyes as they conversed wordlessly. He was amazed that they could still understand each other this way; it conflicted with his sense of them as being irreparably estranged. Maybe they did still love each other. If being able to communicate on this subvocal, subgestural plane wasn't love he didn't know what was.

"Would you be open to us helping you?" Mark asked.

In the depths of Alistair's consciousness he'd predicted this offer, hoped for it even, but he didn't like the way it was being phrased, as a question, and a hypothetical one at that. "It wasn't my intention to ask."

"I know," Mark said.

Elijah caught Alistair's eye. He scrunched his brow, inclined his head at Mark, and gave a little nod. He seemed to be saying that Alistair would be an idiot not to accept, that it was a drop in the bucket, that he would do himself no favors by being proud. Alistair was grateful for the encouragement. He felt that for all Elijah's pampered privilege he understood Alistair better than Mark ever could. He was a child of the middle class who'd stumbled into wealth, and he had a scrappiness, a take-what-you-can-get ruggedness, that Alistair appreciated. "I'd pay you back."

"Only if you want to," Mark said.

"And I don't need much."

"Whatever sounds right to you."

Elijah raised his glass in a ridiculous cheers. "So there," he said. "Great."

For a while they all sipped in silence. Alistair wasn't sure what was supposed to happen next. Should he specify a number? Would Mark send him money on an app, or write a check? He could see Mark writing a check; it would square with his suburban-dad affect. The more the silence went on the more frustrated he grew. They seemed not to understand that he was humiliated and that to have to initiate this transaction, to do all the work in this exchange, would only humiliate him further. They were thoughtless, thoughtless. He'd opened his mouth, having decided he couldn't wait any longer, when the intercom rang.

Mark and Elijah looked toward it with proprietary alarm.

"Is that a package?" Elijah said.

"It's eleven o'clock," Mark said.

Elijah went to the intercom and answered the phone. After a moment his eyes widened.

"What?" Mark said.

Elijah covered the receiver. "It's Jay."

Mark stood and planted his hands on his sides. "Don't let him up."

"I can hear him in the background. He sounds like he's wasted."

"Tell him to go away."

"I'm not telling the doorman to send him away."

"Then go downstairs."

"I don't want to make a scene in the lobby."

"Elijah, if you let him up—"

"Send him up," Elijah said.

After Elijah hung up the phone he and Mark stared at each other, and Alistair walked back his theory: you could communicate on this subvocal, subgestural plane and not be in love at all.

They turned their eyes to him, as if he were a stash of drugs they didn't know what to do with.

"We'll just say you're our friend," Elijah said.

"He is our friend," Mark said.

"Should I leave?" Alistair said.

"Jay's going to leave," Mark said.

"I can hide in the bedroom."

Mark threw himself back into the armchair and fumed through his nostrils, and Elijah, waiting by the door, folded his arms. "Well," he said to Alistair, "now you get to see what all the fuss is about."

A minute later there came four loud knocks, a stagey *rat-a-tat-tat*. Alistair kept his eyes on Mark until the interloper had entered his field of vision. Jay Steigen was thin, about Alistair's height, and somehow at once off-putting and transfixing. His wore his sandy hair center-parted on top and buzzed at the sides, and he had on a strange assortment of clothes—black cashmere hoodie, cruddy slim jeans, multicolored Bally sneakers reminiscent of bowling shoes— that suggested either a recent cash infusion or lack of mirror or both. All the same he had an undeniable glamour. He moved with a celebrity's assurance of electrifying every room he walked into; and indeed the room seemed suddenly brighter, the edges of its surfaces more defined. He looked around and with a flick of his hair turned to Alistair.

"Who's *this*?"

Elijah, standing behind Jay, laughed uneasily. "Alistair, Jay, Jay, Alistair."

As Jay stared at Alistair he smiled with barely parted lips, revealing braces. "What is he?"

Elijah brought over a chair from the dining table, pressed Jay into it, and resumed his spot next to Alistair on the couch. "He's our friend."

Jay pulled out a vape and twirled it. "Wait a second," he said. "Were you all just fucking?"

"Hadn't gotten there yet," Elijah said.

Mark, across the room, whispered, "Jesus."

Jay sucked on his vape. "Very interesting," he said. The drag in his voice suggested he was indeed wasted. "Do you come here a lot?"

"Often enough," Alistair said.

"Have they told you about me?"

"They've told me some."

"Oh goodie. What have they told you?"

"Believe it or not," Mark said, "not everyone is obsessed with you."

"No," Jay said to Mark, "that's just you." He faced Alistair. "What have they told you?"

"You went to school with Elijah," Alistair said. "You just moved to New York." Jay looked crestfallen.

"Where are you coming from?" Elijah asked.

"Howie and I had dinner at his place," Jay said. "Then we went to Townhouse. The last bastion of proper Greek relations. All old men and sprightly twinks looking for substitute fathers."

Alistair had been informed that Jay lived off the patronage of an "older man," and now he had a name with which to fill in that blank.

"I helped Howie find a son, and then I left," Jay said. "I felt extraneous." He moved his eyes around the room. "A feeling I'm used to." He faced Alistair again. "What else do you want to know?"

Alistair held his hands in his lap, pulling at his fingers. "What do you do?"

Jay smiled at Elijah with crinkled eyes. "That's cute," he said. "He thinks I *do* something."

Alistair felt an inclination to dislike Jay as Mark did, to express his loyalty to Mark by sharing his distaste. But despite himself he found Jay intriguing. He was performative, pretentious, not entirely convincing: he had a teenager's way of experimenting with grown-up gestures and turns of phrase. But performativity implied boldness, a will to surpass one's preordained limits, and Alistair understood this; he sympathized with it. What had he been doing for the past three years if not performing the person he badly wanted to be?

"What do *you* do?" Jay asked him.

"I think that's enough for tonight," Mark said. "Nice to see you, Jay. As always."

"I'm in school," Alistair said. "I go to Stern."

Jay snorted. "How terrifying," he said. "I love it. I'm assuming you're bound for Goldman. You have it written all over you."

Alistair could feel Mark and Elijah tensing, shouldering as much of the awkwardness of this moment as they could. But Alistair had pledged to be more open with people, to crawl out of his shell, and he didn't want to make things more awkward for Mark and Elijah by lying. "I'm not bound for anywhere," he said. "Turns out I'm not a good Sternie."

Jay took in Alistair's smart clothes, his trim body, his clean-cut face. "You don't look like a slacker to me," he said. "Quite the opposite."

"Alistair isn't a slacker," Elijah said. "That world is just very tough."

Mark, sitting silently in the corner, seemed chagrined that Elijah and not he had been the one to step in as Alistair's advocate.

"But you don't look like a softie either," Jay said. "Or maybe that exterior hides a soft center." He sucked on his vape. "One knows a little something about that."

Mark leaned forward. "It's getting late."

Alistair was torn between his loyalty to Mark and his undeniable curiosity about Jay. He was interested to see what Jay, obviously eccentric, possibly intelligent, might make of him. "I wasn't good at playing the game," he said. "There are things you have to know how to do. You kind of have to go into it knowing how to do them."

Jay's eyes shone with something like recalibration, something like understanding, something like sympathy. "Yes," he said after a moment. "It's almost like you have to be—born into it."

Alistair stared at him. "I think that helps."

"And you—were not born into it."

Alistair continued to stare. "No."

Jay pulled on his vape and emitted a thick cloud. He spoke to a point above Alistair's head. "The tragic dimensions are in place," he said. "The promise, the yearning, the great hunger unsatisfied. The beautiful boy enchanted, the beautiful boy crushed. The more I think about this idea, the more I see it in everything. In you, Alex—"

"Alistair," Elijah said.

"—in everything. Increasingly, even the news!"

Alistair had to assume Jay was reading different news than he was, and he was jealous. Every day in class he drowned out his professors' ramblings, which increasingly seemed to bear no relevance to his life, by scanning the *New York Times*, and every day he found himself keeping tabs, with Pavlovian helplessness, on the election. He'd followed Trump's string of gleeful offenses—his vituperations about Mexicans, his paroxysms of misogyny, his tossing of slops to fringe right-wing pigs—with awed disbelief.

"Of course Elijah knows something about this idea too," Jay said. "Elijah, have you told him about your paintings?"

Elijah's eyes widened. "That's the cue," he said. "Good night, Jay."

Mark remained miserably in his chair. He seemed disappointed in Alistair for taking Jay's bait, and perhaps disappointed in himself for not intervening more forcefully, for remaining hostage to his timidity.

"One more question," Jay said. He inclined his head at Elijah and Mark. "Why them? I can't imagine you have much in common. They're not strivers. Only failures."

Now Mark stood.

"I get it, though. They're very glamorous. Paragons of the other half. You're getting a vicarious taste. Of that and more! From what I've heard, there's a rather large dick in this room. I think it's behind me. I think it's about to stab me."

Elijah also stood. "Thank you for stopping by."

Jay put out his hands in surrender and, taking his time, made for the door. "You should bring him to dinner at Howie's sometime," he said to Elijah. He faced Alistair and smiled, braces glinting. "I'm happy they found you. They obviously could use some fun."

After Jay had left Alistair waited for Mark and Elijah to sit back down, but they remained standing. Jay's last words hung thickly in the air, and their embarrassment was evident: the secret of their sexual experiment was out, the romantic failure it attested to laid bare.

"So," Mark said to Alistair, avoiding his eyes, "that's Jay."

Elijah had collected their empty glasses and brought them to the sink. "He likes to get a rise out of people," he said to Alistair. "I hope you didn't find him offensive."

"Not offensive," Alistair said. "More kind of fascinating."

"Don't tell him that," Elijah said. "It would be the highest compliment."

"He's rude," Mark said. "He's rude, hollow, and immature."

"He's my friend," Elijah said. "Maybe you don't understand that because you don't have any."

"I'd rather have no friends than be friends with someone like him."

"Well, then I guess you got what you wanted."

Alistair stood too. He saw that the night was over, that Jay had ruined the mood. But he wavered. He waited for the men to remember their offer, the unfinished business of the loan he didn't have to repay, in whatever amount sounded right to him.

"Sorry about tonight," Elijah said. "We'll see you soon."

Alistair looked at Mark, but Mark was too consumed in his irritation to notice him. "Sure," he said in a small voice and left.

He walked up Third Avenue at a clip. He was angry at the men for their obliviousness, angry at himself for indulging Jay, angry at Mark for being disappointed in him, for holding him to his vague moral code. He took long strides and clenched his jaw. The night had suddenly turned cold.

He'd made it three blocks when he heard behind him a heavy, clumsy patter. He turned and saw Mark jogging toward him, a slip of paper in his hand.

"I didn't forget," Mark said, panting.

"It's OK," Alistair said. "I don't want it."

"Take it," Mark said. "Please."

Alistair hesitated and, when he finally accepted the check, took great pains not to look at it.

"I just guessed," Mark said. "I can write another one."

Alistair peeked, with effortful dignity, at the check. Never in his life had he been so unable to assign value to a number. $1,000 was more than he'd expected. By his present standards it was lifesaving. But what was it by Mark's standards? A little, a little more than a little, a lot? Was it anything more than a pleasingly round figure? Was this the basic denomination in which he traded? "I'll pay you back," he said.

"Please don't."

A group of kids Alistair's age walked by, faces he'd seen on campus but couldn't put names to. "I didn't like him either," he said to Mark. "I didn't want to be unfriendly. I'm sorry if I upset you."

Mark stepped forward and embraced Alistair. "You don't have anything to be sorry about," he said and walked off.

Alistair wasn't surprised when he didn't hear from the men for the next three days. By learning of Alistair's existence Jay had sullied the sanctity of their entanglement and at the same time made it realer: they'd been caught, as it were, with their pants down. He suspected it would take them time to recalibrate their feelings about the arrangement, to decide just how real they were prepared to let it be.

He passed his days in jittery apathy. He discovered how barren his life away from the Eros Ananke was, how much he'd come to organize his rhythms around his nights there. He studied only as much as was necessary to earn passably decent grades. He submitted applications to variously depressing work-study jobs: manning the IT service desk, tutoring in the math department, digitizing microfiche earnings reports for a historian of corporate mergers. He scheduled appointments at the career center to discuss his vanishing job prospects. He cashed Mark's check, hoping Mark would notice and reach out. But he heard nothing. He suspected Mark looked at his checking account about as frequently as he cooked.

Elijah called him Friday morning.

"What do you think about Jay's idea?" he asked.

"That I'm 'tragic'?" Alistair said.

"Dinner at Howie's."

What Alistair had most feared was that the men would decide to end things, and what he'd most hoped was that they would invite him over and resume their entanglement on its original terms. He wasn't sure where on the spectrum between these things this unexpected proposal lay. "That would be new."

"Cat's out of the bag," Elijah said. "We have no reason to hide you anymore. And Mark hates these things. He'd feel better if you were there."

"Mark is willing to have dinner with Jay?"

"We've been talking," Elijah said. "We have an idea. There'll be someone else there. Someone Mark doesn't hate so much."

"An idea?"

"We'll see you tonight."

Later that evening, on his way out, Alistair passed through the living area, where Vidi was watching *Wheel of Fortune*.

"Another date?" Vidi said. "With your mystery boyfriend?"

"Who said I had a boyfriend?" Alistair said.

"You're gone every night. You come back with sex hair."

"I don't have a boyfriend."

"I'm happy for you."

Outside, as Alistair approached the Uber, Elijah got out, motioning for him to take the middle seat. Only when Alistair was squished between the men did he realize fully how much he'd missed them. He spread his legs just to feel their thighs against his.

"So, a little context," Elijah said as the car lurched around Union Square. He explained that Howie Gallion was from North Dakota, that he was the brother of a fracking titan named Herve who a few years before had sold his company for some unspecified billions, that Jay had met Howie over the summer in Miami, and that he'd slept with him, charmed him, and persuaded him to bankroll his life and illusory art practice: some "project" about which he was dubiously disinclined to provide details.

"Sounds right," Alistair said. He was relieved to see a reluctant smile appear on Mark's face.

"You'll eat well, you'll drink well, the view is pretty spectacular," Elijah said. "And you'll meet Nikolai."

Alistair felt a surge of social anxiety in his throat. For a loner he was certainly meeting a lot of new people. "Nikolai?"

"He works for Howie's brother," Mark said. "Seems to do pretty well for himself. Comparatively tolerable."

"We were thinking," Elijah said. "Maybe he can give you advice."

"What does he do?"

"Fuck if we know."

"It's just a thought," Mark said. "No pressure."

"And if it doesn't go well, blame Mark," Elijah said. "It was his idea."

Mark lifted his shoulders. He avoided Alistair's face. "I don't want to see you struggle," he said.

The Die Kinder, as Alistair learned Howie's building was called, rose forty stories over Midtown West. He followed its wall of glass, its thousand variably illuminated windows. When his gaze hit the sky, the nighttime clouds passing overhead, he felt dizzy.

"He's all the way at the top," Elijah said.

Mark stared at the entrance. "Let's go."

Upstairs, they were greeted by a petite old man who smiled kindly but struggled to meet their eyes. Alistair assumed he was some kind of butler.

"Howie, Alistair, Alistair, Howie," Elijah said.

Howie let them in and shut the door without answering. The room Alistair had walked into was magnificent by any measure, but Howie's smallness and meekness made it almost comically vast. He was wearing a navy striped button-down of expensive material and khaki pants that his spindly legs barely filled. He had silver hair, cut boyishly neat, rough skin, and piercing blue eyes. His eyes were so youthful, so at odds with his shriveled frame and weathered face, that for a bizarre moment Alistair wondered if they were implants. Howie patted the men's arms limply and then took Alistair's hand in both of his. Alistair, confused, moved it in something like a shake and then withdrew it.

"No," Howie said, his voice thin and languid. "I was going to kiss it."

Alistair gave him back his hand and permitted it to be kissed. He laughed, and Howie finally looked him in the eye. "Oh my," he said, his face reddening. "Oh my."

In the kitchen a trio of caterers sliced and stirred, and near the base of a curved glass staircase a bartender manned a table arrayed with liquor. The windows looked onto a cityscape that seemed oddly flattened, like an infinite, overelectrified circuit board. On the long deep couches beneath the windows sat Jay and a dark-haired man in a white dress shirt who appeared to be in his late thirties.

Elijah and Howie joined Jay and the other man, but Mark lingered and beckoned Alistair toward the bar. While the bartender made them drinks Alistair put his lips to Mark's ear. "Does Howie always hire caterers?" he asked.

"Every time I've been here," Mark said. He glanced behind him. "He's a little weird, but harmless. The other guy is Nikolai. Also weird, also harmless."

"Is everyone here weird?"

"We can be not-weird together."

When they made their way to the couches Jay raised his glass. "Everyone, welcome Alistair!" he said. "Mark and Elijah's seven-year itch. Finally the men have decided to live. But what will they do with their sanctimony, now that they can't gloat about being monogamous?"

"I was never sanctimonious," Elijah said.

Jay's eyes passed over Mark. "Well, *you* weren't." He resumed the story he'd been telling Nikolai, which was about Howie's days in Williston, North Dakota, during the height of the late-aughts oil boom. "You had these men coming in droves, from all over the country," he said to Nikolai. "Colorado, Pennsylvania, Alaska. They lived in—Howie, what were they called?"

"Man camps," Howie said.

"Man camps!" Jay said, clapping. "The women were terrified. They refused to go out alone."

Nikolai squirmed in his chair. "Yes, yes, I have heard this story!" he said. His accent was Eastern European and thick, his movements jumpy. He kept his gaze lowered and gave his head exasperated shakes. With his babyish face and antic energy he seemed almost like a child at a parental dinner party: weary of the adult chatter, desirous of his quiet room.

Jay redirected his story at Alistair. "Howie was living in Fargo," he said. "When he heard about the man camps, he went back to Williston. He couldn't resist."

"We still had my father's place," Howie said dreamily. "Down the road from my brother's house. The rents in town were so *high*. I thought I could be of service."

"Oh, he wanted to be of service," Jay said. "Imagine these men, working a hundred hours a week in the oil fields. The Carhartt jackets, the beards and sweat, the furious storms brewing in their long johns."

"There were rooms in my father's house," Howie said. "I thought I could help."

"He lodged them for free," Jay said. "He watched them come and go. He almost bit his lip off, listening to them at night—drinking, burping, pissing, shitting."

"My God!" Nikolai said. "I have heard this, yes!"

"He couldn't sleep," Jay said. "He could hardly breathe."

Howie smiled, aloft in his reminiscence. "They were such nice men."

"He didn't get very far," Jay said. "Such a waste."

"One let me give him a neck rub," Howie said. "They worked so *hard*."

"They squandered you," Jay said. "You would have let them do anything."

"Oh my," Howie said. "Oh my."

Alistair was trying to keep the repulsion out of his face. He looked at Nikolai, who continued to squirm in his chair, and at Mark, who stared at Jay with steady disdain. For his part Elijah appeared to be listening both squeamishly and keenly.

"What Howie should have done," Jay said, "is tell them who his brother was. A few of them worked for Herve's company. That would have done the trick."

"How?" Elijah said.

"Class antagonism can overcome any sexual barrier," Jay said. "If they knew Howie was the big man's brother, this prince living in splendor off all their hard work, they would have looked at him and seen only a willing backside."

"Ugh, ugh, ugh!" Nikolai groaned.

"And they would have discovered the secret of gay sex," Jay said. "It's really a shame more people haven't learned it."

"What's the secret?" Elijah said.

Jay raised his chin and took a preparatory breath. "That there exists no better metaphor for the world we live in," he said. "Top and bottom, lord and serf, boss and peon, victor and vanquished. A totally unnatural and therefore creative act. Two individuals inclined by instinct to dominate, locked in a struggle for power that brings even its winner sorrow and even its loser ecstasy."

A brief silence fell. Jay looked around, searching for reactions, his cheeks flushed. Alistair wasn't sure Jay really believed these clearly much-considered and preformulated words. They seemed calculated not to persuade but to provoke. Maybe that was the only goal that he, an "artist" of uncertain output and doubtful merit, set for himself. And yet for all his skepticism Alistair felt he couldn't fully discount Jay: couldn't forget how thoroughly, even generously, Jay had seen through him.

He stood and made for the drinks table. After the bartender had topped him up he lingered for a moment, taking in the room. The walls were hung with various abstract artworks that he neither knew nor doubted had cost millions. He realized the penthouse was more or less an exact approximation of the kind of place he'd fantasized about one day owning himself. For how many years had he pictured himself in a room just like this, standing just like this, raising his glass just like this? He waited for some appropriate feeling to wash over him, but if he felt anything it wasn't what he'd expected to feel. He simply stood.

Elijah came toward him with an expression of jovial helplessness. "Sorry for Jay's rambling," he said. "I think he may have—" He snorted.

"How much did this place cost?"

Elijah turned to the bartender. "Don't want to know."

Alistair went to the bathroom, Googled for thirty seconds, and learned that it had cost $15 million.

When he emerged everyone was filing into the dining room, where the ceiling was lower and the lights dimmer. Alistair sat between Mark and Elijah. Jay and Howie each took a head. Across the table Nikolai ran his finger around the rim of his glass and stared at the table with twitchy boredom. Other than a few glances his way in the living room he hadn't much registered Alistair's presence. Alistair wondered if and when Mark would introduce him. The topic of careers, of brute material need, seemed alien to this place.

The caterers brought in wine and small plates piled high with salad. One caterer, a lanky man with sharp cheekbones and thick glasses, stood in the doorway after everyone had been served. "The produce has been sourced from a worker-owned farm up—"

"We don't care," Jay said.

The salad, all endives and huge Bibb leaves and coral profusions of frisée, looked like an exam in a cotillion class. Alistair could see no way of forking a leaf without bringing the whole structure down. He watched Nikolai pick out his frisée and toss it onto the table.

"Alistair," Elijah said to Nikolai, "is studying finance."

Nikolai munched on an endive with pursed lips. "My goodness," he said. "I am sorry!" With his wrinkled dress shirt, caffeinated eyes, and oily face he looked as though he'd been flying business class for forty-eight hours straight.

"Nikolai, tell them about your finance days," Jay said. "Tell them about your *scandal*."

Finally Nikolai looked at Alistair. "This asshole!" he said.

"Now he's just a houseboy," Jay said. "How's our Herve?"

"He is fat," Nikolai said.

Howie let out a pleased chirp.

The main course was an orange stew of unintelligible ingredients. It tasted how Alistair had always imagined rich-people food tasting: too interesting to register as good. As he broke up a mysterious nonpotato tuber with his spoon he felt homesick for Maura's pasta salads, her breaded chicken cutlets. Spices he'd never tasted before inflamed the back of his throat. While Howie described his most recent trip to Miami and Jay cut in with remarks about Howie's South Beach "harem" Alistair looked around the room and took in the various artworks and objets—sepia-toned photographs of frolicking men, forbidding wooden masks frozen in gapes or crazed rictuses—with what he knew to be too obvious and rube-like an amazement. Mark, sensing his bewilderment, nudged him with his elbow and smiled. Elijah, seeing this, gave him a rivaling nudge in turn.

"Enjoying yourself?" Elijah whispered to Alistair.

"We're surviving," Mark answered for him.

During a lull in the conversation Jay set down his fork and began digging in his braces with his pinky nail. Having failed, apparently, to dislodge whatever morsel was stuck he turned to the sideboard behind him, plucked up from a silver tray a very old-looking pocketknife, and applied it to his teeth.

"Jay," Howie said maternally, "why are you cleaning your teeth with a *knife*."

"I forgot my toofpicks," Jay said, moving the knife in his mouth.

"That is a whalebone knife from the nineteenth century," Howie said. "It has been *painstakingly* restored. It cost me almost—"

"He's doing it to get our attention," Elijah said. "He can't even clean his teeth without a spotlight."

Jay proceeded to wriggle the knife under the wire of his braces.

"Yes," Nikolai said. "And now he has it! Here we all are, watching him!"

Jay smiled brightly, the knife glinting between his lips.

After dinner the group returned to the living room. Dessert was fennel-and-artichoke ice cream. Alistair grimaced through three small spoonfuls before abandoning it for his drink. Jay and Howie took Elijah to another room to goggle over a recent art purchase. Once they'd left Mark approached Nikolai. Alistair sat in a distant armchair, trying to eavesdrop, but they spoke too softly for him to hear.

After a few minutes Mark caught his eye, beckoned him over, and made for the bar, leaving him alone with Nikolai. Alistair sat on the couch stiffly, glancing at Nikolai's disheveled clothes and lumpy figure.

"Mark tells me you are feeling hopeless," Nikolai said, swirling his drink. "But he also tells me you are at Stern. These facts do not make sense together. Stern is a good school."

Alistair, now practiced in confessing his failure at JPMorgan, found he could state the facts plainly enough.

"No offer?" Nikolai said. "My goodness. Then you are hopeless."

"Precisely."

"But you are also lucky."

"How's that?"

Nikolai dipped his face toward his drink. "You do not want a job in banking," he said. "Those people—they are terrible. Someday, somehow, they will fuck you."

Alistair recalled Jay's oblique comment about Nikolai's "scandal."

"Anyway," Nikolai said, "I do not know what advice Mark thinks I can give you. I am just as hopeless."

"I was told you work for Howie's brother," Alistair said. "Herve."

Nikolai grunted. "I have to make a living," he said. He gestured at the bar, where Elijah, Jay, and Howie had reconvened with Mark. "I am not like them."

"What do you do for Herve?"

"I will bore you to tears."

"You won't," Alistair said. "At all. It sounds like you found an alternate path. That's what I'll have to do too."

Nikolai smiled. With drunken liberty he reached up and patted Alistair's head. "Listen to you," he said. "Look at you! You are not hopeless. You are still full of such hope."

"I have to be," Alistair said. He lowered his voice. "I'm not like them either."

Nikolai stared at him with fleeting sobriety. "You are young," he said. "Do you know what you should do? You should be a waiter! Or a lifeguard. Something fun. You should be free."

There was something about Nikolai, a kindness, a knowing sadness, that invited abject honesty. "I need to make real money," Alistair said. "I have a lot of debt. And I have family. That I need to support."

There came into Nikolai's face the same fleeting sobriety. Then he turned away and retreated into himself. "You have people in your life," he said. "People who love you. That is so nice."

Alistair, feeling conversationally adrift, looked toward the door. The possibility of getting useful advice out of this person seemed to be quickly vanishing.

"My work," Nikolai said. "It is so—lonely."

"And what is your work?" Alistair asked.

"I am a secretary, more or less," Nikolai said. "Send money here, arrange this meeting. Advise, consult, weigh in, blah, blah. It is not so bad. The money is fine. Three million a year. But it is not so fun."

A familiar note of resentment rang out in Alistair's head. Any job that paid three million a year was more than not so bad, however not so fun. Seeing no way of steering Nikolai's attention to more fruitful territory he made to stand. "I appreciate your taking time to talk to me."

"Wait!" Nikolai grabbed Alistair's arm. "I am sorry. I am just—I get so down."

"I can see that."

"Especially when I meet someone like you. So young, so full of hope."

"Appearances aside, I'm feeling pretty down myself."

Nikolai averted his gaze. "Sometimes I wish," he said. "Sometimes I think it would be better, a little better, if I just had—" He shook his head.

Alistair got the sense that he was the first person Nikolai had talked to, really talked to, openly and feelingly, in a long time. "A friend?"

Nikolai stared at him, his eyes traveling across his face. "Yes."

Alistair couldn't help it: he was being drawn into Nikolai's self-pity. Nikolai was lonely, and there was no sadness Alistair understood more.

Nikolai sat in silence. For a while only his eyes moved, back and forth, back and forth. Finally he breathed in and looked down his nose at Alistair. He stared at him wistfully, almost yearningly, for a rather long time. "You say you are really desperate?"

Alistair wasn't sure where this was going. "Very."

"And what do you think of grunt work?"

"I'm starting to think there's no other kind."

Nikolai pulled out his phone. He studied it for a moment before speaking. "Why do you not give me your number," he said. "I will give it some thought."

A conversation that had been utterly aimless until now had come to a point, a sunbeam of possibility, that Alistair hadn't even anticipated. "Are you offering me a job?"

"Who knows," Nikolai said. "Maybe you will like it more than I do. Herve likes hopeless people. He believes they make the best workers."

Alistair hesitated for a moment, then typed in his number. "Thank you!" he said. "I mean, I'll understand if you reconsider. But thank you!"

Nikolai pinched his cheek. "There is that smile," he said. "Yes, you make me happier already."

Alistair shook Nikolai's hand, took his leave, and found Mark and Elijah by the door.

"Jay says the night is just starting," Elijah said. "So I think we should go now."

Alistair said his goodbye to Howie. He looked back at Nikolai and gave him a nod. Nikolai smiled goofily, then stared at his drink, his mouth flat.

Jay, noting this exchange, put his arm around Alistair's shoulders. "I hate to break it to you, but Nikolai's straight," he said. "Are Mark and Elijah not keeping you satisfied? Or does your hunger just have no limits?"

In the Uber downtown Elijah ridiculed the food, which he'd found too farm-to-table ("More needs to happen in the 'to' part, I think"), excoriated Howie's new painting ("The Zombie Formalists have their next dupe"), complained about Jay ("How many bags did he snort?"), and then said he'd had a great time and hoped Mark and Alistair had too.

"How did your conversation with Nikolai go?" he asked.

"At first weirdly," Alistair said, "and then, by the end, very well?"

"Did he give you advice?" Mark said.

"I think he gave me a job?"

"I'm not surprised," Elijah said. "You're very seductive."

"Past experience suggests otherwise," Alistair said. "And I wasn't even trying for that. I think he just wants a friend."

"What's the job?" Mark said.

"Not sure," Alistair said. "I don't even know what Herve does."

"My question," Elijah said, "is why a billionaire would want to 'do' anything at all. Enjoy your money! Herve should take a lesson from me and Mark."

Mark said nothing. He put his forehead to the window. In the darkness he reached for Alistair's hand.

Alistair, aglow in his tentative excitement, slept more deeply than he had in many weeks. Yet when he woke the next morning he found that his relief, the sunbeam of possibility he'd glimpsed the night before, had somewhat dimmed. He thought again about Nikolai's "scandal." He recalled Nikolai's sadness, his loneliness, his litany of vague complaints. He worried that if he went to work for Nikolai the man's misery might rub off on him. He was feeling miserable enough as it was.

He spent his weekend in nostalgic studiousness, took comfort in the familiar wholesomeness of short essays, of problem sets. He wondered if it wouldn't be better to spend his senior year as a senior: studying, clocking in and out of a lame part-time gig, enjoying whatever scant academic thrills remained to him. But then he remembered how pointless his studies were, how much his lack of offer had rendered them an exercise in futility. And then he looked at his checking account, which after a further textbook purchase and a toiletry replenishment had sunk back down into the hundreds. And on Saturday he received a response from the historian of corporate mergers asking when he'd like to come in for an interview and clarifying that the position paid $9 an hour. And all weekend long the skies threatened rain and the wind blew down Fourteenth Street in cold, terrible bursts. And then on Sunday evening he received a call from a 646 number.

"So," Nikolai said. "How about you come to my place. Tomorrow morning."

Alistair paused before answering. "Can it be the afternoon? I have class."

"My goodness," Nikolai said. "So young!"

His reservations didn't ebb much when he arrived at Nikolai's apartment the next day. Nikolai lived a few blocks south of the Die Kinder, in a one-bedroom with views no less stunning than Howie's for being closer to the ground. His ceilings were high, if not penthouse-high, and he had much the same au courant fixtures and appliances that Howie did. But he was a slob. The kitchen counter was crowded with half-empty liquor bottles and unwashed takeout containers. The floor was strewn with dry-cleaning bags and cairns of magazines and manila folders. T-shirts and dress pants and worn-looking boxer shorts hung from table edges and backs of chairs. Alistair breathed through his mouth and scanned the room with dismay but didn't blame Nikolai. Apartments this bright and open and sterile weren't designed with human habitation in mind. Any sign of life that wasn't promptly rubbed out was bound to spoil them.

Nikolai cleared some newspapers from the couch and gestured for Alistair to sit. "Home," he said, pointing to the couch and the kitchen, "and work," he said, pointing to two adjoined desks by a window. The desks contained a Bloomberg terminal, four Lenovo ThinkPads, snarls of disconnected charger cords, and a jumble of loose papers. Midafternoon sunlight revealed water rings and pushed-around dust.

Nikolai sat across from Alistair in a silver bistro chair that rocked for lack of a rubber cap on one of its hind legs. "I am sorry for the mess," he said. "I guess I live like a college kid too."

"Must be hard," Alistair said, "when you work where you live."

Nikolai giggled. "Who says that I live!"

"I'm happy to lighten your load," Alistair said. "Whatever you need me to do."

"Yes," Nikolai said. "You make me feel lighter already."

There passed a moment of silence during which they only looked at each other: nearly a whole strange minute. "So," Alistair said, "what's the load?"

Nikolai nodded as if at the reasonableness of this question. "I told you I am a secretary, more or less," he said. "But Herve has many of those. For the most part, I am focused on one project. A very big project. Very new."

Alistair had worried his job would entail helping Nikolai with such frivolous tasks as the booking of chartered jets. A project—a big project, a new project—intrigued him.

"You are familiar with Maslow's hierarchy?" Nikolai said. "I remember it from a psychology class I took in college. I find it to be a very useful concept."

"I might have heard of it," Alistair said.

"It is a pyramid," Nikolai said. He put out his hand and made it into a flat plane. "At the bottom, you have the base needs. What will I eat? How will I put a roof over my head. Yes?" He moved his hand up. "In the middle layers, you have the more advanced needs. How will I be liked? How will I get rich?" He moved his hand up again. "At the top, you have what comes after the needs. You have everything all people want. You can see everything clearly. And now you can focus on helping others. You are familiar with this concept?"

Alistair said nothing—only watched, from his slouched position on the low couch, Nikolai's hand move up and up.

"Herve," Nikolai said, "has reached the top. He has worked hard, very hard, all his life. He has succeeded in every way you can imagine. And now, he would like to see others succeed."

"Is this philanthropy?" Alistair asked.

Nikolai barked. "The first thing you must know about Herve is that he likes to control his money. With philanthropy, you give fifty million to some fancy group. How does that group spend it? You do not know. Most likely, they spend it on themselves!"

Alistair smiled. If he were capable of giving millions to fancy groups he might harbor the same suspicion.

"Herve does not want charity organizations," Nikolai said. "He wants to do this himself, with his own people, in his own way. Besides, he would like to help people that, he believes, all those fancy groups have neglected."

"And who might those people be?" Alistair asked.

"Herve is from North Dakota," Nikolai said. "Have you been? I do not recommend it. I am from the shit part of Europe. I have seen enough depressing places for a lifetime. But Herve is interested in these places, and the people who live in them. Being in fracking, he knows all about the depressing places in this country. Pennsylvania, Arkansas, upstate New York. He feels for these places. He feels that they have—did I say something?"

Alistair became aware only then of doing something with his face. "Nothing."

"I said something. What did I say?"

"You mentioned upstate New York. That's where I'm from. I can confirm that it's depressing."

At this Nikolai relaxed—seemed, almost, to feel relieved. He moved his head in a slow nod and spoke more softly. "Herve feels that these places have been forgotten," he said. "This makes sense to you? This feels true, of where you are from?"

Alistair lifted his shoulders. "I certainly can't recall a billionaire ever taking an interest in it," he said. "What does Herve have in mind?"

Nikolai raised his voice again. "Herve believes these places have untapped potential," he said. "If only you lay the groundwork, invest in the existing infrastructure, then industry will come. He sees opportunities in"—he searched his mind—"shipping, manufacturing. Semiconductors. Lithium batteries. Herve has many associates, from all sorts of fields. He believes all they need is for someone like him to show them the way, to give them a lead to follow. If he shows curiosity about these places, they will show curiosity too."

This was even more intriguing to Alistair. Historically he'd framed his future in finance as a panicked flight from his homeland. But that dream had gotten him nowhere, and now the idea of becoming that pastless self had lost its shine. This sounded like an opportunity to do something radically other. If he worked for Herve he might, surprise of all surprises, be in a position not to escape but to help places like Binghamton. Kirit had suggested he go to work for the SEC to take his revenge, but this seemed like a sweeter revenge against the field he'd failed in. Maybe he could still do it, still succeed in his own way, and maybe he could do it without turning his back on his origins, without his old tangle of resentment and alienation. To turn the means by which he'd hoped to escape his shame back onto the source of that shame: this was intriguing.

"I'm interested," he said. "What would I be doing?"

If Nikolai had looked relieved a moment before he now, at the sight of Alistair's enthusiasm, stiffened. "Well," he said, "we will start you slow. Little things at first. Herve, you have to know, has some eccentricities. Discretion is paramount. We will see how you do at first. See how you like it."

Alistair only nodded. He was sure he'd do well, sure he'd like it. And now that he was prepared to take the job the problem of his finances swam back into view. "And what would be the, uh, structure?" he asked.

"You mean the chain of command?" Nikolai said. "It is a mess."

Alistair registered some surprise at this, and not a little early competitive aggression. He'd gotten the sense that the project was a lean affair, too embry-onic to have a hierarchy already in place. "I mean the payment structure."

"Ah!" Nikolai said. He seemed gladdened by this change of topic. "What did your internship pay? With the bank. I will pay more. I hate banks!"

JPMorgan had paid Alistair $1,500 a week. But Nikolai's insistence on one-upping it had opened a negotiatory lane, and Alistair felt he wouldn't be a good Sternie if he didn't exploit it. "Two thousand a week."

"Twenty-five hundred, then," Nikolai said. "I will pay you monthly. I will give you ten today."

Alistair tried to contain his amazement. The sunbeam of possibility widened and brightened. $10,000? All at once? Today?

"And Herve," Nikolai said. "He is always looking for good people. If you do well, if you are loyal, if you are smart, once you graduate? He would start you at one, one-point-five, I have no doubt."

Alistair nearly spat. "One-point-five what?"

"Oh," Nikolai said, slapping his thigh. "Look at you. So young. One-point-five mil, my friend! Oh, how much I like you."

The sunbeam brightened gloriously. It was practically blinding. "Are you shitting me?"

"Why would I shit you?" Nikolai said. "You see how much he pays me."

Alistair looked away, trying to collect himself. He surveyed the pigsty of Nikolai's apartment. "I know how much he pays you," he said. "Though if I'm being honest I don't exactly see it."

Nikolai hooted. "You are wondering where my millions are."

"I'd assume you'd be able to afford a housekeeper."

Nikolai turned his gaze. "I do not need someone coming in here," he said, "messing with all my shit. Besides, I am being smart about my money now. When I worked in banking, I lived like a crazy person. Booze, women, booze, women. Then, when I was fired, I was fucked! I could not refuse Herve. Do you think I want to do this forever? I mean—to work? When I have enough, I am done. Early retirement. Do you see?"

Alistair saw, and he didn't see. He found it odd how Nikolai had characterized his lucky break, as something he might have refused if he were able to, and he was nagged again by the question of Nikolai's days in finance, of the matter of his "scandal." But the figure Nikolai had invoked blazed unabated, blocking out everything else. Whole realities he'd only ever fantasized about and, more recently, dismissed as unattainable filled his mind.

"We will get you started the next time you come," Nikolai said. "There is just one more thing we must do. But first, let us have a drink. I may be smarter now, but I have not given up booze. And it is only the women"—he patted his flab—"who have given up me."

It was two p.m., and Alistair had a long night of homework ahead of him. But he felt he couldn't refuse a person who'd just promised to change his life. "OK."

Nikolai went to the kitchen, returned with two glasses filled halfway with clear uncarbonated liquid, and sat next to Alistair on the couch. *There is no way this is just plain vodka*, Alistair thought. But he took a sip and it was just plain vodka.

"What's the one more thing?" he asked.

Nikolai wiped his lips. "It still surprises me, you know, that you are so desperate. You look very fresh. You have on nice clothes."

"These clothes," Alistair said, "are part of the reason I'm desperate. I've been incredibly stupid."

"I know something about that," Nikolai said. "But you are really on your own? No one even to buy your clothes?"

"My mother is broke."

"And your father?"

"He's dead."

Nikolai took this in with refreshing matter-of-factness. "How old were you?"

"Six."

"Mine is gone too," Nikolai said. "I was not so young. But so you understand."

"What do I understand?"

Nikolai looked out the window. Clouds moved briskly against a cold blue sky. Underneath them the city rose in stalagmites of glass and stone. "You are free," he said. "But you would like, maybe, not to be so free."

He let a moment pass and then, as if to brighten the mood, offered Alistair a capsule biography. He'd been born in Plovdiv, Bulgaria, he explained, and moved to Chicago when he was sixteen, living with well-off cousins before applying to US colleges. Back home his father had worked in IT at a university hospital. Three months before he was due to retire, he'd died of a heart attack at his desk. His mother now lived in Sofia, in a luxury apartment Nikolai had bought her, but he rarely spoke to her. He had a brother in Kraków he hadn't seen in a decade. Until his midthirties, he'd been a trader at the London-based Bank of Zarathustra (BZ for short). He'd started out at the bank's New York offices ("Hell on earth") and then transferred to its desk in Moscow ("I have stories that would make your ears burn"), but then—

"Then?" Alistair said.

Nikolai took a large, unwincing gulp. "It is a silly story," he said. "Look me up. You can read all about it. Run for the hills if you like."

"Is that when you met Herve?"

"My group had dealings with him," Nikolai said. "When he learned what happened, he reached out and made his offer."

"I guess he read all about it and didn't run for the hills."

Nikolai smiled. "I was involved in what you might call a regulatory offense," he said. "Herve is no fan of regulation. In his industry, regulation is the enemy."

Alistair found that, in order to maintain his enthusiasm, he had to suppress the fact that Herve had made his billions in fracking. The Sternie part of him knew that natural gas was an important transition fuel and that extraction of it created jobs, tempered prices, and bolstered the US's energy independence. But another part of him, the Maura part, knew that fracking caused earthquakes, contaminated groundwater, released cancer-causing toxins into the air. He was relieved to be boarding the Herve train after it had left the fracking station. "What's the one more thing?" he asked again.

"You are with me, then?" Nikolai said. "You will work with me? You will be my friend?"

Alistair looked into Nikolai's forlorn eyes. Even if there weren't $10,000 on the other side of this question it would be impossible to say no to them. "We're friends already," he said.

Nikolai yipped, set down his glass, and put his arms around Alistair, engulfing him in scents of vodka and BO. "We will have such fun!"

Alistair wasn't sure when he'd last embraced a straight man like this. It might have been the last time he'd hugged his father.

"The one more thing," Nikolai said, peeling away and fetching his drink. "It is such a little thing. It is more silly than anything."

Silly, Alistair noted, was also the word Nikolai had used to describe his career-ending "regulatory offense."

"Herve is very private," Nikolai said. "He can be paranoid. When you are successful, you must be. You make enemies, you draw scrutiny. You attract the attention of competitors. And such a big, new, exciting project—he would like to keep it under wraps, until he is ready to show and tell."

"I'll be very discreet," Alistair said.

"You will be very discreet," Nikolai said. "And you will have a work name."
Alistair narrowed his eyes.

"For your emails," Nikolai said. "For your meetings, when you have those.
All of us, we all have these work names. Herve does not want people to learn
about the project by keeping track of who is helping him. They might be able
to put it together. He is very private, very paranoid—about competitors."

"You want me to use an alias," Alistair said.

Nikolai flapped his hand. "Work name."

"Why do I need one? I could see if he poached an industry executive. But
I'm just a student. I'm no one."

"No one yet!" Nikolai sang. "It is a top-down policy We must all comply."

This sounded to Alistair paranoid in the highest degree, eccentric beyond
reason. But then maybe this was how Herve had climbed to the top of the
human heap, by being more paranoid, more eccentric, than everyone else.

"It is only for the time being," Nikolai said. "The blander the better. If you
could think of one now, that would be best."

In the blur of his disorientation, in the haze of his vodka buzz, Alistair
could think of only ridiculous contenders. He thought of Kirit, of Paddy, of
Lloyd, his first-ever lay. He thought of the two videos he'd treated himself
to that morning, before class. He'd gone for his favorites, his trusted hobby-
horses, Connor Maguire and Vadim Black. In the first video, Connor reunites
with a former teacher. Connor thanks him for being such a good teacher, the
teacher thanks him for being such a good student, and then the two men begin
fucking. In the second, Vadim plays a cop interrogating a suspect. Vadim asks
the suspect a question, the suspect spits in his face, Vadim throws him to the
floor, and then the two men begin fucking.

"Connor Black!" Nikolai said. "That is a great name. Nice to meet you,
Mr. Black. Hee-hee."

"'Hee-hee,'" Alistair said.

"Now." Nikolai stood and went into the bedroom. Through the open door
Alistair could see more liquor bottles, more clothes tossed around as if by a
tornado. Nikolai returned with a thick envelope. "Your first payment."

Alistair accepted the envelope, feeling its thickness tentatively, as if it had
just come out of an oven. "Cash?"

"Processing a new hire is a chore, and you are only assisting me," Nikolai said. "And this makes things easier. For tax purposes."

"Right," Alistair said. "Easier."

Nikolai went to the desk, dug in the mess of cords and papers, and handed Alistair a phone. "From now on, you will use this to contact me."

If Alistair had been surprised by the cash he was even more surprised by the plastic black flip phone he was now holding. "This thing must be older than I am," he said.

"His first day," Nikolai said, "and he is already complaining."

"Just wondering again where your millions are."

"Be here same time Wednesday," Nikolai said. "I will be waiting, my friend!"

That night, after hastily dispatching his homework, Alistair Googled Nikolai. He'd hoped to find nothing, to be forced to forget about Nikolai's "scandal," but the internet was merciless in its riches, and Google was merciless in its ordering of search returns. The first page of results looked like a rap sheet. According to *Reuters*, *FT*, and a slew of wonkier financial outlets, Nikolai had been involved, three years earlier, in a multibillion-dollar money laundering scheme at BZ. It was case study fodder: a complex web of semilegal financial maneuvers—bad loans, shell companies, nonsensical forex trades—all aimed at helping this or that Russian oligarch or suboligarch smuggle his wealth out of his homeland. Watchdog authorities of various nationalities had descended on the Moscow desk, and one supervisor had fled to no-extradition-treaty Bahrain. Nikolai hadn't been charged with anything—he was guilty only of executing his boss's orders—but Alistair understood why he'd had to find a new line of work. The blot of this scandal had darkened his name, and he was unlikely to find a job in banking ever again. He was an outcast, if only in the obscure world of high finance. Like most financial scandals this one had escaped public comprehension and therefore notice. Crimes that should have incensed the plebeian masses went straight over their heads, cloaked in expert pedantries and stupefying jargon.

Alistair himself could have been incensed, he knew, but he struggled to summon much outrage. Even with this information in hand he still liked Nikolai, still pitied him, found it hard to judge him too severely. High finance was replete with regulation-defiers and exploiters of legal gray zones. Nikolai and his colleagues' only mistake was that they hadn't been more careful. Now he'd been blacklisted, now he was isolated and defeated, even if he'd staged a remunerative second act, and even if that act, by its altruistic nature, promised a chance at redemption. He was woefully, abjectly in need of a friend. Alistair saw that he could make serious money, contribute to a worthy and ambitious project, and give Nikolai companionship all at the same time. He could see no losses in this equation. Only a triplicate of wins.

In the rush of his renewed enthusiasm he briefly forgot about the matter of his "work name," of Nikolai's insistence on paying him in cash. Even as he recalled Nikolai's justifications for these things, even as he tried to rationalize them himself, some internal voice made a sound of complaint. The voice came from somewhere deep in him, beyond justifications and rationalizations, somewhere animal.

He Googled Herve Gallion. Unfortunately, here the internet's riches dried up. Aside from a cryptic profile on the website of his fracking company and a spot on *Forbes*'s 2015 billionaires list (#577, $3.1 billion), there was nothing about Herve—no photos, no interviews, not even a mention of a board seat. Alistair felt confirmed in his sense, formed during his years of pornographically researching billionaires, that online knowability was inversely correlated with wealth except at the very top end: that if graphed it would follow a skewed U. Most people in the bottom ninety-nine percent either publicized themselves of their own volition or were eminently findable, and the very richest people, your Bill Gateses and Warren Buffetts, were famous to the point of immortality. But in between was a nonnegligible slice of world-movers, heirs and investors and minor moguls like Herve, whom it was almost impossible to learn anything about. Like Nikolai's scandal they evaded public comprehension and therefore notice—as was, no doubt, their strong preference.

But surely, at some point soon, Alistair would meet Herve. He'd figure out for himself if Herve's insistence on "discretion," his "eccentricity," was really anything for him to be worried about. And in the meantime he'd see what it was like, to penetrate the sanctums of these world-movers, to understand their prerogatives, to breathe their air. He looked out his window at the old Consolidated Edison Building, at its blue light shining brightly. He stuck his hand in Nikolai's envelope and fingered the green leaves.

The next evening, after making his grand deposit at Citibank, he walked to the Eros Ananke with a check for $1,000.

"You really don't have to," Mark said when he handed it to him.

"I insist," Alistair said.

Elijah, on the couch, followed this exchange with the same amused expression he'd worn while sitting in the Stern plaza. "Big man," he said. "You're in a good mood."

Alistair sat down. "Nice not to be broke anymore."

"So I take it you accepted the job?"

"I guess so," Alistair said.

"What are you doing for him?" Mark asked.

"Besides restocking his vodka," Elijah said.

Alistair realized only then that he was reluctant to tell Mark and Elijah much about his meeting with Nikolai. He felt as if his excitement about the job and his reservations about it were mixed together in the same chamber, and that if he opened the chamber's valve too wide he might not be able to control what came out. "It's a revitalization project," he said in a pinched voice. "Investing in underleveraged local economies."

"You've lost me already," Elijah said.

"He wants to help depressed places," Alistair said. "Direct new business toward them."

"He should start with my hometown," Elijah said. "I can't think of a more depressing place."

"Brookhaven, Long Island, is not depressed," Mark said.

"I should know," Elijah said. "My parents are some of the poorest people in it."

"What kind of places?" Mark asked.

Alistair struggled to meet Mark's eyes. They shone as ever with his intelligence, his private judgments and ideals, his dignity. Surely he'd balk at Nikolai's scandal, at the "work name," at the cash. He was pure, and even if this purity was only an effect of his privilege, of the fact that he'd never had to dirty his hands in work, he was nevertheless forbidding. Alistair far preferred Elijah at this moment. He offered a more forgiving surface, a softer landing, with no sharp crags of high standards. "Not sure yet," he said. "I'm getting the details little by little."

"Mark can name dozens of depressed places," Elijah said. "It's the family business. Maybe Herve should consult with Mark's dad. Though I guess that wouldn't be good for Arty's company. If the people in those places weren't so poor, they wouldn't have to live in his parks."

Mark slumped further into the armchair that, every day more and more, seemed to be eating him. He looked wounded, and not just by Elijah's comment. Alistair wondered if the real reason for his dejection was that he, Alistair, had found a job, paid him back, didn't need his charity, didn't owe him the gratitude and obligation that it entailed.

"Anyway," Elijah said to Alistair, "congratulations. I'm not usually into do-gooders. But don't worry, I still like you."

In the bedroom Alistair again found that he wanted only Elijah's soft landing. He made handsy, mouthy, tumid use of all his forgiving surfaces. He rubbed, he tongued, he grabbed, he spanked, he took a breather, wiped his forehead, recommenced. Mark sat on the sidelines, stroking himself drearily in all his unyielding flaccidness, saved from embarrassment only by the fact that he was well-endowed and a shower. At the end of twenty minutes Alistair came inside Elijah and then submitted, at Elijah's direction, to a sick little procedure that involved a condom turned inside out over a tongue.

"Mm," Elijah said, licking his lips. "Mm."

As Alistair was leaving Mark approached him and touched his arm. He looked at Elijah until Elijah got the message and, shrugging, walked out of earshot.

"I'm not cashing this check," Mark said to Alistair. "I want it to be a gift."

Alistair focused his gaze on Mark's chin. He was afraid of Mark's moral discernment, but he was just as much afraid of his love. It grew larger and darker, like an unhealing bruise, every day. "I don't want to take money from you," he said. "Especially if I don't need it."

"Maybe you don't need me at all," Mark said. "You and Elijah seem to have enough fun on your own."

Alistair looked down at the floor. "I wouldn't want that," he said. "If things are getting too complicated, we can take a pause."

Mark opened the door for him and stepped aside. "I wouldn't want that either."

When Alistair returned to Nikolai's apartment the next day he found that Nikolai had tidied, put on business-casual clothes, and prepped. Alistair was relieved. He was excited, rather insistently so, to *work*.

Nikolai sat him down at one of the ThinkPads and stood over him. He spoke professionally, even brusquely, and quickly, as if he were holding his breath. "This will be your computer," he said. "No need to bring your own laptop."

"Got it," Alistair said.

"And this is your email." He reached over Alistair's shoulder, typed in a URL, and brought up a bare-bones webpage with an empty inbox. It looked like something a distracted engineer had built in a day. At the top left-hand corner were the word PHAKELOS and, below it, the account address, connorblack@phakelos.com.

"What's Phakelos?" Alistair said.

"That is your LLC."

"'My' LLC?"

"This project has a complicated structure," Nikolai said. "If I am being honest, it is like a fucking matryoshka. You do not want to know how many holding companies are on top of this one. Off the top of my head, I cannot even tell you. But this you do not need to worry about. You are Phakelos. Do not bother looking it up. Beyond a few legal documents, it does not exist."

Alistair glanced at the desk, at its chaotic spray of papers. He saw a sliver of what looked to be a contract: *The corporation shall have perpetual existence.*

"Now," Nikolai said. He minimized the email server and brought up an Excel spreadsheet. "We are dealing with several different teams. I have labeled them alphabetically. Some of these teams have sites already, which I have labeled accordingly. Some are still scoping out possibilities. It is easy enough. Team A, Site A, Team B, Site B."

"The sites," Alistair said, "are in the regions Herve is interested in?"

"Yes."

"Which regions?"

"We are still determining the full list."

"What's the process?" Alistair said. "They scout resources and infrastructure, do labor-market research, if there's growth potential bring on investors, pitch executives?"

Nikolai swigged from a bottle of Poland Spring, moving the water in his mouth experimentally, as if waiting for the burn of alcohol. By the time he swallowed he appeared to have forgotten Alistair's question. "Each team has a point person," he said. "As you can see from the names"—he indicated a column of point persons—"they all have work names."

William Wilde, Brandon White, Jeremy Law, Jimmy Barnes—they sounded like the members of a boy band. They sounded like the muscled stars of a porn film about sodomite frat boys. How on-brand Alistair had been when he'd chosen Connor Black.

"The point persons will be contacting you for three reasons," Nikolai said. "They will ask permission to make purchases, they will report on their progress, and they will tell you about any problems. You are to relay any and all communications to me, and I will tell you what to say."

"Understood."

Nikolai scrolled to a column of number salad. "These are the credit cards and bank accounts for each team," he said. "Connected, of course, to their respective LLCs. If a point person requests to make an expenditure, and I grant permission, note it in the cells to the right. You will be compiling weekly expense reports."

"What are they paying for?" Alistair asked.

"They are researching," Nikolai said. "Traveling, arranging consultations, bringing on helpful people. These things cost money."

Alistair looked at the sea of cells, at their dizzying area of inputs. "I'm a little confused by the matryoshka," he said. "All these different LLCs—is that really necessary?"

"If you ask me," Nikolai said, "this entire project is not necessary."

"But what's the purpose? Is Herve trying to dodge taxes?"

Nikolai smiled. "Every penny Herve has to give to the federal government makes his heart break. The federal government is his sworn enemy."

"But the project isn't even profitable at this stage. All he's doing is spending. How much in taxes could he be dodging?"

"This is the way Herve does business," Nikolai said. "It is the way he has always done it. It is the way all people at his level do it. Do you not know this? Are you naive?"

Alistair shrugged. He knew Nikolai had a point.

"Herve likes privacy," Nikolai said. "He likes discretion. He does not need people nosing in on him. The federal government least of all."

"If he's investing in whole communities," Alistair said, "he's going to have to interact with the government in some capacity."

"Oh," Nikolai said, "I am sure."

Nikolai went into the kitchen, where he refilled his water bottle from the tap and then, furtively, topped it off with a pour of Stoli. When he returned he sighed, as if he'd just now let out his breath. "Look at us!" he said as he sat across from Alistair. "Two friends, two happy boys, working!"

Alistair dug in his pocket, pulled out his phone, and brought up an email to himself in which he'd made a frenzy of notes. "I've been doing some research of my own," he said. "I have some ideas that might be of interest. You mentioned shipping? I was looking into southeastern Pennsylvania. That region was absolutely gutted when manufacturing jobs dried up. But geographically it's a supply chain sweet spot. It's equidistant from New York, Philadelphia, and DC, and there's a ton of land there. It's practically begging to be a fulfillment center hub. That could create a lot of jobs. There's already some action happening in that regard. We could speed it along. And you mentioned lithium batteries? With electric cars, that demand's going to skyrocket over the next decade. With enough investment a shuttered manufacturing facility could easily accommodate production, and a single lithium battery factory can employ as many as twenty-five hundred people. That could bring a whole small town back to life. I've been making a list of places with underutilized manufacturing infrastructure. I've been making a list of places adjacent to underutilized rail freight lines. I've been making a list—"

"Excuse me," Nikolai said, holding up his hand. "Excuse me. Why do you have your personal phone out?"

Alistair glanced between his phone and Nikolai. "It's where I have my notes."

"Put it away," Nikolai said. "Do not use it for work. You say you are making lists, you are making whatnot, on your personal devices—you will not do this. You will use only the laptop and phone I gave you. Am I clear?"

Alistair slipped his phone back into his pocket. The shock of Nikolai's interruption, the severity of his tone, had activated his tear ducts. "I don't see why it's such a problem."

"If you use only the phone and laptop I gave you, there is no problem," Nikolai said.

"But why are you such a freak about it?"

"Me!" Nikolai said. "Me, the freak? These are not my rules."

"Then why is Herve such a freak about it?"

"It just makes everything easier," Nikolai said. "To keep it all in the network. This is the way Herve operates."

"Herve seems very particular about the way he operates," Alistair said.

"Yes," Nikolai said. "He is extremely particular. I do not enjoy it either. But maybe that is why he is a billionaire and I am a sad drunk. Though, if you ask me, I would rather be a sad drunk."

Alistair stared at his screen. Nikolai's mandate that he do work only on the ThinkPad made him reluctant, somehow, to do anything on it at all.

"Our point persons know I have an assistant now," Nikolai said. "You should start receiving emails soon."

"What did you think?" Alistair said in a small voice. "Of my ideas?"

Nikolai had sunk into his own screen. "They are good ideas," he said. "You are a good kid. I am happy you are with me."

Minutes later Alistair received his first email. It was from Tyler Forest, who according to Nikolai's spreadsheet was the point person for Team F, which as yet had no site.

> Connor,
>
> Welcome aboard. Please let GC know I've narrowed the short-list down to three, all within an hour of South Bend. Prices range, but there are some other variables to consider. Everyone I've met with here is very excited. I think we could make a real difference. If GC can talk today, I'm around.
>
> Onward,
> TF

Alistair relayed the message to Nikolai.

"Tell him I will call him at seven," Nikolai said.

Alistair typed this message to Tyler Forest, signed it CB, and pressed Send. "You're GC?"

"George Crawford," Nikolai said. "Cindy Crawford—when I was a teen? How many socks I ruined to thoughts of her. Let a boy dream!"

"Who's Tyler Forest?"

"He is someone who knows that region."

"What's he doing there?"

"You read his email."

"That area is rife with manufacturing facilities fading into obsolescence," Alistair said. "You could say the same about parts of Ohio, parts of Michigan. This is what I've been looking into. With investment, with retraining, you could bring these communities into the new economy in a matter of years. Is that what Tyler Forest is working on?"

"I do not know why you bother asking me questions," Nikolai said, "when you are so prepared to answer them yourself."

Alistair read Tyler Forest's email again. He thought about writing him another message, peppering him with the questions that Nikolai wouldn't answer, forging an alliance with someone closer to the ground, nearer to the beating heart of the project. But he sensed that if Nikolai found out he'd go apoplectic.

"You mentioned I might have meetings at some point," he said to Nikolai. "Will I have a chance to go out into the field? Get my own region? Maybe my own team? I'd really like that. I think it would be a great use of my skills."

"My friend," Nikolai said. "You talk of skills. You have written one email, and you have made a whole fuss about it."

Over the next two hours Alistair received four more emails. Hunter Newman, Team B, asked for phone time with Nikolai to describe a recent "very promising" meeting. Gary Washington, Team J, asked permission to add $100,000 to his "site budget." Cody Lightman, Team D, asked permission to spend $15,000 on travel and lodging. Jimmy Barnes, Team A, asked permission to bring on three more team members at a salary of $65,000 each.

"Permission granted," Nikolai said each time.

"You don't run these numbers by Herve?" Alistair asked.

"Herve has allocated a hundred and twenty-five million to this project," Nikolai said. "Not that he will spend all that." He swigged from his bottle of vodka-water. "In fact, I am making sure he does not."

"What do you mean?"

"I do not hear you typing."

Alistair fired off his replies. He looked out the window at the silent city, the sinking sun. He thought of questions, pushed them away, thought of more questions, pushed them away. He knew that, when it came to his questions, he was already skating on thin ice. But when the day had nearly ended he decided to hazard one more.

"What's Herve's work name?" he asked Nikolai.

"Herve does not have a work name," Nikolai said. "He has no name at all. As far as we are concerned, he does not exist."

"He doesn't want credit? This is reputation-burnishing stuff."

"He does not want it, he does not need it, he does not care about it," Nikolai said. "All he cares about is the result."

"That's noble of him."

Nikolai hackled. "Be sure to tell him that when you meet him."

"When am I meeting him?"

"Soon," Nikolai said. "I have a feeling he will find you quite interesting."

Alistair left that day in a mix of low and high spirits. He was frustrated, no doubt, by Nikolai's continual stonewalling. He was also increasingly daunted by all the layers of "discretion." He didn't see why the project had to be so *very* hush-hush. But he foresaw the solution to both these problems in his future meeting with Herve. He felt sure that when he was face-to-face with him he'd get a deeper understanding of his peculiarities and a firmer, more granular sense of his project. In the meantime, he knew, he had little reason to complain. As he exited the subway at Fourteenth Street he walked with a buoyancy and purpose that he knew had everything to do with the ten thousand unborrowed dollars in his account. For once he didn't feel horribly poor anymore; for once he was in a position, even, to be generous. And yet, under all the noise of his speculating and celebrating, he heard again the dim plaint of the animal voice. The voice wanted a little more information about where the $10,000 had come from and what it was for. Failing that, the voice wasn't sure yet whether the $10,000 was really a good thing. And so, the next day, partly in concession to the voice, Alistair decided to put the money toward something he knew with certainty was good.

"No," Maura said to him on the phone. "I shouldn't have told you anything. No."

Alistair hadn't so much made an offer as issued a declaration. He would be sending Maura $3,000 to help with her home equity loan and credit card payments. He would send her $3,000 every month until she was out of the red. He decided to tell her the truth but to keep the details light, to open the valve only as much as he needed to. He said that he'd landed a job with a billionaire's peon and that the peon was paying him too much.

"Is this a job you got through school?" Maura asked.

"I got it through friends," Alistair said.

"Who's the billionaire?"

"No one you've heard of. An industrialist. Energy sector."

"I don't like the sound of that."

"I don't think you'd like the sound of any billionaire."

"Fair enough. But what about the bank?"

Alistair tendered what was, technically speaking, another truth. "I'm not on the bank's payroll currently."

"I thought they paid you nicely this summer," Maura said. "Enough so you wouldn't have to work."

"I didn't want to pass up this opportunity. Especially since now I can help you."

"I don't want you doing anything on my account. Working for a billionaire least of all."

"I can do something for my benefit and have it benefit you too," Alistair said. He pried open the valve a smidge. "This is a really interesting project. It's all about putting money into places that have suffered economically, that aren't sharing in the country's wealth. Places like Binghamton. The man we're working for—he wants to help."

"Don't you think there's something funny about that?" Maura said. "Amass billions, and then decide how you want to help people. But always amass first."

"Unfortunately, that's how the world tends to operate."

"Doesn't mean there isn't still something funny about it."

"I found a job doing something commendable," Alistair said. "I thought you'd be happy for me."

"I am happy for you," Maura said. "But you should save this money. You should put some of it toward your own debt."

"I will save some. I will put some of it toward my own debt. But there's plenty to go around."

"How much is plenty?"

"Enough."

Maura fell silent for a moment. "I'm sorry, Alli," she said. "I can't accept this. I don't want you worrying about me. I want you to live your own life."

Alistair sat at his desk with his face in his hand, pushing at the skin of his forehead. He was getting tired of having his higher purpose frustrated, of having his love refused. He saw himself at this moment as a kind of Herve in microcosm. He'd amassed, yes, and now he wanted to help. Maybe this was only a degraded kindness, the least of all evils in an economically unjust world, but it was a kindness all the same, and it was the most meaningful kindness he felt he could offer to the person he cared about most. He didn't find there to be anything "funny" about this. "You talk about me living my own life," he said, "but my life is you. It always has been and it always will be. You're the reason for everything I do. I know you don't like that, I know it makes you feel guilty, but it's true, and there's nothing you can do about it. And there's nothing you can do to make me happier, really nothing, than let me help you. If I can't help you, then what is all this for?"

"What is all this?" Maura said.

"Please just take the money."

Though she said nothing Alistair could sense her standing down. "I'll let you help me this month," she said. "Next month, I don't know. We'll have to talk about that."

Their conversation veered into intergenerational comedy. He had her put him on speakerphone and walked her through the steps to download a money transfer app, upload her banking information, and accept his friend request. By the time the money went through it felt like the punch line to a joke.

"What are you doing, by the way?" she asked. "For the billionaire's peon?"

"Being a peon to the peon," Alistair said. "Secretarial work, more or less."

"Look at that," Maura said. "Continuing in the family trade."

After he said goodbye Alistair brought up his Citibank and Great Lakes accounts and thought about taking a stab at his debt. But after his gift to Maura his checking account was back down to four figures, and if he kept his promise to her he had another $3,000 due the next month. He saw no reason to rush. If he really did secure a full-time job with Herve and a salary of $1.5 million he could vanish his loans in a matter of months.

When he returned to Nikolai's apartment the next day he resisted his urge to ask questions. He sat at his desk and performed his drudge duties. He relayed requests for permission to make ever-vague expenditures ("materials research," "focus groups," "expert consultations," "incidentals"), rattled off ever-vague details about new hires, meetings, sites of interest, "opportunities." He read and typed words whose basis in reality he had no access to. He set up phone calls between point persons and Nikolai that, being scheduled for the evenings, he would never be privy to. He completed all manner of minor and meaningless tasks—compiling expense reports, researching flights and business credit card rewards programs, making lists of hotels and restaurants in far-flung cities—that brought him no closer to the hard details of the project. He performed these same duties the next week and the week after that.

Nikolai continued to take pitiful joy in his presence, to marvel at his having found a friend. On evenings when he had no phone calls scheduled he convinced Alistair to stay afterward and drink with him. He told rambling stories about his boyhood in Plovdiv, his days at BZ. He enumerated the various Muscovite women who'd broken his Bulgarian heart. He asked Alistair about his homosexual exploits. He asked him to refill his glass. In mid-November he asked, by sliding him another thick envelope, if Alistair wanted to stay on, and Alistair answered by accepting it.

Meanwhile, Alistair used his earnings to do a few kindnesses for himself. He bought himself cashmere sweaters, he bought himself excellent boots. He got an American Express card so as to be a person who had one. He bought $98 running tights and $42 hair cream. He spent unholy dollars on a Canada Goose parka. He told himself if he was being irresponsible and indulgent it was only because the money was so novel, and because, according to Nikolai, there was so much more of it on the way. He told himself he needed to get his financial exhilaration out of his system before he began the sensible work of tackling his debt. He was finally living the life his father had always wanted to give him, and he felt that to satisfy his cravings, to fulfill his father's highest wishes, was a moral good of greater import than prudence.

Only when he went home to Binghamton for Thanksgiving did he encounter a challenge to his bright mood. Maura raised her eyebrows when he drove up in a rental car rather than taking his usual ShortLine. When he got out of the car she raised her eyebrows and asked if he'd really needed to rent a BMW. She raised her eyebrows when they went food shopping at Wegmans and he selected the priciest version of every item on their list; she raised her eyebrows when he insisted on paying the $325 total himself; she raised her eyebrows when he returned from the liquor store not with Yellow Tail but with bottles that looked to be in the $50 price range. She raised her eyebrows so much Alistair worried they'd get stuck that way. Nevertheless she enjoyed herself, this unexpected and uncalled-for but undeniably sumptuous meal. She thanked him. She patted his head as if to say, "This was nice, I'll always remember it, now we can go back to normal." But Alistair had no intention of going back to normal. His broadened financial horizons had opened his eyes. He decided Maura needed new furniture, she needed new clothes. Until such time as he could buy her a new house she needed new wall paint, new bathroom floors, a new kitchen. When he loaded himself into the BMW on Sunday he smiled at her as if in warning.

Upon his return to the city he paid a visit to the Eros Ananke. He'd been seeing Mark and Elijah less frequently lately, in part because Nikolai ate up much of his free time and in part because his bright mood had diminished his need for petting—the money did seem weirdly sexual in the way it lit up his brain's pleasure center. But he'd also grown more shy of seeing the men because, amid their deepening connubial misery, they'd grown less shy of fighting in front of him. Tonight was no different. It transpired that the men had been invited to a party at Howie's, that Mark had refused, and that Elijah had given it a miss too, if only so that he could complain about having missed it.

"Howie flew up some of his boys from Miami," Elijah explained.

"'Boys' being the operative word," Mark said.

"Jay's been torturing me with anecdotes."

"I have no interest in seeing Howie play Caligula."

"They had a great time, and we stayed at home, glaring at each other."

"You could have gone," Mark said. "I would have been happy here by myself."

"Yes," Elijah said. "I think you'd be very happy by yourself. Which raises the question of what I'm doing here."

Mark hazarded a glance at Alistair.

"I don't understand why you're so opposed to making friends," Elijah said. "To having fun. Even with Jay and Howie. Even if the fun gets a little dirty. God forbid."

"I just don't want that," Mark said. He hazarded another glance at Alistair. "I don't need it."

Elijah noted Mark's glance at Alistair and looked away. He seemed to register that by mentioning the prospect of rolling around with Howie's boys he'd crossed a line, broken an unspoken rule. The three of them operated under the tacit assumption that they slept only with one another. For all its experimentalism their entanglement was traditional in this way, and he'd profaned its uneasy sacredness. Alistair suspected, as he watched him pout, that a part of Elijah was unhappy to have profaned, unhappy that his inclinations put him outside the sacred. After a moment he turned and eyed Alistair sheepishly. "Jay tells me your boss is coming to town soon," he said.

Alistair stiffened. "Herve?"

"You didn't know?"

Alistair tried to keep the surprise out of his face, the surprise and the trepidation. Like so much about the project this impending visit, too, had been kept from him. And though he'd looked forward to it, though he'd been keen to get a clearer understanding of Herve and his plans, something about this meeting—about its being withheld, about its promise to reveal things withheld—made him nervous.

"Don't worry," Elijah said. He looked between Mark and Alistair, linking them ruefully with his eyes. Whatever they felt for each other he knew he had no part in it. "I'm sure you'll charm him."

When Alistair arrived at Nikolai's apartment the next day Nikolai confirmed Elijah's intel. They sat on the couch, which in Nikolai's home office served as something of a conference room: this conversation was serious. Outside the first snowflakes of the year drifted sideways, tarrying, as if forestalling their descent.

"He is coming in two weeks," Nikolai said. "He and I have some business, and then the three of us will have dinner. I have picked a very nice place. Herve will hate it."

Alistair spoke calmly but insistently. "I'm excited to hear more about the project," he said. "I have so many questions."

"Yes, well, let us have you keep those questions to a minimum," Nikolai said. "The purpose of this dinner is so that Herve can meet you and make sure you are a good fit."

Alistair felt a pang familiar to him from his days as an intern—a good "fit" he'd never been. "How will he judge that?"

"Who knows what goes on inside Herve's head," Nikolai said. "He sees, he listens, he decides."

"But I am going to learn more about the project, aren't I?"

"This is really more of an introduction."

Alistair shook his head in exasperation. "I've been working for you for six weeks, and I know basically nothing about what's happening on the ground. I don't understand why you insist on keeping me out of the loop."

"It is not just you," Nikolai said. "For so long—it is not just you."

"It doesn't make sense," Alistair said. "This is a large-scale project, involving multiple teams, multiple communities, multiple industries. He can't keep it a secret forever. Eventually he's going to need more help."

"He will put off that day for as long as possible," Nikolai said. "Herve sees point A, he sees point B, and the fewer people he needs to get from one to the other the better. He hates relying on other people."

Alistair was unsettled to hear in Nikolai's description of Herve an echo of his own pathology, his own erstwhile dream of summiting the mountain himself. "But I can bring serious value to this project," he said. "Just because Herve has all the money doesn't mean he wouldn't benefit from other people's counsel."

"It is precisely because he has all the money," Nikolai said, "that he feels he does not need to listen to other people. People telling other people what to do, what is right and what is not, how the world should be, what they must accept—this is everything he stands against. Herve does not care about luxury. You should see how he dresses, how he lives. Money, to him, means only one thing. The freedom to do what he wants, how he wants."

"He didn't make his billions all by himself," Alistair said.

"No," Nikolai said. "But somehow they ended up in his pocket."

"I'm finding it hard to square Herve's dislike of people with the fact that he wants to help people."

"The people he dislikes," Nikolai said, "are different from the people he wants to help. And when it comes to the people he wants to help, he believes he knows best."

Here Alistair recalled his mother's remark about the "funniness" of this logic, and found that he now saw its merit. Herve was only part of a larger trend, an increasing concentration of wealth and decision-making power in the hands of an unelected few, a self-appointed peerage of benevolent billionaires. People put faith in these billionaires to grow the economy, advance innovation, preserve institutions, cure all manner of sicknesses and social maladies, believing their success to be a measure of their genius, of their efficiency, of their superiority to the lumbering, blundering government. But this faith was born of self-spiting optimism. It ignored the fact that these billionaires had accrued their wealth and power at the expense of the government and of the people themselves, that their genius and efficiency lay in shirking taxes, suppressing wages, militating against antitrust reform, busting unions. It ignored the fact that the problems they'd been entrusted to solve were often ones they themselves had created, and that very possibly they'd created them so as to solve them and thereby reorder society however they pleased. Not least it ignored the fact that these billionaires were, for all their benevolence, ultimately unanswerable to the people, mysterious in their intentions, inscrutable—that, really, no one knew them at all. Alistair was aware, as he sat slumped on the couch, that he might not have felt so dubious about this faith in billionaires if it weren't for the billionaire that everyone *did* know, the real estate tycoon who'd pledged to return the country to its former glory, who convinced more and more people every day that he alone could do it, who metastasized his following by stirring hate, who smacked the people with the same hand out of which he promised to feed them. He was the public face of this private peerage, revealing in his grotesquerie.

"Wear something nice," Nikolai said. "But not too nice. I have told Herve about you. He thinks of you as the kind of person he would like to help."

Alistair wasn't sure what this meant and, knowing further questions wouldn't get him anywhere, didn't ask. He stood from the couch, went to his desk, and got to work. He would save his questions for Herve. *This is really more of an introduction*: he'd see about that.

The following week he went to Brooks Brothers with the intention of buying something "nice" but not "too nice." In the store, however, his senseless craving got the better of him, and he walked out with an elegant navy blazer that, with the tailoring fee, came to $725. On the day of the dinner, to counteract its elegance, he paired it with old chinos and scuffed shoes.

Nikolai had made a reservation at Viceroy, an absurdly priced steak house in the Time Warner Center. When Alistair arrived he picked out Nikolai easily enough: his antic gestures and disheveled hair put him at odds with the otherwise staid and combed patrons. Sitting across from him, facing away from Alistair, was a broad back and a large head.

Nikolai stood, made introductions, and gestured for Alistair to take a chair. The guest of honor remained seated. Herve wore a tan suede blazer, a blue twill shirt with pleated pockets, and light jeans. He was the least dressed-up person in the room and very possibly the richest. His head was buzzed, his chin weak, his mouth set into a firm pout. He had Howie's skin, chapped and festooned with snaking red capillaries, and Howie's eyes, teary and blue. But he was bulkier than Howie, stout and sturdy. Alistair knew Herve was older than Howie by two years, but for a moment he imagined him as a twin who'd taken the lion's share of nutrients in the womb, who before long might have eaten his brother whole.

"This is my boy," Nikolai said, grabbing Alistair's shoulder. "Our boy. My friend. Our friend. My goodness!" He waited for Herve to say something, but Herve simply stared, moving his eyes between them. Nikolai turned to Alistair. "Herve is a man of few words."

"And you are a man of many," Herve said. He spoke as if chiseling loose fragments of stone from his mouth. He looked around the room and followed a gallant waiter with suspicion. He faced Alistair. "Nikolai tells me you're a good worker."

Alistair had come prepared to charm, but he saw already that pleasing Herve would require a different attitude. Nikolai's advice about "nice" but not "too nice" applied as well, it appeared, to demeanor. "I just follow his orders," he said.

"That's a good worker," Herve said. "Harder and harder to find them."

"He is so ambitious, so steady," Nikolai said. "He will do anything. He takes after me!"

Herve sat very still, his hands folded on the table. "You'll certainly do anything," he said.

The gallant waiter paraded to their table. He began to speak to Herve but then, registering his chilly expression, directed his speech at Nikolai. The speech was about wine, and Alistair heard it through Herve's ears: French this, Argentinian that, get this schmuck away from me.

"What brings you to town?" Alistair asked after the waiter had left.

"I have dealings here," Herve said. He nodded at Nikolai as if pointing out a building in disrepair. "And I went to see my brother."

"You have been to Howie's place?" Nikolai asked.

"Lot of space for a small man."

"And Jay? You have met the terror?"

"The boyfriend," Herve said. "The whatever. He has a lot to say."

"Next time I will give you earplugs," Nikolai said. "Or drug him! He is a fool."

Herve gave a shrug that was at once small and momentous, like a mountain shifting amid tectonic disturbance. "He said some interesting things."

"Hopefully not too interesting," Nikolai said. "That guy, he is always out to shock."

"Every man must plow his own field," Herve said. "Mr. Steigen knows how to plow his."

"Oh, he plows all right!" Nikolai said.

The waiter brought the wine. He poured Nikolai a tasting sip and then filled their glasses, explaining as he did the wine's flavor notes. Alistair found the waiter pretentious and sad, a victim of an economy in which the number of elite brains exceeds the number of jobs requiring them. He described the specials with a verbosity better suited to the defense of a thesis. Alistair glanced at Herve and saw that he was barely suppressing his annoyance. They all ordered the same nonspecial steak.

After the waiter had floated away Herve returned to the subject of Howie. "He's buying rather a lot of art," he said to Nikolai. "I suspect it's the influence of the whatever."

Nikolai shook his head in commiseration.

"The whatever seems to have plans for an art project himself. All I gathered is that he won't be frugal about it."

"I will put a stop to it," Nikolai said. "I will talk to Jay. A silly man like that, spending your hard-earned money, it is obscene."

Herve waved his hand dismissively. "Let Howie do what he wants," he said. "I don't understand art, and I don't really care to, but Howie likes it. Let him be free."

"For you, the whole *world* is an art project," Nikolai said.

Herve ignored this and turned to Alistair. "You like art?"

"Absolutely," Alistair heard himself say. How to steer this conversation toward the particulars of the project: this was all he could think about.

Herve looked out the window. "There's a certain satisfaction," he said.

"A satisfaction in what," Nikolai sang.

Herve's mouth moved uncertainly, then resumed its firm pout. "You don't need to understand something to take hold of it," he said. "Don't even need to understand it when you have it in your grasp. All that matters is now it understands you."

"Oh," Nikolai said, "that is all that matters."

When their steaks came Alistair tried to think of ways to bring up the project, but every time he looked at Herve he lost his courage. He'd been given to understand that Herve was private and even prickly, but he'd expected him to be at least a little more enthusiastic, a little more animated in conversation, a little more boastful and forthcoming about his plans. Instead he was closed off, wary, grim. Alistair struggled to align the person in front of him with the ambitious, uplifting project of which he was the brain. Where was the idealism, the boldness, the generosity of spirit? He wanted to know.

Nikolai, who'd drunk the majority of the wine, flagged down the waiter and ordered a second bottle. He stood, stumbling out of his chair. "To the loo!" he said.

After he'd left there followed a long moment of silence.

"I'm told you attend New York University," Herve said. "What craziness are they foisting on you?"

"I go to the business school," Alistair said. "So my curriculum is craziness-light."

Herve took in Alistair's elegant blazer, his fastidiously pressed shirt and delicately arranged hair, with a hard expression. "I did half a semester at Williston State," he said. "I decided I knew everything I needed to."

"Your success certainly bears that out," Alistair said.

"And you're from north of here," Herve said. "That's what Nikolai tells me. Small town?"

"A city in name only."

"Nikolai tells me you don't come from very much."

Alistair felt himself tense. That word of his lowly origins had made its way to a billionaire, not to some rich classmate at Stern but to a billionaire: a year ago this would have been his worst nightmare. But he'd grown tired of his shame, and he sensed, somehow, that this particular billionaire would treat his origins with care. "I'm having to make my own way," he said.

Herve's eyes crinkled with satisfaction, and the hardness left his face. "It must be difficult for you," he said. "Living in a city like this."

"Nikolai pays me nicely."

"Seeing all these people with more money than they know what to do with. Who never had to struggle for it. Who don't appreciate it."

Alistair thought this was an odd comment coming from a billionaire. But he also thought of Mark and Elijah, of their featherbed despair, of the irony of his falling for two people who would never see the world as he did. "It can be hard," he said.

"And when they find out where you're from they give you that look," Herve said. "Don't they. That amusement. That pity. That little loss of interest." He gazed at Alistair intently, with a kind of conspiratorial snarl. "You'll never be one of them. They know it and you know it. It must make you angry—doesn't it."

Alistair found that, for all his discomfort, he was able to look directly into Herve's eyes, and to answer honestly. "Yes."

"But in your heart you know you're stronger than them," Herve said. "While they're flouncing around, you're building, you're planning. They have no idea what's coming—isn't that right."

Alistair wondered if this interrogation was Herve's way of determining whether he was a good "fit," and he wondered what determination he was coming to. He had the sense that Herve was drawing conclusions about him over which he had no control. He also failed to see how this discussion bore any practical relevance to the project. He failed, yet again, to connect Herve's disposition to his charitable aims. The man seemed not just grim but *bitter*, *disgruntled*, and this confused Alistair. Righteous fury he could understand, but there was nothing righteous, nothing cause-oriented, in Herve's snarl. His rancor seemed personal, petty even, a matter of score-settling.

"Your project is very exciting to me," Alistair said. "I'd love to talk more about it."

Herve's features went slack, as if Alistair's question had bored him. He sat in silence, looking out the window. After a while he spoke. "My father thought I was a piece of shit," he said. "I don't blame him. He thought he was a piece of shit himself. But he could be very hard on me. He would have been hard on Howie too, if I weren't there to protect him." He faced Alistair again. "But we love them, don't we."

"Who?" Alistair said.

"Our fathers." Herve put his hand to his wineglass, from which he'd taken small, laboriously tentative sips all through dinner. "He was an angry man. Very fearful, very suspicious. He knew the world wanted one thing, and that was to take advantage of him. That he did teach me. That I did take from him. Their laws—they're made by them, and for them."

"Them?" Alistair said.

Herve looked around at the glowing dining room. "If he could see the way things are now, he would have counted his blessings. His era—that was the last time you could really have that. The last time you could really live that way."

"What way?"

"Free," Herve said. He spun his glass counterclockwise. "He was a bad farmer, my father. We were poorer than we really needed to be. I had my ideas, I thought he could run things a little differently. He wouldn't have it. He said, 'The fuck you think you are? Some fancy boy, some genius? You're dirt.' To my father there were two worlds. There was Williston and there was everywhere else. He said I'd be in Williston forever, so I'd better stop thinking I could change the world." He spun the glass another turn. "He was right about one thing. I will be in Williston forever. But he was wrong about the other thing."

Alistair only listened.

"Williston and everywhere else, it's a false choice," Herve said. "I can change the world from my plot of dirt and I will." He pushed the glass away and looked Alistair in the eye, but he seemed to pull into his gaze the opulent room, the magnificent city, around them. "The way you feel, the way I feel? We're not alone, and it isn't right. Isn't right for us to be crushed, condescended to, exploited and then neglected. So you know what I say? I say fuck 'em. I say unzip your pants and fuck 'em."

The waiter approached with the second bottle and made to top up Herve's glass. But Herve, without looking at him, put his hand out in refusal, and then an apocalyptic blunder ensued. Herve's hand collided with the waiter's arm, the waiter lost his delicate grasp, and a gulp of wine flew from the bottle down Herve's shirt.

Herve stood and shot back, knocking his chair on its side. He gave it a small, furious kick. Nearby diners craned their necks in alarm. The waiter, issuing horrified, mellifluous apologies, reached for a napkin but Herve fended him off. Alistair could see it in Herve's eyes: he was humiliated. Some fragile nerve, forever exposed, had been struck, and he was helpless against his own fury.

Nikolai materialized. "My goodness!" he said. He waved the waiter away and stood at a distance from Herve. He seemed to know not to try to help him. "Let us get out of here. I will pay the bill later. After this, they should pay us!"

Improbably the sound of Nikolai's voice seemed to soothe Herve. He stopped wiping his shirt, stood straight, and put his hands on his waist. He looked at Alistair and held his gaze.

On Nikolai's orders Alistair went downstairs to wait. In the lobby he stood by the entrance to Williams-Sonoma, next to a bronze statue of Adam whose penis had been fondled to the point of turning gold. Nikolai came down the escalator and guided Alistair outside to an Uber he'd already ordered.

"Herve never forgets an insult," Nikolai said as the car rounded Columbus Circle. "He will remember that for the rest of his life."

"I don't think it was meant as an insult," Alistair said.

"No," Nikolai said. "But it fits the story he tells. About himself. About the world."

"I thought he was about to tackle that waiter."

"Be glad that he did not. When Herve is angry, he can be reckless."

The car made its way along Fifty-seventh Street, where seemingly every day construction began on a new needle for the superrich.

"In any case," Nikolai said, "he likes you. We can move ahead."

"With that?"

"By now you must be sick of secretary work. We will get you on the ground."

"To do what?"

Nikolai put his arm around Alistair, releasing fragrances of sweat and wine. "My friend," he said. "Digest your steak."

The car cruised down Second Avenue, toward Palladium. At every stoplight Alistair looked east, toward the river, but he could never see it.

———

Alistair and Maura landed on a signal, the only one they could think of that struck the right balance between suspicious and random. Maura would install a new porch light. She would do this in full view of the men in the SUV. The next day, after they'd seen her return to work after lunch, Alistair would flip the porch light on and then quickly turn it off. Suspicious: it would be enough, they hoped, to convince the men that a non-Maura person was inside. Random: if they came inside and turned up no sign of Alistair they'd be left to assume that the new light was glitchy, or that this ineffectual woman, with no men around to help her, had botched its installation.

"So we're assuming they'll think I'm stupid," Maura said.

"We're making misogyny work for us," Alistair said.

"I'm glad it's working for someone."

She bought the light and hooked it up, making a show of her struggle, keeping her body turned toward the SUV up the street. They barely ate dinner that night, or breakfast the next morning, or lunch the next afternoon. Before she returned to work Maura held up the prepaid phone she'd bought along with the new light.

"You'll text me on this," she said. "You'll tell me everything."

"Everything," Alistair said.

She took his hand. "I'll see you tonight."

All Alistair could do, by way of a promise, was nod.

This was June 29. After a week of gray and sultry skies the clouds had cleared, and sunlight shone in the slivers around the window shades, and hazardous peeks at the backyard showed hydrangeas and marigolds and lavender in quenched glory. After he heard Maura's car pull away Alistair stood at the front door, his hand on the light switch. He wondered if the men had tools that would blow his cover, technologies that detected heat or very low sounds. He looked into the living room, fixing on his father's picture of Rio de Janeiro. He took a sharp breath, flicked the light on, flicked it off, and ran to the basement.

Cillian's secret room had no windows. With the light off Alistair could barely see his hand in front of his face. He struggled to secure the lock he and Maura had installed on the inside and, after a few moments, gave up. If literal push came to literal shove it would be pointless anyway. He sat on the concrete floor, regulating his breathing. He reached for the objects he'd gathered and placed in the room the day before, the only household items he'd been able to find that could be put into service as weapons: a kitchen knife, a hammer, a bat. He put his hand to his pocket and felt the hard bulk of the burner. He listened.

Very quickly he lost sense of time. He wasn't sure if he'd been sitting in the room for two minutes or ten, five or twenty, fifteen or thirty. Then he heard a sound.

It was a rustle, something like a shoulder against a low branch, from what seemed to be one of the rear corners of the house. He heard a second rustle from what seemed to be the opposite corner. The sounds came from far enough apart and in quick enough succession for him to deduce that there were at least two of them. They were casing.

He heard the opening of the back door in the kitchen—the drag of its adhesive draft stopper was unmistakable. For days now he'd lived with shallow breathing and a tight chest and he'd expected, when the moment came, to hyperventilate, quake, break out in a sweat. But some hitherto uncalled upon defensive mechanism, a phenomenal composure, came to his aid, and he listened calmly as they traced the route he'd predicted. They covered the rooms on the first floor, thudding, stopping, shifting furniture, opening doors. They went upstairs and sent down muffled versions of these same sounds. He heard no voices.

It wasn't until they returned to the first floor and came back into the kitchen that his body froze, and his throat thinned to the diameter of a straw, and it occurred to him that he might well be listening to the footsteps of the men who'd murdered the groundskeeper. He heard the pivot of a shoe; he heard it almost before it happened: the swing of the basement door, careful steps on the rickety wooden stairs, on the same concrete floor on which he was huddled.

Sounds were more muted down here. He shut his eyes and turned his head. He heard steps approach the pile of furniture at the far end of the room, heard hands lifting and lowering objects. His legs tingled, his arm itched, a booger in his right nostril was giving his breath the slightest wheeze. He discerned steps along the other side of the wall. They came to a stop near the hidden door. If his pursuer put his hand to the wall, Alistair knew, he would feel a slight give. He and Maura had applied a strip of padding to the inside of the jamb; they'd experimented with running it along the threshold. But nothing they'd done had succeeded in neutralizing this give, and this give, he knew, was all his pursuer would need.

He listened. He felt sure he would detect a hand on the wall. But he heard nothing, and he heard no movement away from the wall either. He formulated the only possible thought, a magical one: the man on the other side *knew*, by some sixth sense, that he was near. And then a composure came over him again, not of defense but of resignation, because he felt sure he was in his final minute. But the minute stretched, improbably and intolerably, until he heard steps retreating up the stairs, into the kitchen, and out through the back door.

His best guess was that he waited an hour before he shifted out of his position and stood. His muscles were wrecked. It took him another half hour to switch on the light, listen at the door, and gently open it, and another half hour to walk to the foot of the basement stairs, and, at a rate of one step a minute, take them up to the kitchen. He stood for a while, looking where the men had looked, listening to the silence they'd listened to, trembling.

He texted Maura, telling her they'd come and gone and giving her the all-clear. Then he did something strange: he descended the basement stairs and returned to the secret room. He wasn't sure why. All he knew was that, even freed, he wanted to go back to his cell.

Maura arrived at five. She called for him, but she must have seen the open basement door, because she flew down the stairs and materialized at the door to the secret room.

"Why are you in here?"

Alistair, sitting on the floor, only shook his head.

She came to him, sat, held him. He slid down, putting his head in her lap and his arms around her waist. All at once the fright in his body swam free. He let out a whole summer's worth of tears. She said, "It's OK, it's OK." She looked at her lap and told him he'd cried so much she looked like she'd wet her pants. He laughed and then cried even harder.

"They're gone," she said.

Alistair couldn't bring himself to reply.

Later that evening he texted Nikolai and received a response immediately. He would wait a bit, he told Alistair, just to be sure, and then he would come for him. Probably, being Bulgarian, he didn't realize the significance of the date he specified. Or maybe, being Bulgarian, with a European's disenchanted irony, he did. He told Alistair to expect him the night of the Fourth.

Alistair would wait; he would hear out Nikolai's plan. But the courage he'd taken from the cross in his desk drawer had been building, every day more and more, and he had a plan of his own. All he'd have to do was convince Elijah. And if he and Elijah decided they needed help, as seemed likely, then he'd have to convince Mark. But he wouldn't tell this to Nikolai or Maura. He hardly even articulated it to himself. All he did was let his courage grow. He knew he'd need a great deal of it.

They never saw the SUV again.

———

On the morning of December 23, a week after his dinner with Nikolai and Herve, Alistair found himself cruising up I-81 in yet another rented BMW. He knew Maura would raise her eyebrows again, just as she would raise them at the bounty of presents in gift-wrapped boxes on the backseat. But for now he could put off the image of her skepticism. Binghamton wasn't his first stop.

Next to him, on the passenger seat, was a folder containing specs about five commercial properties, various documentation relating to Phakelos Consulting should he need to present any, and directions Nikolai had insisted on printing out. "It is safer this way," he'd said to Alistair. "For driving."

Alistair knew I-81 well enough: he'd followed its dreary length back and forth between Binghamton and New York a dozen times. But right now he was headed to points north of Binghamton, to the hinterland of his homeland, to places of single thoroughfares and single hotels, and these were routes he'd never learned. He kept the directions within easy reach. In his near future, he knew, were missable signs, narrow roads, strange turns.

He passed Scranton, which the world made fun of only because it had never heard of Binghamton. He passed Clarks Summit and signs for Waverly and Scott. Frigid winds blew unobstructed over acres of dormant fields. Occasionally he saw a barn with a wreath over its door or a rundown home with a blow-mold Nativity scene in its front yard. For hours now he'd driven under the same sheet of slate clouds.

The Wednesday after the dinner at Viceroy, Nikolai had explained to Alistair just how fortuitous it was that he was from upstate New York. This, he explained to Alistair, was a region he and Herve saw much opportunity in. Surely Alistair, knowing the region, agreed?

"I told you as much when we started working together," Alistair said flatly.

Nikolai bowed his head. "It took me time to catch up with your brilliance."

"So I'll be a point person?"

"This could be the beginning of that. Herve would like to see you more involved. See how you do."

"What's the opportunity?" Alistair asked, again flatly.

"There are so many," Nikolai said. He consulted a list in his mind. "The area has quite a robust defense contracting industry, with room to grow. There is some promise in the healthcare sphere. Some promise in manufacturing. But the idea here is to secure a few properties while we explore investment potential. Herve likes to move quickly. If things get going on the investment side, he wants to have the foundation already in place."

If Alistair was speaking in a flat voice it was because his enthusiasm was quickly flagging. Nikolai's evasiveness had wearied him, and the informational uselessness of his meeting with Herve had wearied him further. All he'd gotten for his meeting with Herve was more confusion. The man's anger and resentment, vague but potent, continued to contradict the nobility of his plans. It did thrill Alistair a little, to have his resentment shared and recognized, to see what heights of wealth and power it could lead to. But it also unsettled him, because he didn't want to be that way anymore. For him all it had led to was failure and need.

"Seems like an unnecessary financial risk," he said to Nikolai. "If nothing pans out investment-wise, you have this property on your hands and nothing to do with it."

"We will cross that bridge when we come to it," Nikolai said. "Besides, real estate in this region is quite cheap. I am sure you of all people know this."

Alistair gave a smirk. "What am I looking for?" he said.

"We have already identified five properties that meet our specifications."

"Which are?"

"Your job is to make sure they are in good working order. Check the plumbing, the heating and cooling, the electricity. Find the best one. I have scheduled appointments with local people. At these places, there is always some sad guy taking care of the property, maintaining the grounds, repairing things. They will be able to tell you if there is anything wrong with the place. Real estate agents will just BS you. They will tell you there is nothing to worry about. You know this about real estate agents?"

"I know," Alistair said. "You'd make a great one."

"Just remember," Nikolai said. "You are Connor Black. They have your Connor email and your Connor phone number. You work for me, George Crawford, at Phakelos. And the biggest rule of all."

"Don't mention Herve."

"Who is Herve? There is no such person as this."

Alistair couldn't help it. He jerked his head in frustration.

"I know it is all so peculiar," Nikolai said, touching his arm. "But if you do well, this will mean something for Herve. It will mean something, perhaps, for your future."

If Alistair had any enthusiasm left it was reserved for the riches Nikolai had assured him could be his. But even here, much to his surprise, his enthusiasm was lacking. He'd come on board believing he could both do good in the world and achieve financial success at the same time. But with so little access to the particulars of the project, with so little involvement in the worthy core of its mission, the only thing for him to be excited about was the money, and compared to the prospect of doing meaningful work the money excited him little. For the first time he failed to see it as its own reward. Yet he was in no position to pass it up.

"I'll do my best," he said.

"You will do your best, my friend," Nikolai said, "because you are the best."

Alistair had expected Nikolai to give him the info packet on the sites then and there. But for whatever reason Nikolai had insisted that he pick it up the morning of his departure, at six a.m., which Alistair had grumblingly done, taking the folder from a boxer-shorted, hangover-encrusted Nikolai at his door. In his haste to get on the road—his first appointment was at eleven—he'd put off looking at the specs, and now, driving at a flow-of-traffic eighty, he could only imagine what kind of properties he would soon visit. Shuttered mills, abandoned factories, empty office parks awaiting new tenants? Whatever he was driving toward he was glad to be driving toward *something*: something seeable, feelable, concrete. His days of being kept in the dark were over. Finally he would be able to give the animal voice some good answers.

But if there were any good answers to be found at his first destination, near the town of Dryden, an hour northwest of Binghamton, he missed them. The property lay three miles beyond Dryden's small downtown, on a road lined by houses covered in Tyvek wrapping, fields gouged by ATV tracks, and blank billboards. Along the way he passed only three vehicles and saw no people. The farther he drove the emptier the landscape became. He failed to visualize a booming enterprise sprouting up out of this nothingness, and he failed to visualize any enterprise finding a home in the dumpy warehouse to which, following the directions, he pulled up.

He came to a stop in the warehouse's gravel parking lot, empty except for a rusted Ford pickup. The driver of the truck stepped out, took in Alistair's BMW, and gave his eyebrows a Maura-reminiscent lift. Presumably this was the groundskeeper, who according to the spec sheet in Nikolai's folder was named John Laddis. He wore a camouflage coat, a pilled gray sweatshirt, and a Pittsburgh Steelers hat with a tattered bill. His beard, longish and wiry, was flecked with gray.

"Howdy," John said as Alistair emerged from the car. "You George?"

"Connor," Alistair said. He tucked the folder under his arm.

John nodded and turned toward the building, the sole of his boot crunching the gravel. "So," he said, "here it is."

The warehouse had tan corrugated siding, four drive-in bays, and no windows. In various places its foundation was cracked, its hinges rusted, its paint chipped. The property itself was large, two acres or so, and was bounded on three sides by dense trees. What these trees were meant to offer privacy from was something of a mystery—in all directions lay endless carpets of brown. Who'd picked this site? According to what specifications? It had to be a mistake.

John led him through a door next to a drive-in bay and flicked on the fluorescent lights, revealing a bare, concrete room under a ceiling of corroded trusses. Alistair sensed, his limited knowledge of warehouses notwithstanding, that the space was small: enough, maybe, for a modest farm-supply concern but no more.

John turned, hooked his thumbs into his front pockets, and looked Alistair over. "Built 1983, ventilation good as new, floor could hold a cruise ship, all up to inspection. Bathroom's over there, got another sink there, hookups for plumbing there, there, there. You could do a walk-in freezer, you could put in a bigger bay door. You want shelving, you want walls, I could give you names."

Alistair glanced around, trying and failing to imagine how this warehouse could be the seed of a regional rebirth. Defense contracting? Healthcare? Manufacturing? He didn't see it. "What was in here before?" he asked.

"Trailer park company," John said. "Put all their equipment in here. Pulled up stakes a few months ago, put this place on the market. Found somewhere cheaper I guess. Everyone's always out for a bargain, couldn't give two shits about the community. We look after ourselves around here. Everyone takes care of each other. We're like a family."

Alistair opened the folder and glanced at the spec sheet. 12,000 square feet, $24 per, asking price $288,000. "And what do you do here?" he asked.

"Mow, check the lights, smooth the gravel, odds and ends."

"Full-time?"

"Shit," John said. "What do you think they pay me?"

Alistair studied his folder for fear of meeting John's eyes. John and his community, his so-called "family," were precisely the sort of people Herve's project was meant to help. But he could see no salvation coming from the building in which he was standing.

"What are you guys putting in here anyway?" John asked.

"I'm on the finance side of things," Alistair said.

"You work for a bank or something?"

"Sort of."

"You guys really screwed everyone over back in oh-eight."

"I was fourteen," Alistair said.

"Well," John said, "you're probably still screwing everyone over."

Alistair returned to the BMW and drove to his next appointment, in Blodgett Mills. He considered calling Nikolai and reporting his misgivings about the first site, about asking him some firm questions, but he held off, hoping the Dryden warehouse was an anomaly. But the next three sites he visited were all empty warehouses with more or less the same dimensions, and each groundskeeper he met with was more or less another John Laddis. They described the spaces with listless shrugs as if to say: *Nothing to see here.* And there was nothing to see. The only function Alistair could imagine for any of the buildings was storage. He drove to his final appointment, in Richford, with an anxiety he could as little quell as explain. Something terrible, long in the making, seemed to be pushing its way into his consciousness. He kept his eyes on the road, checked his mirrors fastidiously, if only to keep his focus turned outward, away from the thought forming in his head. But when he arrived in Richford, amid a sharp late-afternoon wind that shook loose dead leaves and scattered them across the road, the thought burst forth, victorious over his denial, and he saw: this was all a ruse.

All a ruse, all a ruse! The facts fell into place with astonishing speed. Herve wasn't helping anyone; no one that bitter could. He cared only about himself, his battered ego, the war he waged in his head against imagined enemies—the government, the elite, anyone who condescended to him, anyone who constrained his free will. He had no generosity to offer, only his wounds to nurse, only an amorphous "them" to get back at; and now he would pad his fortune at their expense. He'd dump his money into wholesome causes and reap the tax benefits that came with them. He'd take government grants, nonprofit money, investor cash and squirrel it away, promising to use it to revive the backwaters of the nation but in reality keeping it for himself. Clearly he expected to reap gains enough to justify employing his point persons, employing Nikolai, employing him. He was doing it all over the country, his gains could be enormous, and it was a ruse! Alistair couldn't see yet exactly how it all worked. But it explained everything that had perplexed him up to now. The aliases, the insistence on keeping everything in the "network," the clunky phones, the homespun server, the nesting-doll holding companies, the cash. It explained Nikolai, who'd shown his willingness to skirt the law in his banking days, and it explained Nikolai's hiring of him. Nikolai felt guilty, he was alone with his guilt, and he'd brought on a "friend" to assuage it. It explained everything, it was all a ruse, and Alistair hated himself for not seeing it earlier. The animal voice had been telling him all along, but the money had been telling him something else.

By the time he returned his attention to the road he was at the entrance to the fifth and final warehouse. Waiting for him in the parking lot was a kid not much older than him. He had blond hair, blue eyes, and a reedy frame buried in a large Carhartt jacket. Alistair thought about sticking his head out the window and canceling the appointment. But he felt he needed to leave the car, clear his head, get fresh air.

When he stepped out the kid came gamboling toward him and introduced himself as Andy McCurdy. He shook Alistair's hand vigorously.

"Nice whip, man!" he said, looking at the BMW. "Fuck!"

Alistair smiled dismally. "It's a rental."

"Whatever, man!" Andy said. "You're *living*."

Alistair gave Andy his full attention. He was disarming in his earnestness. He stood with his hands in his pockets, smiling brightly, letting out vaporous breaths. Alistair decided to go through with the tour. He didn't feel like disappointing him.

"You want to see my kid?" Andy asked.

Alistair looked around for a small human.

"Here," Andy said. He pulled out his phone, swiped for a moment, and turned the screen. The baby had pudgy cheeks, a drooly mouth, and a cyclone of almost translucent blond hair. "He was born a month early, so he definitely had problems?" Andy said. "But honestly I feel lucky because my girlfriend's sister has two kids and they're both retarded. Both of them."

"He's very cute," Alistair said.

Andy swiped to another photo, this one showing Andy and presumably the girlfriend sitting on a brown couch with the baby between them. The girlfriend was, like her son, pudgy, with dyed red hair, narrow eyes, and a thin mouth spread into a disingenuous smile. "That's Amber," Andy explained. The next photo he swiped to showed the three of them in front of their house: a mobile home on a tiny plot of dead grass.

"Happy family," Alistair said.

"Never thought I'd be a dad at fucking twenty-*four*, man," Andy said. "I leave the Army after my contract is up, a year later my girl's got a bun in the oven. Out of the fire, into the flames. That's what my dad always says. But that's life, man. Wild!"

Alistair could hardly bear to listen. His anger at Herve's skullduggery still loomed large in his mind, and his pity for Andy, this young father raising a baby in a glorified shack, was threatening to magnify it. "Would you like to show me inside?"

"You got it, man!" Andy said.

While they toured the warehouse Andy peppered Alistair with questions, displaying a curiosity that Alistair, still operating as Connor, struggled to navigate. He admitted that he lived in New York. He recycled the lie John Laddis had supplied him with and told Andy that he worked at a bank. Andy laid on the extolments. He said it was *so* cool that Alistair lived in the city. He said he must make *so* much money. He told Alistair he'd been to New York twice, once for SantaCon and once for the St. Patrick's Day parade. "*Wild* fucking city," he said. "You must be *living*."

"So this is what you do?" Alistair said. "Look after this place?" He was asking only out of concern for Andy. He couldn't have cared about the warehouse if he'd tried. All he perceived was that it was small, inauspicious, ruse-like in its unsuitability.

"Yeppers," Andy said. "Check the lights, check the pipes, do the lawn, clear the snow. I'm your man. I'm very professional. Whatever you need me to do, I can do."

Alistair realized, with a swell of nausea, that Andy was hoping for a job. "What happens when this building gets sold?" he asked. "You move on to another one?"

Andy's sunniness faded. "I'm not betting on it," he said. "Not a lot of work around here. Took me three months to find this gig."

"Do they pay you OK?"

"Thousand a month," Andy said. "I know, it's shit."

The math was too much for Alistair. He thought of Andy's baby, of bottom-shelf diapers, onesies from Goodwill, canceled doctor's appointments. He thought, as he turned away, of an idea. No matter what Herve was planning to do with these buildings he'd have to hold on to them for some time, and for as long as he owned them he'd have to pay for minimal upkeep. Surely Nikolai would insist on using someone of his own choosing, on keeping everything in the "network," but his treachery had given Alistair nothing if not leverage. The least Nikolai could do, after bamboozling him, was let him give a desperate kid a job. The least he could do was let him help someone in the way that Herve was only pretending to.

"I'll talk to my boss," he said. "I imagine we can do better than that."

Andy was all smiles again. He rubbed his hands together. "That would be *sick*, man," he said. "You won't regret it. I'm super-professional. Just like you!"

In the face of Andy's gratitude Alistair began to feel regret. He couldn't be sure Nikolai would let him put Andy on the payroll, even if he had the moral high ground—moral high ground didn't seem to matter much where Nikolai and Herve were concerned. He needed to talk to Nikolai, he needed to lay into him, and he needed to do it now. When they exited the warehouse he paused in the parking lot. "Mind if I make a phone call?" he said.

Andy seemed not to hear him. He gazed at Alistair's BMW with a sensuous fixation, as if he were scrolling through porn. Some hitherto unapparent aspect of his character revealed itself in this gaze: a grasping, almost devious curiosity.

"Maybe some privacy?" Alistair said.

Andy nodded sharply. "I gotta check something in the back anyway."

Alistair waited until Andy had walked the length of the warehouse and turned the corner. He stepped across the lawn, toward a clump of bare trees, and, covering his mouth, called Nikolai.

The phone rang six times before Nikolai answered. "Yes?"

"I visited your little sites," Alistair said.

Nikolai, perhaps hearing the venom in Alistair's voice, hesitated before responding. "Did you find a good one?"

"Depends on what you mean by good," Alistair said. "Good for investment? I don't see it. Good for what Herve is actually doing? I can see that."

"What are you talking about?" Nikolai said. "What Herve is actually doing—what is this?"

"That's what I'm calling to ask you."

"I can hear that you are angry," Nikolai said. "I do not know why, but maybe it is better—"

"Don't fuck with me," Alistair said.

Nikolai hesitated again. "The way you are speaking to me—it is unprofessional. It is not right."

"Not right?" Alistair said. "You're telling *me* what's not right? Why don't you skip that and tell me what Herve is doing buying up dinky warehouses. Where are the factories? Where are the production facilities? Huh? What's the real reason for the 'work names,' the holding companies? You tell me. You tell me what Herve fucking Gallion—"

Nikolai waited for him to finish and then began responding calmly, but Alistair didn't hear anything he said. The reason he'd paused was that he'd sensed footsteps behind him and, turning, noticed Andy standing not ten feet away. Alistair hung up and stared at Andy, trying to keep a calm face.

"I was gonna ask if you wanted to see the back," Andy said. He directed his words at the black flip phone in Alistair's hand.

"That won't be necessary."

Andy looked up at Alistair, gazing at him the way he'd gazed at the BMW, with the same devious curiosity. "Trouble at the office?"

Alistair shook his head. "It's nothing." He looked toward the parking lot and stepped forward, but Andy didn't budge.

"Is that your boss?" he asked. "Herve Gallion?"

Alistair froze. Andy had so perfectly realized his worst fear that for a moment he wondered if he'd imagined it.

"Is he like, your CEO?"

Alistair had no desire to protect Herve's identity, not anymore, but he remembered the man's anger, he knew his power, and he feared leaking his identity could lead to ugly consequences. That he couldn't, right now, imagine what these consequences might be made them seem all the uglier. "Herve?" he said, pretending to struggle with the word. "I think you misheard me."

"Huh."

Alistair knew that he should drop the matter, that prodding it would only raise suspicion, but his fear got the better of him. "I really think you misheard me," he said again.

Andy tilted his head curiously. Then he laughed. "I got a baby crying in my face all night," he said. "My hearing's shit."

As they made their way to the parking lot Alistair wondered if the wisest thing would be to walk back his promise of a job and wish Andy a good life. But he thought again of Andy's baby, and Andy, as if reading his thoughts, spoke again.

"You're gonna do so much for me," he said to Alistair. "This is a lifesaver. And you won't regret it. I got you, man. I'm very professional. All business!"

Alistair opened the car door. He couldn't walk back his promise: he couldn't and he wouldn't. He was determined in his rage, determined to make at least one good thing come out of this scheme. "I'll be in touch."

"Thank you, man!" Andy said. "Merry Christmas!"

Alistair sped out of the parking lot, kicking up loose pebbles behind him. He thought about calling Nikolai again but knew it would be futile. Only when he had him face-to-face could he hope to penetrate his wall of bullshit. He drove to Binghamton at eighty-five, passing on the right, listening to carols the whole way.

His Christmas was a disaster. He'd come with plans of treating Maura, of making improvements to her life, and he'd decided to start with her clothes, which were too dull for such a pretty woman, and her furniture, which was shabby and out of date. Knowing he'd come on too strongly in his extravagances over Thanksgiving he'd decided to proceed carefully. He'd bought Maura fewer clothes than he'd wanted to, and when they went furniture shopping the day after Christmas, which he'd insist they do, he'd exercise restraint. He'd buy her either a couch or a dining table and maybe one other small thing and leave it at that: this had been his plan. But his discovery of Herve's treachery had made restraint impossible. His long-held fantasy of doing right by Maura now felt like a moral imperative, an ethical counterweight. The money in his checking account felt newly filthy, tainted by Herve's venality and his own willful blindness to it, and he felt a compulsion to launder it in kindness, to do as he planned to do with Andy and make something good come out of this scheme. He would exchange his dirty dollars for wholesome offerings, would exchange his complicity for generosity, and the exchange would be absolute, the things he bought severed from the labor he'd sold by means of an intermediary abstraction: this was the magic of money. One couch and one small thing wouldn't do it, he decided. He had in mind a Christmas miracle.

He kept to this new plan even when, on Christmas morning, Maura opened her presents with evident dismay. Alistair had taken care to remove the tags from the spoils of his SoHo spree—a Burberry jacket, a Longchamp tote, a Theory silk blouse, a pair of Tory Burch flats, three Eileen Fisher sweaters, a YSL clutch, a Ralph Lauren evening gown that, truth be told, Maura had no reason to wear—but now he wondered if this had been a mistake. As far as Maura knew the total was as likely $1,000 as it was $10,000. (In fact it was $3,114.)

"These things are awfully . . . nice," she said.

Sunlight was pouring into the living room, exposing the tree in its dryness, the plates of cookies they'd made in their homeliness, the gingerbread house they'd assembled in its structural fragility. Amid the luxurious clothes spread on the floor at Maura's feet the room looked embarrassed—embarrassed for him. "Not awful," he said. "Just nice."

"They seem very . . . expensive."

"They were on sale," Alistair lied. "They were a steal."

"I don't wear things like this."

"Now you can."

"Who am I wearing them for?"

"Wear them for yourself!"

Maura smiled tactfully. With an air of dutifulness she stood, held the Theory blouse over her torso, and looked in the mirror, appraising herself with cool equanimity. She had an attractive person's ability to take in her reflection without fear. If she was afraid of anything right now it wasn't her own image. "I don't want to seem ungrateful," she said.

"Then don't be," Alistair said.

"How about I keep a couple of things, and you take the rest back. I don't want you spending so much money on me."

"I like spending money on you," Alistair said. "And I plan to keep doing it. You have more presents coming."

Maura stared at him agog.

"Tomorrow we're going to Ethan Allen," he said. "We'll get some things for this room, maybe the dining room, maybe the bedrooms."

Maura laid the shirt in its box and put her hands on her waist. "We don't need new furniture."

Alistair had expected this and, having expected it, reacted with pent-up feeling. "Yes we do," he said adamantly. "Our furniture is old. It was old when you and Dad got it and now it's falling apart. The couch is stained, the coffee table is scratched, the leaves of the dining room table don't work, we're getting new furniture."

Maura should have been insulted by this outburst, and probably was, but she seemed, again, mostly frightened. She sat next to him. "What's going on?"

"I've done well and now I'm helping you," Alistair said. "This was always the plan and now I'm doing it. That's all that's going on."

Maura listened to him as if intaking a psychiatric patient. She touched his shoulder. "Are you OK?"

"I'll be OK if you let me help you," Alistair said. He put his hands to his face, made a steeple over his nose, and shut his eyes. "Please let me help you. You have no idea how much it means to me. Especially now."

"What do you mean 'now'?"

Alistair shook his head. "It's Christmas!"

Maura considered for a moment. She seemed to be negotiating between contradictory motherly instincts. "Were these clothes really on sale?"

Alistair nodded mendaciously.

She considered for another moment. "Fine," she said. "But here's the deal. We'll go look at furniture. We'll get one thing—maybe. If we see something that we like and that's reasonably priced. And then that's it for the gifts. Deal?"

"Deal," Alistair said.

The next day, when they walked into the Ethan Allen in Vestal, Alistair retrieved a registry scanner from a cashier. When Maura objected that they didn't need one since they were getting only one thing, he replied that he merely found the technology interesting and thought it looked fun.

He faced further objections by the couches, where he expressed a liking for a handsome cream sleeper that cost $2,800 and she a synthetic-looking gray loveseat that cost half that. He proposed they compromise on a marginally less handsome sleeper that cost $2,400.

"This is just cotton," Maura said, fingering the armrest. "It's outrageous."

Alistair pointed the scanner at the tag and clicked. "Oops."

Maura stared at him with her chin raised. "Thank you, it's very nice, I'm so happy," she said. "Now let's go."

When they neared the checkout line Alistair told her to wait.

"Wait for what?" she asked.

"I want to look at a few other things."

Maura regarded him icily. "We agreed we're buying only one thing, and we couldn't even agree about the one thing."

"Little stuff," Alistair said. "I'll be right back."

When he returned at the end of ten minutes Maura seemed relieved that he'd been so brief. "I guess you didn't find anything," she said.

"So many options," Alistair said. He joined the line and nodded at the front doors. "You can wait outside. You can warm up the car."

Maura followed his shifting gaze. "No," she said, "I think I'll wait."

Alistair turned away, toward the cashier desk, and awaited his doom. She'd find out soon enough anyway. In those secretive ten minutes (in his senseless craving they'd felt like ten seconds) he'd in fact found a great many things. He'd scanned a dining room table and six matching chairs, two end tables, a coffee table, three rugs, two sets of curtains, a media display, an armchair, an ottoman, another ottoman, and a number of throw pillows and blankets that even in his senseless craving he'd known to be excessive: he hadn't been lying when he'd said there were so many options.

When he reached the front of the line the cashier, a girl his age, accepted the scanner. Oblivious to the delicacy of this moment, to the contracted muscles in Alistair's face, she read out the total with clarion frankness. "That comes to eleven thousand three hundred and forty-six dollars and fifty-two cents," she said.

Alistair felt he could hear, behind him, the very opening of Maura's eyelids, the very parting of her lips. Certainly he could hear her turning on her heel and walking at speed through the front doors.

Alistair gave the cashier his American Express. Having never confirmed his credit limit, and having already charged his SoHo purchases to the card, he wasn't entirely sure the sale would clear. Nor was he entirely sure he was happy when, with a beep of the reader, it did.

He crossed the parking lot with heavy footsteps. He felt his adrenaline crashing and the reality of his actions settling. His craving had been satisfied, and now his sense had returned.

When he got into the car he glanced at Maura furtively, fearing tears. But Maura's face was dry, steady, and hard-set, which seemed to Alistair somehow worse. For a few moments they said nothing, only stared together out the windshield, at the gray skies and sooty mounds of shoveled snow. Finally she spoke.

"Tell me everything," she said. "About your job."

Alistair had anticipated several things, a demand that he return the purchases, a tirade about their agreed-upon terms and the insult he'd dealt her by violating them, but not this. "I told you," he said. "I'm a secretary. I schedule meetings. I write emails."

"Emails to who?"

Alistair saw cosmic comedy in the fact that, even if he hadn't wanted to evade this question, he wouldn't have been able to answer it anyway. Yet he evaded it nonetheless. "I know in your personal experience secretaries don't make a lot of money," he said. "Which is unfair. But we're talking about New York money, and the people I'm working for have even more money than that."

Maura brushed this away. "I don't care how much money you make," she said. "It's how you're spending it. That's what I care about. That's what angers and frightens me."

"I've spent most of it on you," Alistair said, not untruthfully.

"You tell yourself it's for me, but it's for you," Maura said. "If this were a normal job, a job you felt good about, you wouldn't be acting like this. You're acting like you want to get rid of the money as fast as you can."

This deduction didn't surprise Alistair: Maura was the smartest person he knew and the person who knew him best. But she didn't know everything, and for now Alistair preferred to keep it that way. "If I were ever to learn that I'd been asked to do something improper," he said, speaking with great grammatical care, "I would quit."

"See, I'm not sure you would," Maura said.

Alistair didn't know how to respond to this.

"And what really astounds me," she said, in a hiss Alistair had never heard before, "what really infuriates me, is that you think *I* would ever want any of this—any of this crap. How could you get that idea? You know my mother was materialistic and you know I hated her for it. You know your father cared only about his job, making more and more money, and you know that hurt me. You know he did terrible things for a terrible man, and you know that if he weren't so blinded by his obsession with making us rich—which I never cared about! Which I never wanted!—he might still be alive. You know I tried, very hard, to raise you to care about other things. I'd say you're a bad son but I think the truth is I'm a bad mother. It's very clear to me that I failed with you."

Alistair found it in himself to look at her, and for a while he simply stared at her face, seeing with new clarity the shape of her mouth, the texture of her skin, the wrinkles around her eyes. "The furniture is an investment," he said grotesquely. "You'll never have to replace it. We'll never have to do this again."

"You're right about that."

"I wanted to set you up nicely, while I can. I wanted to do something kind for you."

"The kindest thing you can do right now is take me home," Maura said.

As he drove out of the lot and onto the parkway Alistair thought of more things to say, more ways to explain, but he knew there was no use. And he knew the things he'd said, however grotesque, were true. His expenditure may have been extravagant and the moral calculus behind it flawed, but it really had meant the world to him. At some point in the future, no matter where he landed, he would be able to look back on this day and be glad that he'd done something grand for his mother. But when he left the next morning without even a goodbye, with barely a glance from Maura as she washed dishes at the sink, he understood that she would never see it this way.

When he returned to New York he spent three days in largely empty Palladium, pretending he was still in Binghamton and so unable to confront Nikolai face-to-face. But something about the energy of the city on New Year's Eve—an acceleration of traffic, a multiplication of sirens, a special gravity in the air, a solstice lament and a solstice madness—made him pick up the burner, which it was now obvious to him was what the flip phone was.

"I'm coming over," he said to Nikolai. "I don't care if you have plans."

Nikolai answered through a vodka fog. "Why would I have plans?"

"It's New Year's Eve," Alistair said.

"Is it?"

When he arrived Alistair saw that Nikolai had outdone himself. His apartment looked like a redemption center. Empty bottles on the counter, on the coffee table, on the desk. Empty bottles on the side tables, on the floor, on the stove. Most were vodka but a few were Bulgarian plum brandy—maybe this was Nikolai's version of getting into the Christmas spirit. After he let Alistair in he collapsed onto the couch. Something about the readiness with which the couch accepted him suggested he'd been sitting on it for days. Outside the sky was dark and the lights of the city bright. Midnight was an hour away.

Alistair pulled up the silver bistro chair and sat. He dropped the folder containing the site specs onto the floor. He avoided looking directly into Nikolai's eyes. He'd had every intention of letting his anger fly, of screaming at Nikolai if he felt moved to. But the sorrow in Nikolai's face, the chaos of bottles around him, was moving him in a different way. For all his anger he found he still pitied Nikolai, still felt a marginal fidelity to him. At some point in the past ten weeks he'd become, without realizing it, the thing Nikolai had wanted from the very start: he'd become his friend.

"I did some thinking upstate," he said.

Nikolai poured the remaining finger of vodka from a near bottle into a coffee mug. "What was that like?" he said. "I do not do much of it myself."

"I know what Herve is doing."

Nikolai, with the mug to his lips, looked at Alistair with amusement. Yet he held his face still.

"It's all fraud," Alistair said. "Herve is defrauding investors, he's defrauding the government. He's using this project as a vehicle to hide his millions, and to steal more millions. It explains everything. I figured it out."

Nikolai turned his face but kept his eyes on Alistair. "You have figured this out."

"You don't seem remorseful," Alistair said. "Not that I expected you to be."

There came into Nikolai's eyes a strange levity. "It does explain everything, does it not."

"Give me one good reason I shouldn't go to the authorities."

Nikolai set down the mug. "You will not do that," he said. "You will not cross him. I have seen—you will not."

Alistair cast his eyes to the floor. The image of Herve's face, of his embarrassment at the restaurant, his deep humiliation and outsize rage, blazed in his mind. "I mostly just want to forget about it," he said.

"That is best."

"How could you work for him? Knowing all this?"

Nikolai drained the mug and looked around for more nonempty bottles. "My friend," he said, "you and I are the same. I have no choice either."

"But how could you involve me in this? You call me your friend—how could you do that?"

In his search for alcohol Nikolai was becoming agitated. "I seem to remember you telling me you were hopeless," he said. "I seem to remember you looking at me with your little-boy eyes and telling me you were broke! And do you know what I did for you? I gave you money. I gave you an easy job. I kept you away from everything. I have protected you. I am protecting you still."

"You didn't do it for me," Alistair said. "You did it for yourself. You were lonely. You felt guilty." As soon as he'd said this he realized he'd recycled, more or less, the same words Maura had said to him.

"God forbid!" Nikolai said. "God forbid anyone wants to be Nikolai's friend! And now I am alone again. With this, with what you tell me you have figured out, I am alone with this again. Do you think I am happy, working for that man? I have told you, I am trying to get out too. But now I am alone with it again, and you do not care. You do not see that I was tricked too!"

"I don't believe that," Alistair said. "You knew. I know you knew."

Nikolai was up on his knees, shuffling along the couch, searching the bottles on the windowsill. "You know less than you think," he said.

Alistair watched Nikolai give the bottles useless swirls. He began to fear, however preposterously, that if he left now Nikolai might not live to the morning. "What am I supposed to do?" he said. "Keep coming here? After everything? Just to spend time with you?"

"You make it sound so horrible!"

"I don't want to see you like this. I really don't. But there's nothing I can do."

Nikolai quit searching. He moved his eyes around the room, chasing a thought as if following a mouse, and then caught hold of it. "There is something you can do," he said.

"I'm not doing one more ounce of work on this project."

"No," Nikolai said. He gazed at Alistair with excitement, with naked need. "I will give you something else. That is what I will do. You can manage my money! It is a complete mess. Use whatever they teach you at Stern. I will pay you the same. After you see my accounts, you will probably ask for a raise!"

Nikolai had hit on another reason Alistair found it hard to muster anger. His principled fury had become diluted by certain material facts that he'd uncovered, slowly and wincingly, in the preceding days. In his weeks working for Nikolai he'd made $30,000, and he'd spent two-thirds of that on his mother's bills and various craving-fueled indulgences. Now, after his SoHo and Ethan Allen sprees, he had some $15,000 in credit card debt, and this was not a sum he was content to pay off slowly. He'd checked the interest rate on his American Express; it made his student loans look interest-free by comparison. He also had those, his loans, and the $3,000 a month he would insist against every refusal on sending Maura, and the rest of the school year to get through, and no six-figure salary awaiting him. He'd done it again, he'd dug himself deeper in. He seemed to have an extraordinary talent for fucking himself financially.

"I would have absolutely no involvement in Herve's project," he said.

"None!" Nikolai said ecstatically.

"No fake names, no weird phones. I guess I don't—mind the cash."

Nikolai giggled and clapped.

"If I hear even a whisper about the project, about Herve, I'm gone."

"Who is Herve?" Nikolai said with a glimmer in his eye. "There is no such person as this."

"If you ask me to do anything shady with your accounts, you'll never see me again."

"There is nothing shady in the accounts you will be looking at," Nikolai said.

Alistair glanced at the folder at his feet. "There's one more thing, before we forget about the project."

"Yes," Nikolai said less ecstatically.

"If Herve is determined to buy a warehouse, he should buy the one in Richford. Out of the five it's in the best shape, and it'll cause the least headaches maintenance-wise." This was a lie—Alistair could barely remember the warehouse—but it was means to a good, and it was, he hoped, the last lie he'd have to tell for a while.

Nikolai seemed surprised by Alistair's diligence in the matter but nodded. "I trust your judgment."

"I'm assuming Herve will just let it collect dust while he collects investor cash and tax savings. But someone will need to look after it. There's a groundskeeper who already works there, and I think you should keep him on. You could pay him nothing, two thousand a month, and it would change his life."

Nikolai began shaking his head before Alistair had even finished. "Absolutely not," he said. "You know Herve. He will use his own people. You do not want—absolutely not."

Alistair shrugged, nodded, and silently formed a plan. He'd tell Andy he could keep looking after the warehouse, and he'd pay him himself, at least for now. Even with his credit card debt he could afford to, as long as he kept working for Nikolai. "I thought we could help someone," he said. "But Herve isn't really interested in helping people, is he."

"Not in a way that makes sense to me," Nikolai said.

A while later they heard a swell of cheers, possibly from a neighboring apartment, and Nikolai turned on the TV. There it was, in bright gold numbers, atop One Times Square: year of our Lord 2016.

The next day Alistair called Andy McCurdy on the burner, his last task before he ended his involvement in Herve's project for good.

"Connor!" Andy said. "Happy New Year!"

An unfortunate aspect of Alistair's plan was that, in order not to raise Andy's suspicion, he had to continue operating as Connor Black: had to carry that residual taint of Herve. "My colleagues will buy the warehouse," he said. "I expect the sale will go through soon. We're happy to keep you on."

"Oh man, oh man," Andy said. "That's sick!"

"We can pay you more than you're being paid now."

"Oh man, oh man."

"How does two thousand a month sound?"

To Alistair's surprise Andy fell silent. When he answered he spoke with exaggerated sweetness. Apparently he knew he was pitiable, and apparently he knew how to wield this. "I have this baby, man," he said. "Two thousand would be huge. But three thousand? Three thousand would be *perfect*."

Alistair breathed in and out. Three thousand a month for his mother, three thousand a month for Andy, four thousand minus necessities left for his credit card bill: Jesus. He'd hatched his plan quickly, without forethought, without considering how long he could sustainably carry it out. But he felt he couldn't turn around now. "Fine."

"Dude," Andy said, "you're *saving* me."

"I'm happy to hear it," Alistair said. "There are two things you should know."

"I'm all ears," Andy said.

"First, the warehouse might be empty for a while. Maybe for a long time. But you should just keep doing your thing. Obviously, since there won't be anyone around, don't kill yourself. This should be an easy job."

"Dude, this is *sick*."

"Second thing. At some point, you might see someone else, maybe one person, maybe a whole contracted service, coming to do your job. They'll have been hired by my colleague, George Crawford. You can give them his name and tell them we hired you too. You can divide the labor between you, or you can just give yourself the day off."

Andy laughed, in disbelief at his good luck, and then again fell silent. "So wait," he said. "You're telling me your company bought a three-hundred-grand property, isn't gonna put anything in it, and hired multiple people to take care of it?"

"That's correct," Alistair said.

"What's this company?" Andy said. "It sounds like muh-*nee*."

Alistair heard in Andy's voice the same devious curiosity he'd picked up on in Richford. He diverted his attention to technicalities. He explained that he'd be sending Andy his salary via a payment app (on which he'd already created a Connor Black profile) and that Andy should contact him via email (he gave him his Phakelos address) rather than by phone: Alistair was hoping never to use the burner again. Thankfully Andy saw in none of these details cause to pose more questions.

"Thank you, man," he said. "Thank you! Thank you!"

"Unless you have any problems, no need to reach out," Alistair said.

"You got it, man," Andy said. "I'll talk to you soon!"

After he hung up Alistair opened his American Express profile and put $7,500 toward his bill, nearly emptying his checking account. He opened a notebook and did the math. From here on out he'd need to be thrifty, thrifty. But he couldn't deny his relief. If he was financially squeezed it was because he was helping people, and if he was able to help people it was because he had a good job, one that was straightforward and legitimate and that bore cheerful relation to his studies. He was done with Herve. He could breathe easy again.

And, for a blessed few months, he mostly did.

He began the semester with a spring in his step that he hadn't felt since freshman year. In class he sat in the front row, took assiduous notes, and introduced himself to his professors with toothy smiles. He wrote his essays and completed his problem sets and populated his presentation slides with glee. He didn't care that he was the only person in his class putting in such effort: didn't care that his peers, with job offers in hand, had given themselves over to senioritis. He'd forgotten the simple joy of being a student.

He visited Nikolai's apartment three times a week and, little by little, organized his money, which as Nikolai had warned was a dog's breakfast.

"You have nine hundred thousand dollars sitting in your checking account," Alistair said. "Accruing absolutely zero interest."

Nikolai lay on the couch, hiding his face in the cushions, shielding his eyes from the brutal January sun. Whatever elation he'd felt upon securing Alistair's continued friendship had faded.

"You have six hundred thousand in your savings account," Alistair said. "The interest rate there is a whopping oh-four percent."

Nikolai looked at him with all the abasement of a starving dog. Maybe it was an effect of the light, but his eyes looked teary. He picked a mug off the floor and held it out. "Refill," he said, "please."

"Your Vanguard funds are all passively managed."

"Passively managed funds outperform actively managed ones," Nikolai said. "They will not tell you this at Stern."

"Your few high-risk positions are, shall we say, low in rewards. Have you not been reading the news? Brent crude is cratering. You've lost fifteen thousand in three months."

Nikolai searched the room desperately for drinkable liquid. "I do not care!" he said, swinging his mug. "I do not care! And that is not all of it anyway. Not by a long shot."

Alistair recalled something Nikolai had said a few months earlier: that he was "making sure" Herve wouldn't spend the full hundred and twenty-five million he'd allocated to the project. But he didn't care to ask Nikolai what he meant, because he didn't care to talk about Herve. Who was Herve? There was no such person as this.

Nikolai sat back, holding the mug to his chest, breathing heavily. "You have abandoned me," he said. "With all of this, you have left me alone."

Alistair pushed this away with a bright, hard smile. "I'm right here," he said. "I'm helping you. Let's talk about your portfolio."

Nikolai gazed at him wistfully. Then he sprang from the couch, ran to the bathroom, and vomited.

At the Eros Ananke, too, Alistair's new optimism ran into a brick wall of misery. Mark and Elijah had gone to Ho-Ho-Kus for Christmas and returned with fresh resentments.

"He'd leave me with his family for *hours*," Elijah said, as Mark sat stoically in the armchair. "He'd go up to his room and wouldn't come out until dinner."

"I can only take so much of my family," Mark said.

"So he puts it on me!" Elijah said. "Eddie, Mark's brother, private equity schmuck. He'd say, 'Elijah, how's your *fart* going? Working on any new *fart* projects? Thinking of going back to *fart* school?'"

"You can see why I can only take so much," Mark said. "And don't pretend you don't find Eddie's assholery titillating."

"Did you get nice presents?" Alistair asked.

Elijah opened his mouth, caught Alistair's gaze, and then shut it.

"How was your Christmas?" Mark asked Alistair.

"I'm looking forward to a new year," Alistair said.

The men's Christmas did sound genuinely awful, but Alistair understood, perhaps more clearly than they themselves did, that it was only one more advance in a trend. Follow their relationship's daily performance closely and you saw only minor fluctuations. Zoom out and look at it YOY and you saw a precipitous leakage of value: this stock was crashing. The longer the men stayed together the more each warped his personality in opposition to the other's, and the more each warped himself the stranger he became. Elijah's restlessness and risqué impishness had hardened Mark into a dullard and prig, and Mark's dullness and priggishness had hardened Elijah into a disciple of Jay Steigen. Elijah continued to frolic with Jay, to invite him over against Mark's wishes, to relay bizarre and incendiary things he'd said. He relished Jay's bad-ness, borrowed it and dressed himself in it, flaunted it before Mark's eyes. He wanted to be interesting, and confusing Mark's goodness for tediousness he confused Jay's badness for interest.

As the weeks went on Alistair felt his loyalties shifting. When he'd been flush with cash and flush with reservations, when he'd had the animal voice whispering incessantly in his ears, he'd loved Elijah. He'd sensed he'd become involved in something unsavory and he'd loved Elijah for tolerating, nay for lustily delighting in, unsavory things. But now that he'd extricated himself from Herve's project and returned to the straight and narrow he loved the hopelessly straight and narrow Mark. He wanted to be good, wanted this as never before, and his desire to be good awakened his desire for the soft-hearted introvert in the armchair. He wondered, sometimes, if he should say some choice words to Mark, nudge him toward the inevitable end of things with Elijah. But intervening in the men's relationship, bringing about certain heartbreak, seemed like a decidedly *not* good thing. And so he stuck to the program, drank with them and slept with them, as if their bedroom activities hadn't been part of the problem all along.

The sex became unbearably competitive. If Mark butted in while Elijah was kissing Alistair, Elijah would push him away. In the inverse situation Mark would do the same. Mark appeared increasingly unwilling to sit on the sidelines while Alistair plowed Elijah. Once, while Alistair was lying on his back, Mark crept toward him, hovered over him, brought his genetic jackpot perilously close to Alistair's ass, and looked at him with the never-broached question in his eyes. Alistair, closing his legs, shook his head regretfully. The answer was no, had always been no, maybe wouldn't be no forever, but was certainly no now. Elijah, following this exchange, lowered his head to the mattress and raised his backside in the air, brandishing his goods. He had the monopoly on points of ingress, and he smiled with a monopolist's cruel confidence.

As he plowed Elijah and thought about plowing Mark and thought about letting Mark plow him, Alistair recalled the speech Jay had made about gay sex at the Die Kinder. Now that he wanted to be good Alistair wanted something gentler, something more tender, but Jay was right, and Alistair was never sorrier to be wrong. There seemed no way to fuck Elijah without violating him, and Alistair rued this, however much this violation was desired. Their body parts were such that their congress was never without the quality of domination, of submission, of war. Straight sex was life, beauty, and nature, but gay sex was history: it was dialectical. Inheritances of male aggressions and humiliations, conquests and invasions, takeovers and dispossessions, seemed definitely to be at play. He brought to the act the same single-minded rapacity that he'd brought all his life to his studies, his work, his upwardly mobile grasping, but he wanted just one place to exercise different instincts, to spread the wings of his better angels, and he wanted the bedroom to be it.

One night in late February, while Elijah was in the bathroom, Mark rolled over, stroked Alistair's face, and, summoning new courage, parted his lips to say something—to say everything, it, the thing they were both thinking—but Alistair put his hand to Mark's mouth.

"I know," he said. "I know."

On the increasingly rare occasions when he spoke to his mother, Alistair encountered yet another challenge to his optimism. He'd called Ethan Allen and confirmed that the furniture had been delivered, but Maura said nothing about it and Alistair didn't ask. He continued to send her $3,000 a month, but neither acknowledged this either. He told her he'd quit his job, which he felt was only half a lie, but she asked no questions and he volunteered no details. To tell her that he was engaged in aboveboard tasks now would be to admit that his previous tasks had been dodgy. They exchanged dull pleasantries and hung up after five minutes. They spoke without saying anything at all.

And the wider world, the ceaseless onslaught of news alerts: this too was an enemy of Alistair's optimism. Trump, by now the presumptive GOP nominee, continued to inundate the country with deranged invective, and the media, fascinated in its indignation, continued to magnify his voice. Alistair did his best to tune it out. He'd check back in after the election, at which point the nightmare, the political glitch, would be over. He focused his attention on the signs of spring: the crisp morning breeze, the leafing of trees, the stretching and yawning of the earth. He moved the bulk of Nikolai's money into sensible diversified funds and, thanks to a roaring Q1, reported immediate if moderate gains. He ate away at his credit card bill. He went for runs along the river. For days at a time he forgot he had no job offer. He felt the world broadening and reopening to him its vistas.

Then, one night in late April, he heard a strange buzzing, as if a giant fly were trapped in his room. He'd put the burner into semiretirement by keeping it on the floor under his desk but turned on at all times. He worried Andy would call him, regardless of his stated communication preferences, and now he had.

"Did you see my email?" he said when Alistair answered.

Alistair thought Andy sounded unusually urgent. "I asked you not to call me."

"Well, I emailed," Andy said.

"Well, but you're calling."

"Did you see what I sent?"

"Why don't you just tell me now."

"I can't explain it over the phone," Andy said. "You have to look."

Alistair opened his laptop instinctively, as if it were his hands heeding Andy's directive. He brought up an email to himself in which, months before, he'd written the URL of his Phakelos account, thinking he might in some emergency need it. He remembered Nikolai's command to use only the devices he'd supplied him with; but he wouldn't have access to Nikolai's ThinkPads until the following afternoon, and Andy's voice told him this might be an emergency.

Andy had sent him an email with a subject line reading: *WTF?* Enclosed was a photograph of the warehouse in Richford. Six or eight men were walking from the parking lot toward one of the bay doors, each carrying two large bags. The photograph had been taken from a distance and was blurry, but

Alistair could see that the men were young, in their twenties or thirties, and wearing camouflage.

"Do you see?" Andy asked.

"I see," Alistair said. "What is it?"

"That's what I'm calling to ask you."

It occurred to Alistair that Herve had already turned around and sold the warehouse, or that Nikolai had simply gone with a different site altogether. "Have you talked to these people?"

"More like they talked to me," Andy said. "I showed up last Friday to cut the lawn, and they were there, bringing in tons of shit—computers, desks, boxes, bags. When they saw me they put their arms up. They go, 'Whoa-whoa-whoa, who are you, what are you doing here?'"

"What did you say?"

"What you told me to say. Mentioned George Crawford. They go, 'George Crawford?' They still looked suspicious, but they said if it was OK with George Crawford it was OK with them."

Alistair's heart was racing. This put his hopeful theories to rest.

"Told me I could cut the lawn, do whatever," Andy said, "as long as I don't go in the warehouse. They were pretty adamant about that. 'Don't even come to the door.'"

Alistair looked again at the image. All the men were wearing sunglasses, even though the sky was its usual central New York gray. "Did you ask them who they were?"

"I was too freaked out," Andy said. "I was hoping you could tell me."

"Beyond picking the warehouse and managing your payment I'm not involved."

"You told me the warehouse would be empty. It's not empty. There's a lot of guys standing around, driving up, going inside. There were about twenty the first time I saw them, and yesterday there were even more. That's when I took this picture."

Alistair's immediate instinct was to tell Andy not to take more pictures. But that would only fan his fear, and he wasn't sure there was anything to be afraid of. He wasn't sure his heart had any reason to be beating wildly. He thought it was critical to recognize just how little he knew—and how unpleasant, how familiar, this thought was.

"There's something I don't like about these guys," Andy said. "If I'm being honest, they scare the shit out me."

"Have you seen them do anything weird?"

"It's just the way they look at me," Andy said. "The way they look at each other. I don't like it."

"Just stick to your job," Alistair said. "Don't hang around longer than you have to. Let me know if anything changes, and I'll talk to George."

"What's this company, Connor?" The question was piercing in its intelligence. "I looked up Herve Gallion. Wasn't much, but I see he's a billionaire. Must be a pretty powerful guy."

"As I told you," Alistair said, "you misheard me."

"I'll let you know if anything changes."

At the moment he'd said it, Alistair really had planned to talk to Nikolai. But when he arrived at Nikolai's apartment the next day he lost his nerve. If he asked Nikolai about the men at the warehouse he'd have to tell him how he knew they were there, and if he told Nikolai he'd kept Andy in his job Nikolai would surely erupt. But more than the prospect of angering Nikolai he feared the prospect of reentering Herve's world.

Andy called again the next evening. "Check your email," he said.

This time Andy had sent two photographs, though Alistair froze on the first. Like the one from two days before it showed a group of men carrying goods into the warehouse. But this time the goods weren't bags.

"Those are assault rifles," Andy said. "I thought maybe these guys were setting up some kind of hunting lodge. You don't use those guns for hunting."

The thing clearest in Alistair's mind, as he stared at the photograph, was that he wasn't shocked. The facts had been few, but the empty space around which they'd been organized had been ready to accommodate, he saw now, something of this order.

"I don't want to sound like some crazy liberal," Andy said. "But I was in the Army. I've handled those kinds of guns. I don't think any old Joe Schmo should be using them."

"You need to stop taking pictures," Alistair said.

"Look at the second one."

The second photograph at first looked comparatively harmless. It showed a pickup truck parked in front of the warehouse from behind.

"You see that bumper sticker?" Andy said. "You know what that is?"

Alistair zoomed in. The sticker featured a simple design: a black cross against a black circle on a white background.

"I looked it up," Andy said. "White Pride Worldwide. Some of these cars have Confederate Flag stickers. There were guys like that in the Army. Total psychos."

Alistair said nothing. He heard his blood in his temples.

"Did you talk to George?"

"I think it's best if you quit," Alistair said.

"I think so too," Andy said. He spoke with a tremble, something like stage fright. "But I've seen things. I think I should be compensated."

Alistair was almost glad of the threat. It shook him from his terrified torpor. "Don't go back to the warehouse," he said. "We can do a one-time payout, and then we can part ways."

"How much are we talking?"

"I'll come up with something."

"When?" Andy said.

"Soon."

"Better be soon. I'm sure Herve Gallion doesn't want these pictures out in the world."

After he hung up Alistair went to his bed, slipped under the comforter, and pulled it over his head. His idea was to take fifteen minutes to calm his heart and gather his thoughts. But he ended up staying there all night and well into the next morning, with a mind none the clearer for his self-cocooning. The comforter became a kind of interior cognitive membrane. On the far side of it were all the things he was too afraid to think about, all the pieces he was too afraid to fit into place. On the near side was only his oldest, closest, most familiar, most private self. He sensed that as soon as he pulled the comforter down some part of this self would be lost.

In the afternoon he texted Nikolai to tell him he was sick and couldn't come to work. He checked his funds. The last time he'd looked he'd had some $8,000 in his account, and he wouldn't receive his next payment from Nikolai for another two weeks. He thought about asking Nikolai for an advance but decided against it. He didn't want to field questions about why he needed it, and he worried he didn't have much time. He sent Andy $7,000 via the payment app. He waited for his reply. Outside the sun sank and darkness followed it. The light of the old Consolidated Edison Building across the street blazed. At eleven the burner vibrated to life.

"Seven thousand isn't gonna do it," Andy said. "Check your email. I went inside."

"You what?" Alistair said.

"I went in a few hours ago. The guys were all gone. I checked for cameras, didn't see any. Don't think they want a record of what's in there anyway."

Alistair brought up his email. This time Andy had sent three photographs. The first showed a smallish room in a corner of the warehouse with thin, makeshift walls and no ceiling. Guns of every variety hung from pegboard panels. There had to be at least two hundred of them. There were pistols and rifles, small guns and large guns, simple guns and guns equipped with reinforcements. Along the walls were cubbies holding boxes of ammunition, nylon straps, and magazines of varying capacity. In a large crate beneath a center table, stacked like dry laundry, were a dozen or so black Kevlar vests.

The next photograph showed the remainder of the warehouse's interior. Alistair saw a dozen widely spaced desks, festooned with laptops and hard drives. He saw chairs pulled together in loose circles. He saw, pinned to bulletin boards, various large sheets of paper, some bearing indecipherable images, some bearing maps. He saw, against one wall, four bookshelves in a row, crammed with hardcovers and paperbacks, a miniature library.

The third photograph showed a close-up of one of the maps on the wall. It depicted downtown Albany, at its center the state capitol.

Andy spoke. "I want a hundred thousand dollars," he said. "That's in addition to the chump change you sent me today. Don't know how you'll get that to me, but I'm sure you can figure it out."

Alistair said nothing, only listened to Andy's stage-fright tremble. He had the sense that Andy had rehearsed these words, spent desperate minutes whipping himself up. He didn't know that Alistair was as much a desperate upstate kid as he was. He saw him only as a powerful stranger from a powerful world—fearsomely, dauntingly other—and he'd calibrated his speech accordingly.

"Once I get the money, I go my merry way," Andy said. "Won't say anything. If I don't get the money, I send these pictures to the police. I give them your name, I give them George Crawford's, and I give them Herve Gallion's. Maybe they won't care about you or George, but I have a feeling they'll care about Mr. Gallion."

For a moment, as he scrolled back and forth between the photographs, Alistair had an instinct to refuse Andy. Let him go to the police, let him expose whatever this operation was. But then he wondered what the chances were that law enforcement would be able to connect "Connor Black" to him—he suspected they weren't nil. And he pictured Herve, leaning forward at Viceroy and telling Alistair to fuck the world, barely containing his rage as the waiter doused him with wine. He had a feeling he had things other than law enforcement to be afraid of.

"You listening?" Andy said.

"I'm listening," Alistair said.

"You have twenty-four hours."

"I didn't know any of this. I'm as shocked as you are."

"I figured. But I also don't care."

"I need some time. I need to talk to people."

"You have twenty-four hours," Andy said.

Alistair took a cab to Nikolai's, holding his head in his hands the whole way. He blew past the doorman and, when he got upstairs, pounded on Nikolai's door until it opened.

"I guess you are not sick anymore," Nikolai said.

Alistair took him by the shoulders, turned him around, and marched him to the living room.

"What is this?" Nikolai said. "What are you doing? This is unprofessional."

Alistair pushed him onto the couch and went to one of the ThinkPads. In the thirty minutes since they'd spoken Andy had sent him another email. *Last warning*, he'd written. *And if you think I'm making an empty threat, then you are so fucking sadly mistaken. 100K by tomorrow or I tell the authorities about Herve Gallion and whatever he's doing in this warehouse.* He'd included three more photographs: the gun room from a different angle, a map of DC, and a tall metal bucket holding a quiver of flags, like a bit of pomp at a meeting of diplomats. Alistair saw a Confederate flag, a flag bearing the same symbol as the bumper sticker Andy had showed him, and unrecognizable others: ominous mysteries of black and green, blue and white, red and yellow. He picked up the ThinkPad and delivered it into Nikolai's lap. "Fuck you," he said.

While Nikolai scanned the email Alistair pulled up the bistro chair. He told Nikolai everything: how he'd let slip Herve's name, how he'd secretly hired Andy, how Andy had inched toward his threat. "Your turn," he said. "No point in bullshitting me anymore."

Nikolai moved his head back and forth very slowly. "My friend," he said. "You have made a terrible mistake."

Alistair pressed his elbows to his thighs to keep his legs from wobbling. He spoke in a whisper. "What is this?"

Nikolai closed the laptop. He retrieved a mug of vodka from the coffee table and sipped. He was drunk, he was always drunk, but when he opened his mouth he spoke with disarming sobriety. He had always had it in him, no matter how tanked, a little viper of lucidity ready to spring. "This all started a few years ago," he said. "Though if you asked Herve, he would say he has been working toward it all his life."

"Working toward what?" Alistair said.

"When he hired me, he gave me the same story I gave you," Nikolai said. "'I want to help people. People who have been neglected, oppressed, taken advantage of.' He said he wanted to 'invest' in these communities. He said he wanted to secure 'infrastructure.' He let me figure out what kind of infrastructure he had in mind, what kind of communities he was talking about. He connected me to the people he had already begun working with—our point persons—and it did not take me long to put it together. But by then, I was already sworn to him. I knew too much, I could not back out. Herve made that very clear."

Alistair was practically folded over in his chair, at once impatient for Nikolai's explanation and dreading his every word.

"Herve had always been cynical about politics," Nikolai said. "He made his donations, to his senators and his congresspeople, his PACs and his whatnot. But he felt the country was doomed. He had no hope of anything changing."

"Changing how?" Alistair said.

"All his life, Herve has hated the government," Nikolai said. "His father taught him it was the enemy, and when he went into fracking he saw this for himself. His whole career, it was one long war. Not only against regulators, the EPA, but the liberal activists, the media—the bureaucrats, the elites. These people, Herve felt, they looked down on him, on everyone, wanted to control them, and every year they gained more power. Over how you can make your money, how much of it you can keep. Over what you are allowed to say, what you are allowed to think. These cozy elites, they oppressed the ordinary men and women of this country, kept them down by taking away their economic opportunities, by telling them that they had no place in the future, that they were dirt. Herve was sick of it. He had had enough."

"Then what?" Alistair said.

"He should never have stopped working," Nikolai said. "When you are working, you have no time to think. But he sold his company, and around that time the Tea Party movement was in full swing. He felt things might be turning around, and he began to pay more attention. All the Party's ideas—a crippled federal government, elimination of income tax, of environmental regulations, a return to absolute freedom, a country ruled by the people and for the people, as it was meant to be—these are ideas he had always held dearly. He had never dreamed of seeing his vision gaining such wide appeal, such urgency. But then the fever broke, the Party's ideas became co-opted by politicians in Washington and watered down, and business as usual returned. Herve was not surprised—he was too cynical for that—but a fire had been lit in him, and a fire had been lit, he believed, in millions of people like him. The politicians in Washington would never do anything. To bring about real change, revolutionary change, you had to go to the people, you had to find them where they were hiding. He had unlimited time and money at his disposal, and he began to think of his legacy."

Alistair breathed slowly, fighting back his nausea.

"He put out feelers," Nikolai said. "To people he knew of, groups he had heard of, always through intermediaries. Groups that shared his interests—antigovernment people, separatists, gun rights activists, visionaries of the libertarian state. Groups that he didn't care for so much—white supremacists, Confederate freaks, guys with Nazi memorabilia—but that he knew could be useful. Futurists, survivalists, preppers, militias. He saw at once what needed to be done, if only there were someone to do the work. All these people, these men, they were lying low, festering, hiding out on the internet. Herve wanted real action. And these groups were disorganized, they did not work together. They had no larger aim, no guidance, no leader. Herve felt that if you gave them a common mission, gave them structure and funding, they would be more effective. No one had ever tried it before, no one had tested their collective power. Let them have their little philosophies, their little flags. As long as their eyes are on the prize, they will be useful."

Alistair worked to open his throat. "Useful for what?"

"For a while it was not going anywhere," Nikolai said. "I assumed the project would die out, and I hoped it would. But then, last year, Herve got a lucky break. Right away, before anyone else, I think, he saw how valuable he could be."

"He?"

Nikolai took a sip from his mug and smiled bitterly. "Their candidate," he said. "Their big blond buffoon. He spoke to all these people, all these different groups. The man is so hollow, so vague, so meaningless, you can make him mean anything you want. Herve saw this. All these different groups, he could unite them under that man. He could tell them that their day had come, and that now they had to band together, so that they could make the most of this moment."

"Make the most of it how?"

"For the last year or so, the point persons—ex–law enforcement types, ex-military types—they have been recruiting," Nikolai said. "They have been buying up sites—camps, compounds, warehouses—where they can gather these groups. Where they can train them and lay out their plan." He caught Alistair's eye and looked at him pleadingly. "You must understand that I am not on board with this plan! I am only the money man. I am only the mediator. I set up the holding companies, I keep the books, I keep track of the point persons' progress and I report back to Herve. And I am the only one who speaks to him. The point persons know who Herve is, but the recruits know nothing about him, and they never can. That is my job—to make sure Herve's identity remains a secret."

"What is the plan?" Alistair said.

Nikolai shook his head. He laughed the way people laugh at funerals: strangely, helplessly. "Herve speaks of phases, and we are in the first," he said.

"Bring the men together, organize them, train them, arm them, and then start small. A demonstration here, a protest there. Show up at polling sites, show up at the next land dispute between the government and a rancher. Occupy a state capitol building, block roads, be seen. Get the message out. Recruit more followers, bring in more money. Show that you are many, that you are unified, that you are not going anywhere. Do this consistently, in every corner of the country. Show leaders at every level that you must be reckoned with. Bring more and more of them over to your side. Divide their loyalties. Sow chaos. Lay the groundwork."

"The groundwork for what?"

Nikolai sipped from his mug and exhaled slowly. "Herve talks of a final phase," he said. "The libertarian wet dream. The federal government brought to its knees, a new constitution, an America you would not recognize—a very old one. Herve likes the way America used to be, all separate communities, living as they please, by their own rules, with their own laws—'city-states,' he calls them. Unrestrained self-interest, unchecked will. He likes the idea of the vacuum the destruction of the federal government will create, because he knows what will fill it—free enterprise. The freest you can imagine."

"If that's the final phase," Alistair said, "what comes in between?"

Nikolai fell silent for a moment, turning the mug in his hands. "I have been to Herve's house, in Williston," he said. "He has big windows that look onto his property. The land there is flat, and you can see all the way to the horizon. He gets up early, he stays up late, he hardly sleeps. And all day he looks out those windows, and he can see nothing standing in his way."

Alistair pitched forward. "You're telling me about demonstrations," he said. "You're telling me about land disputes and occupations. And then you're telling me about a new America, with no federal government, with different laws. You're telling me about the first phase and the last phase and Andy's showing me guns, he's showing me maps. Tell me. Tell me what happens. What comes in between?"

Nikolai set down the mug and put his face in his hands. "I do not know!" he said. "Herve does not tell me, and I do not ask! I do not want to know— I cannot! Thousands of these people, eventually tens of thousands, all armed and angry. You can imagine, can you not? That is all I can do. That is enough!"

Alistair could hardly breathe. He put his own face in his hands. Attacks on federal buildings, kidnapped politicians, rogue networks in the military and police, a counter-media and a counter-trade, sieges and demands, secessions and barricades, contests over goods and natural resources ending in devastating, map-redrawing concessions: on and on his mind raced.

"My only comfort," Nikolai said, "is that I know it will never work."

"How do you know that?" Alistair said. "You just said he can't see anything standing in his way—how do you know that?"

"The men Herve is recruiting," Nikolai said, "they may be motivated, but they are stupid. They are only little boys. Their candidate will lose, and they will lose their fighting spirit. Herve cannot change the world, not by himself. Sooner or later his self-preservation instincts will kick in. He will see the futility of the project and cut his losses. And he has lost quite a bit already. He has spent ten million, though as far as he knows he has spent double that."

"As far as he knows?"

"As soon as I learned the truth, I began planning my exit," Nikolai said. "I have been putting money offshore. I guess my time in banking was not so useless. I am almost ready. If you want to live a long life and never work again, you need a lot."

"How can you be so sure he'll fail?"

Nikolai retrieved his mug and swirled it. "I am not so sure of anything," he said, "except that your country's future does not look good. The things Herve believes, the things his men believe, even if the election does not go their way, even if the project comes to nothing—I am European, I am familiar with all of this. I am afraid it is coming for you."

Alistair turned to the window, to the vast, twinkling city, and turned back. "Why didn't you go to the authorities?" he said. "Why aren't we going to the authorities right now?"

Nikolai sat upright. "You will not," he said. "We will not. Herve will do anything to protect the project, anything to protect his secrecy. If it were ever discovered that he is funding this operation, he would go to prison, and he would lose access to his billions, and then he would not be able to do anything at all. He will take any action to protect himself. He will, and he has."

Alistair held himself still. "What do you mean?"

"When you are dealing with so many people, there are occasional indiscretions," Nikolai said. "People who learn things they should not. People who open their mouths. I have seen people come, I have seen them go. And I have never heard from them again."

Alistair fixed his eyes on the floor. He willed it to break open, pull him down and swallow him, whisk him, by means of a magic portal, to any other reality.

"If Herve gets wind of any mistake, any betrayal, any deviation from absolute loyalty," Nikolai said, "he will act quickly. He will not tolerate liabilities."

Alistair said nothing.

"You were wrong the first time," Nikolai said. "How much better it would have been, if Herve was only cheating investors. But you were also right."

Alistair looked up.

"I have been living with this for three years," Nikolai said. "It is eating me alive. I cannot sleep, I cannot talk about it to anyone. And then you come along. Your face is like the sun. I thought, 'As long as I protect him, I can be less lonely.' And you did make me less lonely, and I have protected you. There is no trail connecting you to this project. There is no evidence you had any involvement with it. You should not have used your personal computer—Herve has people who can track these things. But I think, for now, that you are safe."

"Why me?" Alistair said.

"I told you. For three years, I am living—"

"Not you," Alistair said. "Herve. If he cares so much about secrecy, why would he let you bring me on?"

"He was not happy at first," Nikolai said. "But I assured him I had worked it so that you would not find anything out. I think he felt bad for me. He has his soft spots. And when I told him about you, where you are from, how you had struggled, he became interested. When he met you, he liked you. The men he is recruiting, he understands them, he feels for them. But there is something special to him about a person like you."

Alistair spoke over a lump in his throat. "Like me?"

"A person who tries to join the world Herve hates, to succeed among the elites, to play by their rules, but who is turned away at the door. Herve saw your desperation. He saw your pain, your anger. He believed you understood each other. He hoped you might join his cause."

It was somehow the worst thing Nikolai had said, somehow the very worst, because it was true. Alistair and Herve had, in a certain way, understood each other. And now the nausea returned. "What about Andy?"

"I will take care of him," Nikolai said. "I will pay him off and I will scare him. He will go quietly." He took the last sip from his mug and caught Alistair's eye. "And you will go quietly too. I will give you your last payment, when I have it. And then we will say goodbye."

Alistair held his gaze briefly and then looked away.

"I am sorry," Nikolai said. "I am sorry to see you go."

Alistair went. He returned to his dorm, pretending not to hear Vidi's greeting when he entered. He escaped to his room, rebuilt his cocoon, and remained in it all weekend. That he could do nothing, say nothing, forget nothing: the thought kept him pinned to his bed and kept him awake.

On Monday, in an access of terror and need, he accepted an invitation to the Eros Ananke. As he was preparing to leave Nikolai called him on the burner and told him he could come for his last payment. Alistair thought about refusing it, but having given almost all his money to Andy he knew he'd be in dire straits without it. It seemed the ultimate testament to the ultimate intractability of money that amid everything his mind should go here: that the homo economicus in him should never be diverted from the one object to which it gave absolute meaning. He told Nikolai he'd come but left the burner at home. In his hand the thing felt like fire.

When Nikolai opened the door to his apartment he handed Alistair the envelope. "I am taking care of it," he said. They lingered for a moment, staring at each other silently, and parted ways without a goodbye.

At the Eros Ananke he told Mark and Elijah that he'd quit his job with Nikolai. He felt he had to publicize his break from him, however vaguely, to make it real. Elijah proposed a meal out, and as they were leaving Alistair left his jacket, containing his envelope, on their couch. He assumed he'd return, he needed to return: to be naked with them again, a clean babe in the woods.

But things between Mark and Elijah had reached their logical end. At dinner they fought loudly, continuously, hideously. Alistair barely listened. He glanced up only occasionally and only at Mark. Even in his anger Mark's face still shone with tenderness, with discernment, with goodness. From where Alistair sat such goodness seemed a galaxy away.

Amid the men's arguing he gave up hope of returning to their apartment. He'd retrieve his cash the next day. Because he hung his head the whole way back to Palladium he didn't at first notice Nikolai when he arrived.

"I have been waiting here for hours," Nikolai hissed to him on the sidewalk. "I called you a hundred times."

Alistair noticed Nikolai was carrying a bag.

Nikolai said he'd contacted Andy and offered to get him his money. But Herve's tech hounds, it appeared, had seen Andy's emails before Nikolai had had the chance to delete them. Nikolai had begun to suspect something had gone awry, he told Alistair, when he'd kept calling Andy and getting only voicemail. Finally, hours before, just after Alistair had picked up his cash, Nikolai had thought to look up local obituaries. Andy's crucial mistake, Nikolai said, had been mentioning Herve by name in his last email. It wasn't about the money: a hundred thousand was nothing to Herve. But his name, his protection from the authorities, was everything to him, and there was nothing to stop a blackmailer from taking things too far.

"They made it look like a suicide," Nikolai said. "I do not know how, but I do not doubt they are professionals. A twenty-four-year-old kid with no money and a new baby—no one will second-guess it."

Alistair's panic kicked in with cruel immediacy. It gave him not a moment to feel anguish, to feel grief.

Herve's men were surely coming for them, Nikolai said. He himself was leaving that night and he suggested Alistair do the same. "I do not believe they know where you live," he said, "but it is only a matter of time." He went on, his voice a sharp whisper. They'd made a mess, he said, and Herve didn't like messes. Surely Herve believed he'd be better off if they were simply no longer around. "You have seen what he is willing to do. Now he is coming for us."

After Nikolai left Alistair went upstairs, spurred by his terror, slowed by his paranoia. The news of Andy's death came to him only as a fact that his fear processed with computational disinterest. Even all through the following day, as he said his goodbye to Mark, as he unloaded on Maura, as he boarded a ShortLine to Binghamton, he struggled to wrap his mind around Andy, to contemplate him as anything other than a factor in his panic. It occurred to him, as the bus made its way upstate, that he'd lived his whole life in one state of panic or another: a panic to get away, a panic to get rich, a panic to help his mother, a panic now to survive. His heart had been so consumed by panic that it had hardly been able to let in any other feelings. Little did he know, as he hunkered down in his seat, that when he arrived home he would have a whole summer to feel them.

On the Fourth of July Maura and Alistair made cookout food for their indoor, sunless holiday: pigs in blankets, a watermelon salad, a sheet cake with patriotic frosting. They didn't know when Nikolai would arrive, but they were ready. Alistair's duffel lay open by the couch.

Maura, peering at its contents, noticed the wooden cross lying atop a stack of T-shirts.

"What's this?" she asked.

"An experiment," Alistair said. "Maybe a replacement."

"For what?"

"Whatever I believed in before."

All day they talked aimlessly, letting the dread fact go unacknowledged: they had no idea when they would see each other again. Alistair hadn't yet told Maura what he had in mind; he'd hear out Nikolai's proposition first. But he was sure no proposition, however attractive, would deter him. Maybe previously he'd lacked the evidence to go after Herve, the evidence and the courage. But now that Herve was in New York, accessible if only indirectly, Alistair had an opportunity to gather proof, and the cross in his duffel had given him all the courage he could reasonably hope for.

He stared at his father's picture of Rio de Janeiro. He thought about asking Maura if he could take it with him, but it was as dear to her as it was to him, a living testament to Sean's dead dreams, and he'd remember it well enough.

At nine they heard the fireworks show at Recreation Park. From behind the shaded windows Alistair listened: imagined brilliant bursts, spreading pom-poms of red and blue, corkscrewing tendrils of dying sparks. He felt the grand finale in his chest.

The knock at the back door came shortly after ten. Alistair and Maura found Nikolai crouching on the patio, clutching a bag, looking back fearfully at the yard. He scurried inside, slamming the door behind him, and stood straight, taking in the kitchen. He wrapped his arms around Alistair and picked him up off the floor. "Oh!" he cried. "My friend!"

Nikolai was fresh-faced, fattened, energetic. Apparently two months on the run had done him good. "I must say," he said, setting Alistair down. "I understand why you got away from this town. It is a complete shithole."

"Mom, Nikolai, Nikolai, my mom," Alistair said.

Nikolai looked back and forth between them. "My goodness," he said, his face reddening. "The two of you."

Maura folded her arms and smiled guardedly. "I'll let you two talk," she said and went upstairs.

Alistair and Nikolai sat at the breakfast nook. Nikolai dug in his bag. "My friend," he said, "I have come through for you." He slid across the table a thick clasp envelope. "Driver's license, birth certificate, Social Security card, passport, debit card, all under a new name. It takes a while to get these things together. Even longer when you are on the run."

Alistair opened the envelope and inspected the documents. When he saw his ID he jolted. "How did you come up with this name?" he asked.

"I had to come up with something," Nikolai said. "It is a simple name. You know the kinds of names we use. George, Connor, Joey, Charlie. I am David. I always liked this name. David and Goliath—and look who won!"

Alistair stared at the ID in disbelief.

"You do not like your last name?" Nikolai said. "Miller does not have the same ring as McCabe, I agree."

"It's the first name," Alistair said. He shook his head. "It doesn't matter."

"Now," Nikolai said. "We have what we need to leave the country. We will stick to places with no extradition treaties, starting with Indonesia. After a year, we will begin putting out feelers. Try to figure out what Herve is thinking, what is happening with his project, if he will lay down his sword. But even if we never come back, we will be OK. I have enough money for us to live on for the rest of our days. I am thinking, almost, that it will be fun! You and me, on the beach. No jobs, no worries. But we must leave now."

Alistair studied the tabletop, measuring out his silence. He listened for the sound of Maura moving around upstairs but heard nothing.

"Hello?" Nikolai said.

"It's a big decision," Alistair said.

"Decision? You talk like we have a choice."

Alistair gathered the documents into a neat pile. "I have some demands."

"You are kidding me," Nikolai said.

"If I'm leaving, maybe for good, I need to make sure things are taken care of around here."

"What do you want?"

"I know you have an offshore account. I know you can move that money easily."

"And you are lucky for that!"

"I want you to set up an account for me."

Nikolai grunted. "How much?"

"A million," Alistair said.

Nikolai hooted. He slapped the table. "You are crazy, my friend. You are on another planet!"

"You destroyed me," Alistair said. "I have to go into hiding because of you. And I know you have it."

Nikolai looked around at the dingy kitchen, shaking his head and fluttering his eyes. "Fine."

"Good," Alistair said. "Now I want a second account. This one with two million."

Nikolai practically leaped off his seat. "Are you insane?" he said. "You are insane. How much do you think I have? You will leave me broke. Us—you will leave us broke!"

"I don't believe that for a second," Alistair said. "You led me to understand you have ten million hidden away, all stolen from Herve. Plus the millions in your personal accounts that I oversaw." He cocked his head. "How far off am I?"

Nikolai breathed furiously through his nose.

"You owe it to me," Alistair said. "You say you're my friend, then be a friend. You say the money's ours to live on in Indonesia, then deduct this from my half."

Nikolai gestured around at the cramped house. "Three million?" he said. "Who is this for? Who in your life could possibly need that?"

"Why do you need it?" Alistair said. "Why you and not them?"

"Because it is my money!"

"Is it?"

Nikolai sat silently for a while, clenching his jaw, stealing guilty glances at Alistair.

"Do it now," Alistair said. "Set up the accounts right now."

"It is late," Nikolai said. "Do you think I have twenty-four-hour service?"

"Yes," Alistair said. "With an account like yours, I think you do."

Grumblingly Nikolai took out his burner. The transaction was at once complex and strangely frictionless. To the person on the other end of the line (Alistair thought he heard a woman with a British accent) he rattled off a series of long numbers and passcodes from memory, an astonishing feat. He requested the establishment of two new accounts, funded with the amounts Alistair had specified, endowed with full owner capabilities. He grabbed Alistair's documents and read off his identifying information. With the phone still to his ear he mouthed "pen" and then wrote down, on Alistair's clasp envelope, the bank name and the account numbers and passcodes. He thanked the woman and hung up. He slid Alistair the scrawled-upon envelope. "Happy now?"

Alistair stared at the numbers. "You can easily move this money out of my accounts."

Nikolai tossed him the pen. "I can," he said. He sighed heavily. "But I will not."

For once Alistair knew he could trust him. He had him by the heart. "Where are you leaving from?"

"We," Nikolai said, "are leaving at six a.m. from Syracuse. Apparently your little airport does not do international flights. Which is for the best, I think. Imagine coming to this country, and landing here!"

"If I decide to come with you, I'll meet you there," Alistair said.

This was finally too much for Nikolai. He lowered his face almost to the tabletop and seethed. "What are you telling me? What are you telling me! You are being crazy, crazy, stupid!"

At this point Alistair was only letting Nikolai down easy. He wasn't going to Indonesia with him. He just needed him to leave the house with hope enough not to make a scene. "You should go now."

"You are thinking of not coming with me?" Nikolai said. "You would do that? I do all this for you, I give you all this money, I risk getting killed coming here for you, I promise to support you for the rest of your life!"

"Would have been a lot easier not to offer me a job," Alistair said. "Don't you think?"

"You will leave me all alone? You will abandon me? My friend?"

Alistair couldn't help it. He gazed at Nikolai's face. He tucked his accented voice away for permanent keeping in his mind. "I'll always be your friend," he said. "If I'm not at the airport, leave without me."

"I will!" Nikolai said. "I will not wait for you! You are being very stupid!"

"I know," Alistair said with a smile.

After Nikolai left, darting across the dark yard, Alistair sat at the breakfast nook, studying Nikolai's scribble. Maura came downstairs and sat across from him.

"You heard—"

"Everything," she said.

Alistair nodded. "Not everything yet."

"The money—"

Alistair held up a hand. "Later."

"You're staying here? Please tell me you're staying here."

Alistair shook his head. A few blocks away an illegal firework went off: an accelerating scream, then a silence, then a bang. "Let's have that cake," he said to Maura. "And then I'll tell you what I have in mind."

PART THREE

HO-HO-KUS

MARK'S MOTHER, JANET, was turning sixty. Her party was scheduled for the night of Friday, July 8, three days from now. The eighty-odd guests would convene at the Ridgefall Country Club, where they would sit at tables centered by vases of white peonies, dine on filet mignon with a zinfandel reduction or grilled halibut with a tomato coulis, listen to a local jazz band that specialized in "soothing" selections, and, should they step outside, find an outdoor bar and a lawn scattered with illuminated white spheres. The party planner, whom Janet had hired at a cost of $5,000, had managed every detail and done a fair amount of coercing in matters of taste. But the night before, while watching Fourth of July fireworks with Arty and Mark, Janet had decided she wanted balloons, something loudly and wholesomely festive, even if the planner had suggested, in so many words, that balloons were cheap. Earlier that day, then, Janet had gone to Party City and then dug out from the garage a helium tank left over from her much-ballooned thirtieth anniversary dinner, and now Mark sat with her at the kitchen counter, surveying piles of variously colored rubber. They inflated blue balloons, green ones, white ones, and black ones, holding their ends and studying them before letting them deflate.

"I like the white," Janet said.

"Everything is white," Mark said.

"White is nice. White is simple."

"This party is costing you thirty thousand dollars," Mark said. "Its connotation of simplicity goes only so far."

Janet squinted as if to shield her eyes. Money, Mark knew, was a gnat of complexity forever hovering at the edges of her vision, encroaching on what she considered to be simple pleasures. She was neither proud of her wealth nor protective of it; she would have liked everyone to have as much money as she did, if she thought about money at all. But her preference was not to think about it.

Mark attached a blue balloon to the nozzle of the helium tank. "Let's see how they float."

"Careful," Janet said. "Don't let it get away."

Mark tied the end, waited until the balloon had stilled, and sent it aloft. But the balloon had its own ideas. It bounced and bobbed toward the double-height great room behind them, passing the lip of the kitchen ceiling and drifting out of reach. As Mark watched it climb, putting his hand out helplessly, he had a memory of some kindergarten celebration, maybe a graduation ceremony, at which the children were encouraged to blow up balloons and release them into the air. He remembered panicking at the sight of his balloon flying away, vanishing into the sky. He remembered realizing, with a sense of injustice, that no adult force could stop it. He wondered now if that was his first-ever inkling of loss—the permanence of it, the inability of higher powers to redress it. The balloon rose and rose toward the great room ceiling and came to a stop between two wooden beams, twenty feet up.

"Shit."

"I told you to be careful," Janet said.

"I'll get it. I'll get the ladder from the shed."

"Let your father do it," Janet said. "Or Eddie, when he gets in."

Eddie was due in an hour. He'd stop in at Ho-Ho-Kus after landing at Teterboro—he'd spent the Fourth in Maine with friends from Boston College—and then return on Friday to make his appearance as the star child at Janet's party. At the mention of his name Mark felt his chest tighten.

"I'll get it," he said.

"Let Eddie get it," Janet said. "You'll fall."

Before Mark could reply he heard the garage door and the sleek machine heave of Arty's car. He looked down at the balloons, his gym shorts, his bare feet. He was supposed to have spent the day reading the CommonWay handbook. Instead he'd gotten up at ten, watched TV, and abstained from showering. The only real task he'd completed was a certain nonwork email that had taken him ninety minutes to compose.

Arty entered beaming. He saw the helium tank and the clumps of vaguely condom-like sacs on the kitchen counter and gaped cartoonishly.

"I want balloons," Janet said. "I don't care what the planner says! I want them!"

"If the birthday girl wants balloons, she gets balloons," Arty said.

"She does!" Janet said.

Arty looked around, possibly in search of Eddie, and noticed the blue balloon resting against the ceiling. "Oopsie?"

"One got away," Janet said.

"I'll get it down," Mark said.

"Let Eddie get it," Arty said. He inclined his head at Mark. "Give me a second and then come to my study. We'll have a little chat."

"About what?"

"Just a teensy-weensy chat."

Mark watched Arty disappear down the hallway. He helped Janet gather the balloons.

"What do you think Eddie wants for dinner?" she asked. With every minute that his arrival drew closer her eyes shone more brightly.

"I can't speak for Eddie," Mark said.

"Fish? He doesn't like fish."

"I like fish."

"I'll make steak."

Mark went into the great room and stood listlessly by the windows. He pulled out his phone, brought up his email, and scrolled to his conversation from earlier in the day, looking again at the address in Binghamton. He stared out at the placid pool, at the sinking sun, at a lawn boy hunched over a malfunctioning mower, hurling inaudible curses.

"Markie!" Arty bellowed.

In the study Mark found Arty perched at his desk, flanked by two green banker's lamps. On either side of him ran bookshelves outfitted with rolling ladders. Mark took a seat in one of the chairs opposite.

"Take a seat," Arty said.

Mark settled himself more fully to confirm his seat-taking.

"All ready for tomorrow? Yes? You're ready?"

"Yes," Mark said.

"Let's do a quiz."

"I'd rather not."

"Let's see if you've been studying."

"I've done this five times."

"But this is your first solo visit," Arty said. "This is a big step!"

"I can handle it, Dad."

"Question one," Arty said. "What's the first step in a park visit?"

"I do a drive-through," Mark said.

"Wrongo!" Arty said. "First thing you do is read the park file."

Mark breathed out slowly. "I don't have the park file."

"Good!" Arty said. "You need the park file. And here it is." He slid across the desk a thick black folder. "After you've read the file, and done your drive-through, what's next?"

"I talk to the park manager."

"And when do you talk to the residents?"

"After I talk to the park manager?"

"Wrongo!" Arty said. "You never ever talk to the residents."

"I feel like that was a trick question."

"It's a tricky business!" Arty said. "No talking to residents. Never ever. That's the park manager's job. Sometimes park managers ask regional managers to talk to the difficult ones. That's a deviation from protocol. But this park manager, Tricia, she's a good one. I don't think she'll pull that."

Mark tried to think of ways to terminate this conversation. "Any news on the sale?"

"What do you do after you leave the park?" Arty asked.

"I file my report."

"By when?"

"Within twenty-four hours."

"The sooner the better."

"I can handle it," Mark said. "It all sounds pretty easy."

Arty made a face of comic indignation that nevertheless shone with pricks of sincerity. "Easy!" he said. "You try building a company from the ground up. You let me know if it's easy."

Mark gave his flat, close-lipped smirk. He'd been wearing this smirk around Janet and Arty so much he worried he'd given his face new creases. "So the sale," he said. "Any news?"

"You sound like your brother," Arty said.

"I'm just curious."

"As is Eddie. Very curious."

"I think as an employee of the company I have more right to be curious."

"If you were only an employee I would say it's insubordinate of you to ask."

"Well, but I'm also your son," Mark said.

"Well," Arty said, swiveling in his chair. "Well."

Such were the awkwardnesses and ambiguities of Mark's new nepotistic employment. A week after he'd returned home in early May, Arty had sat Mark down in this very chair and made him his offer. He was willing to put more quarters in Mark's piggy bank, he'd said, but this time Mark had to work for them. After Mark had spent some time in the fields, put in his oar, touched his nose to the grindstone—Arty's speech was rich in obsolete work metaphors—then, well, maybe. Mark had had no choice but to accept, to work until Arty decided what came after "maybe." His impression was that after he'd toiled at CommonWay for a few months Arty would refill his piggy bank to its previous level out of the goodness of his fatherly heart. But in the weeks since he'd begun to doubt this impression. Arty had given him no timeline, no sense of what Mark had to do to prove himself, no hint of what rewards might come to him when he did. Mark felt that Arty was toying with him. He felt like a hostage whose kidnapper was also his ransomer. He languished all day in his dungeon hoping for a change in his keeper's whims.

And CommonWay did feel like a dungeon. Currently Mark was eight weeks into his three-month regional manager traineeship. He'd read less of the CommonWay handbook and worked fewer days than he was supposed to—Arty wasn't so hard-hearted as not to let his feckless son slack—but he'd learned enough to be repelled by his father's business. By now he'd gone on five park visits with the regional manager, Joey Spera, whom he would be replacing. Joey, a unibrowed divorcé from Metuchen, was being promoted to "district manager" (according to the handbook CommonWay had no fewer than nine managerial classes) and he was more than happy to leave his area of coverage, a vast swath stretching from Allentown to Rochester, in Mark's hands. "You'd think," Joey had said to him on his first visit, gesturing at the grim environs of Wilkes-Barre, "that if you lived in a mobile home you'd move your ass to a park in Florida. But that's the thing about these people. They stay put."

Joey, of course, knew as well as anyone that there was nothing mobile about mobile homes. Outfitting one for transportation and relocating it could cost upward of $10,000, and selling and buying elsewhere wasn't much of an option for many CommonWay residents: their dilapidated double-wides afforded them little purchasing power in greener pastures, and they had trouble enough paying the slim rents on their lots without the added burden of saving for better digs. Retirees with no pensions, single mothers on assistance, grizzled bachelors with half a dozen minimum-wage jobs, shut-ins subsisting on the charity of their relatives, couples with children of uncertain parentage, the occasional destitute newlyweds beaming with pride at their first home: every park Mark visited offered another Hieronymus Bosch of the American underclass, and with shame at his former naivete (artfully constructed, artfully maintained) he realized it was this underclass he had to thank for his top-notch schooling, his eight years of dissipation with Elijah in New York, and the palatial home in Ho-Ho-Kus he now returned to each day.

If initially Mark had been shocked by the CommonWay residents he now felt defensive on their behalf, because Joey Spera could be outright cruel to them. In referring to residents Joey made use of various zoological metaphors: the overweight ones were belugas, the disgruntled ones toads, the ones living six to a single-wide anchovies, the community agitators rats. In his conversations with park managers Joey clung with unwavering smugness to the clean lines and rigid bounds of bureaucracy. His favorite sentence was *The rules are the rules*. He signed off on evictions and advised fines and denied maintenance requests with spirited, merciless efficiency. He pried park managers for whispers of rebellion among residents, and when he heard tell of meetings or petitions or planned rent strikes he sent word to the district manager and waited with glee for the rainstorm of ominous letters from legal. Mark had decided that if he ever did take up his post as regional manager he would reign with a softer touch. He thought residents were rather justified in complaining about potholes or random extensions of "quiet hours" or inexplicable and immiserating rent hikes. But mostly his hope (and it turned the screw of his shame to entertain it) was that his father would bail him out before that happened.

Hence his interest in the sale. Not long after moving home Mark had learned that after thirty-five years at the company's helm Arty was ready to cash in. For six months now he'd been taking meetings with various private equity firms. Mark had gathered that mobile homes were something of a fashion on Wall Street (it amused him to imagine Alistair dissertating, with bountiful statistics and breathless jargon, on why), and he'd gathered, based on the numbers Arty was fielding, that CommonWay was seen as a prized get. The provisional offers on the table averaged $80 million. The firms were currently wrapping up their market research and had pledged to announce final figures shortly after the Fourth. Mark couldn't help but wonder if such a windfall might induce Arty to end his paternalistic theatrics and reopen his wallet. Indeed he couldn't help but wonder if such a windfall might induce Arty to give him a few more quarters than he had last time. But he never said this directly, because another thing he'd gathered was that the sale of the company was a touchy subject.

The reason for this was Eddie. Apparently, Mark's brother had labored for some years now in the delusion that when Arty retired he'd hand the company down to him. When Eddie had discovered that Arty was confabbing with private equity firms he'd begun showing up to Ho-Ho-Kus on weekends, cornering Arty, trying to persuade him to rethink his decision. Mark wasn't sure why Arty had decided not to bequeath the company to Eddie, though surely Eddie's alcoholism, amoral ruthlessness, and all-around terribleness were factors. He also wasn't sure why Eddie had such a keen interest in taking over the company, though it seemed likely that, with his firsthand knowledge of Wall Street fads, he understood CommonWay's salability and hoped to share in the $80 million himself. (To add insult to injury, one of the firms courting Arty happened to be Rend Kurtz McCrave, Eddie's employer.) Another thing Mark didn't understand was why Eddie had continued making regular visits to Ho-Ho-Kus and posing questions about the sale even after failing to bring Arty around to his side. It seemed possible that Eddie's curiosity about the deal was now much the same as Mark's: that he too wondered if Arty's windfall might mean a second round of generosity. But Mark didn't like the idea of him and Eddie having a shared motive, and he felt that Eddie's questions, in their needling persistence, had something else behind them.

Arty tapped his desk. "The more these conversations go on," he said, "the more I have my doubts."

Mark stiffened. "You're thinking of not selling?"

"Oh, it's too late for that," Arty said. "But I have my regrets. I've gotten up at the crack of dawn and looked after my little shingle every day for thirty-five years, Markie. I'm exhausted, I'm spent, I'll admit that. But I'll tell you, it gives me the heebie-jeebies."

Mark inclined his head in a show of sympathy. "What does?"

Arty looked up at him, with naked but unguessable emotion, then looked back down. "Going to my little shingle, every day for thirty-five years, and now—" He fell silent, as he did whenever he approached a thought that tested the verbal limits of his cartoonish persona. There was another person under that cartoon, but by nature or design Arty never let it come to the surface, not with his family, and for Mark this made him, especially where the sale was concerned, a source of continuing interest. He pitied his father for having as vast an interior as anyone but so pinched an expressive aperture. More to the point, he wanted to know what he was thinking. "You get up at the crack of dawn, every day, for this *thing*, this thing that means everything to you, and when you don't have that thing anymore—what then?"

"Maybe you can start by not getting up at the crack of dawn," Mark said.

Arty laughed. "I may have something to learn from you."

"I doubt it."

"And you have this too," Arty said. "You go about it differently, a little more slowly, sure, but you have it. Your writing! Markie the writer. I do hope, you know, that you're still finding time to write."

Mark said nothing.

"That's what I'll do," Arty said, palming his desk. "I'll read more. Write your book, so I have something to read."

Mark gave his smirk. He turned his eyes to his father's bookshelves, which contained photographs, binders, folders, paperweights, sports memorabilia, and maybe ten books. Five of these were John Grisham paperbacks, and the only one that showed signs of handling was *The Firm*. Mark had revisited his boarding school novel exactly once since moving home and been reminded afresh of its awfulness. It struck him as a dense, occasionally pornographic retelling of *A Separate Peace*. Paragraph upon paragraph clogged with ten-dollar words and impenetrable unnecessary subclauses. Everywhere the fusty odor of E. M. Forster and Henry James. For pages at a time not a concrete noun or active verb in sight—just terrible. He doubted he'd ever write again, but if he did he suspected a plunge into John Grisham might be useful. Maybe that was the way forward. Maybe he could put his antiquated prose into the service of a crude plot, throw together his tortuous abstractions with cheap thrills and stir, risk being rude and stupid.

He took the park file from Arty's desk and stood to leave.

"One more thing," Arty said.

Mark half sat.

"I know this is supposed to be your first solo visit. But tomorrow you'll have company."

"Dad, no." If Mark had to spend another day with Joey Spera he felt he would perish.

"RKM, as you know, is doing its market research."

"Eddie's firm?"

"Well, technically, yes," Arty said. "Though I'm sure Eddie has no dealings with the team working on this. Conflict of interest. I'm sure they put up a Chinese wall."

"I'm sure."

"They'd like to send one of their people with you tomorrow. Get a better sense of the parks, how they're run, that sort of thing."

"Who are they sending?"

"Name is Cliff Warnung," Arty said. "I've emailed with him. He sounds very . . . young. He shouldn't be a bother. You'll pick him up at the train station tomorrow, let him follow you around, then drop him off at the train station on the way back."

Mark thought of his email exchange from earlier in the day. When he'd learned he'd be visiting a park in central New York he'd looked up the town, Whitney Point, and seen that it was only a half hour from Binghamton. "I was hoping to make a stop on the way back," he said. "I want to see a friend. She lives in the area."

Arty seemed incredulous. "This a Hamilton friend?"

Mark, deciding he could make peace with a white lie, nodded.

"I love to hear that you're in touch with friends," Arty said. "But it'll have to wait. You need to bring Cliff back to the train station. And you have to file your report. The sooner the better, remember."

Mark said nothing as his mind worked. He gave another white lie. "I'll reschedule."

"And one more thing," Arty said. "This Cliff person—keep an eye on him."

Mark turned his head. "What do you mean?"

"He's a guest," Arty said. "I want you to be an attentive host."

Mark waited for Arty to explain further, but he simply stared.

"Understood?"

"Got it," Mark said.

On his way to the pool house he passed through the kitchen, where Janet was feverishly applying marinade. "Go change," she said. "Eddie will be here any minute!"

Back in May, after Elijah had decamped from the Eros Ananke, Mark had hired movers to collect his remaining furniture and deposit it in the pool house, where it had sat in haphazard, toe-stubbing arrangements ever since. He picked his way now past the deconstructed dining table, the stacked side tables and rolled rugs, and sat at his desk. He opened the park file, flipping through the tedious stuff—the financial stats and property stats, the legal matters and maintenance issues—until he got to his favorite part: the park manager's rundown of troublesome residents, the dramatis personae of rule-breakers and reprobates.

A man named Guy Noonan (lot 55, duration of residence three years, rent $375/mo.) refused to remove the black tarpaulin from his windows. *Neighbor in 56 says she smells something chemical*, the park manager, Tricia Lindquist, had written. *I'm worried it's some sort of drug lab. What if he blows the place up?* A woman named Yvette Collier (lot 226, duration of residence nine months, rent $475/mo.) refused to clear her children's toys from the yard. *Grass is ruined*, Tricia had written. *Toy guns, toy soldiers, toy tanks everywhere. Looks like D-Day.* A woman named Amber Osgood (lot 188, duration of residence two years, rent $425/mo.) was three months behind on her rent. *Her husband committed suicide in April*, Tricia had written. *My heart goes out to her. But the woman is a banshee. She's convinced her husband was murdered (!). Won't talk about anything else. Says she can't even think about her rent until she figures out what happened to him. Meanwhile, the eviction clock is ticking. I know this isn't protocol, but maybe the regional manager can talk to her? I wouldn't ask, but she's just so difficult.*

Not a chance, Ms. Lindquist. Mark was planning to be in and out of the park in two hours. He'd stick to his original plan. He'd help the kid from RKM find some other way back to New York, make his stop in Binghamton, then race back so as to arrive in Ho-Ho-Kus at a suspicion-averting hour. If Tricia pestered him about Ms. Osgood he'd simply instruct her to reset the eviction clock. He had no interest in making a grieving woman's life harder.

He opened his laptop and reread his email exchange. He wasn't sure why it had taken him so long to contact Alistair's mother. For the past two months he'd spent the good part of his waking hours wondering fruitlessly where Alistair was, whether he was safe, whether he was alive. Needless to say he no longer believed the story Alistair had given him in early May. That Alistair was going home for his mother's birthday, in the middle of the week during finals season, had seemed dubious then and seemed still more dubious now. He remained convinced, on the evidence of Alistair's anxiety that day, on the evidence of his evasiveness and his desperation to retrieve his cash, and on the evidence of a few details Elijah had reluctantly thrown his way, that Alistair had been in trouble. And yet Mark had been slow to reach out to the one person who might have had something concrete to tell him. He knew this to be his chronic problem: the stronger his feelings were the more afraid he was to act on them.

The easy part had been finding her email address: all he'd had to do was give $25 to a sketchy but impressively data-rich lookup site. The hard part—never a surprise for him—had been figuring out what to say. How to extract more information, any information, without scaring her away. How to explain that if he couldn't have Alistair he wanted, at the very least, to talk to someone who would understand his love for him. The draft he'd ended up sending was his eighth.

Dear Ms. McCabe,

I'm not sure if you know about me, but I know your son. He and I and my boyfriend Elijah were all friends, of a sort. (Sorry, trying to strike a balance between candor and discretion here.) Alistair left New York pretty abruptly in May, and I haven't been able to reach him since. I don't know where he is, or what he's doing, and I'm worried about him. If he's at home with you, I'll be happy to hear it, but I have the sense that's not the case.

I'm writing because I'll be near Binghamton tomorrow—I'm passing through for a work trip—and I was wondering if I might stop for a visit. Obviously, I'm hoping you can shed light on the matter, but even if you can't I'd still like to come. Just to meet his family, see where he grew up, would mean something. Maybe that sounds crazy, but your son was important to me—is important to me—and his vanishing has me feeling pretty crazy.

Best,
Mark Landmesser

He'd received a reply in the afternoon, shortly after two.

Hi Mark,

Don't worry about sounding crazy. Alistair has that effect on people. Of course he's told me about you, though he tried to strike the same balance you did, as if a mother can't fill in the blanks. I'm glad he found someone—two people, it sounds like!—to, shall we say, be close to. Sometimes I worry I'm the only person he'll ever be close to, and I worry that's my fault. But now I'm rambling.

You'll be coming to Binghamton. I'll admit that surprises me. One reason being that I can't imagine anyone coming to this part of the state for work. But if you'll be here, please do stop by. And if something comes up, I'll understand completely—really. The address is below. I get home from work at five. (Apologies to the Binghamton tourism bureau: we do in fact have an economy.) You can see our little house. It feels littler every day.

I'm afraid, though, that if you're hoping to see Alistair you'll be disappointed. He's hiking the Appalachian Trail. I know that sounds bizarre—believe me, I know. But that's the story on him, and I have no other information I can offer. But it sounds like you have mushy reasons to come anyway. It takes a mushy person to know one. And now I'm rambling again.

Really, though, if something comes up, I'll understand completely. Repeat: *I'll understand completely*. Otherwise, I'd be glad for the company. It's been a lonely summer.

Ramblingly,
Maura

Mark hadn't picked up a book since moving home, and Maura's email gave him a fresh opportunity to exercise his undergraduate enthusiasm for textual analysis. He noticed, to his relief, that she used the present tense in referring to Alistair—maybe she didn't know where he was, but she at least appeared to think he was alive. And when it came to his whereabouts Mark detected what he thought might be a sly admission. The idea of Alistair hiking the Appalachian Trail was indeed bizarre, and Maura's stressing of this fact suggested that she didn't quite believe the explanation herself, or that she was tendering it only out of obligation. The last thing he picked up on he couldn't make much sense of at all. Why clarify, three times in the space of a short email, that she'd understand if he couldn't come? Maybe she was only being modest; maybe she was only trying to find a kind way to put him off. But the repetition nevertheless struck Mark as strange. It was as if she'd divined, somehow, that he would be derailed.

Two weeks before, during their silence-breaking phone call, Elijah had advanced his theory about Alistair: he believed he and Nikolai had stolen money from Herve and absconded. He'd told Mark that Nikolai had disappeared too, that Herve had come to New York with the aim of determining where they'd gone, and that he dropped by Howie's apartment every few days to subject Howie, Jay, and Elijah to useless queries. Mark struggled to imagine Alistair committing high-level theft, and the idea clashed inconveniently with his sunny image of him, but he had no better alternative to offer. The only detail that weakened Elijah's theory was the fact that Alistair had been so insistent, that day in early May, on collecting his cash. If he and Nikolai had stolen enough money to merit going off the grid, why would he have needed five or ten thousand in loose bills?

In his desperation Mark had done some useless querying himself. He'd Googled Nikolai and found nothing relevant—only a spate of articles about some heady controversy from his banking days (apparently what Jay had been referring to whenever he'd ribbed Nikolai about his "scandal") that was several years in the past and that as far as Mark could tell bore no relation to his work for Herve. He'd Googled Herve and found almost nothing at all. He'd hunted for evidence of whatever obscure project Alistair had been working on. He'd tried to think of places Alistair would go, aliases he would adopt. He'd scoured the internet for any pictures of his social media–spurning infatuation. He didn't know why he loved Alistair as much as he did and he didn't care. His sense was that in the course of life every person got one preoccupation, one obliterating fascination, one call or cause or catastrophic exhilaration, and for whatever reason Alistair was his.

At the same time he knew this couldn't go on forever. If Alistair never turned up he'd have to find a way to move on, to trade his fascination for a different if surely dimmer one. Maybe that was why, two weeks earlier, he'd finally broken his silence and called Elijah, and maybe that was why he'd continued to lose sleep over Elijah's increasingly appalling life with Jay Steigen in New York.

Much of what Elijah described of this life during their call Mark already knew. He'd kept tabs on the unfolding of Jay's art project via Jay's Instagram. He'd seen beautiful models in grotesque getups, he'd seen photos of lurid parties peopled by strange men, he'd seen advertisements for Jay's "opening" at Howie's penthouse later in July. But Elijah had nevertheless told Mark everything, sparing him no detail—and there were grotesqueries beyond the ones that Mark already knew about, that never surfaced in Jay's posts, that Mark could never have imagined and that he suspected he would never forget—as if explicitness were the price of absolution. And Elijah was indeed sorry. He was sorry, he said, to have pushed Mark away, sorry to have traded their life for vacuous thrills, sorry to have quenched his thirst for freedom, to have seen his most perverse desires to their most perverse ends, at the expense of Mark's constancy and comfort. He'd had his fun and now he wanted to come home. He needed Mark, needed his ballasting goodness. He'd wanted to see who he'd be without it, and now he had, and he didn't like what he saw.

For all his revulsion Mark listened dutifully. He heard the pang in Elijah's voice and he felt the same pang himself. The truth was that he missed Elijah no less than Elijah missed him. In losing Elijah he'd lost the person who knew him most deeply, he'd lost his best friend, living without him was like living with a phantom limb—no grotesquerie Elijah described could change this. If anything the details Elijah self-castigatingly relayed only revived Mark's instinct to protect him. But he couldn't tell this to Elijah, not until he settled the matter of Alistair. He had his own thirst to quench, his own desire to see to its end, before he decided he needed Elijah in turn.

He stood from the desk. He went to the closet and selected his least wrinkled khakis and his least cheerful button-down shirt. He inspected himself in the mirror. Since moving home he'd acquired a summer tan and lost maybe ten pounds, chiefly by skipping meals with his parents and drinking his dinner instead, but he detected a new haggardness in his face, a new slackness in his body, as if his cells were replenishing themselves with inferior product. In such an access of mortal depression he almost looked forward to dinner with his family, who'd never stopped seeing him as a child.

He made his way across the backyard under an apricot-colored sky, amid darting birds and flickering fireflies, as all around him shadows darkened and evening gathered into a mournful, greenish-blue haze—New Jersey had no business being this beautiful.

When he entered the house he found his family in the kitchen, his parents sitting on stools and his brother standing at the counter, holding court. Eddie was telling a story and appeared to be winding down, which Mark was grateful for, but upon seeing Mark he started back up.

"Markie," Eddie said. "Listen to this." He wore a voluminous white polo and loose coral shorts. His hair, sun-blonded and long with summertime overgrowth, was tucked in pomaded clumps behind his ears. He'd poured himself a whiskey that, to judge by the flush in his cheeks, was not his first of the day. "Guess who my Uber driver here was. Just guess."

Janet and Arty turned to Mark. Janet was ablaze with motherly rapture. Arty was crinkling his eyes painedly. "Why don't you just tell me," Mark said.

Eddie gave the counter a hard slap for each word. "Robbie. Fucking. Malloy!"

"Do you remember Robbie?" Janet asked.

"No," Mark said. Robbie Malloy had gone to junior high with him and Eddie. He'd been a football wunderkind, preternaturally fast and strong, and before he'd transferred to boarding school in the ninth grade Mark had used him often for masturbation material.

"Oh, come on, you remember him," Eddie said.

"Such a wonderful kid," Janet said.

"Wonderful," Arty said. "Wonderful athlete."

"I don't remember him," Mark said.

"Yes you do," Eddie said. "Can you believe it? Robbie Malloy."

"If you'd asked me fifteen years ago, I would have bet on him going pro," Arty said.

Eddie sipped his whiskey and grinned. "Dude was a god," he said. "Now he's driving a fucking Uber."

Arty bowed his head. "Driving is honest work."

"So *handsome*," Janet said.

"What does he look like now?" Mark asked. He picked a piece of lint off his shirt as he said this, trying to disguise the homosexual interest in his question. Officially his parents accepted and supported him, but whenever he betrayed even the slightest desire, stared at a passing jogger or smiled at an attractive waiter, they looked away and fell silent, as if he'd splattered HIV-infected blood on the floor. Eddie, in all fairness, had never said an unkind word about his sexuality. He reserved his unkind words for everything else about Mark.

"He's an athlete," Eddie said with less spirit. "Guy's fucking ripped."

"I guess he has that on you," Mark said.

Eddie's eyes lit up briefly with hostility, but he said nothing. In the six months since he'd been dumped by his former girlfriend, a New School graduate named Eugenia, Eddie had put on conservatively twenty pounds. He'd had a dozen such girlfriends, but he was approaching thirty-three and had clearly been hoping to marry this one.

"Well," Janet said, flapping her hand, "he has *time* for that. He drives an Uber! He has *time* for the gym. That's why."

Eddie smiled reluctantly. He and Janet loved each other, rather creepily so, but it clearly dented his ego to have to lean on her for support. "Yeah," he said. "What a life. Driving an Uber. Good luck with that."

Arty rubbed his face and looked out the window. "I think life today can be very hard for someone like him," he said. "That hometown celebrity, those team values, that strength—it doesn't always translate into prosperity anymore. I'm sure he's struggling. I'm sure he's as surprised as we are."

Eddie met Arty's sympathy with revived arrogance. "Maybe you can help him out, Dad," he said. "Give him a rent discount. Find him a lot in one of your parks."

"Oh, Eddie," Janet swooned.

While Janet finished dinner Arty and Eddie went into the great room and disappeared into their phones. Mark poured himself wine and lingered awkwardly by the kitchen table. Where to sit, where to stand? How close to

the woman and how close to the men? All his closeted youth Mark had staged
this debate with himself. Mostly, as now, he'd staked out a neutral position, a
no-person's-land of gender equidistance, where he could be neither woman
nor man and where, as an added benefit, he could be alone.

"Boys," Janet called, to Arty and Eddie. "Dinner's ready."

In the dining room Eddie refilled his whiskey. Janet put her hand out
when the liquid neared the glass's brim. "I just worry you won't be able to
taste your food."

"Steak is excellent," Arty said.

"Delicious," Mark said. He eyed Eddie as he gave Janet's hand a pat.

Eddie observed this with a sneer and turned to Arty. "I hear you're meeting
one of our boys tomorrow."

Arty replied grudgingly. "Yes, well, I won't be meeting him. He's visiting
one of the parks."

"Joey taking him?"

Arty chewed a piece of steak slowly, as if savoring the excuse it gave him not to
answer. "Let's put this aside," he said. "I know you work at the same firm, Eddie,
but you can see how a conversation like this might not be—let's put it aside."

Eddie nodded and looked down at his plate, but Mark noticed he was
tensing his jaw. He seemed to have altogether stronger feelings toward Arty
than Mark did: a deeper hunger for his approval, a deeper resistance to his
reprimands. "Sure," he said. "We'll talk about it after dinner."

"Who is the friend," Arty said to Mark, "you were hoping to visit?"

"Just a friend," Mark said.

"Is this a friend," Janet said, "or a friend?"

"The former," Mark said. "It's a woman."

"A woman!" Eddie said. "Markie, you switching teams on us?"

Mark sipped his wine and set his glass down with a rigid arm. "Eddie," he
said, "have you heard from Eugenia?"

Eddie looked back and forth between Janet and Arty. "Are you seeing this?
Are you seeing this aggression? I don't say anything about Elias—"

"Elijah," Arty said.

"I don't say anything about Elijah, I'm very respectful on that front, and
here Markie comes, bringing up my ex, trying to make me feel bad."

"I was only asking if you'd heard from her."

"I haven't heard from her," Eddie said. "And I'm glad. If you want to switch teams, maybe you should date her. You'd be perfect together. Two kids with trust funds and hearts of gold. All spring she was volunteering for Bernie's campaign. You should've seen her Twitter. She was a fucking maniac. 'Soak the rich.' 'Fuck the one percent.' Meanwhile, she's rich! Richer than we are! She was going to rallies in Margiela sneakers. She was putting these long things on Instagram. 'Donate now,' 'Feel the Bern,' blah, blah, blah. And then you look at the picture, always a selfie, and she's on her dad's plane. Her dad's fucking plane!"

Mark often felt that if Eddie were a stranger he would mostly pity him. He would see in his brashness a panicked awareness that nothing he did and nothing he had would protect him from life's futility and certain end. Unfortunately, he was his brother, and he did not enjoy a stranger's privileges.

"Speaking of planes," Janet said. "I have given up on Colleen."

"She's not coming?" Arty said.

Janet shook her head gravely. "I tried once more yesterday. I have given up. I said, 'Colleen, I want you at my party. You're my sister, you're the only family I have left. I want you there.' She totally went off! She said she was *offended* that I would expect her to fly all the way from California for a *birthday* party. I said I'd pay for her plane ticket, and she said she was *offended* that I'd offer. I said, 'Colleen, what choice do I have? I want you at my party, and you can't afford the plane ticket, so—'"

"What happened to the ten thousand we gave her last year?" Arty said.

"She said she was *offended* that I'd assume she couldn't *afford* the ticket. I said, 'Well, isn't that what you're telling me?' I said, 'Colleen, you know I don't like to make an issue out of money, so why don't I just pay for your ticket and then it won't be an issue?' She said if I really wanted to see her I could wait until she comes back east for the holidays. She said it wasn't her fault that I live all the way across the country and that my birthday is in the middle of the year. As if those things are my fault? She said she couldn't *believe* the position I was putting her in. She said I had *no* respect for her. Meanwhile, every time I talk to her, I tell her how incredibly much I respect her! Being a teacher's aide, helping children, I think that's *great*. I think that's *so* important."

"Very important," Arty said.

"But here I am, coming out like the villain. For wanting her at my party! For offering to buy her plane ticket!"

"Honestly, I think you dodged a bullet," Eddie said. "I love Aunt Colleen, but she's a wet fucking blanket. All she does is talk about 'the children.' She's obsessed. The children! Oh, oh, the children!"

"Children are very important," Janet said.

"Very important," Arty said.

"This is my problem with Hillary," Eddie said. "She rattles on and on about 'the children.' Everything is about 'the children.' 'They're our future!' 'We have to leave them a better world!' Blah, blah, blah. As if there aren't adults living in this country too. And that's one thing I don't mind about Trump. You'll never hear him talking about children."

"Unless they're his children," Mark said.

"I assume," Arty said to Eddie, "that's the extent of your affection for Trump."

Eddie shrugged. "He's interesting," he said. "Would he be a terrible president? Maybe. But he's interesting."

As a rule Mark's family almost never discussed politics. But all summer long news of the election had invaded the house, spreading itself like a mist over their food, their conversation, every quiet domestic hour.

"I'm not sure we need our presidents to be 'interesting,'" Arty said.

With every sip of whiskey Eddie grew less restrained. "Don't get your Reagan Republican panties in a bunch," he said. "Maybe Trump is a little wild, maybe he's not the mannequin we'd all prefer, but he's classic GOP."

"Oh, I don't think that at all," Arty said. "He's emboldening some very scary people. Angry people, hateful people."

"Yeah, well, like it or not, those people are your party too," Eddie said. "And he's making them feel heard. You watch. They'll vote for him in droves. And he knows what he's doing. If he wins, he'll win on their votes, and then he'll do all the things someone like Jeb Bush would have done. Cut taxes, clean up bureaucratic self-dealing, put entitlement programs on a much-needed diet."

Mark eyed Eddie's bloated corpus and smiled.

"And those scary people?" Eddie said. "Those angry, hateful people? He'll throw them bones, he'll keep them under his thumb. But he won't help them. And neither would Jeb Bush."

"Well," Arty said, "I've always put more faith in private enterprise to help people. What those people need is jobs, homes, and opportunities. Government can only do so much. Why else do you think I go to work every day? I feel for those people, even if a few of them are bad apples. I like to think I'm helping them."

Mark had drunk quite a bit himself and was also feeling less restrained. "Do you really think you're helping them?" he said.

Arty turned his head as if it were on a revolving cake stand. "I'm sorry?"

"I just wonder if you really think you're helping your tenants. They don't seem to have very happy lives. They're stuck in their little homes. They can barely afford their lot rent. And every day we give them a new rule."

"Those homes may be little," Arty said. "But they're homes, and they own them. And if we make rules it's only in the interest of creating a safe, clean neighborhood. Isn't that what everyone wants? To own a home? To live in a safe, clean neighborhood? Isn't that what we give them?"

"I just think if you really want to help people there might be other ways to do it."

"Do you have ideas?" Arty said. "Because I'd love to hear them. Have you ever done anything to help people? I must have missed that. Have you worked tirelessly for thirty-five years? Have you built a company from the ground up?"

"No," Mark said. "And I won't be getting an eighty-million-dollar payout either."

Eddie glanced at Arty, then looked at his lap, sinking for a moment into some private thought. He turned to Janet. "This is what I mean," he said. "Mark and Eugenia. Perfect match."

After dinner and another drink refill in the kitchen the four of them gathered in the great room. Janet griped for some minutes about her party. Eddie listened avidly and impatiently. He stole repeated glances at Arty and parted his lips every so often, desperate for an opening. When Janet concluded a diatribe about the ever-recalcitrant party planner he spoke.

"Dad," he said, "can we have a minute? In your study?"

Arty avoided his gaze. "Maybe later. We're having family time."

"I'm leaving soon."

"So let's have family time."

Eddie sank into the couch with a huff. It was obvious to Mark, and obvious to Arty apparently too, that he wanted to ask about the sale, and Mark wondered again: Why? Why so curious? Eddie had reason to be angry at Arty, but Mark didn't see how nosing about the sale was supposed to offset his sense of injustice. He watched Eddie look fitfully around the room, down at the floor, up at the ceiling. His heart sank even before Eddie opened his mouth.

"What's that?" Eddie said, pointing at the blue balloon.

"We were testing colors," Janet said. "I told Mark to be careful. I really do think I like the white."

Eddie turned to Mark. "You let it get up there?"

"It was an accident," Mark said. "I'll get it down."

"No you won't," Eddie said.

"Mark will get it down," Arty said.

"No he won't," Eddie said. "He'll let one of you climb up there. He'll let Mom climb up there."

"Whoever goes up there should dust," Janet said.

Eddie downed his whiskey. "I'll get it," he said.

"No," Arty said.

"You've been drinking," Janet said.

"I'll get it," Mark said.

"No you fucking won't," Eddie said.

Eddie stood from the couch, barged through the patio door, and stomped across the backyard. Through the windows they watched him make for the shed. He emerged a minute later with the ladder over his shoulder, stumbling and careening under its weight. In his meandering passage he activated a security light, and for a moment, in the white glare, he looked like a killer in a horror film, a marauding, lame-gaited villain, hauling a signature if cumbersome weapon, intent on massacring them. As he passed through the patio door he banged the ladder against the jamb.

"Oh, Eddie, no," Janet said.

Arty sipped his drink and shook his head.

Eddie set the ladder up under the balloon. In his drunkenness he accidentally kicked it but caught it before it fell.

"Oh, I don't like this!" Janet said. "I don't like this at all!"

And yet her eyes, Mark felt, told a different story. Janet watched Eddie climb the steps with an alacrity, a consuming fascination, that seemed to him positively pelvic in origin. As he watched with her he entertained a cruel thought. He wanted his brother to fall, to crack his head open on the floor, not to die but to sustain a near-mortal wound, a frisson of death that would scare grace into him and dampen permanently his cocksureness.

At the top of the ladder Eddie fished out his keys. He separated one from the rest, reared back, and then lunged toward the balloon and stabbed it. Skins of blue shot to the floor.

"Oh!" Janet said with a spasm.

Eddie turned and looked down at Mark, relishing his height. "There's your balloon," he said. "Go pick it up."

Mark set his glass on the coffee table. "I'm going to bed."

"We have dessert," Janet said.

"Good night, Mark," Arty said.

In the pool house Mark waited for the sound of Eddie returning the ladder, but the yard remained quiet. He wondered if Eddie had succeeded in muscling Arty into the study, if he was swamping him again with his mysterious curiosity. Finally, a half hour later, he heard the squelch of Eddie's footsteps and the ruckus of his fumbling in the shed. But the steps that followed didn't seem to be retreating toward the house. They seemed to be getting closer. There came a knock.

When Mark opened the door Eddie had tears in his eyes. His breathing was heavy and his cheeks red. He jabbed Mark's chest with his finger, stabbed and stabbed at his sternum. "Don't you ever mention her again," he said. "You hear me? Ever." Without waiting for a reply he marched off.

Mark closed the door, went to the window facing the house, and watched Eddie reenter its glowing interior. He had a masochistic desire to observe his family in his absence: his strong parents and strong brother relieved at last of their weak link. What shared understandings, what easy air and knowing glances, could they exchange now that he was out of the room? But even as Janet went to Eddie and hugged him fulsomely goodbye Arty remained at a distance, standing at the window and staring out at the backyard. It took Mark a moment to realize that his own lights were on, that if he could see into his parents' great room they could see just as easily into the pool house, and that

Arty, with an expression impossible to make out against the backlight, was staring not at the backyard but at him.

––––––––

Mark arrived at the Ho-Ho-Kus station at ten. He slumped in the seat of his mother's "old" (2013) Mercedes, savoring his last minutes of peace. When the train from Secaucus Junction pulled in he watched the thin reverse-commute crowd scatter itself in the parking lot, looking for anyone who smacked of youth and private equity braggadocio.

Before Mark had left the house Arty had caught him in the kitchen. He seemed to have delayed his usual early departure to speak with him. He put his hand to Mark's shoulder, looked around for Janet, and spoke softly, pointing his gaze just north of Mark's eyes.

"It occurs to me," he said, "that I never actually gave Cliff your name. I told him what time you'd be there and the make of the car, but I only ever said he'd be picked up by the regional manager."

"I'm capable of introducing myself," Mark said.

"It occurs to me," Arty said, "that it might be interesting if he didn't find out quite who you are."

Mark narrowed his eyes.

"That he might say something," Arty said. "About the deal. To a regional manager that he wouldn't say to the CEO's son. And it seems possible that Eddie has mentioned his brother Mark. It seems possible that Eddie has said more to his colleagues than he should about a lot of things."

"Are you asking me to give a fake name?" Mark said.

"I would never ask you to do that."

"It sounds like you're asking me to do that."

"I just think it could be interesting," Arty said. "Maybe it could be useful."

"Useful how?"

Arty maintained his smile. "Maybe that's what I'm hoping you can find out."

It dawned on Mark, as he searched his father's face, that Arty had tasked him with this visit not so that he could acquire more field experience but so that he could carry out this peculiar errand. Joey Spera would happily do reconnaissance for Arty—he was ever the loyal hound—but he was clumsy, an aggressor lacking in scruples, liable to interrogate heavy-handedly rather than wait for information to come to him. Mark, by contrast, was nothing (to Arty's mind really nothing) if not delicate. "Is there something you want to tell me?" he asked Arty. "About the deal?"

Arty briefly met Mark's eyes. For a moment his mask of jollity slipped, and something else—something quicker, something older, something needier—broke through. But he only gave Mark's shoulder a shake and smiled again. "Markie the writer," he said. "Always watching, always listening. I think it's wonderful when a father and son can help each other out."

Mark freed himself from Arty's grip. This was a perplexing request and a daunting one. But he'd heard Arty's message, and he saw no reason not to play along. He was desperate for any inroad into his father's good graces, any chance to impress him and be rewarded accordingly after the $80 million came through. "I'll see what I can do," he said.

Now, in the parking lot, a fresh-faced boy came gamboling toward the Mercedes. He looked through the passenger-side window, nodded, and got in, bringing nostril-assaulting clouds of cologne and shampoo. He wore navy slacks and a pink button-down and carried a large backpack. His hair was parted at the side into two glistening dark shields.

"Sup man!" he said. "Cliff!" He shook Mark's hand as if he meant to break his fingers.

"Joey," Mark said. He'd thought of the lie on the way over. Cliff had no way of differentiating between Mark and his foulmouthed superior, and if Eddie asked Cliff whom he'd met with—as he'd tried to ask Arty the night before—Cliff's answer would raise no suspicion.

Cliff looked through the windows. "Beautiful out here," he said. "All these trees and shit? Feel like I'm skipping school. You live here?"

Mark reversed out of his spot. "For now."

"You're lucky, man. Can't imagine the square footage you get out here."

Mark turned onto Sheridan Drive and headed toward the New York State border. "We do have space going for us."

"I just bought this place in the East Village?" Cliff said. "Christ, dude. Half a mil for a *studio*. Seven-sixty a month maintenance. I can walk from one end to the other in twenty steps. Twenty. When I do my lunges, I have to move the coffee table. I don't even have a street view. All air shaft. Terrible. The mort-gage isn't bad because my parents helped me with the down payment? So I'm like, why not, right? But all my friends are like, 'Cliff, you're twenty-four. You don't need to buy yet.' But I think that's stupid. So fucking stupid. Buy if you can buy. Otherwise you're just throwing away money. I'm like, 'OK guys, let's check back in a few years. You'll still be renting, my place will have doubled in value, I'll probably have sold it already and gotten something bigger, and you'll all be sitting there feeling like fucking idiots. We'll do the math. We'll see how much money you threw away.' You know what I mean?"

The hours before Mark dilated into an eternity. "It's a long drive," he said. "Feel free to get in a nap."

"Oh," Cliff said, "I am *so* skipping school."

Cliff did shut his eyes, and somewhere between Goshen and Middletown did emit a dry snore, but after an hour he was awake again and refreshed. He fidgeted in his seat restlessly and looked out the window, but the breeze-stirred trees and magnificent high clouds failed to hold his interest.

"All right, Joey," he said. "Tell me your story. How's a guy like you end up a regional manager for CommonWay?"

By now they were approaching Monticello, which on previous visits Joey Spera had called the "gate to hell." Past this point upstate New York took on its true neglected character. No more New York City bedroom communities, no more Hudson Valley towns propped up by Manhattanites and Brooklynites with second homes. On either side of the highway lay miles of green whose untaintedness came at the expense of commerce. "A guy like me?"

"You're a good-looking dude," Cliff said. "Sound smart, got this car. I was expecting something else."

"What were you expecting?"

Cliff unwrapped a piece of gum and chomped. "I was picturing, like, a New Jersey dad? One of those Italians who's all like, 'Mozzarella!' 'Buon amici!' But he's never even been to fucking Italy?"

This was a scarily precise description of Joey Spera. "It's a job," Mark said. "It's fine for now."

"I get it, dude. You're probably interested in real estate development, and this is an in, right?"

"You got it."

Alongside them ran a blur of unmowed grass, flecked here and there with plastic bottles, fast-food bags, Styrofoam cups.

"You ever meet Arty?" Cliff asked. "Mr. Landmesser?"

"A few times," Mark decided to say.

"What about Eddie? His son."

Mark suppressed a smile. He felt a space of play opening inside him. It reminded him of how he'd felt, eons ago, when he'd put together the first, halfway promising sentences of his novel. "Don't think so."

"He's at RKM with me," Cliff said. "Fucking love that guy."

"Is he working on the deal with you?"

"On the record, no."

"And off the record?"

"He's got some information the other firms don't have. Being the guy's son and all. You think we'd pass that up? It's all very hush-hush, but he gives us what he has. In a competitive market like this, you need all the intel you can get. MH is the fucking rage now."

Mark had assumed only Joey Spera used this gratuitous abbreviation for manufactured housing. "Why is it the rage?"

"Dude," Cliff said, gesturing at the barren landscape around them, "open your eyes. You've got the bottom eighty percent of earners in this country taking in less than half of national income. You've got a workforce whose quote-unquote skills will be meaningless a generation from now, if they're not meaningless already. And there's no way they can get the sweet deals they used to. Back before oh-eight? All those fun mortgage structures? Interest-only? NINJA loans?"

"What's a NINJA loan?"

"NINJA," Cliff said. "No income no job no assets."

"I see."

"Point is, those days are over. Couple decades ago the American dream was a whatever. Four-bedroom attached two-car garage big lawn thirty-year fixed rate. No more. You have a huge number of people, growing every day, who not in their wildest dreams can swing that. Meanwhile government-subsidized housing is going poof. So now, what we're driving to see? That's the new American dream. I think in fifty years half of Americans will be living in mobile homes."

"You really think people will dream of owning a mobile home?" Mark asked.

"If they're not already, they should change their dreams," Cliff said. He lowered his window, letting in currents of manure-inflected air. He projected his voice over the wind. "Problem is, the companies who run these parks aren't used to Wall Street attention. They're totally old school. Way too fucking generous."

"Generous?" Mark said. This was the last word he'd use to describe his father, at least where his residents were concerned.

"Dude," Cliff said, "your CEO is *hemorrhaging* money. He's not playing this smart at all. We come in, we play it smart."

"How is he not playing it smart?"

"Uh, well, let's see. First of all, he takes Section 8 vouchers. Which is idiotic. Legally he doesn't have to, and they're a *huge* fucking administrative burden. Does it out of the kindness of his heart, which, whatever. And he's way below market on lot rent. We come in, those rents will go up thirty, forty, fifty percent *easy*. We'll charge extra for water and trash removal. We'll pull out all his pools, playgrounds, clubhouses. Total money pits. Eventually we'll sell off all the parks in New York and California. The tenant rights are just too ridiculous. And we'll give his home financing program a nice little makeover. He's missing an easy fucking opportunity on that one."

"How?" Mark said.

"You tell these tenants they qualify for financing, you tell them what they'll owe for the first couple of years, you see the stars in their eyes. Then, little ways down the road, their payments skyrocket. They're all like, 'What the hell!' And you pull out the contract and flip to page five thousand or whatever and point. 'It's all there! You signed!' Not our problem. These people can read. Most of them, at least. We give them all the information. But Arty won't do anything like that. Says it gives him the 'heebie-jeebies.' He loves that phrase by the way. 'Heebie-jeebies.' Guy's a total dork."

Mark said nothing. He fantasized about an eject button that would fling Cliff into the passing fields.

"And he's super fucking shady," Cliff said. "Very nontransparent. We like our deals *clean*."

DANIEL LEFFERTS

"What do you mean nontransparent?"

Cliff shrugged. "There are some gaps," he said. "Discrepancies. Things Arty doesn't seem to want to disclose. I don't blame him. I'd do the same thing if I were him. But if he wants the big one he'll have to open his mouth a little wider."

Mark was surprised to feel a throb of indignation. "Is that why you're here today?" he said. "To look into these discrepancies?"

Cliff turned in his seat. "You're not gonna say anything?"

"I don't care enough about this job to bother."

"That's the spirit. Sounds like you're ready to make your next move."

"As soon as I'm able to," Mark said.

"I get it, man. Before RKM, I was at JPMorgan? In I-banking? Fucking terrible. *Zero* involvement in strategy. That's why I love private equity. I'm in the field." He pointed out the window. "I'm literally in a field! I'm making things happen. It's all on the buy side now. The buy side is where it's at."

"I know someone who worked at JPMorgan," Mark said.

"Yeah? What's his name?"

Mark immediately regretted alluding to Alistair. Some strange competitive instinct seemed to be working through him. He wanted Cliff to know that he could speak his language, even though he couldn't and would never want to. "You probably don't know him."

"Well, I hope he left," Cliff said. "Sooner or later, that place will kill him."

They arrived at the park shortly after one.

"I'll do a little drive-through," Mark said, "and then meet with the park manager."

Cliff had taken a laptop out of his backpack and was shuffling between various spreadsheets. "Sure."

Mark eased up the main road, surveying the spread of shallow-roofed homes, columned and rowed in a tight grid. On either side of the park lay acres of hayfield.

"Listen," Cliff said, "while you talk to the park manager, I think I'll walk around on my own."

"And do what?" Mark said.

"You know anything about these PO homes?"

Mark worked to recall the relevant section of the CommonWay handbook.

The majority of homes in CommonWay's parks were resident-owned, but occasionally, to offset vacancies, the company bought homes and sold them to buyers directly. At any given time a fraction of homes were as yet unsold park-owned ("PO") homes. "What about them?"

"So the rent roll CommonWay gave us," Cliff said, gesturing at one spreadsheet, "is telling me that just twenty-one out of three hundred homes here are POs." He switched to another spreadsheet. "But this other rent roll is giving me only a hundred and ninety-three heads of household."

Mark continued up the road. The numbers passed through one ear and out the other, finding no purchase in his math-averse brain—and yet he felt the start of a tingling on his neck.

"The rent roll CommonWay gave us tells a totally different story," Cliff said. "Two hundred and seventy-nine heads of household. Which fits with their math."

Mark kept his eyes on the road as the tingling spread. "What's the problem?"

"Both rent rolls are from last month. There's a difference of eighty-six heads of household between them."

"What are you saying?"

"I'm saying it'll be really interesting to knock on some of those eighty-six doors," Cliff said. "Find out if anyone actually lives in those homes. I'm not seeing anything about a third-party LLC owning them. And in any case a third-party LLC couldn't own more than five percent of homes in a park, and the park itself couldn't own more than fifteen percent—no bank would touch that. Eighty-six plus twenty-one is what? A hundred and seven? And a hundred and seven is what? What percent of three hundred?"

Mark pursed his lips.

"Thirty-six percent? Thirty-six percent! I'm *definitely* walking around on my own."

For a moment Mark said nothing. In fits and starts the half-glimpsed facts and dim conjectures settled. He knew, of course, that his father would never want him to let Cliff go off on his own—he now suspected Arty's cryptic guidance the day before had been tailored precisely to this eventuality—but in light of this new information he also no longer knew where his loyalties lay. Everything Cliff had told him had redoubled his disdain for his father's line of business. That the incoming firm would make the residents' lives even worse than they already were sickened him; that Arty surely knew this but was too keen to cash out to care sickened him further; and that he himself had agreed to be Arty's ear, to help protect his exploitative and (if he was understanding Cliff correctly) possibly spurious gains in the hope of sharing in them: this sickened him most of all. He saw, as he stared up the sunbaked road, no obvious course of action, no obvious choice of whom to help and whom to harm. His mind was a wash of obscure, ambiguous instincts—some valorous, some cynical, some an uneasy mix of the two—that in the end manifested only as a paralyzing inertia. He put up no resistance to Cliff's declaration. All he did was ask one more question, though he had a guess already as to the answer.

"Who gave you the other rent roll?" he said.

Cliff shrugged. "It's ours now. That's all that matters."

Mark fell silent and began the drive-through. He fished a notebook and pen from the backseat and, using his steering wheel as a desk, jotted down every violation in sight. He was supposed to drive past all three hundred homes, but out of laziness he subscribed to a pollster's logic: a quarter of them probably offered an accurate enough picture of the rest. Trash bags left outside at lot 3, porch steps broken at lot 17, grass too long at lot 26. Artificial flowers at lot 33, for some reason a violation. Men tinkering with a car in the driveway at lot 40, for some reason also a violation. As they turned onto the next lane they saw a Trump sign in the yard of lot 51.

"Christ," Cliff said.

CommonWay had a long-standing rule against political paraphernalia. But in recent months park managers across the country had reported vociferous pushback from residents with Trump signs. After a park manager in Indiana had sustained a punch to the face the company had announced a moratorium on the rule until after the election. The moratorium was technically politically agnostic, but there were never any Hillary signs to ignore.

He came to a stop in front of the park office. Cliff got out, holding his laptop open on his arm, and began walking up the main road.

Mark let him go. Compounding his paralysis was his fear that if Cliff joined him in the park office and heard Tricia Lindquist address him by his real name his cover would be blown.

"Wish me luck!" Cliff called back.

Mark did wish him luck. He noticed a few nearby residents staring at Cliff, this business-attired brat walking with princely pomp through their park. He wouldn't have been surprised if some of them gave him trouble, and he wouldn't exactly have blamed them.

He entered the park office. Tricia Lindquist, blond and bespectacled and clad in a robin's-egg blouse, stood behind the counter. The first thing Mark noticed was the conspicuous flatness of her chest, and then he remembered something Joey Spera had mentioned: a long sick leave, a double mastectomy.

"You're Mark?" she said.

Better, obviously, not to have let Cliff come in with him. "That's me."

"The scion?"

"Today I'm just an employee."

Tricia eyed him half maternally, half flirtatiously. "And tomorrow you'll inherit the earth."

Mark took the flirtational bait. "I thought that was the meek."

"Maybe you're a meek scion," Tricia said.

He approached the counter, passing tables festooned with pamphlets and a window darkened by a chugging AC. He laid his notebook on the counter and rattled off the violations he'd noticed. "Little things, mostly."

Tricia peered at the notebook with a frown. "I've never understood the rule about fake flowers."

"Neither have I," Mark said. "But it's a rule."

"You sound like Joey."

"Please don't say that."

Tricia smiled briefly and then frowned again. "And I enforce the rule. Everything you've written here I've told residents about time and again."

"You can always impose fines."

Tricia looked up at him searchingly. "These people have so little money," she said. "You saw my report. I'm as annoyed as you are."

"I'm not annoyed. If it were up to me—"

"If I started handing out fines for every little thing I saw, I'm telling you, there'd be an uprising. People would leave. The park would be empty. It's a third empty already."

Mark thought of Cliff's one hundred and seven PO homes.

"I already stopped taping the mailbox shut at five p.m. on rent day," Tricia said. "Even though Joey would go berserk if he found out. Just to collect a hundred-dollar fine from someone who tries to drop off their check at five-oh-five? Some of these people don't get off work until midnight. It's cruel."

"Your secret is safe with me."

Tricia reached under the counter and brought out a ream of crinkled papers. "Lot of maintenance requests."

Mark uncapped his pen. Technically he was supposed to read each request and study each cost estimate carefully. One of CommonWay's "goals of the year" for 2016 was to reduce maintenance expenses by twenty percent. But Mark had no interest in contributing to this goal, and as ever he was lazy. He signed the whole pile in minutes.

"I guess you're not like Joey," Tricia said. "Now for the big problem."

"The woman who isn't paying her rent."

"You need to talk to her. I can't anymore. At this point I fear for my safety."

"Just forget the last three months," Mark said.

"That'll only embolden her."

"I'm not supposed to talk to residents. You know that. That's your job."

"She frightens the daylights out of me," Tricia said. "But I don't want her evicted. Joey is always on my case about being soft. You seem a little soft yourself, so. This woman lost her husband. I think she quit her job. She's got a baby. I lose sleep thinking about what goes on in that house. She's driving herself crazy with all these conspiracies about her husband's death. She can't punish whoever she wants to punish, so she's punishing anyone in sight. Frankly, I get it. But I think a visit from top brass might put some fear into her."

Something about Tricia, her kindness, her recent brush with death, gave her an air of irrefutable moral authority. "Is she home now?" Mark asked.

"She never leaves."

"You have one of those payment forms?"

"You think she'll pay now?"

"Easier for her to sign a paper than drop off a check."

Tricia rooted around under the counter and handed him a form. "Don't be too hard on her," she said. "Don't force her hand."

"I'm taking it just in case."

"In case of a miracle."

Outside Mark listened for Cliff's voice, but all he heard were distant TVs, syncopated sprinklers, singing insects. As he walked up the main road he passed lot 51, of the Trump sign, and this time saw the owner outside, hunched over a lawnmower. The man was young, shirtless, and exquisitely built. When he noticed Mark he stood and revealed unexpectedly patrician features. They nodded at each other and Mark walked on. He fought off a tingling in his groin. He'd seen such men on previous visits, rakishly handsome, fatless and firm, sheathed in veiny muscles. They were gods to their fellow residents, idols to the men, blessed botherations to the women. They enjoyed an esteem within the park's limits that they enjoyed nowhere else: went to their jobs and suffered the humiliations of a corporatized economy and then returned here, where they ruled according to an older system, a politics of virility, an erotics of martial law. He wasn't surprised that such a man would display such a sign, swear his loyalty to such a person. Trump alone promised, however emptily and self-servingly, to extend his dominion back into the wide world.

He arrived at lot 188, stepped onto the porch, and knocked.

The woman who opened the door had dyed red hair and a preemptively hostile expression. She wore a ribbed yellow tank top that seemed designed to do the opposite of flatter her figure and complexion. Behind her, in the living room, a baby boy sat on the floor, playing with a ring of rainbow-colored keys. "Yes?"

"Are you Amber Osgood?"

"Who's asking?" Amber said.

"My name is Mark Landmesser. I'm with CommonWay."

"Landmesser? Like, the CEO of this place?"

"I'm a relative."

Amber's expression grew more hostile. "What do you want?"

"I'm wondering if we can have a little chat," Mark said. Only when he heard the wobble in his voice did he realize how much this woman intimidated him.

"About what?"

"About how you're doing."

"I'm doing fine."

"May I come in?"

"I don't have to let you in."

"I know," Mark said. "That's why I'm asking. I'm here to help."

The baby boy on the floor made a paralinguistic sound, something like *hunter* or *hundred*.

Amber stepped two inches to the side and turned. "Be my guest."

The home was a single-wide, fifteen by seventy-two, and its interior was a model of light absorption: burgundy carpet, chocolate brown furniture, dark oak cabinets and tables. The curtain was a microfiber Buffalo Bills blanket cinched with a hairband.

Amber heaved herself onto the couch and nodded for Mark to take the armchair. She shut off the TV and put her hands in her lap. "So."

Mark laid his notebook and the payment form on the floor. The baby boy stared at him dumbfoundedly. Mark wondered if he was the first non-Amber person he'd laid eyes on in months. "I understand you've been having trouble paying your rent," he said.

"I've been having all sorts of trouble," Amber said. She pulled from the coffee table a clunky plastic object, put its end in her mouth, and emitted a plume of vapor. She spoke to the wall. "It doesn't hurt the baby."

"Are you working?" Mark asked.

"Nope."

"You were let go?"

"I quit."

She had no interest, it appeared, in presenting a sympathetic case. "Any reason?"

"I was night shift at a hospice," Amber said. "You think I wanted to be around all that death?"

"Right," Mark said. "After your husband."

"We weren't married," Amber said.

Mark waited a moment, wondering whether to push on this subject or skirt it. "Are you on unemployment?"

Amber emitted another plume. "Here's a lesson for you, rich boy. You don't get unemployment if you quit."

"There are programs for single mothers," Mark said. "Assistance programs."

"You try filling out all that paperwork."

"Can I ask when your husband passed away?"

Amber glared at him. "We weren't married," she said, "as I told you. And he didn't 'pass away.' He was murdered."

"When did this happen?"

"End of April."

"I'm sorry," Mark said. "I'm sure he was a wonderful father. A wonderful husband."

Amber brought her palm down on her thigh. "We were not! Fucking! Married!"

Mark shrank back in his chair. He glanced at the baby, who continued to stare at him. "I don't mean to upset you."

"You're doing a wonderful job of it."

"I was under the impression that your—partner—"

Amber rolled her eyes.

"—that he took his own life."

"Yeah, well, everyone's under that impression," Amber said. "The police, his family, everyone in this hellhole park, everyone in fucking town. But they're wrong. He was murdered."

"Why do you think that?" Mark said. He didn't like asking these questions, and he didn't like hearing Amber's answers, but he hoped that if given the chance to vent she might become more reasonable.

"Weird fucking shit happening in that warehouse," Amber said.

"Warehouse?"

"He was taking care of this warehouse," Amber explained grudgingly, "over in Richford. Mowing the lawn, shoveling snow, that kind of shit. New company moves in, pays him triple what he'd been making, and nothing goes in the warehouse. So that's all fucking weird to start. Then, end of April, he comes home saying there's weird people there now, going in and out, doing weird shit. Won't tell me a thing, doesn't want me to worry. I keep asking him, he keeps his mouth shut. But I could tell from his face, he was scared. Then, boom, week after he tells me about all these weird people, doing their weird shit, cops find him in his car, off the road in the woods, with a hose going from his exhaust to his window, everything all duct-taped. You tell me. You tell me."

She reached for a framed photograph on a side table and chucked it at Mark. The corner of the frame jabbed his stomach. "That was taken in November. You tell me that's the face of someone who'd fucking gas himself to death."

The photograph showed Amber, her boyfriend, and the baby outside the home Mark was now sitting in. He was struck at once by the resemblance. The dead man had Alistair's hair color, his eye color, his bright smile. His face shone with the same skyward yearning. Amber was right: he didn't look like someone who would take his own life. But then Alistair didn't look like someone who would disappear.

For a minute the only sound in the room was the aimless murmuring of the baby. Mark stared at the stained burgundy carpet. The picture of Amber's boyfriend had left a ghostly image in his mind, and it was this image, maybe, that finally sunk him, finally brought home to him what he couldn't deny any longer: he would never see Alistair again. If he wasn't dead he was in hiding, and he had no desire to be found. All at once the delusion he'd been subsisting on for two months collapsed. He shut his eyes and breathed out quietly. He felt his shoulders fall, his stomach drop, his blood slow.

"And now you're here," Amber said, "and you're probably trying to evict us, aren't you."

Mark heard himself reply as if from afar. "You're three months behind."

"Like you need my four-twenty-five a month," Amber said. "Like you and your family will starve without it."

Mark opened his eyes but kept his gaze on the floor. "I understand your pain."

"You don't understand," Amber said. "You could never. You don't!"

Mark looked up at her. "I understand," he said.

Amber may have seen his dawning realization in his face. She fell silent. When the baby began crawling into the kitchen she reached down and hoisted him onto her lap. She looked at Mark defensively, as if afraid that in showing tenderness she'd forfeited an advantage. "What am I supposed to do?" she asked softly.

Mark took his things from the floor. He laid the payment form against his notebook and reached for his wallet. He couldn't keep asking Tricia to ignore Amber's delinquency on his questionably authoritative orders. He went for the company American Express but he couldn't do this either. His father's accounting team was scrupulous and he wouldn't be able to explain the charge. He slid out his personal debit card and copied the numbers onto the form. He tried to multiply $425 by some generous number of months, but his mind was a fog of grief and he gave up and wrote $5,000.

He stood and held out the form. "Give this to Tricia."

Amber rocked the baby. "I don't want your charity."

"Take it," Mark said. "Please."

Amber reached out and snatched the form quickly. She seemed to fear that the moment she made for it he'd take it back.

"I'm sorry to have bothered you," Mark said.

Amber made no reply and he left.

When he emerged onto the main road he saw Cliff sitting on the hood of the Mercedes, speaking into his phone in a hot whisper. When he saw Mark he leaped off the hood, raised an index finger, and scurried down one of the lanes. Mark decided a conversation Cliff didn't want him to hear was one he might like to hear, and a minute later he followed.

Cliff, standing at the end of the lane with his back to the main road, spoke quickly, jubilantly, with astounded shakes of his head. Mark crept halfway down the lane, for now devoid of residents, until he could hear his every word.

"Not a one," Cliff said into the phone. "They're fucking *empty*, dude." He listened to the person on the other end of the line. "No shit. If this is happening at all the parks? Eighty? They're fucking delusional." He listened and nodded. "That's what I'm saying. This is an ideal situation. Tainted asset, solid fundamentals. We can get this thing *cheap*." He nodded again. "Let's talk to all of them. Anyone in the running. Race to the fucking bottom now." He hooted. "I still can't believe it. In your dad's fucking study! I could kiss you, man. Seriously, I could kiss you!"

Mark, having heard all he needed to, walked back to the car and waited. When Cliff returned his face was glowing. It seemed beyond him to imagine that Mark had eavesdropped on him, or that it would even matter if he had. As far as Cliff knew Mark was Joey, and Joey was a nobody, a negligible sub-urbanite with a crap job. When he got into the car his eyes passed over Mark's face as if he were a server obstructing his way at a party. All at once Mark understood how Amber must have felt standing at the door of her trailer. *This person doesn't see me. I'm no more real to him than a gnat. An hour from now he'll go back to his life and forget he ever met me.*

Mark drove out of the park and turned onto the highway. Cliff, typing madly on his phone, deigned to make small talk.

"How was your—whatever you did," he said.

"Less interesting than your whatever, I'm sure," Mark said.

Cliff, deaf to Mark's words, put down his phone and breathed triumphantly. "Let's pick up the pace a little. I have to go back to the office."

"I'm not taking you back to New Jersey," Mark said.

Cliff turned to him. "I'm sorry?"

"I'm stopping in Binghamton. It's a half hour away. I'll drop you off at the bus station."

Cliff gaped. "Are you kidding me?"

"There's a ShortLine," Mark said. He remembered Alistair's griping about the bus, about the economy-stifling lack of commuter rail to his hometown. "It leaves every two hours."

Cliff hackled. "You're out of your fucking mind. You're taking me back to New Jersey. I'm not getting on a bus."

"People ride buses all the time," Mark said.

"Not me!" Cliff said. "I don't!"

"Well, you can start today."

"You can't be serious," Cliff said. "This is unacceptable."

"I'm sorry you feel that way," Mark said.

Cliff fretted in disbelief for another minute. Then he thumbed his phone and dropped it with a clatter into a center cupholder. The screen showed Google Maps directions to an Enterprise outside Binghamton. "Guess I'll rent a car!" he said. "Since I'm being stranded in Shitsville! Gotta say, CommonWay, impressing me more every minute!"

They drove in silence. When they arrived at the Enterprise, in a town called Vestal that seemed mainly to consist of a parkway, Cliff got out with a huff. He put his face to the open window. "Just want to say, for clarity's sake, this is so fucking unprofessional."

Mark saluted him and drove away.

At a quarter after five he made his way to Binghamton proper, cruising down a wide riverfront road flanked by crumbling mansions. He entered a neighborhood of narrow houses on cramped lots. In winter the place was surely bleak, but now a yellowing sun was bearing down on the trees, brightening their leaves, raining coins of gold onto the sidewalks. For all its postindustrial decay the city radiated nostalgia, evoked a midcentury Arcadia of friendly neighbors, young families, Cronkite in the evenings and Mass on Sundays, children playing games in the street.

He was gladdened but not surprised to see that Alistair had grown up in the best-cared-for house on his block. When he came to a stop he took in the bright white siding, the black shutters and tall windows, the small but flourishing garden, and the deep tidy porch on which, he saw, a pretty blond woman sat.

As he emerged from the car and crossed the street Maura stood. Mark couldn't believe how much she resembled Alistair. She seemed to have made him all by herself. On the porch they greeted each other awkwardly, putting both hands in the other's, smiling with fleeting eye contact, and sat.

"So you came," she said. "I guess nothing kept you."

Mark wondered again at her insistence that he'd be derailed. "I wouldn't miss this," he said.

Maura looked out at the street. "I hope it's not a disappointment."

"It's lovely," Mark said. "I'm sure it was a great place to grow up."

Maura laughed this away. "I'm glad the weather cooperated," she said. "We don't get a lot of days like this. Usually it's pretty cold and gray. Sometimes I look at those scary maps? Here's where temperatures will go up, here's where sea levels will rise? Apparently not much will happen to Binghamton. Not even climate change wants to come here."

The irony in her voice, the acuity, the appealing hint of hauteur: she sounded just like him too. "Alistair did always talk about it as a place he was . . . eager to leave," Mark said.

Maura smiled to herself. "And leave he did."

There passed a moment of silence during which they only played with their hands and made the same fleeting eye contact.

"We can go inside in a minute," Maura said. "I'm trying to maximize my fresh air. I've been pretty cooped up all summer."

Mark thought to ask why but then swallowed the question. He imagined weeks of wondering, Googling, catastrophizing, sitting in dark rooms in despair. "I'm assuming you haven't heard from him," he said.

"Since we emailed yesterday? No."

They fell silent again, looking at each other and looking away.

"You want to ask me a million questions," she said.

"But you don't have any answers," Mark said.

"Probably not to the questions you want to ask."

Mark thought he saw in her face the same sly admission he'd detected in her email. She seemed to be all but confessing, in the warm intelligence of her gaze, that the story about the Appalachian Trail was bogus. Yet he didn't want to push too hard. "What did Alistair tell you about me?" he said.

"I asked what you did," Maura said. "How you spent your time. He was pretty vague. He gave me the impression you don't do much at all."

"That's not vague," Mark said. "It's accurate."

"He said you're handsome, which I can now verify. He told me about Elijah. He told me about things between the two of you. Listed your virtues, listed your faults."

"What are my faults?"

"Too good for your own good."

"And Elijah's?"

"Too excitable."

Mark had to laugh. It embarrassed him to think of Alistair describing him and Elijah, translating their affair into mother-appropriate language—embarrassed and touched him.

"And are the two of you," Maura said, "still in New York?" The question seemed strangely half-hearted.

"We're on a break," Mark said. "I'm at my parents' in New Jersey."

"And Elijah?"

"Unfortunately, still in New York."

"Unfortunately?"

Mark raised his shoulders and shook his head.

"What is he doing there?" Maura asked.

Mark heard in her voice a curiosity more pointed than he would have expected. He noticed that she'd now asked more questions about Elijah than about him. "I can tell you if you want," he said, "but I think I might need a drink."

She led him inside and through the living room. The house was old, narrow, and poorly ventilated. Humidity-bloated floorboards gave prewar creaks beneath his feet. But it was handsome, well-swept, self-respecting. He was surprised to see that it was more graceful, less self-embarrassed, than the boy who'd grown up in it. The only ugly thing in the living room was a magazine picture of Rio de Janeiro in a frame. But its ugliness seemed somehow a part of the room's integrity.

In the kitchen Maura brought out two glasses and a bottle of Yellow Tail, a brand Mark hadn't drunk since college. They sat at a breakfast nook. He noticed a rolled-up blackout shade at the top of the window frame; looking around he saw another one over the window above the sink. Outside the air was growing thicker, sultrier, suffused with the threat of near storms. He hoped Maura would drop her question about Elijah but she broached it again: what was he doing in New York?

"Can I ask," Mark said, "why you're curious about him?"

Maura reddened slightly and nodded. "As you know, I can ramble."

"I'll tell you whatever you want to hear."

"Tell me whatever you want to tell me."

Mark sipped his wine, finding it as juice-like as he remembered. "He's very unhappy," he said. "He seems lost. And I feel like it's my fault."

"As someone who blames herself for everything," Maura said, "I'd advise skepticism about that."

"I let him live off me for years. He never really had a job, we never had a lot of people in our life. I don't think I understood how lonely and desperate he'd be without me. But now I'm seeing it loud and clear."

"And what are you seeing?" Maura asked.

"He's living with a friend," Mark said. "He's very much under his influence."

Maura eyed him steadily. She seemed to have an almost practical interest in Elijah's doings and well-being, and this Mark found confusing. "How is he being influenced?"

Mark tried to think of a way to answer without mentioning Jay's project, the models, any specifics of the grotesqueries Elijah had divulged. "They're having fun," he said. "Pleasures of every variety. The issue is one of degree."

Maura nodded circumspectly. She appeared, to Mark's further confusion, relieved.

"I want to help him, but I don't know how," he said. "I don't think I can get back together with him, not yet." He paused, and Maura let him know by her gaze that she understood why. "And for once in my life I can't throw money at the problem."

Maura refilled his glass. "Does this explain why you're working?"

Mark bowed his head.

"Tell me about it."

"We just met, and here I am spilling my guts to you."

"I'm getting to know the person my son loves," Maura said.

Mark felt a flush rise to his cheeks. No words could have made him happier and, under the circumstances, more depressed. He leaned back and obliged her, made a therapist out of her. He told her about CommonWay, his regional manager traineeship, his visits to the parks. In a kind of rehearsal of his looming meeting with his father he told her about his conversation with Cliff Warnung and everything he'd learned by being Arty's ear.

"You're confirming my worst fears about the world of finance," Maura said. "I do wish Alistair could hear this."

"I thought my father was bad," Mark said. "But whichever firm comes in will make him look like a saint."

"Did you ever tell Alistair about your father?"

"He's not my favorite topic."

"He sounds very successful."

"My slumlord dad."

"Alistair loves a success story," Maura said. "He used to read those absurd memoirs. Bill Gates, Richard Branson, Mark Cuban."

"I pray to God my father never writes one."

"He could call it *Upwardly Mobile*."

Mark laughed. With every passing minute he liked this woman more. It occurred to him that in another reality, with a smaller age gap and a remixing of body parts or orientations, they might have been a couple. Two people in their middle years talking about their beloved twenty-two-year-old: there was something inescapably parental about the picture.

"Did Alistair ever tell you about his work?" he asked.

Maura held her face still. "He told me some," she said.

Mark waited for her to go on but she simply stared. "Do you wonder?" he said.

"Wonder what?" Maura said. "If Alistair is really hiking the Appalachian Trail?" The tone of her voice killed that story definitively. "I wouldn't say the word is 'wonder.' But I'd really rather not talk about it."

Mark wanted to ask her more questions, but he knew he wouldn't get answers, and he didn't want to cause her undue pain.

"And what about his own father?" Maura said. "Did Alistair ever tell you about him?"

"Just that he passed away."

Maura emptied her glass and reached for the bottle. "He worked for a slumlord too," she said. "A cousin of his. Sort of a bigwig around here. I'm sure Alistair didn't mention this—it's all very speculative, and all very painful—but I think there's a chance, a very good chance, that his father's work is what got him killed. Did he tell you this?"

Mark shook his head.

"Someone ran him over. No suspects, no leads. But his cousin gave him the dirtiest work you can imagine. He had all these people who owed him money, or who he'd screwed over in some way, and it was Sean's job—that's Alistair's father—it was his job to bully them, or threaten them, or give them their bad news. He was a hunting dog, more or less. I think someone got very desperate, or very angry, or just had nothing else to lose, and lashed out. Either he mistook Sean for the person responsible or he knew Sean was just a deputy and figured he'd be an easier target. Honestly, my experience of the world tells me it's the second one. It's like how people don't marry outside their class. I don't think they go to war with people outside their class either."

"I'm sorry," Mark said.

"Sean was convinced that someday, just around the corner, he'd have enough money to break free. He had all these totally unrealistic plans. He wanted to build a real estate empire, here, in Binghamton! I think you've seen enough of our city to be as dubious as I was. He was a great husband, a great father, he loved us both very much. I don't want to say the problem was that he loved money more than us. I don't think that's true. But I think money was his *way* of loving us. And I think that's just as much of a problem."

"He sounds like Alistair," Mark said.

"And Alistair sounded like him. From about the time he could do multiplication. Money, money, money. That's all he wanted. Money explained everything, it justified everything, it solved everything. And when he finally got his hands on some he became obsessed with it in a whole new way. He insisted on buying me all this stuff, taking care of me, making my life better, as if my life was bad. I wondered, sometimes, if he ever really saw me. Saw what actually made me happy."

"And now you're worried he ended up like his father," Mark said.

Maura stared at him in silence. She had the slightest, strangest smile on her face. For the first time Mark realized that she was far less bereaved, far less wrecked and ravaged, than he'd expected her to be. "I love your son," he said. "And I'm worried I'll never see him again."

"That makes two of us," Maura said.

Mark folded his arms on the table. "What will you do?"

Maura gestured around the house. "You're looking at it," she said. "I think for you that's a bigger question."

Mark slid his glass away and stared out the window. "I don't know," he said. "By the end of the week I probably won't have a job anymore. I certainly can't keep doing this one. And I think I'll have outstayed my welcome at my parents' house. But I have nowhere to go. I'm not needed anywhere."

Maura looked at him almost reproachfully. "I can think of someone who needs you."

Mark smiled. All day, he realized now, his thoughts had been leading him here. "I guess Elijah could use a friend."

"Yes," Maura said. "I think it sounds like he could."

Before he left Mark asked to see Alistair's room. Maura went upstairs first, telling him that she'd been going through his things and wanted to straighten up, After a few minutes she called for him, showed

him the door, and left. He stood still until he heard her reach the bottom of
the stairs.

Alistair's room was small, with light blue walls and dark cherry furniture.
A waist-high bookshelf held textbooks and layperson's finance guides and
organizers crammed with papers. On the floor by the dresser were three
black JanSports arranged in order of deterioration, like an exhibit in the
museum of his schooling. Mark looked around, turning and searching,
but he saw only necessities, only supplies, only tools of sustenance and
self-invention: no hobbies, no indulgences, no waste. Even the tennis
racket propped in one corner felt like a concession to some ideal of well-
roundedness. This was the refuge of a scholarship student: provisional
and barren.

He sat on the bed. He listened for Maura, heard nothing, and then lay
back, staring at the plastic glow-in-the-dark stars on the ceiling. He turned
his head and buried his nose in the pillow. He was amazed by how richly
it smelled of Alistair. The last time he'd been home, Mark had to assume,
was in the winter or early spring. He caught the sweetness of his shampoo,
the savoriness of his sweat. He lay frozen for a moment in deranged consideration. Maura would notice, he decided, be perturbed, and then understand, in that order. He slid off the pillowcase, folded it, and stuffed it into
his pocket.

He made a quick getaway. "I want to stay in touch," he said by the door,
keeping his body turned and the offending pocket out of sight. "I'll visit
again."

Maura shrugged resignedly. "I'll be here."

The sky broke open two hours later, as he was passing through Middletown.
Band after band of merciless rain. Twice he put on his flashers and pulled
over. All the usual landmarks of his approach, the brightening lights of greater
commerce, the densification of houses, were invisible now. Everywhere the
same afterworld of drear. In the thirty seconds it took him to run from the
garage to the pool house he got soaked. He stripped and put on sleeping
clothes. He hastily filed his park report. Then he turned off the lights, lay in
his bed, draped the pillowcase over his face, and five minutes later had the
most pitiable orgasm of his life.

———————

He'd planned to talk to his father the following evening, after Arty had returned home. But at seven a.m. he woke to a knock at the pool house door and, opening it, found his father hovering in the frame, blocking the sun.

Arty glanced at Mark's underwear. "RKM emailed me last night," he said. "They want to have a phone call this morning. They were rather vague." He waited for Mark to speak. "Did something happen yesterday?"

It occurred to Mark only now that he was about to ruin his father's day, and perhaps in some sense his life, and that he felt bad about this. "Do you want to come in?" he said.

Arty's features fell. "I'll be at my desk."

Mark trudged to the main house in gym shorts. When he entered his father's study he realized he'd seldom seen the room in the morning. The light streaming in through the east-facing windows was diminishing, desacralizing, in its brightness. He felt as if he were in a church lit by fluorescents. Arty leaned over the desk with his hands in a tent, looking expectant and agitated and altogether not like himself.

"So," he said.

"So," Mark said.

"Did the visit go well?"

"The visit went fine."

"Did Cliff enjoy himself?"

"I actually think he did."

"And did you—"

"Give a fake name?"

Arty looked down.

"Yes," Mark said. "And I learned quite a lot."

"And Cliff—"

"He learned a lot too."

Arty raised his eyes. "What do you mean?"

"You wanted me to get information," Mark said. "Cliff did some exploring, and now I have some."

A vein in Arty's neck pulsed. "I told you to keep an eye on him."

"You told me to be attentive," Mark said. "You weren't very clear. But then if you were clearer you might have had to tell me things you didn't want me to know."

Arty continued to stare, but his gaze retreated. "Why don't you get to your point," he said. "It's a workday. For most of us."

"Cliff went to check on some of the lots," Mark said. "He seemed to think that the park's rent roll was doctored. That a few of the residents listed on it weren't real, and that those homes were in fact empty. More than a few, actually. Eighty-six."

Arty seemed to be taking great pains not to move his face. "And how did he come to that idea?"

"Because he was given another rent roll. With a very different list of residents. He thinks that in the run-up to the sale you've padded the rent rolls to try to inflate the value of the parks."

"And this other rent roll," Arty said measuredly, "if it's actually a real rent roll, which I can tell you it's not—how might he have gotten that?"

Mark took no pleasure in this conservation, but he knew the next moment would live in his memory as one of his finest. "Your son," he said. "Eddie is trying to sabotage you, Dad. I think that's why he's been coming here so much. He's been trying to get information out of you that he can pass on to RKM. I think he's broken into this room and taken documents off your computer. He's angry that you didn't hand the company off to him, and now he's trying to knock down the offers to get back at you. RKM will give this information to the other firms. They'll try to go as low as they can. I got all this from Cliff."

Arty stared in silence, evidently burying whatever direct response he had to Mark's words. "You're enjoying this," he said after a moment, "aren't you?"

"I assure you I'm not."

"You think this is true, which I can tell you it's not. I'm horrified by the accusation. It's a clerical error. It'll be cleared up immediately. There's been nothing untoward."

"I'm just telling you what I heard from Cliff," Mark said. "Why does it matter what I think?"

"Because you think it's true, and it's not," Arty said. "You think I've lied, and I haven't. You think I don't deserve what the firms are offering, and I do.

You might hate your brother but you're just like him. He sabotaged me? You sabotaged me. You say I wasn't clear? You knew exactly what I meant. You knew, and you let that brat from RKM—"

"So is it true or not?"

"You're just like him," Arty said. "You want to see me fail."

"Frankly, I don't really care what happens to your company," Mark said. "But I think you should know if your own son is betraying you."

"What did you say to Cliff?" Arty said. "When you heard all of this?"

"Nothing."

"You didn't think to defend the company?"

"He didn't know I'd heard him," Mark said. "I eavesdropped on a phone call. And again, I don't really care."

Arty seemed momentarily impressed by Mark's sleuthing. But his disdain for him quickly returned. "Well, if you don't really care," he said, "then I'm not sure you're really right for this job."

"I'm not," Mark said. "I quit."

At this Arty's anger boiled over. He shook his head in tiny movements. "You're unbelievable," he said. "Unfuckingbelievable. You've never worked a day in your life, you put in two measly months, and you can't handle it."

"It's not that I can't handle it," Mark said. "I can't condone it."

"'Condone'?" Arty said. "You—don't 'condone'?"

"Those people's lives are miserable and you know it," Mark said. "You treat them like serfs. And the firms will treat them even worse. You know that and you don't care. You just want your money."

"This is rich," Arty said. "This is really rich."

"I don't think it's right that you've made millions off their backs. I know you didn't invent this business, but you could choose not to be a part of it."

"As could you," Arty said. "I didn't hear you complain when we moved into this nice house. I didn't hear you complain when I sent you to boarding school and college. I didn't hear you complain when I give you a million dollars with no strings attached. I didn't hear you complain when you spent eight years doing God knows what in New York with your little boyfriend. I didn't hear you complain about any of that, not once. The first time I heard you complain is when I put you to work. When I sent you out into the field to see how all the money you've gladly taken from me gets made." He palmed his desk. "*That's* when you complained. When you had to get off your ass and do something. You disapprove of what I do? Go ahead, disapprove. Let's see how long your little crusade lasts. I'll be counting the seconds. If you want to quit, fine, but pack up your stuff. You don't get free room and board anymore. And don't expect another fat check from me. I wouldn't want to damage your integrity. We'll see how long you last. A month from now you'll be sitting in that very chair with your head between your knees. We'll see what you 'condone' and don't 'condone' then."

"I don't want your money," Mark said. "I don't want another dollar out of you."

"Go start your little crusade," Arty said. "The rest of us need to get to work."

Mark returned to the pool house. He began preparing for his departure. He reconstructed the moving boxes he'd had the laziness or possibly the foresight not to chuck. He tossed in unfolded clothes, books, bottles of liquor. He might as well have been back at the Eros Ananke. He might as well have never left.

At three he heard a car pulling into the garage and footsteps approaching over the grass. When he answered the door he found his mother in her tennis gear.

"Are you busy?" Janet asked.

"Very," Mark said.

She entered unbidden. Perhaps expecting disorder she avoided looking at the room. With her hair pulled back and sweat crusting on her face she looked frightful, she looked old. "Your father left this morning in a huff, and now he's not responding to my messages," she said. "Eddie isn't responding to my messages either. Strange things happening the day before my party—I don't like it. What's happening?"

Mark stood with his hands on his waist. "I think there might be a problem with the deal."

Janet narrowed her eyes.

"The deal, Mom. The sale of the company. You have to know something about that."

"I don't see why it should interfere with my party."

"Your party will be great."

Janet finally glanced around and noticed the open boxes. "Markie," she said, "you still haven't *unpacked*?"

"I unpacked," Mark said. "Now I'm packing again."

"I'm sorry?"

"I'm going back to New York."

Janet looked at him in terror. She was a like a small battalion being surrounded on all sides by approaching forces. Everything was going wrong, everything, on the day before her party. "What about your job?"

"I quit."

"Oh, Markie," she said. "I know it's a change for you. But you have to give it more time."

"If I hadn't quit Dad would have fired me. We have irreconcilable differences."

Janet spoke reluctantly. "What happened?"

"Don't worry about it."

"Is this why your father isn't responding to my messages?"

"Yes and no."

"Is this why Eddie isn't responding to my messages?"

"Yes and no."

"What are you saying?"

Mark knelt over a box and loaded in the ebony-and-boxwood chess set he still hadn't opened. "I don't really know," he said. "But I think the next time you talk to Eddie you should ask him why he's been making all his little 'visits.' I think you'll be disappointed to learn that it's not because he loves seeing you. I think you should ask him why he's been so 'curious' about Dad's deal. I think it'd be really interesting to hear what he has to say."

"I stay away from work stuff," Janet said. "You know that."

"Well, I don't think this work stuff will stay away from you."

"I have no idea what you're talking about."

"Let me pack."

Janet fanned her shirtfront. She'd started sweating again. "Where will you go?"

"I'll figure it out."

"How much money do you have?"

As a trainee Mark had made some ten thousand in nine weeks, and he'd just blown half of that on Amber Osgood. He was more or less back to where he'd started. "I'll be fine."

"But Markie," Janet said, "how will you support yourself?"

Mark heard her maternal worry, the biological sincerity of it, and when he answered he felt his throat catch. She was willing to think about money after all, if only when it came to her children. "I'll figure something out."

"Let me give you money," Janet said. "Your father doesn't have to know."

"Please leave me alone."

"Be realistic," Janet said. "What are you going to do, write a book? You've never worked. I don't think you realize how much things cost."

"Like you do?"

"Let me give you money."

"Go away," Mark said. "Just go away."

Janet put up a finger. "I don't want to see this attitude at my party."

"Go away! Go away! Go away!"

He spent the rest of the day in the pool house. At seven he heard his father pull into the garage, but when he glanced at the kitchen window an hour later he saw his mother eating alone, a stark break from tradition. The lights in Arty's study burned bright.

Before he went to sleep he visited Jay's Instagram page and saw an update: a picture of a video shoot in Howie's apartment with a caption teasing the exhibition party—*One week until Daddy comes home.* The picture was centered on a group of models, predictably underdressed and horrifically hatted, but Mark could see, at the edge of the frame, a sliver of Elijah's face. He was still there, waiting for his rescue. And rescue him Mark would.

He slept terribly. When he finally left bed it was time to put on his party gear. Though he couldn't remember when he'd last eaten his body felt bloated, and the old tuxedo he'd taken from his childhood bedroom fit like a vise. As he studied himself in the mirror he entertained a cruel fantasy. He imagined that he was dressing for his wedding, that Alistair was suiting up in another room, that all of their friends and family were waiting.

He drove to the club. The rain from two days earlier had given the greenery a fresh stimulus. Everywhere he looked he saw verdant lawns, blooming flowers, trees as thickly tufted as pom-poms. The blue of the sky was fading toward a pumpkiny sunset. It was vast and caressing in its embrace.

In the parking lot of the club he joined a line of buffed Benzes and BMWs prowling for spots. White-shirted caterers walked with chafing dishes toward the service entrance. Under the portico women in dresses and men in better-fitting tuxes loitered. Mark parked and made his way toward the front doors, keeping an eye out for Eddie. The closer he got to the clubhouse the more his dread increased, the more he resented these glitzed-out suburbanites and his unwilling if unresisting association with them. He slowed and veered, desperate for a minute more of peace. He followed a footpath to the pool, which to his relief had been cleared. He could hear the sounds of the party, greetings and clattering cutlery and musicians waking their instruments, but the pool was encircled by tall shrubbery that shielded his view.

An unavoidable fact about the Ridgefall Country Club pool was that it was shaped like a dick. It consisted of a long four-lane shaft with a glans-like semicircle at one end and two testicular semicircles at the other. Mark stood at the lip of one of the testicles and stared at the artificially blue water. He reached into his pants, adjusted himself, and had an infernal idea. He looked in the direction of the club, heard an eruption of laughter, and peered through the shrubbery in search of passersby. Seeing none, he unzipped his pants and spilled into the pool a thick stream of dehydration-amber urine. He watched it discolor the water and dissipate and felt pleased.

When he entered the club he kept his eyes raised, ignoring the clumps of suntanned retirees. He nevertheless caught sight of faces he recognized: tennis partners of Janet and golf partners of Arty, parents of classmates from junior high and boarding school. He heard, "Mark! Mark? Mark!" but kept walking. He saw no sign of Eddie.

Everything really was white: the flowers, the tablecloths, the curtains, the balloons. Mark noticed the party planner, her hair and forehead skin pulled back into a tight bun, counting table settings with vicious concentration. He grabbed a flute of Champagne from a passing tray, found an unoccupied corner, and surveyed the crowd. He wished Elijah were here. He'd offer a sumptuous, murderous appraisal of every person in the room.

He saw Arty standing by the bar, whiskey in hand, pretending to listen to a leather-skinned woman in a blinding Lilly Pulitzer dress. Arty caught

Mark's gaze, stared at him blankly, and turned away. He looked handsome in his tux and loomed as large as ever, but some change, perhaps perceptible only to Mark, had come over him. Wrinkles and age spots previously disguised by his ebullience showed cruelly on his face. The long march of his life had hit an obstacle, for the first time possibly an insurmountable one, and Mark wondered, with unexpected pity, if he would ever recover.

Janet, glittering in a bejeweled navy dress, emerged from a cluster of guests and approached Mark. She put her lips to his ear. "I haven't heard from Eddie."

"He'll be here," Mark said, though he didn't know if his brother would come, and he suspected it would be best if he didn't. Janet walked off.

He had his suspicions, which in time would be confirmed. Months from now, long after he'd returned to New York, he would learn everything. He would learn that the day before Janet's party there'd been a conversation between Arty and Eddie: an accusation, an inquiry as to the source of this accusation, a divulgence of this source, and a remorseless vitriolic confession. He would learn too that there'd been a conversation between Arty and RKM, and between RKM and Eddie, and that earlier that day RKM had pulled out of the deal with CommonWay and, upon learning of Eddie's skullduggery, fired him. But that was later.

Shortly before seven the party planner sent out a contingent of servers to persuade guests into their chairs. Janet lingered at the center of the room, standing alone, turning her head and giving forced smiles, searching for Eddie, glancing at Arty and Mark, looking for all the world like a lost child.

The music softened. Servers struggled to settle guests. Mark walked to the head table but remained standing. Arty, sitting at one end, pretended not to see him. Mark looked in vain for Janet, who'd disappeared, and then he heard by the entrance a small fracas.

The guests standing by the doorway grew silent and turned. Some began shuffling, moving backward, making way. Mark saw a body advancing chaotically through the crush, and then Eddie appeared, breathless and red-faced. He was drunk, drunker than Mark had ever seen him, though he'd managed to put on a tux. Janet materialized and approached Eddie, opening her arms for an embrace, but he brushed her aside. Arty stood. Eddie cast his eyes around the room lustily, and it didn't take Mark long to realize he was looking for him. Mark stepped away from the table, ducking his head, and slipped through one of the lawn-facing doors onto the terrace. He heard his mother say, "Eddie! Eddie!" and his father say, "Hey! Hey!"

He descended to the lawn. He cruised past the outdoor bar at a steady clip. He glanced back at the terrace, saw that it was still empty, and picked up his pace. He weaved around the illuminated white orbs as if he were navigating an obstacle course. He walked toward the pond and then turned toward a line of trees, hoping to cut around to the parking lot under their cover. He tried to jog but the tuxedo constricted his movements. His shoes slid on the grass.

He felt his phone buzzing in his pocket. He expected it to be Janet or Arty, but when he reached for it he saw—incredibly—that it was Elijah.

"Hold on," he said, panting. He tried again to jog.

"I have some news for you," he heard Elijah say.

Mark looked back at the terrace. A dozen people had gathered there, with Arty, Janet, and Eddie at the head. Arty was clutching Eddie's arm, trying to hold him back, but Eddie freed himself. His gaze had alighted on Mark.

"It's Alistair," Elijah said.

Eddie barreled down the terrace steps and charged toward Mark at a sprint. Janet and Arty followed him, putting their hands out and shouting. Eddie was saying the same word over and over, but Mark couldn't make it out. All he could hear was the word Elijah had just uttered. He started running as best he could.

"He's here," Elijah said.

Eddie was approaching quickly, and now Mark could hear him. "Fucker, fucker, fucker," he was saying.

Mark could barely speak for his panting. "Where? Where?"

"What's going on?" Elijah said.

Before Mark could respond he lost his balance and fell. He jammed the phone against his cheek, tried to stand, settled for a backward crabwalk.

"Fucker, fucker, fucker," Eddie said. He was twenty, ten, five yards away.

"Alistair is here," Elijah said. "He wants to talk to you."

Mark tried again to stand, but Eddie closed in.

"We need your help," Elijah said.

Then the phone was in the grass and blood was in the air.

PART FOUR

THE DEMAGOGUE

ELIJAH STOOD IN the shadows, fingering his stack of folders, trying to look diligent enough to earn his bread but not so involved as to attract the attention of the journalist. Though by today, July 7, Jay had plenty of videos, and though the exhibition party was only one week away, he'd insisted on calling back some of the models for another shoot. He'd decided, for reasons obscure and abstract, that he needed a final installment with a large cast.

Jay spoke to the models, naked except for their hats and skimpy white briefs, from behind the camera. "As you may or may not know," he said, "in the classic Freudian account, the band of brothers rises up against their father and kills him." His voice was grating, self-conscious, his words prepared. He smiled with lips over braced teeth. "In this retelling, though, you have come together in titillated subservience to your father. You have risen up against all that is tender and feminine. You have killed your mother."

The models, ranging in age from nineteen to twenty-two, stunningly beautiful, woefully uncredentialed, stared at Jay dumbly. One, a tan boy with large nipples and a mop of curly brown hair, turned up one corner of his mouth and said, "The fuck?" He scratched the part of his head where MAGA hat met ear.

"I'm just giving you context," Jay said.

"I have to leave in an hour," another boy said.

Jay cleared his throat tersely and began choreographing. "Griffin, I want you to get down on your knees. Turn your body toward Howie. The old guy."

Howie, sitting with legs together on a chair from the dining room, bowed his head and smiled.

"Tommy, I want you to crouch down and put your hand behind Griffin's head. Like you're holding him up. He is overcome by wonderment and idolatry. He has collapsed."

Tommy followed Jay's instructions, then turned his head and burped.

"Adam—sorry? Aidan. Fine, 'Aidan,' I want you to put your arms around Mike's shoulders. No, more around his neck, like you're hanging on to him. Good. Emilio, I want you to face in the opposite direction. You're afraid to look at what the other boys are looking at—it's too bright, too sublime, you're overwhelmed. Now, finally, Blake, you're cowering in fear, but you're ready to act at the first sign from your father. I want you to get on your haunches."

"The fuck are those?" Blake said. He was the one with the curly hair.

Jay looked at Elijah and almost said his name but stopped himself. "Can you show him?"

Elijah stood still, folders in hand. He glanced at the journalist in the corner, at his recording iPhone, his steady gaze.

"Show him?" Jay said. "Please?"

Elijah lowered himself to the floor and modeled the posture.

"Oh," Blake said, "so like when you're in the woods and you gotta shit."

The other boys laughed. Jay blinked rapidly. "Sure."

Blake got on his haunches.

Jay crossed the room and switched on a high spotlight near Howie's chair. "Now," he said, returning to the camera, "everyone put on your blindfolds." The boys raised the black cloths they'd tied and hung around their necks and fitted them over their eyes. "When I begin shooting, I want you to take off the blindfolds one by one—I'll call out your names—and look directly into the spotlight. Emilio, I want you to keep your blindfold on—remember, you're afraid. Mike and Tommy, when I give you the cue, I want you to turn to Emilio and try to untie his blindfold. I want the three of you to struggle for a moment—don't use force, we don't have insurance—until Emilio finally submits and looks into the light. Emilio, I want you to imagine, for all your fear, for all your refusals, that you have never seen anything more beautiful."

The shoot began. One at a time the boys removed their blindfolds, staring into the spotlight until tears formed in their eyes, their red hats glowing radiantly in the merciless white glare. After surrendering to the prying hands of Mike and Tommy, Emilio looked with them, affecting, with a performative skill that far exceeded Elijah's expectations, an expression of gratified terror. Jay took some twenty minutes of footage, occasionally instructing the boys to rearrange themselves and try new positions. After snapping an iPhone photo for Instagram, which Elijah tried his best to stay out of, he told them they could get dressed and collect their checks from Elijah, again almost mentioning his name but then remembering. "From the pretty one," he said. "With the dark hair, hiding."

The boys tossed their MAGA hats and blindfolds onto the floor, put on their clothes, and lined up to receive their wages. The folders Elijah held contained checks for $1,000 and info sheets advertising the exhibition party with strongly worded encouragements to attend. A bolded, asterisked line on the info sheet promised another $1,000 if they did.

"Here you go," Elijah said to Mike, then Emilio, then Aidan, then Tommy, then Blake. They thanked him mumblingly. Back in May, after he'd moved with Jay into Howie's penthouse and agreed to work on the project in exchange for $1,500 a week, Elijah had helped Jay find and handpick these boys. They'd recruited on Grindr, distinguishing themselves from the numberless other contraband commercial accounts (johns, sex workers, small-time pornographers, solicitors of foot pics or sweat-crusted jockstraps) only by the relative generosity of their offer. Altogether they'd received more than three hundred responses. After scanning profiles and requesting photographs they'd narrowed the pool down to seventy-five. The majority of the candidates, after Jay had explained the project (which Elijah had insisted he do), had said no thank you, often with sanctimonious expletive-laden invective, and two New School students had agreed with suspicious alacrity: a half hour of snooping on social media suggested they were would-be antifa operatives trying to infiltrate the project. But by and by they'd landed on twelve models ("My disciples," Jay had said), the six handsomest of whom were now gathered around him.

"Can we leave?" Blake said after he took his folder.

"You can leave," Elijah said.

The five boys who'd already retrieved their checks made for the door of Howie's bedroom. The journalist approached them with questions on his tongue but Jay intercepted him: he'd promised the boys privacy, and he didn't want them talking to media anyway. He was keen to manage the narrative.

The last boy, Griffin, Elijah's favorite, stepped forward and held out his hand. He was shy, doe-eyed, smoothly contoured, with a choppy haircut that smacked of cost-saving self-shearing. Elijah had never flirted with him explicitly—the project made him feel creepy enough, and Jay had forbidden relations—but he spoke to him kindly, paternally, with a curiosity that appeared not totally welcome and that was in any case never reciprocated.

He gave Griffin the folder and asked what else his day had in store.

"I have work," Griffin muttered, opening the folder and locating his check.

"Starbucks?" Elijah said.

Griffin kept his eyes lowered and nodded.

"Maybe I'll stop by sometime."

Griffin peered up. "I'm new, so they only let me pour drip."

Elijah smiled. "Then I'll order drip."

"Can I leave?"

"Don't forget about the exhibition party."

"Yah," Griffin said and walked away.

Elijah remained in the shadows, avoiding the eyes of the journalist, and watched the models shuffle out. Over the course of the now ten shoots he'd collected their stories, each one depressing him more than the one before. None of the boys had gone to college and most had only barely finished high school. They'd come to the city on buses from faraway places, found squalid living arrangements, and now spent their time scrounging together whatever degraded sources of income they could. One boy had arrived from Kansas, forged a membership to the University Club, and offered unspecified varieties of friendship to various geriatrics he met there. Another was a camboy who'd once been asked, he'd told Jay and Elijah, to urinate onto a photograph of Henry Kissinger (this performance had netted him $150). Another had recently finished a yearlong stint as a server on a Disney cruise ship during which he'd contracted chlamydia and gonorrhea twice each. He was now busing tables at a steak house in the Time Warner Center and shoplifting his clothes from the SoHo Uniqlo.

Aside from one boy from south Texas who shared his family's yeehaw conservatism, and who'd asked to keep the MAGA hat Jay had provided, the models made no comment on the political nature of the videos. Elijah suspected most of them ignored the news (as he himself tried to) and he suspected the ones who did feel distaste for Trump judged their integrity to be less useful than their paychecks. In their abject desperation the boys sometimes reminded

Elijah, unhappily, of himself. Wasn't he, as surely all of them were, waiting for someone to rescue him?

He hadn't heard from Mark in two weeks.

After the models had left the journalist approached Jay. "Should we talk here?" he asked.

"In the living room," Jay said. "I'll be there in a moment."

Howie sprang up and offered to show the journalist to the living room, probably so as to steal a last glimpse of the boys. Jay and Elijah had to keep an eye on Howie. Occasionally they had to slap his wrist.

Jay watched them go and turned to Elijah. "What did we say your name was?"

"Charlie," Elijah whispered. "You're the one who came up with it."

"Right, Charlie. You look like a Charlie. Who couldn't love a Charlie?"

"Charlie himself, maybe."

"I'll do all the talking," Jay said.

"You absolutely will."

"And you'll stop me if I say anything—"

"I absolutely will."

For weeks now Elijah had been trying and largely failing to secure Jay media coverage. Using the nameless project email account he'd fired off press releases to art publications, mainstream publications, and a bevy of websites with conservative leanings and tabloid instincts. Predictably the art publications and mainstream publications had ignored Elijah, unless you counted the response he'd received from a journalist at *New York* magazine: *Thank you for your interest in ruining my day.* Several of the trashy conservative sites had expressed interest, but in the end Jay had decided it would be a mistake to unveil his work in *Breitbart* or the *Daily Wire*: he didn't trust such outlets not to frame the project as mere propaganda, and he judged their readers to be, to use his word, "icky." Nor had Jay been especially thrilled when they'd finally gotten a bite from the *Grift*, an effortlessly hip online magazine that specialized in stories about obscure subcultures, gasp-seeking travelogues from combat zones and bacchanalian desert raves, and movie reviews written under the disclosed influence of illegal substances—"lame" was Jay's assessment. But the *Grift* had the right audience and at least a marginal degree of cachet, and ultimately it was their only option. They'd offered the magazine access to a shoot, admission to the exhibition party, and exclusive clips of Jay's videos, and now one of their writers, one Spencer Vaught, sat waiting for them in the living room.

Elijah had read some of Spencer's articles: a feature on a college student who sold 3D-printed guns emblazoned with the Louis Vuitton monogram, a profile of a former cartel leader who now taught Vinyasa yoga, a dispatch from a Portland furries convention that had descended into violence. He was a shock jock, a Jane Goodall of fringe characters and lurid appetites. He would write about Jay as if he were a zoo animal and he would surely get clicks. Hence Elijah's request, earlier that day, for an alias.

"Ready?" Jay said.

"No," Elijah said.

Jay inspected himself in the mirror, smoothing his hair, neatening his center part, running a wet finger over his braces. Though he professed to love his "disciples" he always cheered up whenever they left. Once they were gone he could resume his status as the star, the center of attention, the bright young thing, if not (Elijah smoothed his own hair) the beauty.

"This is my moment," Jay said. His face was flushed and his hands, Elijah noticed, were trembling. Deep down Jay knew, had known for some time now, that he was out of his depth—Elijah felt sure of this. But it was too late now, and whatever regret Jay acknowledged he did his best to convert into gleeful impenitence.

"Let's get it over with," Elijah said.

He followed Jay at a distance, dragging his feet, whispering to himself, *Charlie, Charlie.* All summer long he'd demanded anonymity: he forbade Jay to include him in his Instagram photos, he communicated with the models and pitched the media outlets without ever giving his name, he ate and drank and rolled around with Jay's new "friends" without ever introducing himself. So far Spencer Vaught hadn't shown much interest in interviewing Elijah or even mentioning him in his article—he appeared to have gathered, as much to Elijah's chagrin as to his relief, that Elijah was merely a peon, the wind beneath Jay's wings—but if he did turn his reportorial attention his way Elijah would simply present himself as a tight-lipped "Charlie." Soon enough Elijah would be gone, and he wanted to leave no sign that he'd been here. His plan was to resign from the project and leave the Die Kinder the day after the exhibition party. By now he'd padded his bank account sufficiently. He'd get an apartment, take his graphic design business off ice, go his merry way and forget his bizarre summer as best he could. He hadn't told Jay this yet, and he wasn't sure when he'd get up the nerve to. He envisioned leaving, like a miserable spouse, like a kidnapped child, in the dead of the night.

Spencer was sitting on one of the long deep couches, his back to the windows overlooking Midtown. The night before it had rained violently and the air above the cityscape was still steamy. Howie sat on a stool in the kitchen playing a game on his iPad. For his part Howie had introduced himself to Spencer willingly. Elijah awaited the day when Herve learned that his surname had been dragged through Spencer's report.

In preparation for the exhibition party Jay had had five large TV screens mounted on the walls of the living room, sending Howie's Abstract Expressionists into temporary storage. In the coming days he'd install several more, filling every available space with his videos on infinite replay. Elijah peered at a video in which two boys stood over a kneeling third; again and again the kneeling boy tried to stand only for the other boys to press his head down. In the neighboring video two boys played cat and mouse. One, blindfolded, crawled around on the floor, reaching out his hands in increasing desperation, while the other evaded him, sidestepping gingerly, his stern gaze fixed on his pursuer. From wall to wall the boys moved, lolling and strolling, glaring and beckoning, immaculate in their near-nakedness, crushed beneath their red hats.

Jay sat on the couch opposite Spencer as Elijah took an armchair. Spencer moved his eyes between them. "Am I interviewing both of you?" he said.

"Charlie's just listening," Jay said.

Elijah's purpose was to listen and, if need be, to lean forward or clear his throat or make some other silencing gesture. Jay believed wholeheartedly in the political agnosticism of his project, but he was aware that, when provoked by needling liberal pieties, he could slip and give grist to the idea ("unhinged," to his mind) that he actually harbored pro-Trump sentiments. He needed Elijah to keep him from saying things he'd assured him he didn't believe, from crossing a line he'd assured him it wasn't in him to cross. If Elijah had agreed to babysit him it was because this line—between aesthetics and politics, between "interest" in Trump and support for him—mattered direly to him. All his flimsy self-justifications would fall apart if it didn't hold.

Spencer laid the recording iPhone on the coffee table and leaned forward with his notebook on his knees. He wore a threadbare black T-shirt, black jeans, and black combat boots. He reminded Elijah of the punk boys from high school and he countered Elijah's sense that eventually all punks grew up. His journalistic portfolio suggested an appetite for rebellion, an increasingly doomed hunt for filth and grunge in a professionalized and homogenized and sterilized world. Elijah wondered if the path of the avant-garde had progressed to the point where an artist flirting with reactionaryism was the nearest thing to cool.

"So," Spencer said. He spoke with affected man-to-man candor, as if they were dockworkers at a pub. Having already collected the basics of Jay's biography over the phone a few days earlier, he got to the heart of the matter without preamble. "The RNC will take place later this month. Do you think Trump will get the nomination? And, if he does, do you think he has a chance of winning?"

Jay put up his hands. "Whoa," he said. "Whoa, whoa."

Spencer turned his head. "What's the problem?"

"Why are you asking *me* about this?"

Spencer looked at the videos on the walls, as if pointing to evidence for his confusion. "You seem fascinated by Trump."

"Fascinated, yes," Jay said. "At all concerned with his electoral prospects, no."

"You don't care whether he wins or loses?"

Jay lifted his shoulders at the apparent lameness of this question. "I don't care whether he lives or dies," he said. "He's an idea to me. His reality as a person is immaterial."

Spencer smiled. "Why don't you tell me about your idea."

Jay sat straight and breathed with relief. "I'm interested in the erotic dimension *of* politics," he said. "Never *in* politics per se."

Spencer scribbled feverishly, which Elijah thought was a little theatrical. Couldn't he just listen to the recording later?

"I've been working toward this idea for years," Jay said. He pulled his vape from his pocket and expelled a white plume. "But only now have I found the perfect moment, and the perfect subject."

"Tell me what you mean by 'erotic dimension,'" Spencer said.

Jay responded chipperly. "The libido is central to our experience of the world," he said, reading off the cue cards in his head. "And it's central to our experience of politics. That we never think to reckon with this fact is only proof, I think, of its centrality. We can't see it because it's what we see politics *through*."

Spencer continued scribbling. "Go on," he said.

"We don't realize it," Jay said, "but we choose political systems and leaders that organize our erotic energies. Sometimes we choose systems that stimulate them, sometimes we choose ones that suppress them. It depends on what the historical moment demands. But if the libido itself were a form of government, it would, I think you'll agree, be an authoritarian one."

Elijah squirmed in his chair.

"Come again?" Spencer said.

Jay, briefly rattled, shuffled his mental cue cards. "The libido understands only submission and domination," he said. "It's fixated on a singular object, either its would-be prize or its would-be ruler. It loves strength, beauty, and power and it abhors everything lacking these qualities. It loves violence. Think of the last time you had sex."

Spencer actually did seem to think about this.

"Think of the kisses and the caresses and the kind words. And then think of what those things were a means toward, or a compensation for."

"What does this have to do with your project?" Spencer asked.

Jay reddened, then shook his hair and resumed. "We can all agree that authoritarian governments are bad for society," he said. "That liberal-democratic governments are the most conducive to health, safety, and prosperity."

"Yes," Spencer said.

"But the liberal-democratic system provides no erotic satisfaction. The violent, discriminating, hierarchal libido has no outlet in a world of kindness, peace, and civility. At different times and in different circumstances, maybe in the face of erotic excesses in authoritarian governments elsewhere, this is a good thing. But the libido is incorrigible, it's unrepentant, and we're due now, I think, for a carnal correction."

Spencer's eyes were aglow. He was already selecting pull quotes.

"The interest of Trump, for me, is that he's unleashed the libido," Jay said. "And after decades of well-mannered liberal-democratic governance, the

libido has a lot of time to make up for. Think about Trump. He thrashes, he
rages, his grasps, he hates. He quickens the blood, he makes people hard. He
speaks the language of the groin. He has that on his opponent. Where sexual
excitation is concerned, there's really no contest. If he wins, it'll be a triumph
of the eros over the psyche."

"Are you saying people want to have sex with Trump?" Spencer asked.

"Speak for yourself," Jay said.

Spencer smiled but let the question hang.

"Maybe not literally," Jay said. "But maybe, in a deep sense, yes. Have you
watched his rallies? I've watched clips. I can only take so much. Speeches
bore me."

Unless they're your speeches, Elijah thought.

"You know what those rallies look like to me?" Jay said. "Like the first three
minutes of a fantastic orgy. Bodies shifting, hands traveling, gazes leering—
clothes are about to come off. Those people, they're tired of their daytime lives.
They're tired of being browbeaten, of being on their best behavior. They're
ready to express their most beautiful, most brutal instincts. And they're looking in awe at their dear leader, with their mouths open and their legs spread,
waiting for him to overpower them, to fuck them into oblivion."

"Wait a second," Spencer said. "That sounds like a contradiction. You're
saying these people are tired of being browbeaten. But you're also saying they
want to be, at least in a deep sense, dominated."

"You're pointing to the wonderful contradiction of the libido," Jay said with
professorial pleasure. "I don't really read the news, but I've heard all the theories
about Trump's popularity. His supporters feel angry, they feel marginalized,
they feel oppressed by the 'elite.' I'm not sure they're right, and I don't really
care. The important thing is that their anger explains their sexual idolatry of
Trump. Ideally, the libido wants unrestricted power and freedom. It wants to
take, it wants to own, it wants to control. But not everyone can live out that
desire, especially not in this country, and the next best thing is to participate
in someone else's domination, even if it means being on the receiving end of
it. For these people, the problem with the 'elite' isn't that they're oppressive. It's
that the elite's form of oppression is too respectable, too educated and sterile,
too *bleh*. It doesn't excite them, it doesn't satisfy them, it doesn't validate their

erotic impulses. Trump, in his swaggering authoritarianism, does. He swings his
dick around in a way that they understand, and they're content to live through
him. Even if he turns around and crushes them, even if he takes that dick and
fucks them with it, they'll be happy, they'll be ecstatic, because *someone* will
have crushed, *someone* will have fucked, *someone* will have claimed his beastly
freedom, and their carnal essence will have found vicarious expression."

Spencer held his pen still. "They do have specific grievances, though,"
he said. "A lot of his supporters come from communities where economic
opportunity has dried up. Manufacturing towns that have been eviscerated."

Jay made a show of considering this by cocking his head. "I'm sure those
grievances are legitimate," he said. "But my point stands. Money is one of the
ways we sublimate the libido. Whenever we talk about money we're really
talking about fucking. That's especially true of America. It doesn't strike me
as coincidental that the country most obsessed with capitalism and ambition
is also the one most riddled with sexual hang-ups. These people may say they
want more money, more power, more whatnot. But that's only a higher-brain
way of articulating a desire that springs from the groin, and that ends in the
groin. Trump won't give them money, and he won't give them power. But he'll
give them sensation, and they'll be satisfied."

Spencer glanced at a video on the wall in which Blake, his waistband lowered
to expose the upper growth of his pubes, walked toward the camera until his
crimson-haloed face filled the screen. "Your project is certainly sex-forward,"
he said to Jay. "But why gay men specifically?"

Jay smiled and sucked on his vape. He searched for his next words and
seemed to find them in the expansive view out the window. "Gay men understand the centrality of the libido better than anyone," he said. "They conduct
their lives with lusting rapacity. They earn good grades, secure jobs and pro-
motions, acquire wealth, climb social ladders, give perfect wedding presents,
curate wardrobes and home furnishings, all with the same ravenous zeal they
bring to their fucking. They know, better than anyone, that fucking is where
the truth of life resides. And they understand the authoritarian nature of desire.
They top, they bottom, they roar in conquest and squeal in defeat. They get
down on their knees and look up at their lords with worship. They know that,
whether they fuck or get fucked, they've made contact with the beating heart

of human experience, and the beating heart of history. My boys understand this. Not the models themselves—they don't understand the difference between east and west—but their representations. They've undressed, they've donned their badge of loyalty, they're ready. Put your boot to my face, tie me to the whipping post. As long as you give me release, I will love you."

"Your ideas are . . . interesting," Spencer said. "But I imagine there are other ways of expressing them. It seems like you've chosen the most provocative way possible."

Elijah caught Spencer's eye and smirked as if to say: *You're telling me.*

"People use the word 'provocation' so dismissively," Jay said, "and I think it shows real intellectual impoverishment. Provocation has inherent value to society."

"So do you think your project is doing a social good?" Spencer said.

"There's another example of intellectual impoverishment," Jay said. "The idea that art must necessarily promote the 'good.' No bigger lie has ever been told."

"So what is this project accomplishing?" Spencer asked. "Or is it just provoking?"

"My project is offering the most truthful statement about America as it exists today," Jay said. "We yearn, we clamor, we pursue our dreams by any ways and means. But it's all futile. We're all fucked, and it feels good to be fucked. The only solution to the pain is to accept it and give in to it, to see the joy in it. The only thing we can do, to save our sanity, is step back from this struggle, this orgy of striving and suffering, and admire it in its cruel beauty."

Spencer paused the recording on his iPhone and closed his notebook.

"You have what you need?" Jay said.

"For now," Spencer said wearily. "I'm sure I'll get more at the party."

"You'll get *everything* at the party," Jay said.

Spencer nodded limply and Jay showed him out.

After he closed the door Jay let out a breath. He looked at Howie, who'd retired to a distant chaise longue and fallen asleep. "Did I sound normal?" he asked Elijah.

"Did you want to?" Elijah said.

"Not really."

"Mission accomplished."

Jay rubbed his hands with firestarter quickness. "I have so much *energy*."

"Speak for yourself," Elijah said. "I need a nap."

Jay fished in his pocket and glanced at his phone. "Be quick. We have guests tonight. They'll be here in a few hours."

"Don't you think we've done enough for today?"

"We've created monsters," Jay said. "They can't be controlled. And we need to keep up momentum until the exhibition party."

"Is Herve coming for dinner beforehand?" Elijah asked.

"I hope not," Jay said. "He really kills my buzz."

Elijah had no burning desire to see Herve or to fend off his persistent questions about Alistair and Nikolai. But he couldn't deny that he and Herve had, over the past two months, formed a special relationship. He dreaded his visits but he also took comfort from them, with something of the eagerness of a child who sees his father too rarely. He offered a distraction from Jay's project and a relief from Jay's antics. Even counting Howie he often felt to Elijah like the only grown-up, the only man, in the room. "I'm going upstairs," he said.

"Sleep tight," Jay said. "My prince."

Elijah ascended the curved glass staircase, sauntered along the gallery overlooking the living room, and stepped into the guest room where he'd been staying, picking his way among the piles of clothes and random objects he'd taken from the Eros Ananke. He lowered the shade, sat on his bed, and dug in the side table drawer, searching for one of the Klonopins that their coke dealer had included as a lagniappe in one of their many bulk orders. To his dismay he saw he'd consumed them all. He lay back and thought of Mark, imagined him pressing down on him, warming him, suffocating him. In lieu of chemicals this fantasy was the only thing that put him to sleep, and a few minutes later he was dead to the world.

———————

Over the past eight years Elijah had seldom gone a day without experiencing some low-level annoyance at Mark—at the way he sighed huffily whenever Elijah took a phone call in a room where he happened to be reading, at the way he put on his running sneakers at noon and then dithered all day until the sky had grown dark and he gave up on jogging for fear of stepping on rats, at his preference for window seats when booking plane tickets ("I like looking at the clouds," he'd explain to Elijah), at the primness with which he ignored any off-color joke Elijah made—but he'd rarely ever experienced *anger*. Yet in the week after Mark left, as Elijah hauled his belongings to the Die Kinder and there took to bed in an agony of grief, he felt his anger asserting itself at last. Up to now he'd never found much appeal in anger; he'd seen it as an ugly emotion, lacking polish and poise. But the more he felt it now, the more he egged it on. He discovered that his anger was more sustaining, more ego-affirming, than his loneliness and sadness, and he discovered, for the first time, that it could be beautiful. It lay at the center of his chest, arousing in its power, burning brightly. It was white-hot.

He was angry that he'd spent *years* urging Mark to take charge of his life only for Mark to turn this advice against him: angry that Mark's inaugural show of boldness should assume the form of his spurning the very person who'd pushed him to be bold. He was angry that Mark had disapproved of his "badness" while taking selective advantage of it. It was Elijah, not Mark, who had suggested they go to Phoenix one night and find themselves a hunky third, and it was Elijah, with his supremely penetrable asshole, who'd kept their entanglement with Alistair from dying out in a whimper of mutual sucking and frottage. Mark and Alistair, in their moony tenderness for each other, in their insufferable decency, had relegated Elijah to the sidelines. They'd dismissed him as a slut, a meal and an entertainment, without acknowledging that it was this slut who made the bedroom gymnastics by which they fostered their affection for each other possible. Elijah sometimes felt, after Alistair had left for the night and Mark had retreated into his postcoital tristesse, like one of the companies Eddie Landmesser bragged about raiding and pillaging on behalf of his firm. He felt that he possessed value for Mark and Alistair only as a leverageable asset, that they used him, squeezed him, wrung from him emotional profits that redounded only to themselves, and then, after he'd fulfilled his purpose, left him neglected and hollowed out: and this made him angry.

He was angriest of all that Mark had wasted so much of his *time*. He'd spent eight years pretending to be someone else—a nice person, a normal person, a paragon of latter-day homosexual respectability—while his real self had languished in a drawer. This real self, he believed, was the self he'd been at Vassar when, in a frenzy of demonic inspiration, he'd painted his outré *Blue Light* paintings. This real self was the self that relished Jay Steigen in all his glittering nihilism and crazed transports. This real self was weirder, darker, more original, and more brilliant than the self he'd pretended to be, and he was angry at Mark for disregarding it and thereby causing him to neglect it himself.

He had no more time to waste. His anger was urgent and, in its urgency, indiscriminate. He would do whatever it took to feel free, to recover his diminished spirit, to become interesting to himself once again. He found the content of Jay's project intriguing, insofar as he understood it, but he also knew it was largely irrelevant. He cared only that it was affronting, that in its provocation it made him feel alive, and he cared only that Mark would be horrified by it. He was aware that a great many more people than Mark would be horrified by it, but in his cloistered rage, in his chronic political blinkeredness, he failed to see these people or their objections clearly: the world of right-minded people (a world of which he'd always considered himself a member, if only for lack of any other card to carry) seemed to him now only like an extension of Mark. And it was Mark's sanctimony that he was rebelling against. His rebellion might have an incidental political valence but it was ultimately, refulgently personal.

He also knew that his rebellion would be short-lived: that being fueled by fury it would have the lifespan of a tantrum. He'd give himself the summer to be as deranged and flippant as he wanted to be and then take stock of how his experience had benefited or cost him. And he saw, that first week, that even in his adamancy he was still in possession of his critical faculties. He found Jay's project intriguing, yes, but he also found it crass, tasteless bordering on sadistic. He'd lend a hand and siphon off vicarious thrills but he would never put his name to Jay's work. He knew that if the videos attracted the kind of attention Jay sought Jay's name would forever be bound up with that of the most hated man in the country, and Elijah had no intention of going down with that ship. In the meantime, though, he would be able to visit regions of himself he'd forgotten about and perhaps never visited before, dark places of dark secrets, beyond the preserves of common decency. He felt, that first week at the Die Kinder, like a tetherball spinning wildly around its pole, faster and faster. He trusted that as long as he spun in the right spirt of levity he would never come loose, that the center would hold.

Jay saw the shift in him immediately. He asked Elijah if he was ready to have fun, Elijah said yes, and they got to work. They set up the Grindr account and began recruiting models. They drafted press releases and drew up a list of media targets. They staged trial shoots in which Elijah happily played the model, experimenting with different lighting and different poses, different ways of positioning the MAGA hat on his head. After they'd shot the first videos they posted stills to Jay's Instagram and watched the opposing tides of opprobrium and encouragement roll in. They read aloud the deranged hate messages Jay received and the (frankly more deranged) messages of support. They noted with curiosity that the project's detractors and boosters often employed identical phraseology. Jay was "unbelievable," they said in outrage or approval, he was "playing with fire," he was "fucking insane!" They watched mentions of the project accumulate on Twitter. They ate Howie's fine food and drank his fine liquor and snorted his premium-grade powder. They contacted numerous spaces-for-hire in Manhattan and Brooklyn in search of a makeshift gallery, attempting to preempt reluctance by offering double the asking price, and were rejected each time. *You couldn't pay us $100,000 to host this exhibition*, one program manager emailed them. And when Jay offered $100,000: *Still no.*

Howie was the one who suggested hosting the exhibition party at the penthouse. "We can fit a hundred people in here," he said. "What's the difference?"

Jay considered this. "I want longevity, though. I don't want this to be a one-time thing."

"You could have this party and another one a month later," Elijah said. "Make it a recurring pop-up."

Jay rubbed the corners of his mouth. He wouldn't admit it but he wanted legitimacy. For all his mockery of the contemporary art world he wanted that world's attention, and without a public gallery show he was unlikely to get it.

"We could fit two hundred people," Howie said. "These boys you're bringing over—they're so *slim.*"

Howie's thoughts about Jay's project were somewhat of a mystery, though his willingness to put unlimited money toward it suggested condonement. If Howie cared enough to have politics they'd probably lean to the right. He was a fruit but he was a fruit from North Dakota, son of a farmer and brother of a fracker, a man of the land as much as a patron of drag shows. If anything the project brought the two sides of him closer together: his heartland conservatism and his godless deviancy, his old man's suspicion of young-people ideas and his irrepressible appetite for young studs. He sat in on the shoots, greeted the models, and blushed at their slightest acknowledgment of him. By his own admission he was having a great summer.

Jay relented and agreed to host the exhibition party at the Die Kinder, and Elijah, who'd always wanted to throw a big party (Mark's eternal, damning response: "Who would you even invite?"), set about planning it. But even in these early days he felt the first stirrings of doubt. He wondered how many people would actually show up to Jay's party, how many people would want to toast this nobody's infernal videos—he imagined a tragedy on the order of an unpopular girl's sweet sixteen. He also wondered why so many of the messages they received had to be so *very* hateful. He wondered why the replies from event spaces had to be so *very* terse. He wondered why so few people saw the videos as he did, infernal but undeniably haunting, undeniably fascinating: why so many people failed to see the fun in them. He wondered, in other words, if his journey away from the preserves of common decency had perhaps taken him a mile too far.

Yet he trekked on. He wrote his press releases, he selected a date for the exhibition party, he labored to schedule shoots in the face of the models' organizational incompetence and calendrical illiteracy ("Is Thursday tomorrow?" Emilio wrote to him on a Tuesday). During the shoots he played PA, spotting Jay to make sure he didn't trip on cords and holding the gimbal when Jay's arms got tired. He swept the refuse of a video involving a pillow fight. He joined Jay during his maniacal editing sessions, advising on shot selection and transitions and color grading. He passed his evenings whipping himself up on coke and putting himself to sleep with vodka. The more he occupied and blunted his mind, he knew, the less chance he would give it to fixate on Mark and Alistair.

Unfortunately, the universe kept finding ways to remind him of them. Every few days, beginning in mid-May, it sent him a carrier pigeon in the form of Herve Gallion. Two weeks after Elijah had settled himself in the Die Kinder, Herve arrived in New York and began making his thrice-weekly visits to the penthouse. On the first of these visits, which he made with only an hour's notice, he told them he was merely visiting the city and tried, unconvincingly, to engage in small talk. But after five minutes of listening to Jay hold forth on his project Herve grew distracted and sullen and put up his hand. To Elijah the man couldn't have looked more out of place, sitting there under the penthouse's magisterial windows in his tan suede blazer and Wrangler jeans, in his agrarian dourness and uncosmopolitan girth. Elijah, who'd only ever heard Herve described, failed to see any but the faintest resemblance to Howie, and he pitied Herve in his hickish alienation. But the longer Herve drew out his silence the more forceful his presence became, the more it dispersed itself and took possession of the room around him. The world he'd come from might be far away, might be laughable in its backwardness and remoteness from cultural nerve centers, but it was realer than the penthouse, older, harder—this was what his stare communicated. And as the silence went on Elijah began to feel as if he were the one in alien territory.

"I'm wondering," Herve said to them, "if you've heard from Nikolai."

The three of them looked at one another and shook their heads.

"Contacted him? Seen him?"

They shook their heads again.

The reason Herve was asking, he explained, was that Nikolai had been unreachable for two weeks now and also appeared to have left the city. Herve knew this because he'd visited the apartment he'd rented for Nikolai a few blocks away and found moldy food and half-empty drawers. He'd since discarded the remainder of Nikolai's possessions, had the place deep-cleaned, and moved himself in. He would be staying in New York, he told them, until the question of Nikolai's whereabouts had been settled.

"And what about the boy?" he asked. "Mr. McCabe. It's my understanding"—he glanced at Elijah—"that he and Nikolai met here."

"Your paramour!" Jay said to Elijah.

"The blond," Howie said musically.

Elijah shrugged and told Herve the truth. "I haven't heard from him," he said.

"Have you reached out?" Herve asked.

Elijah hesitated. He found Herve intimidating, but his anger at having to discuss Alistair, at having to dredge up memories he'd been working hard to bury, was stronger than his fear, and he answered impertinently. "No," he said. "And I have no plans to."

"Well," Herve said evenly, "perhaps you can try."

Elijah fuzzily recalled Alistair saying, on the last day he'd seen him, that he'd quit his job with Nikolai. But now he wondered if he was mistaken, if his memory-burying had in fact been partway successful. Wouldn't Herve, being Alistair's boss, know if he'd resigned? "Why?" he asked. "Is he gone too?"

Herve held Elijah's gaze for a long moment. "I haven't heard from him either."

"I can let you know if he gets in touch, but I really don't see that happening."

"Please do," Herve said. "I would appreciate any news."

Herve left soon thereafter, and Elijah assumed that would be the end of his questioning. But he came by again a few days later, and a few days after that, and by the end of month he'd become a regular at the Die Kinder. He often came for dinner, sitting at one head of the table, chewing miserably and saying nothing as Jay and Howie prattled. Elijah suspected, again with pity, that Herve was growing restless in Nikolai's apartment, in this foreign city, and that he needed, though he would never admit it, a little company. But every night, after they'd finished eating, he made the true purpose of his continued visits clear. He asked the three of them if they'd heard from Nikolai, when exactly they'd last seen him, if he'd said or done anything out of character, given any hint of plans to leave the city. They answered unsatisfactorily each time. Herve, forcing a smile, barely disguising his mounting frustration, thanked them and asked them to let him know if their memories ever ceased to be quite so blank.

Having gathered that Jay and Howie knew even less about Alistair than they did about Nikolai, Herve reserved his questions about the kid for Elijah. After dinner he'd find a way to corner Elijah in the living room or sometimes a hallway, where he'd loom over him with his hands on his waist and put to him various futile questions. Precisely when, he asked, had Elijah last seen Alistair? Precisely what, he asked, had Alistair said? Had he ever mentioned plans to travel? Had he ever mentioned a new job? Had he ever mentioned the prospect of returning to his hometown after graduation? Elijah, still reluctant to devote mental energy to Alistair, answered in a monotone and in brief. Early May, didn't remember, no, no, and no. It seemed obvious to Elijah that Alistair was ignoring Herve, for whatever unaccountable reason, and he sometimes thought to tender this possibility but always stopped short—he had a feeling that Herve would find the idea somehow wounding. Only when, after the fourth of these interrogations, Elijah finally threw up his hands and called Alistair and got a message telling him the line had been disconnected—an errand to be repeated three times over the following days with the same result—did he begin to worry.

His theory fell into place quickly. If only Alistair had gone AWOL Elijah would have assumed that some undergraduate whim had prompted him to cut ties with his social and professional network, in the manner of a teenager melodramatically deleting his Facebook. If only Nikolai had gone AWOL he would have assumed that the Bulgarian had gone on a bender and was lying in some remote tropic with a bottle of Stoli pressed to his chest. The fact that both were missing, the fact that both had left Herve dangling, and the fact that Herve was ever so persistent in his pursuit of them suggested something more nefarious: Elijah believed they'd shaken Herve's pockets and run.

As far as possibilities went Elijah found this one both surprising and not. Alistair may have believed himself a nice boy but he'd always been money-obsessed, and if Nikolai didn't exactly strike Elijah as a high-caliber larcenist he also didn't exactly strike him as a model citizen. Now Alistair's claim that he'd quit his job with Nikolai made sense. He'd been clearing away any bread-crumbs that Mark and Elijah might follow.

His first feeling, upon formulating this theory, was one of delicious, ven-omous schadenfreude. Mark thought *he* was bad, but the boy he'd fallen in love with was an outright criminal—how delicious. He imagined Mark at his parents' house in Ho-Ho-Kus, calling Alistair to no avail, wondering after him with the same hopelessness with which Herve did. He derived no small pleasure from the picture of Mark's certain frustration and certain hurt. But this feeling was quickly replaced by a much less giddy one, a disappointingly human one. He found that he was, despite himself, afraid for Alistair and sorry for Mark. He didn't like the idea of Alistair on the run, he didn't like the idea of Mark stewing in his lovesickness, and he didn't like that he was moved to pity for two people who'd never cared a shred about him. He didn't like that his instinct, during Herve's subsequent interrogations, was to be even less helpful than he'd been before for fear of getting Alistair into trouble. Why protect Alistair? Why feel bad for Mark? Why be generous and concerned? Mere weeks into his program of derangement and flippancy he was already losing his resolve, was already returning to the preserves of common decency. His one concession to his selfishness, to his delicious schadenfreude, was not to tell Mark that Alistair was missing, to let him keep thrashing in his frustration and hurt. But even here he saw nobility imposing itself. His theory was only a theory, and he didn't want to cause Mark undue worry. That he cared to spare Mark undue worry! He didn't like this at all.

And he didn't like that, after each of Herve's interrogations, he returned to the world of Jay and his project with less enthusiasm. Herve's forbidding North Dakotan presence made the penthouse and everything that transpired in it seem frivolous. The very real danger Alistair was possibly in and the very real pain Mark was likely experiencing made his own predicament, his hunger for thrills, his desperation to rekindle his lost vitality, seem trivial. His debauched life with Jay was beginning to feel as hollow, as cramped and inauthentic, as his wholesome life with Mark. He felt the tetherball losing momentum, limply returning to its pole, and sent it spinning again with a half-hearted smack.

Only in the privacy of his bedroom could he work through his confusion in peace. But even here, it turned out, he wasn't safe. One day in late May, after returning home from a brutal ten-mile run that did exactly nothing to clear up his ambivalence, he stepped into his bathroom for a shower and jolted. On the sink, next to his toothbrush, was the nineteenth-century whalebone knife that Howie had bought for some throwaway thousands and that Jay had taken to using as a dental implement.

He took the knife and went out to the hall and called Jay's name with parental severity. Jay bounded out of his room and came skipping toward him.

"Were you in my bathroom?" Elijah said, holding up the knife.

"The housekeeper was cleaning mine, and I'd eaten an apple," Jay said.

"OK, well, I don't really want to come home and see this on my sink," Elijah said. "I don't want to think about you cleaning your teeth in my personal space."

Jay took the knife and looked at Elijah with puppy-dog eyes. "I was leaving you a reminder of me," he said. "So you don't forget about me!"

Elijah stared at the knife, at its refurbished silver blade and handsome cream handle, and felt sorry for it. Hewn by an honest craftsman, intended for such mannish tasks as the cutting of rope or whittling of wood, now stripped of its purpose and rendered an effeminate art object, now used to excavate fruit from a freak's teeth. "We're with each other every waking hour," he said to Jay. "I spend the bulk of my time looking at, thinking about, or talking about your art. You practically live inside my brain."

Jay skipped back down the hall as he answered. "That's good, I'm writing that down," he said. "I want to live inside people's brains. Every man and woman on earth!"

Elijah returned to his bedroom and stripped. In the shower, as he let cords of scalding water beat his face, he saw that what he'd said to Jay was true. Jay had commandeered his brain just as completely as Mark had, filled it with badness just as Mark had filled it with goodness. At no point in this transfer of ownership had there been one second for Elijah to claim his mind as his own. He'd begun his summer with the intention of recovering his real self, but all he'd done was trade one influence, one derivation, for another. It rattled him, it made him tremble, as he left the shower and toweled himself off: the possibility that he was neither bad nor good but nothing, that he was a person without will or ideas or beliefs, that there might be no real self for him to recover at all.

Nevertheless, that evening, he made an attempt to put up a self-delimiting defense. Jay approached him in the living room, where Elijah was trying by means of a fourth cocktail to forget about Mark and Alistair and failing. Jay was wearing a MAGA hat.

"Get your shoes on," he said to Elijah. "We're going out."

"Where?" Elijah said. "No."

"Gay bars," Jay said. "Hell's Kitchen. Chelsea."

"Wearing *that*?"

"If we're having the exhibition party here, we need to find people to invite," Jay said. "This'll be my magnet."

"For punches," Elijah said. "For abuse. What do you think will happen when you show up to a gay bar with that on?"

"I'm sure some people will hector me," Jay said. "And I'm sure others will take an interest."

"There's a difference between putting the hat in a video and wearing it in public," Elijah said. "Anyone who sees you wearing it and takes an 'interest' is insane."

Jay pulled the brim of the hat lower and smiled. "Like you?"

Later that night Jay did, as Elijah had feared, return to the Die Kinder showing evidence of abuse. Explaining the red mark on his face, he told Elijah that a drag queen at Industry had broken her routine and slapped him. Also: a bartender at Boxers had refused to serve him, the bouncer at the Rail had turned him away, a boisterous group at Barracuda had badgered him until he'd left. He relayed all this at two a.m., after waking Elijah and luring him to the living room. He paused occasionally to suck on his vape or sip his drink or inhale a nightcap line of cocaine. He was still wearing the MAGA hat.

"It was incredible," he said. "Every time I walked into a room I could feel its actual physics changing around me. Now I understand what it feels like to be a famous person. What it *will* feel like—when I am famous!"

Elijah was wearing his sleeping clothes, rubbing his eyes, and regretting his own nightcap line of cocaine. "Well, it sounds like it was a failure."

Jay emptied his drink. "Not at all," he said. "I exchanged numbers with ten people. They were shy. I learned to lurk in corners, so they could approach me discreetly. Most I found at the Eagle. That'll be a great scouting location. Those bears and wolves, those leather freaks, they're always up for a fresh experience. They all started with the skeptical song and dance. 'Are you actually,' 'Well if not,' 'Oh art you say,' 'Well if it's art,' 'A party you say,' 'A penthouse you say.' But you could see it."

"See what?"

"Their amazement."

Elijah lowered his head.

"We'll have them over next week."

"The exhibition party isn't until July."

"We need to start courting people, building our following. We need to get the word out."

"What do you know about these people?"

"Age-wise, I'd say they go from twenties to forties. On the hotness scale, five to eight."

Elijah spoke warily. "But are some of them—"

"Trump supporters?" Jay said. He put up his hands in mock horror. "Who cares?"

"I care," Elijah said. "Again, videos, real life—big difference."

Jay shook his head and laughed. "You lived with Mark for too long," he said. "Why be disdainful when you can be curious? Why be righteous when you can be fascinated? Why be dismissive when you can be interested? It's *so* much more fun. I thought you knew that."

Curiosity, fascination, interest: Jay had named Elijah's dearest shibboleths, his cardinal directions, but directions to where? In their vagueness, their capaciousness, their indiscrimination they could lead him anywhere.

Jay leaned forward and spoke to him candidly, with an impish levity in his eyes, a brotherly affection that brought Elijah back to Vassar. "If some of these people are honest-to-God Trumpies, so be it," he said. "Being in the same room with them won't hurt us. If they're crazy enough, it'll make us feel more alive."

Elijah stared into his oldest friend's face. It occurred to him that the crucial difference between Mark and Jay was that Mark was gone and Jay was here, that Mark had abandoned him and Jay had quartered him, and that while there were a million things he could do to drive Mark away there was literally nothing he could do to make Jay cast him off. He could murder someone and Jay's first response would be to ask what it had felt like. He wasn't sure Jay's coat of amoral hilarity was one he really wanted to wear himself, but he also wasn't sure he was done with his summer of his self-inquiry. He felt pulled up, challenged, by Jay's implicit likening of him to Mark. And he had nowhere else to go. "What will we do?"

"Mingle, eat, drink," Jay said. "Half these men had their shirts off. A few of them groped me. I think we should be ready for what usually happens when you put a bunch of gay men in a room. We need to stock up on lube."

A part of Elijah unanswerable to his conscience—his libido, at once the rogue menial and chief executive of his mind—perked up. He hadn't touched another human being in weeks. "You really think they'll come?"

"I worry about the retention rate," Jay said. "Which is why I'm going back out tomorrow. Join me?"

Elijah shook his head. He sat for a few more minutes, until his erection went down, and then escaped to his room.

Jay spent the next three nights terrorizing the gay bars of Manhattan, making his way down the west side, over to the East Village, and back again. On the third night he returned with a bruised eye and swollen cheek. "It appears the many hours a certain go-go dancer puts in at Planet Fitness," he said triumphantly, "have not been in vain."

"Are you OK?" Elijah asked from his bed, where Jay had found him.

"He took my hat and threw it behind the DJ booth," Jay said. "Thankfully I brought a spare."

By this point he'd collected forty or fifty numbers, he told Elijah. Taking into account cold feet and the noncommittal nature of plans laid under strobe lights he expected about a dozen to show up. "I'll tell them next Thursday," he said. "Howie will handle the food and drinks. You—"

"The lube," Elijah said and went back to sleep.

On the appointed day, Elijah went to CVS and all but emptied its shelves of Astroglide, K-Y, and Swiss Navy. He also bought several boxes of Durexes, Trojans, and Magnums, even though his impression was that every gay man from sea to shining sea now swallowed a daily PrEP pill with his coffee. The cashier did him the generosity of not meeting his eyes. Howie ordered several platters of sandwiches and crudités, some thirty bottles of middle-shelf liquor, and enough cocaine to lead their dealer to ask if they were selling. A rush shipment from a website called Mom and Poppers rounded out the provisions: two dozen small vials of Jungle Juice and Rush, officially designated, on the enclosed receipt, as VCR cleaner. The label on the vials of Rush, bright yellow with a red lightning bolt, captured perfectly Elijah's feeling about the gathering: an uneasy combination, so familiar to him now, of arousal and dread.

That evening, while Howie busied himself with the food platters and Jay compiled the playlist, Elijah snuck off to his room for an hour of critical precoital ablutions. The last time he'd been penetrated was sometime in late April, when, for what he didn't realize would be the last time, he'd endured the two-pronged offensive of Mark's grandfatherly pokes and Alistair's jackhammer exertions. In his bathroom he ran clippers over his pubes and a razor over his asshole and balls. Back in the bedroom he took from a moving box his prized three-piece dildo set. The set contained a small dildo, a giant one, and one of

Goldilocks stature. He feared his anus had returned to virginal tightness: if he could squeeze in the biggest one he'd be ready for anything.

He lay on his bed, opened a bottle of Swiss Navy he'd smuggled up to his room, and began the operation: deep breaths, a teaspoon of lube here and a teaspoon there, an ambassadorial finger, more deep breaths, and then, after the wince-inducing surprise of the dildo's coldness, after some resistance from a rectum lately disaccustomed to rigidity, success. He got the little guy in all the way to its flared end in seconds—he was not, it appeared, revirginized. He extracted the little guy slowly, applied fresh lube, and reached for Goldilocks. After another wince and plaint of rectal resistance it slid in just as easily and in fact to greater stimulatory effect: this one was just right. He shut his eyes and moved around in slow innards-adjusting gyrations, turning this way and that, until he felt ready to graduate. But when he looked at the large dildo towering on the side table he balked. For this one he needed poppers, which stupidly he'd neglected to smuggle up along with the lube.

He stood carefully and pulled on shorts and a T-shirt. He left Goldilocks in. A trip downstairs and back up to his room would force his bowels into new movements, new acclimatory challenges. By the time he returned to his bed he'd be as loose as a jellyfish. He walked down the hallway with rigid steps, clenching to guard against expulsion. He passed Jay's room and heard his shower going. With any luck Howie would be in his room too.

When he was halfway down the stairs, though, he heard voices in the kitchen, and before he could turn back Howie called out: "Jay?"

He descended the rest of the stairs. Every step sent a throb of pressure through his abdomen. When he reached the bottom and turned to the kitchen he froze. Howie stood at the counter before the food platters and bottles. Across from him, on the stool nearest Elijah, sat Herve.

Herve eyed Elijah inscrutably. "Hello," he said.

Elijah smiled and nodded. He very much wanted to take himself with rigid steps back to his room. But some minimal sense of manners kept him in place.

"Howie tells me you're having a party," Herve said.

"A party that's starting very soon," Howie said. "So."

Elijah tried to avoid Herve's eyes, which were still trained on him. His rectum seemed unsure of what to do with the dildo in light of this new threat. He felt it quivering with defecatory and constipatory indecision. He looked toward the living room, where Jay had dumped the condoms, lube bottles, and vials of poppers into rattan bowls. On the walls the screens played Jay's videos. Beneath one screen, on a low console, was a pile of MAGA hats.

Herve finally peeled his eyes from Elijah and looked at the screens. "So this is what Mr. Steigen has been up to," he said.

"You'll see more at the exhibition party," Howie said. "Which isn't for a few weeks. So."

"I'm looking forward to it," Herve said. He returned his gaze to Elijah. "Seems like you're expecting quite a crowd tonight."

Howie toyed aimlessly with an arrangement of celery stalks. "And they'll be here any minute," he said. "So."

"And these guests," Herve said to Elijah. "Are they people you know?"

Elijah squirmed. "I've never met them," he said. "They're friends of Jay's."

"How long has Jay known them?"

"Oh, *this* again," Howie said.

"A few days," Elijah said.

"So they wouldn't have—"

"They don't know Nikolai," Howie said. "No one knows anything. When will you stop asking?"

Herve would never stop asking. The longer Elijah looked at his chapped face and unwavering eyes the more clearly he understood this. And though he found Herve overly obsessive, and though he disliked his interrogations, he nevertheless felt respect for his resolve, the single-mindedness of his pursuit, the determination with which he sought to redress whatever wrongs had been committed against him. Presumably this determination explained his billions, his commanding presence. Elijah couldn't imagine himself ever having even a speck of it.

Herve looked again at Jay's videos, at the boys frolicking in their near-nakedness, touching the bills of their MAGA hats. He stood from the stool. "I can't pretend I understand the point of all this," he said.

"Neither can I," Elijah said.

After Herve left Elijah retrieved a vial of poppers, returned to his room, and managed the last dildo with an ease he found unsettling. Poppers did weird things to the mind, he knew. They could make you fall in love with a pillow. But he'd never expected, in that dumb divine haze, to imagine Herve Gallion of all people getting on top of him, baring his belly, putting his nose to his nose and boring into him with his questions. And yet this was precisely what Elijah pictured as he writhed. He imagined Herve penetrating him, drilling deep, breaking up the sediment of his decadence and frivolity, his utter nothingness as a person, and filling him with harder things. He imagined Herve ravaging him with the same tenacity with which he'd built his fortune, bent people to his whims, wrestled the world into submission. He imagined being fucked by Herve until he was all but empty, little more than a shell for Herve to do with what he liked.

And how blissful, how dreadfully familiar, this fantasy was.

Having accidentally come during his turn with the large dildo, he showed up to the party in diminished spirits. Thankfully Jay was too distracted to notice. The first four guests arrived at eight and by nine they'd been joined by seven more. Elijah stood at a remove, drinking heavily and eating nothing, nodding when the men gave their names and saying only "Welcome" in reply. Jay's description of them came in for a heavy edit: they were higher on the age scale and lower on the hotness scale than advertised. In terms of milieu they were a mixed bag. Three of the men, who appeared to be friends, were a familiar type: shaven muscle boys with short-cropped hair and a jittery demeanor that suggested occasional or possibly regular use of meth. They sucked on their vodka sodas, tried on the MAGA hats and laughingly took selfies, eyed the assortment of poppers and lube, and after an hour began impatiently to pull at their crotches. They all wore the same black tank tops, black short shorts, and white Converses. Their names were things like Ricky and Devin and Brett.

Four of the guests were older: two bearded bearish types and two bespoke gentlemen with silver hair and natty attire who, Elijah would soon learn, were married. They sipped their drinks and stood stiffly with middle-aged self-consciousness and said little. Howie, perhaps fearing demographic association with them, kept his distance. He took an immediate liking to Ricky-Devin-Brett.

The rest were closer to Elijah's age: an academic-looking guy with patchy stubble, a rail-thin man with acne and thinning blond hair, a chunky person with a high-and-tight and baby-soft skin, and a short loud redhead with a

Nassau County accent named Paul who led the field in terms of Trumpist enthusiasm.

"Brilliant, brilliant, brilliant," he said of the videos playing on the walls. "The campaign should fucking *hire* you, man."

"Thank you," Jay said. "Though this is not campaigning. It's art."

Paul put out his arms as far as his tight teal button-down would allow. "*Love* art," he said. "Especially when it really *says* something, you know?"

Elijah pursed his lips. Paul sounded like certain people he'd grown up with. Whenever Elijah had to say where he was from he always clarified, however preposterously, that he was from *Suffolk* County, Long Island—yes, the part that included the Hamptons.

"Let's move to the couches," Jay said to the men. "We can all admire the art together."

Before taking a seat Paul grabbed a MAGA hat from the console and fitted it onto his head. Its color matched his hair almost exactly, as if the hat were melting and melding with his skull. He smiled at Ricky-Devin-Brett, who'd turned their own MAGA hats backward and were well on their way to being trashed.

"So are you at all involved in politics?" one of the nattily dressed men asked Jay.

"I'm a nonparticipant observer," Jay said. "I form no alliances, make no judgments."

"So is this, like, satire?" one of the bearded men asked.

"Satire is for suckers," Jay said.

"We were very dubious about Mr. Trump," the nattily dressed man said. "We're longtime fiscal conservatives." He explained that he was a managing director at Goldman Sachs and that his husband—the husband nodded—was a partner at Skadden. "We were excited about Marco Rubio."

"I'm from Florida," the chunky guy said.

"Trump really feels like the lesser of two evils," Goldman Sachs said. "We're alarmed by the direction the Democratic Party is moving in. It puts us in a tough spot. All our gay friends have stopped speaking to us."

"Same here," the man with thinning blond hair said.

"Oh, you just don't have the right gay friends," Paul said. "I'll bring around my boys. You'll fucking *love* my boys."

"We'd be very interested in your boys," Jay said. "We're having an exhibition party next month. We'd love—"

"Who says you have to be liberal to be gay?" Thinning Hair said. "The righteousness is exhausting."

"Not to mention intellectually incoherent," the man with the patchy stubble said. He explained that he was a PhD in history at Columbia, focus modern Europe, and that the incuriosity and uninterrogated Democratic Party fealty of his colleagues made his head spin. He was thinking of dropping out.

"Marco Rubio lives near my parents," the chunky guy said. "One time I saw him at Chipotle."

"The things you're not allowed to say," the PhD said. "Not even allowed to think."

"Well," Jay said, "here you're free to say and think whatever you please. But let's not get bogged down in politics. That's not really what this is about."

Elijah was grateful for the intervention. This sort of discussion was, safe to say, not what he'd signed up for. He felt an instinctive Mark-like horror, an instinctive Mark-like sanctimony. That he could provide no rationale for this sanctimony—that in his political ignorance he could only feel that these reactionaries were wrong, not explain intelligibly why—only made his instinct stronger. And yet even as he sat erect, with self-regardingly squared shoulders, he saw the futility of his disapproval. He would gain nothing by aping the sanctimony he'd always ended up on the wrong side of. Pretending to be like Mark wouldn't gain him readmission to Mark's heart. Pretending to be good wouldn't make goodness any more welcoming to him. He remembered Jay's challenge: *Why be disdainful?* He remembered what Jay had said about the craziness of men like this: *It'll make us feel more alive.* He remembered that he'd come to the Die Kinder, had given himself over to this strange summer, with no other purpose.

"What *is* this about?" one of the bearded men asked.

Jay put his hands together, raised his chin, and glanced at the screen behind him. "My idea is very simple," he said before launching into a fifteen-minute speech about his project. The speech was like a drinking game: every time Jay uttered the words "erotic," "libido," and "carnal" the men took a sip. By the time he was finished their glasses were empty.

"Mostly I just want us to have fun," he said.

Ricky-Devin-Brett cooed in unison.

"I was hoping," one of the bearded men said, staring at the lube and poppers.

"We were wondering," Goldman said circumspectly.

"Interesting," the PhD said.

"Very," Skadden said.

Paul: "I love it! I fucking love it!"

Jay clapped his hands. "Good! So."

Howie went to the bathroom and came back reeking of Listerine. Someone turned up the music. Baggies of cocaine materialized out of nowhere. Jay collected an armful of MAGA hats and distributed them to everyone who didn't have one, and everyone but Elijah accepted.

"You all look so good," Paul said. "*Damn!*"

As he turned his head it dawned on Elijah that every person in the room was white. This was hardly surprising, given the politics that had drawn them here or that they'd felt no compunction about ignoring, and in Elijah's experience it was hardly without precedent: practically everyone he knew was at the spray end of this or that wave from Europe. But here, under the blaze of their red hats, the men's skin seemed to accrue a strange force, to gather and cohere into a comment upon itself, to glow with forbidding, metacomplexional significance. When Elijah noticed several of the men looking his way he wondered if they were thinking the same thing. But then it registered with him that he was the most attractive person in the room.

His next drink, his sixth of the night, carried him safely into oblivion, as did the powder he railed off a key, and the vial of Rush he held to his undusted nostril. From here on out the night was a blur. He didn't remember taking off his shirt, but all of a sudden the two beards were at his nipples. He didn't remember lowering his jeans, but all of a sudden Thinning Hair was on his dick, and then Paul was butting in, making a game of trying to fit both his balls in his mouth at once, and then the PhD had his lips on his neck. He didn't remember going up to his room, but all of a sudden he was on his bed with Goldman and Skadden, submitting to their caresses, their spit-roast theatrics, getting whiffs of well-seasoned crotches and hoary pubes in his teeth. He didn't remember going into his bathroom, but all of a sudden he was in the shower pulling his cheeks apart for Chunky, whose tongue wriggled up inside him like a smoked-out badger. He didn't remember going back downstairs, but all of a sudden he was dancing idiotically with Ricky-Devin-Brett, then bending over and taking them one at a time, like a cream-ready donut on an assembly line. He didn't remember putting on a MAGA hat himself but when he caught his reflection in the darkened windows and saw the red halo over his head he understood, amid his blur, the extent of his derangement. He lost track of Howie and Jay for long spans of time but whenever he spotted them he was unnerved by their discretion: both kept their clothes on and limited themselves to modest pleasures—petting, jerking, furtive sucking. Elijah saw that for all his confusion, for all his ambivalence, he'd gone much further than either of them.

The sky was getting light by the time the last guests left. Jay found Elijah supine on a couch and stood over him.

"Was it fun?" he asked. He seemed very high up, like the summit of a mountain.

"It was a lot," Elijah managed.

"Oh, I don't think so. It wasn't nearly enough. Next week I want twenty people, thirty, *fifty*."

"I need to puke," Elijah said.

"Here," Jay said and half carried him to the bathroom.

A plan was established. During the week Jay would visit gay bars and invite more men. He'd induce enthusiastic attendees to do their own recruiting. Every Thursday he'd host another bacchanal. By the time the exhibition party rolled around they'd have enough fans to fill the penthouse. They'd have to institute a *waiting list*. Jay explained all this the Saturday after the gathering.

"You can decide how involved you want to be," he said to Elijah.

"OK," Elijah said. "How about not at all."

"All you have to do is show your face."

"And if I don't want to show my face?"

"You seemed to have quite a time on Thursday," Jay said. "You showed more than your face."

"Maybe I've had my fill," Elijah said.

"I doubt that."

Elijah's hangover lasted all weekend and was existential in its dimensions. When he wasn't writing press releases or scheduling shoots he sat in bed, drinking and snorting and huffing according to some misguided hair-of-the-dog logic. He wrapped his mind repeatedly around one masochistic thought: he imagined Mark walking into the Die Kinder on Thursday night, spurred by chivalric romantic reconsideration, and seeing him on the floor with his ass in the air and a MAGA hat on his head, waiting for the next stranger to plug him. He imagined the immediacy with which Mark would renounce him forever. And when this thought lost its power to traumatize he progressed to an even worse one. He realized that Mark would never come to the Die Kinder, that he probably wasn't thinking about him at all, that he didn't care enough about him to renounce him more definitively than he already had, and that even this masochistic fantasy therefore partook of hopeful delusion. It was a delusion to think that anyone, Mark least of all, was watching over him. He had no audience to act out for, there was no pole for his tetherball to return to.

On Monday he consumed so much cocaine that he thought about calling 911. But after an hour (so, by eleven a.m.) he'd stopped twitching and sweating icicles.

On Tuesday he moved the tub of bleach out of his bathroom for fear of what he might do with it.

On Wednesday his parents called and alerted him, in bright singing voices, to the fact that it was his thirty-first birthday.

On Thursday night Jay held his second gathering and this time opened the door to twenty-five men, of whom Elijah opened his legs for fourteen.

Herve continued to make his visits, but he asked fewer questions and posed them with less vigor. He grew every day wearier, every day more despondent, which Elijah took solace in—at least he wasn't the only one. And then one afternoon Elijah made his way downstairs to fix himself lunch at Howie's liquor cart. Howie and Jay had gone to see a Francis Bacon show at the Met, and Elijah was relieved to have the penthouse to himself. But when he stepped into the dining room he found Herve sitting at the table, staring blankly at the city.

"Just getting myself a drink," Elijah said as he went for the whiskey. "You have as long as it takes me to empty my glass and refill it to ask me questions. So about a minute."

"Don't worry," Herve said to window. "No questions today."

"You've given up?"

"I didn't say that."

Something in Herve's voice told Elijah that he needed companionship, and that he really would refrain from battering him with questions. "Can I make you one?"

Herve turned to him. "I almost never drink."

Elijah held the whiskey bottle at an angle over a glass. "I heard an 'almost.'"

Herve shrugged, watched Elijah pour, and accepted the glass. Elijah made an effort to sip slowly. Sunlight was beating on the dining table, bringing out the blond in its grain. "You know," he said to Herve, "maybe it is time to give up. I'm sure you have plenty to go back to. I imagine your billions keep you pretty busy."

"People act like having money is an occupation," Herve said.

"It was my boyfriend's occupation for eight years."

Herve sipped his whiskey. "And what was your occupation?"

It occurred to Elijah that in all of Herve's interrogations he'd never once asked a question about him, and he was unexpectedly moved by his curiosity. "I did graphic design," he said. "I hated it, but now I'm thinking it's the perfect job for me."

Herve sat motionless, waiting for him to continue.

"Whatever the client wants, I'll do," Elijah said. "I can make anything look appealing, and I'll shill for anyone. The less thinking I have to do the better. Just make me your vessel."

"Is that what you're doing for Mr. Steigen?" Herve said. "Being his vessel?"

"I certainly would never have come up with this project myself."

"And why is that?"

Elijah smiled. "If you're expecting me to critique his views, you'll be disappointed," he said. "I have no views to critique from."

"Then what do you have?"

Elijah gave up on drinking slowly and gulped. "Nothing," he said. "Just emptiness and nothingness. I'm hopeless."

Herve drew his finger along the rim of his glass, squinting in the warm sun. It occurred to Elijah that there was a quality of flirtation about this conversation, and not for the first time he wondered about Herve. By all accounts he was arrow-straight, but according to Howie there'd never been a woman in his life, and there was something heated in his pursuit of Nikolai and Alistair, something hankering about his quest to grab hold of his missing men. One could be gay without really being gay: Elijah had blown enough Vassar jocks now saddled with wives and children to know.

"Hopeless people make the best workers," Herve said.

"I'll tell that to my next prospective employer."

Herve smiled. He seemed to find Elijah amusing. "Shame to see you waste your talents on jobs you don't care about," he said. "A smart person like you should be more ambitious."

"No one in my life has ever called me smart," Elijah said.

"Maybe no one has ever listened to you."

Elijah lowered his head to his drink. He assumed the tears building from out of nowhere behind his eyes had to do with the whiskey and his lack of sleep.

"Maybe you feel aimless because you've never found a meaningful goal," Herve said. "Something bigger. Something that'll really shake the world." He glanced toward the living room. "What Jay is doing—all I see is 'look at me.' All right, I'm looking. But then what? What's he doing? Where's the action?"

"The action happens on Thursday nights," Elijah said. "You're welcome to join. Clothing very much optional."

Herve shook his head. "I'm sure you could find something more worthwhile if you tried," he said. "There's always work in making things look appealing."

"Got a job for me?" Elijah said. "You'll never meet anyone more hopeless."

Herve glanced at him, naked for a moment in the loneliness that Elijah suspected haunted him always. Then he looked at his empty glass with something like chagrin and sat back.

"Another one?" Elijah said.

"No," Herve said, unsteadily, and left.

Elijah passed the rest of his day in stunning temperance. Only three more drinks and no coke at all. He continued to feel moved by Herve's curiosity. He felt chastised, smacked on the behind, talked to. Maybe Herve was right. Maybe he was smart, or least not impossibly stupid, and maybe it was true that his problem was that he hadn't found a meaningful goal, hadn't pushed himself into concrete action. He kept waiting for Mark to decide he loved him again, kept waiting for his old vital self to resurface, kept waiting, in other words, for life to *happen to* him. And he wondered how much longer he could go on waiting. He wondered if it was his turn to be an agent of happening.

Inspired but incorrigibly himself, Elijah opted to bring these thoughts to bear on the next Thursday gathering. He certainly acted; he certainly happened. He launched himself into the party as if it were his first, because some part of him knew it would be his last. Jay had persuaded more than fifty men to come, and Elijah determined quickly that they were the looniest bunch yet.

He met a man who believed Bill and Hillary Clinton were responsible for the murders of at least sixteen people, who held most of his money in Bitcoin, who described himself as a member of the "Dark Enlightenment," and who claimed to own a sex doll designed to look like Julian Assange.

He met a man who asserted that a shadowy group of elites was seeking to rend national identity everywhere and subject the world's population to its control in part by producing pop songs that included random lists of countries and cities and that thus promoted a "sensibility of borderlessness," citing as an example Fergie's "L.A. Love," which in a single verse referred to Amsterdam, San Francisco, Switzerland, São Paulo, Johannesburg, Mexico, Stockholm, Jamaica, and, naturally, L.A.

He met a man who believed that the Constitution had been a terrible mistake and that the United States would be better off under monarchic rule, who after years of careful genealogical research had deduced that he was a distant descendant of George Washington, meaning that he carried within him the bloodline most nearly invested with divine right, and who therefore believed that, under such a monarchic rule, he deserved to come into princely or at least ducal privileges.

He met a banker who believed gay men were naturally inclined toward finance because the profession allowed them to avenge their alienation from the traditional objects and processes of production (think, he said, of farming, transportation, manufacturing, construction) by pricing, packaging, and liquidating those objects and processes: by reducing, always in a deliciously cold manner, all these things to their unholy monetary value. "You see," he said to

Elijah, with the barest smile on his face, "they do more than make unholy the world they've been cast out of. They eat it."

An important fact about these men was that Elijah slept with all of them, and he slept with a great many more besides. He bounced, he sucked, he moaned, he clutched: his curiosity knew no bounds. As he applied himself to such tasks as the blowing of two men while unseen others treated themselves to his ass, or the scraping with his tongue of fecal particulates from the hairs of an otter's taint, or the inhaling of coke off a man's semierect penis (inadvisable, impossible, terrible waste of drug), or the enduring of spanks and slaps to the face, or the special hell of fellating a man who wanted to see tears, Elijah began to understand, at long last, Jay's philosophy. And he wondered if these gatherings, even more than the videos, served to effectuate his ideas. He wondered if all these men weren't, by dissolving into a heathenish jumble, acting out some deranged model of empire, one with more ancient authority and appeal to the instincts than any infant democracy could lay claim to, one that would satisfy their hunger to be frightened, overwhelmed, dislocated, obliterated. He recalled his *Blue Light* paintings, the fascination in the young men's faces, their yearning for the bright mountain, their craving for destruction. All summer he'd thought of Jay as the original and he as the derivative, but the situation was in fact reversed. He'd had this idea long before Jay had ever come to it. It had always been with him; it was the guiding idea of his life. And now, with his face against the floor, he was seeing it realized.

He wondered if he'd had enough.

He put this question as if sending aloft a prayer, and soon enough his prayer was answered. A few days after the gathering Mark finally broke his silence and called. He told Elijah that he'd seen Jay's Instagram, that he knew what he and Jay were up to. And even as he proceeded to lay into Elijah, even as he chewed him out, Elijah felt a wave of happiness, because if Mark had bothered to keep tabs on him, if he'd bothered to call at all, he must (for all his anger, and he was really quite angry) still care about him. Elijah had waited, and he had been rewarded for his patience.

"I know," Elijah said when Mark had finished. "It's bad, bad, bad. And you don't know the half of it."

Mark spoke warily. "The half of it?"

"The quarter of it," Elijah said. "The eighth of it. The hundredth of it." And he told him all—more than he wanted to; more, surely, than he had to. But he needed, he felt, if he was to clear a new path for himself, if he was to clear the way (and he clung to the hope as desperately, as delusionally, as ever) for a new beginning with Mark, to tell him everything. He started with his first rage-fueled days at the Die Kinder and barreled forward, neglecting no details of his recklessness and debauchery, relishing them even, the very worst of them. He'd gotten as far as recounting the most recent gathering, recounting in particular his thirty minutes with two congressional aides up from DC who'd managed, after much arduous relubricating, to jam both their hideously curved members in Elijah at once, when finally Mark interrupted him.

"I don't need to hear this," he said. "I don't need to hear any of this."

"There's more," Elijah said. "My God, Mark, there's so much *more*."

"I don't need to hear it."

"I'm sorry I was unfaithful to you. I know we're only on a break."

"That is literally the least of my concerns."

"I'm sorry for everything," Elijah said. "I'm sorry I ridiculed you. I'm sorry I made you feel boring. You are boring, if I'm being honest, but that's what's beautiful about you. I was the one who made things between us ugly, I was the one who didn't think you were enough. You're more than enough. You would have been better off if you'd never met me. *I* was the one, *I* was the one—" He wasn't crying. The volcanic rumbling in his chest was the precursor not to tears but to something larger, something more terrible and more wonderful: the full expulsion, after eight long years, of the truth. "I wasted you. You gave me your youth, you gave me the best years of your life, and I wasted them. But you—"

"Elijah—"

"You don't know what it was like. To live with you. To be with you. To love you. You take one look at you, that's all it takes, and you know."

"Elijah—"

"You were born whole. Entirely at peace with yourself, at peace with the world. No brokenness, no self-destructiveness, not a bad or misshapen thought in your head. You don't know what it was like—"

"Elijah—"

"—to look at that, every day, for *years*. I saw you and wanted you from the first second because I knew—even if I didn't really know it then, I knew—that you would save me. You would take me in. I would become part of your wholeness, and I would become whole myself. But it would never work. I figured that out eventually. I'm not like you. I'll never be. And instead of—"

"Elijah—"

"You don't need to tell me what Jay is doing is fucked-up. You don't need to tell me why. I know what you'll say. How—how could I know? I've never read a news article all the way through in my life. But I know, Mark, and the reason I know is that I'm fascinated by it. I love it. That's how I know. There's a sick part of me, there always has been. It's not part of me, it *is* me. And I can't honestly tell you—"

"Elijah—"

"—that I'll ever be any different. I'll never be right for you. I'll never be what you deserve. I'll never be up in that wholesome place where you were born, where you live, never. I'll always be down here, with my twisted compulsions, my resentments, my weaknesses. Intoxicated by all the wrong things, mocking all the wrong things—always. But maybe, maybe, if we—"

"Elijah—"

"If we *start* from that. If we accept that and go from there. If we accept that we're not right for each other but not totally wrong either. That there'll always be something between us, some misunderstanding, some gap, and try anyway, because maybe that gap is exactly, maybe exactly, what pulls us toward each other. Maybe it's exactly why I need you. And I need you. And maybe, for all my weakness, for all my twistedness, maybe you—"

"Elijah," Mark said, and this time Elijah let him speak. "Everything you're saying about yourself—I don't recognize you in it. I love you."

Elijah held his breath.

"I love you," Mark said. "You don't need to tell me we're not right for each other. I know that. I always have. And I've always loved you."

Elijah only waited, teetering, unbreathing.

"But it's not everything," Mark said. "Everything you're saying—the misunderstanding between us, the gap—it's not everything." He paused. "There are other things."

Now Elijah spoke. He said only one word, the only one that mattered. "Alistair," he said.

Mark made no reply, only sighed softly, and after a while Elijah relieved him. What mixed motivations he may have had—whether he hoped that by voicing his concern for Alistair he might endear himself to Mark, whether he hoped that by revealing Alistair's disappearance he might shunt Alistair definitively into the past, whether he hoped for nothing in particular at all—he couldn't at the moment sort out. And he knew that, regardless of his motivations, he was, by giving Mark what little information he possessed, by easing Mark's thirst with what few drops he could, acting as honorably as he ever had, that he was in the midst of perhaps his finest hour. He told Mark about Herve's interrogations, he told him his theory. He told him that while he surely worried for Alistair less than Mark did he worried for him all the same. "Other than stonewalling Herve, I don't know what to do," he said. "I know barely anything. But you should know what I know."

Mark was slow in responding, and when he answered he seemed to speak over an internal rumbling of his own. "Thank you," he said. "Thank you."

They talked for a while longer, working back to Elijah's summer, over to Mark's summer, back to Elijah's pitifulness and his pitiful need for Mark—his undead hope, all his belated realizations—before saying their amicable, inconclusive goodbye. When Elijah dropped the phone onto his bed he understood that nothing had changed. Nothing he said to Mark could circumvent the spectral blond standing between them. Yet he also knew that, where he alone was concerned, nothing could stay the same. He'd said what he'd said, he'd expelled and he'd voided. By now he'd reached a place of clarity from which there was no returning. He stepped out of his room and looked around at the penthouse and knew that he wasn't long for it.

He began, little by little, to pull away from Jay. He counted his money. He scanned Craigslist for apartments. With or without Mark he was getting out of here. He circled the day after the exhibition party in his mind.

Practically speaking he remained a dutiful assistant. He continued sitting in on the shoots and harassing media outlets. At long last he succeeded in getting a lukewarm response from the *Grift*. He wanted to avoid a scene with Jay, and he needed a few more $1,500 checks before he flew Howie's nest.

When he declined to participate in the Thursday gatherings Jay only assumed he was recovering from overexertion. He once asked Elijah, in all sincerity, if he'd sustained anal fissures.

Oddly enough, the one person who seemed to pick up on Elijah's waning commitment was Herve. On the Fourth of July, the elder Gallion joined them for dinner and then stood with them on the terrace to watch the fireworks.

"Elijah," Jay said, leaning perilously over the railing, "why didn't we invite our boys over for a Fourth of July party? Feels like a missed thematic opportunity."

Elijah felt Herve beside him, forbidding in his presence, fatherly in his understanding. When he noticed that Elijah had ignored Jay's question he faced him, and his gaze seemed to recapitulate the gentle chastisement he'd meted out in the dining room. It seemed to say: *Something bigger.* Then his expression hardened and he turned away.

The fireworks began. Though they were being set off from the river they were visible through the intervening skyscrapers, and they were loud enough to rattle Elijah's chest. He heard the bombs and saw the lights, shrank from the cannonade and marveled at the explosions. He was amazed, as he'd been on this day every year since childhood, that such violence could be the source of such beauty.

Four hours after the *Grift* writer had left, the first of Jay's Thursday night acolytes arrived. Elijah listened to them parade in from his bedroom. He chided himself for not sneaking downstairs earlier to grab a sandwich from one of the platters. He settled in for a long night of lying hungrily in his bed, fending off sounds of depravity from below.

He opened his laptop. Over the past week he'd bookmarked a dozen Craigslist apartments, all with leases starting July 15, the day after the exhibition party, all miniscule and criminally priced. A $1,600 one-bedroom in Crown Heights with drooping ceilings and a refrigerator in the hallway. A $1,400 studio in Inwood that overlooked, according to Google Street View, an abandoned lot strewn with weeds and single-use plastics. A $1,300 studio on the Upper East Side whose astonishingly reasonable cost was explained by the fact that it shared a bathroom with two other units. He skimmed the

few unanswered emails that had come into his freelance inbox and realized
with a shudder that he'd have to triple, possibly quintuple, his productivity to
afford even these jerry-renovated digs. He saw his future. His long sojourn
in the land of other people's wealth, a land he'd never belonged in and never
made any lasting claim to, had come to an end. Yet he couldn't deny his relief.
He was tired of mooching, of entrusting his security and satisfactions to other
people and their unpredictable whims. He had to make a life, by himself and
for himself, and he had to start somewhere.

He passed the night fitfully, kept from sleep by the music and guttural
moaning below, with only thoughts of Mark to console him.

The next morning Jay knocked on his door. Elijah opened it only a crack.
He wanted to hide his now halfway-filled moving boxes, the toiletries that like
a hotel guest he'd begun keeping in a dopp kit, all the evidence of his imminent
departure. He feared not that Jay would be angry but that he'd be smooth: that
he'd try to persuade Elijah to stay and would succeed. He remained the person
who knew Elijah best, who loved him most unconditionally, who understood
his weaknesses and how to exploit them.

"I'm looking through yesterday's footage," he said to Elijah. "I want your
input."

"You're the artist," Elijah said.

"I need your eyes. I rely on them!"

"My eyes are struggling to stay open. There was a lot of noise last night."

Jay cocked his head. "Am I sensing a loss of enthusiasm?"

"Only a loss of sleep."

"Well, rest up," Jay said. "The big day is almost here."

Elijah spent the afternoon packing happily in his room. But by four o'clock
he felt stir-crazy. The exhibition party was only six days away but it felt *months*
away, it felt *years* away; he wanted to leave *now*.

He put on his running gear and managed to escape the penthouse unnoticed.
He started down Forty-second Street and followed routes every sane runner
avoids: through Times Square, around Columbus Circle, along the carriage-
clogged border of Central Park. But he was keen to see people, crowds of
new faces, great big chunks of the world he'd soon rejoin. After crossing the
island and wending his way back he stopped on the west side pier next to the
Intrepid. He looked at the scruffy banks of New Jersey.

He took out his phone. Years before, in the prime of his and Mark's relationship, Elijah had saved all the Landmessers' birthdays to his calendar, and earlier that day he'd received an alert reminding him that today was Janet's. He navigated to her Instagram. Surely the family was celebrating, surely Janet was documenting it, surely she'd lassoed Mark into at least one frame. But Elijah saw no sign of him. Janet had posted only one photo, an uncharacteristically cheerless selfie with Arty in front of a building that Elijah recognized as the Ridgefall Country Club, and since then she'd posted no more. Nonetheless Elijah could picture the scene vividly: Mark standing stiffly in a corner of the club's dining room, masticating canapés with all the gaiety of a dying cow, wishing he were anywhere else. Elijah, sweating on the pier, all but doubled over at the sweetness of this image.

He took the last few blocks to the Die Kinder at a walk. His mind was so filled with his vision of Mark, so disconnected from the pedestrian reality around him, that he didn't notice the young man crossing Forty-second Street and bounding toward him. He didn't notice him hopping up onto the sidewalk and following him. He was only shaken from his revery, fifty yards from the Die Kinder's entrance, when he heard a sharp whisper.

"Elijah."

When Elijah turned and saw the face behind him he assumed that he was only imagining it, that his mind had simply shuffled to another vision. But the face, unmistakable, refused to dissolve. Standing on the sidewalk, in a black baseball hat and sunglasses, was Alistair McCabe.

"Come," Alistair said, beckoning with his hand. "Quick."

Elijah stood still. He looked toward the few other pedestrians nearby as if to confirm the reality of what he was seeing.

Alistair stepped forward, grabbed Elijah's hand in his own very real one, and tugged. He glanced fearfully at the Die Kinder. "Let's go."

He led Elijah down the block, across Twelfth Avenue, to a bench overlooking the river. "Face the water," he said.

Alistair was paler than Elijah remembered, his hair less lustrously blond, but it was him, the fugitive in the flesh. Elijah turned to the river and hissed: "What are you doing here?"

"Is there a chance any of them will come this way?" Alistair said. "Herve? Jay? Howie?"

Elijah shook his head dumbfoundedly. "None of them strike me as river gazers."

Alistair fidgeted on the bench. "I've been casing that block for days now, waiting for you," he said. "Do you never leave the penthouse?"

Elijah found the clarity of mind to be miffed by this. "Why are you waiting for me?" he said. "What are you doing? Where have you been?"

"I need your help," Alistair said.

Elijah's stomach turned. "With what?"

"You need to believe me."

"Believe you about what?"

Alistair moved closer, bent forward, and, in a long, unbroken, ten-minute whisper, told Elijah what. Elijah kept his eyes on the river the whole time, creasing his brow in confusion and then, as Alistair went on, feeling the blood drain from his face. The details were terrible upon terrible, and Alistair, in his breathlessness, gave Elijah no time to absorb their shock. No sooner had he finished telling Elijah the truth of Herve's project than he began explaining about the groundskeeper and what had happened to him. No sooner had he finished telling Elijah about the men who'd broken into his house in Binghamton than he began describing, as he best he could, the nightmarish future Herve wanted to usher in.

"Jesus, Jesus, Jesus," Elijah said.

"I'm sorry to unload this on you," Alistair said. "And I'm sorry for what I'm about to ask you."

Elijah could only breathe. Pedestrians continued bizarrely to mosey around them. The sun continued bizarrely to shine.

"I have a plan to stop him," Alistair said. "To make sure he pays for what he did and make sure he doesn't hurt anyone else. But I need your help."

Elijah pitched forward. Clearest in his mind now, clearer than anything Alistair had just told him, was the image of Herve's face in the dining room, and the sound of his words: *Something that'll really shake the world.*

Alistair spoke in another unbroken whisper. The plan he described was so horrifying to Elijah that he disobeyed Alistair's order and looked at him. "Are you kidding me?"

"I've worked it out, I think it's as airtight as can be," Alistair said. "And it's the only way."

Elijah turned back to the water. "No," he said. "I can't do this. You don't want me to do this."

"I do," Alistair said. "You can. I believe in you."

Even as Elijah shook his head, even as his fear coursed through him in cold bursts, he saw that he was not in fact the worst candidate for the job. He'd told Herve he was hopeless; he'd told him he was only a vessel. He'd made evident that he wanted, as Herve had told him to want, something bigger. Yet his fear remained absolute.

"And you won't be alone," Alistair said. "Take out your phone."

Elijah made no movement, only glanced at Alistair in confusion.

"Call him," Alistair said. "We need his help. Call Mark."

Elijah shook his head again. "No," he said.

"He'll help us. He won't want you to do this alone."

"No."

"You belong together. You know it, he knows it, I know it. He'll come. He won't let you do this by yourself."

"No."

"Call him," Alistair said. "Do it now."

In his fear Elijah couldn't help it: he really could only imagine carrying out Alistair's plan with Mark, ever his ballast, ever the pole to his tetherball, at his side. But even as he obediently took out his phone, even as he replayed Alistair's words and felt the stirring of a tremulous hope—and even before the confounding call that in the next moment took place—he saw that his hope was foolish. Alistair wasn't just bringing him and Mark back together. He was bringing all three of them back together, with their same divided loyalties, their same conflicting affections. He saw, as he put the phone to his ear, that the days ahead would be very difficult.

PART FIVE

ON THE MOUNTAIN

ALISTAIR HAD BEEN staying at the Millennium Hilton for only nine days, but already he felt like a resident. He knew when the lobby was least likely to be crowded, he knew which vending machines were broken, he knew the security guards and front desk staff by name, and they knew him by name too. "Good morning, Mr. Miller," they said to him. "Mr. Miller, good to see you."

Every time Alistair had to use the fake credentials Nikolai had given him he was surprised by how well they worked. The ID worked at the hotel desk and the liquor store. The debit card worked at the grocery store and the odd little security equipment store where he'd bought the Wi-Fi–enabled voice recorder. He wasn't sure how much Nikolai had loaded onto the debit card, so he'd also brought with him the $10,000 in cash he'd retrieved from Mark's apartment back in May—what felt like an eternity ago. So far he'd held off on setting up a new bank account into which to transfer the million Nikolai had set aside for him. He was waiting to establish himself in a permanent place, wherever that was, whenever that would be. Before leaving Binghamton he'd given Maura all the information she'd need to access the other two million and instructions for how to disperse it.

He had no idea if his plan would work. As he left the hotel now and emerged onto noon-bright Church Street various contingencies and worst-case scenarios crowded his mind. Yet he'd run out of time to backtrack. Jay's exhibition party was tomorrow night; everything had been set in motion. At the very least, he believed, the scheme he'd devised put Elijah in minimal danger.

He walked north, looking at the spreading wings of the Oculus, the line forming at the entrance to the 9/11 Memorial, the sun smacking off windows and bright limestone walls. With any luck, after tomorrow he'd never see the city again.

He stopped at a convenience store to get more ibuprofen and new bandages. He stopped at a grocery store and filled two cartons at the hot bar. Even according to his own most paranoid calculations a food run here and an errand there posed a fairly minute risk. His disappearance had never become news, not even an alert on NYU's public safety listserv, and if Herve had ever looked for him in the city he'd surely given up some time ago. Nevertheless, wherever he went, he wore his black baseball hat and kept his sunglasses on. For his part he thought he looked awfully conspicuous. But the people he moved among were harried lunch-takers, consumed in their phones, in the work they'd abandoned and to which they would soon return, and no one ever gave him a second glance.

He'd picked a hotel in the Financial District precisely because the neighborhood was so anonymous. Few regular dwellers here, mostly tourists and commuters, no one who would remember his face if he or she happened to see it twice. At night, after the office workers and visitors had dispersed, the streets looked almost abandoned. For all its majesty nobody seemed to want to live here. These few hundred acres had once transacted much of the world's capital, but they offered no solace, no warm refuges or soft surfaces, nothing out of which to fashion a home.

On his way back to the hotel he stopped at a liquor store. He handed over his ID with studied coolness, and as he slipped it back into his wallet he glanced at the name and balked again at the coincidence. Of all the first names Nikolai could have chosen—of all the names! He was led to wonder if Nikolai had been guided by the prankster hand of God.

Alistair hadn't heard from Nikolai, and he doubted he'd ever hear from him again. Surely he was in Indonesia by now, sunning his pale flab, drinking clear spirits, catching the eyes of passing women and foreclosing any chance of action by the adolescent goofiness of his smile. Surely he was lonely, surely he missed his friend. Alistair only hoped he knew how much his friend missed him back.

When he returned to the hotel and reached his floor he made his way past his own room to the second one he'd booked five days earlier. He knocked first, then slid in the keycard and entered. He still hadn't gotten over Mark's face.

"Meds, food, liquor," he said.

"Bless you," Mark said. He lay on the bed, propped against an assemblage of pillows, nursing his wounds. The bruises on his cheeks had passed their peak darkness, the cuts under his eyes were healing, his nose was gradually returning to its precontusion size, and to judge by his restored mobility no bones were broken.

Alistair passed him the ibuprofen and bandages and one of the cartons of food. "Are you feeling better?"

Mark opened his carton, forked a potato, and chewed on the side of his face that his brother hadn't repeatedly clocked. "Now that you're here," he said.

Five days earlier, after Mark had finally called Elijah back and, in his post-beating daze, agreed to come to the city, Alistair had opted to book him a room of his own, lucking into one on the same floor. (The Millennium had turned out to be a rather shitty hotel with an advantageously high vacancy.) Alistair had done this mainly out of respect for Elijah. He'd determined that it would be best for Elijah to continue staying at the Die Kinder for as long as possible, to ward off any suspicion, and he didn't want Elijah spinning masochistic fantasies about what might result from Alistair and Mark sharing a room while he was away. But Alistair's discretion had been for naught. Every night since his arrival Mark had tiptoed down the hall. He spent his days healing in his own bed but he never slept in it.

"Any calls from the family?" Alistair said.

"Eleven from my mom, three from my dad."

"That's less than yesterday."

"I think they're starting to give up."

"And Eddie?"

"Still nothing."

Alistair had pretended to be stunned by the story of Mark's mother's birthday party and all the sordid business that had led up to it. But in truth it had only confirmed things about the world he already knew. "Do you think you'll ever talk to them again?" he asked.

"I'm not thinking about them," Mark said. "You've given me other things to think about."

"Are you nervous?"

"That's not what I'm talking about."

Alistair avoided his gaze. The first knock at his door had come Friday night, just hours after Mark had showed up at the hotel in his bloody tux.

His body was still throbbing, his wounds were still swelling, his bones still felt out of place. But he'd spent two months waiting to hold Alistair in his arms and he refused to delay any longer, even if in his condition he couldn't really hold Alistair, couldn't really do much at all. Every night since then, as he'd recovered, he'd gotten more insistent, more dexterous and ambitious, but he still hadn't gotten what he wanted. The problem was their bodies and what they were and weren't willing to do with them. They were doomed in their stubborn tophood. And the thing Mark really wanted, a life together, Alistair had told him was impossible.

Alistair had spared Mark no detail about Herve's project, Andy McCurdy, and his summer in Binghamton. But he'd been mum about his plans for after tomorrow night. He'd told Mark he was going away, but he hadn't told him where, and he hadn't given him the full range of reasons, some practical and some not, for his wanting to flee. He'd told him as much of the truth as he needed to know: after tomorrow he would be unreachable, and Mark shouldn't wait around for him.

"Tell me where you're going," Mark said to him now.

Alistair stared at his food and made no reply.

"Let me come with you."

"I'm not making you do that," Alistair said. "I'm not making anyone make any more sacrifices for me."

"It'd be a sacrifice to stay here without you."

"Elijah needs you," Alistair said. "He loves you and you love him, and you know it."

Mark glanced out the window. The face he made when he thought about Elijah was all weariness, intractable certainty, resignation—a far cry from the crazed yearning with which he looked at Alistair. But Alistair was sincere in his belief that Mark and Elijah belonged together, in his hope that by convening them here he'd set in motion their reunion, and he felt that weariness and resignation were surer signs of love than fascination. Mark and Elijah no longer enchanted each other, and that was for the best. In the absence of enchantment they would build something more enduring. And after Alistair had gone away he could comfort himself with the image of them.

"He'll be sleeping here tonight," Alistair said.

Mark caught his gaze. "What are you saying?"

"That maybe tonight we should focus on getting a good rest."

"You don't want me to come to your room."

Alistair gave a shrug. "I don't want to complicate anything," he said. "Not tonight."

Elijah was due at the hotel in a few hours. He'd come to the end of his stay at the Die Kinder. Earlier that week he'd put a deposit down on an apartment in Washington Heights. Alistair had hoped that Mark would intervene, suggest they pool their money and get a place together. But Mark had let the transaction proceed, and Elijah, for his part, had moved ahead with unexpected grace. He seemed neither surprised by Mark's reluctance to intercede nor especially dejected about the downward turn of his lifestyle. All he'd said about the apartment, with an equanimous smile, was that it got pretty OK light. Currently he was at the Die Kinder having his breakup talk with Jay and overseeing the movers he'd hired to haul his things uptown. He certainly couldn't count on moving his things after tomorrow night. None of them, for all the care they'd put into their scheme, could count on anything.

"So you'll go wherever," Mark said. "To some country or city. And then what? How will you live?"

"The money Nikolai gave me should last a while," Alistair said.

"I don't see you doing nothing. I did that. You're too ambitious."

"Maybe I'm not anymore," Alistair said. "Maybe I don't want to be. Maybe I don't want to keep grabbing and taking and winning."

"Then what do you want?"

"I don't know yet," Alistair said. "That's my new experiment." As soon as he'd used this word he regretted it, because he knew the question that would come next. That was how he'd described the cross in his duffel: as his "experiment."

"Is this where the God stuff comes in?" Mark asked. On the first night he'd come to Alistair's room Mark had spotted the cross in his bag, and every night since then he'd nodded at it, as if it were a person in the room with them, a shared joke. "I have to admit, that really came out of nowhere."

"I think that's probably where it usually comes out of," Alistair said. "Wherever there's nothing else."

"Do you really believe?"

"At the very least," Alistair said, "it offers a better theory of economics."

"Right," Mark said. "I recall Jesus not being big on rich people."

Alistair smiled. "You need something," he said. "I thought for me it was money. But I don't think that's what I really wanted. And I think a part of me knew that, because I kept fucking it up. Every time I got some I threw it away. Every chance I got I buried myself in debt. You need something, and I couldn't imagine anything else to want. Maybe what I need is a thing that tells me not to want anything at all."

Mark stared at him steadily, forlornly, and then looked away. "Your mother really has your number," he said. "She pretty much said all this when I visited her." He shook his head. "I still can't believe you'd only left the day before. No wonder she kept giving me an out. No wonder she kept asking about Elijah."

"I still can't believe you stole my pillowcase," Alistair said.

Mark laughed, then winced and touched his cheek. Alistair looked out the window at One World Trade, looming imposingly before them. Beyond it the Hudson flowed with geologic aplomb. Everywhere you looked the dumb earth had been stamped out, but it was possible to imagine, on a day like today, when the sun shone brighter than anything, this place as it had been centuries before, wooded and quiet, when the first Europeans (Maura's father's forebears among them) had arrived. All the business that had been undertaken since then seemed to Alistair like a great beautiful error.

"I'll let you rest," he said to Mark and left.

———

Not until Mark had freed himself from Eddie—not until he'd grabbed his phone from the country club lawn and, fending off solicitous shrieks, run to his car; not until he'd driven half-blind and shaking to a nearby CVS and, terrifying the employees and customers therein, bought himself what first aid materials he had the clarity of mind to pluck from the shelves; not until he'd returned to his car and applied bandages and compresses and antiseptics as best he could—did he remember that Elijah had called and what he'd said. *Alistair is here.* Without delay he called Elijah back, confirmed his recollection, and listened foggily to an elaborate speech he couldn't quite process. No matter. By then he was already driving to the train station.

Was he the first person ever to board New Jersey Transit in a bloody tux? He doubted it. Nevertheless the car he entered cleared out immediately. A mother shielded her child's eyes; a teenager took a photo. The ticket agent jolted when he strolled in with his puncher, but he quickly shelved the sight of Mark with all the other sorry things he'd witnessed on the job.

At Penn Station he drew literal screams. When he saw a woman glancing between him and a cluster of police officers, who for their part were engrossed in their phones, he decided the least he could do was hide the blood running down the front of his shirt. He bought the only article of clothing in sight: an I ❤ NY hoodie at a souvenir kiosk. In this still more deranged getup he went outside and ordered an Uber. When the driver arrived he took one look at Mark's battered face and sped away. He reentered Penn Station and boarded the subway, where no one paid him any special attention at all, aside from an elderly Black woman who offered him her seat. He tried to smile, failed utterly, said no thanks.

Only when he arrived at the Millennium Hilton and laid eyes on Alistair did his pain begin to abate. Alistair and Elijah, mortified at the sight of him, decided it would be best to let him rest and run through their plan the next day. But during his train ride bits of Elijah's elaborate speech had returned to Mark. He knew that they needed his help, that Alistair needed his help. He told them he wanted to know everything now.

Alistair sketched out the plan in bare-bones form that night, but it wasn't until the next day, when Elijah escaped the Die Kinder and returned to the hotel, that he laid it out in all its fearsome detail. The three of them sat in Alistair's room, Mark and Elijah together on the end of the bed and Alistair in the desk chair, the laptop he'd bought earlier that week behind him. He leaned forward with his elbows on his knees.

Incredibly, Alistair said, Jay had orchestrated the ideal opportunity for them to entrap Herve, by hosting a party at which Herve would be in attendance. Herve wouldn't pass up the chance to scope out such a large gathering of Jay and Elijah's milieu in search of anyone who might know something about his missing men. And with a movement to grow he wouldn't pass up the chance to scout for possible recruits at a party paying tribute, however winkingly, to that movement's figurehead. Even more incredibly, Alistair continued, Elijah had already laid the groundwork for the plan without knowing it.

"Elijah has been talking to Herve," Alistair said to Mark. "He knows Herve is looking for me. He knows he'll do anything to find me. And Herve knows Elijah is hopeless. He knows he'll take any ticket out of his life."

Elijah smiled pridefully.

"At the exhibition party," Alistair said, "he'll talk to him again. But this time he'll go further, and he'll have a recorder on him."

Elijah's smile faded.

"All he has to do is get him to admit to something criminal," Alistair said. "If not to Andy's murder, then at least to funding his extremists. Backing conspiracies to commit public disorder, facilitating firearm offenses, anything."

It would take Mark some weeks before he made the connection between Andy McCurdy and Amber Osgood, the tenant he'd met with in Whitney Point. And by the time he made the connection he'd have no one, really, worth telling. "How is he supposed to do that?" he asked.

Alistair nodded and began. Elijah, he said, would tell Herve that he knew where Alistair was, had known for a few days, but had sat on this intel while he decided if and how he wanted to use it. Elijah would tell Herve that he'd lead him to Alistair on three conditions. First, he had to promise not to harm Alistair. Elijah would draw Herve's suspicion if he didn't stipulate this condition, and Herve would heartily agree to it: he would have no compunction about lying to Elijah. After that, Elijah would tell him his second condition, and he'd tell him he'd have to comply with it before he told him the third.

"What if he says no right off the bat?" Mark asked.

"He has no other options," Alistair said. "He knows what I know, and he knows I'm not loyal to him. He knows he can't afford to have me walking around freely, tempted to open my mouth."

"What if he doesn't believe Elijah knows where you are?"

"Already a step ahead of you," Alistair said.

Elijah would prove he was in contact with Alistair by showing Herve a photograph—they'd make it look like Elijah had sneaked it—of Alistair sitting on the hotel bed. Elijah would take the photograph before leaving for the party, and the timestamp would prove it had been taken that day. Then he'd tell Herve his second condition, which was that Herve explain to him everything. Why had Alistair and Nikolai disappeared? What had they done? What project had they been working on? Elijah was asking, he'd say, because he was intrigued. He'd pick up where he'd left off during his conversation with Herve in Howie's dining room. He was hopeless, he wanted to be done with his aimlessness, his frivolous fun and games. He didn't really care if what Herve was doing was unlawful or unsavory. As evidenced by his association with Jay moral dubiousness didn't faze him: if anything it aroused his interest. But first, he'd tell Herve, he needed to know what he was getting into.

"So," Mark said to Elijah, "you're posing as an aspiring criminal."

Elijah tilted his head. "The nice thing about being empty inside," he said, "is that you can pose as anything."

"But what if Herve doesn't want to hire him?" Mark said. He turned to Elijah. "No offense."

"Herve likes desperate people," Alistair said. "And Elijah is pretty desperate."

"At your service," Elijah said.

"He'll pluck Elijah up. He'll figure he can use his design background for messaging and recruiting, and he'll be happy to have another person who's sworn to him. He'll know he can figure all that out later—how to make Elijah useful—but by then, hopefully, it'll be too late. Hopefully he'll have already told Elijah something, and hopefully he'll have told him something incriminating."

"What if he lies?" Mark said. "What if he agrees to the second condition but tells Elijah all you did was steal money—something like that?"

"I'll say it doesn't make sense," Elijah said, apparently repeating what Alistair had already told him. "I'll say that Alistair has no money. That he came to New York hoping I could get him some, from Howie. I'll say I know it's something else." He swallowed. "Something bigger."

"Herve's answer to Elijah's question is the only thing standing between him and me," Alistair said. "If he answers to Elijah's satisfaction, he gets his prize. My head on a spear."

Mark's eyes fell to Alistair's neck. "So let's say he admits to something criminal," he said. "And Elijah has it on the recorder. Then what?"

"Then Elijah tells him his third condition."

"I want a hundred thousand dollars," Elijah said. "I'm happy to work for him, be his vessel, but first I need a down payment."

"That gives us time," Alistair said. "Herve can get the money together quickly, but not immediately. Elijah will suggest the next day, at noon. And to show that he's not just extorting Herve, he'll make him a promise. He'll say he'll only take the money when Herve has me in his sights."

"But that won't happen," Mark said.

"The delay should leave me enough time," Alistair said. "Assuming Herve says anything even slightly incriminating, I'll send the recording immediately to the FBI." He explained that a few days earlier he'd called the FBI with an anonymous tip and a promise of further evidence. He'd also written a long document laying out the whole story of his work for Herve, which he would send along with the recording. He felt sure that once the FBI began prying into even the measliest criminal offense they would, in time, uncover the project. His written testimony would lead the way. But to make absolutely sure they launched an investigation he needed an admission on Herve's part, needed hard proof. "Hopefully they'll act quickly. I'll send the recording to media outlets too. A billionaire secretly recorded admitting to a crime—they won't pass that up. I've been making a list of contacts."

"Funny, I've been doing the same thing for Jay," Elijah said. "I think you'll get more bites."

"What if the FBI, the media outlets—what if they don't believe the recording?" Mark said. "What if they think you just staged it?"

"That's where you come in," Alistair said. "At the party, Elijah will steal Herve away and pull him into some private room. You need to take pictures of them entering and exiting. I'll send those pictures along with the recording. The timestamps can be cross-referenced."

"Why can't we just secretly film it?" Mark asked.

"We can't be sure which room they'll go into," Alistair said. "We can't plant cameras throughout the whole penthouse. And we can't plant a camera on Elijah. Herve will think of that. Before he says anything he'll probably frisk him. He'll probably take his phone. That's why we need a recorder, hidden in Elijah's clothes, and that's why we need to be careful about where we put it."

"What if the authorities don't act?" Mark said.

"The media will, and they'll do the authorities' job for them," Alistair said. "If Herve has the spotlight on him, he won't be able to do anything. Attention will incapacitate him just as much as arrest. And if the story spreads widely enough, the authorities will be pressured to act. And it will. It's sensational. It obviously helps that this will have all gone down at a gay MAGA party."

Elijah sighed.

"Why do we have to do it there?" Mark asked.

Alistair lowered his eyes. "Herve clearly has a short fuse," he said. "He had Andy killed, and I think Andy might not have been the only one. And he'd love nothing more than to kill me, which is why I can't be the one to confront him. He might not attack me then and there but he wouldn't let me out of his grasp. He has no particular reason to hurt Elijah, but his conversation with him will be very frustrating."

"If they were alone, he might use force," Mark said.

"That's also where you come in," Alistair said. "You need to stand near whatever room they go into. I'll be listening to the recording. If I hear any-thing like that start up, I'll call you and you'll intervene. Break down the door if you have to. But with dozens of people right outside, Herve probably won't risk that."

"I'm loving the word 'probably,'" Elijah said.

Mark turned to Elijah. "You really want to go through with this?"

"It's something," Elijah said. "It's time I finally do something."

Mark put his hands to his face, not remembering his cuts and bruises, and winced. "Wait," he said. "Elijah is starting out by saying he knows where you are. If the conversation goes nowhere from there, Herve will still believe he does. It's not like he'll let that go. What then?"

"Even if Elijah doesn't get Herve to admit anything," Alistair said, "he can still ask for his hundred-grand reward. On the day after the party, after Herve has gathered the money, Elijah can lead him here, to the hotel. Beforehand I'll book a third room, under my real name, in case Herve's hounds get hold of the guest list."

"But by the time he comes here you'll be gone," Mark said.

"And Herve will be out of luck," Alistair said. "Elijah won't get his money, but he'll be off the hook. If Herve admitted nothing, Elijah will have nothing on him. He'll be just another person I slipped away from."

"So let's say it works," Mark said. "Let's say he admits something, and in the time between the party and the delivery of the money he gets detained.

Let's say he goes to prison. Elijah will have caused his downfall. Herve will be furious at him. What's to stop him from commissioning another killing?"

"If Herve doesn't have his name or his project to protect anymore, there'll be no use in eliminating traitors," Alistair said. "And if something happens to Elijah any sane person would trace it back to him. Having Elijah killed would be stupid."

"How comforting," Elijah said.

"And he won't be able to find me," Alistair said. "Because I really will be gone."

Alistair had already explained that he intended to go back into hiding, this time under whatever false name Nikolai had christened him with, and Mark was eager to persuade him away from this plan. "Why do you have to flee?" he said. "You just said Herve won't risk taking revenge."

Alistair glanced away. He was keen to avoid this topic. "I won't just be running away from Herve," he said. "I aided and abetted this scheme for months. Ignorance may not buy me absolution."

"You knew nothing," Mark said. "You're helping the authorities take him down. There's no way they'd bring a case against you."

"Maybe not," Alistair said. "But then what? My name will get out in some form or other. And I'll live my whole life as Alistair McCabe, known forever as the kid who worked for a billionaire domestic terrorist. I'm not counting on everyone to believe I was totally ignorant. My name will always have a black mark on it. And I've seen what happens when your name is ruined. I saw it with Nikolai. 'Alistair McCabe' is dead. Frankly, I'm looking forward to it."

Mark suspected that Alistair had once set excessive and embarrassing store by his name—Alistair McCabe, senior vice president, CEO, chairman of the board—and he saw no small tragedy in his decision to give it up. Yet at the same time he envied him his freedom, his fresh start. He'd be happy to put his own name, his own burdensome self, behind him.

There were more details to hash out, namely the placement of the recorder on Elijah's person, but they decided they'd done enough for the day and scattered—Elijah to the Die Kinder, Alistair back to his planning, and Mark to his room, to his slow convalescence.

Over the next few days, as he sat on his bed recovering, Mark ignored dozens of calls from his parents. On Friday night he'd sent his mother a curt text explaining that he was OK, letting her know where he'd left her car, and requesting that she leave him alone. But his phone kept buzzing wildly. He knew that at some point he'd have to resume contact with his parents and, at some much later date, make peace with his brother. He couldn't go on raging with hatred toward them forever. But he also didn't have to be a part of their lives. Arty's business revolted him, his fraudulent scheme revolted him, Eddie's sabotage revolted him, and he revolted himself. His ignorance about the source of his wealth, to adapt Alistair's words, bought him no absolution. Arty had been right: he could have complained about his father's company, he could have refused to benefit in any way from it. But instead for eight years he'd sat in his luxury apartment and tried not to think about what paid for it. He'd sat and he'd sat and he'd sat some more and he could sit no longer.

He couldn't afford to, for starters. His remaining money might last him a year. But trying to imagine what kind of job he could get was like trying to imagine a fourth dimension. Who would hire a thirty-year-old with a single internship, seven years in the past, to his name? For nearly a decade he'd been dithering and tracing the curlicues of his malaise, and the whole time, without realizing it, he'd been sealing his fate. Everything he'd done and failed to do had prepared him for a middle age of humiliation. And yet a part of him warmed to this prospect. He was keen, after years of burying his head in the sand, to face reality. He welcomed its bright glare and stinging abrasions. And maybe, just maybe, he'd be jostled enough to give new life to his vegetative aspiration. He *had* felt the old familiar stirring these past few days. If nothing else Alistair had given him quite a story.

For now, though, his mind was all on Alistair himself. Every night he slunk to his room. Given his condition they had to be cautious, maddeningly so. Every other move made Mark clench his jaw in agony. He wanted his body all over Alistair's and Alistair's all over his, but so many parts of his person were off-limits. And the thing Mark really ached for, that Alistair really ached for, the this-in-there consummation that their minds couldn't help straining toward, the terminal insertion that refused to concede its all-importance, was a no-go. Alistair opened his legs and tried; Mark did the same. They could barely get in a centimeter. They told themselves that what they did was enough, that there was nothing special about that particular move. But neither of their bodies would be persuaded away from its object. Everything else felt like prologue. Each seemed to believe that if he could get inside the other he would come away with something to hold on to after they'd parted ways. And night after night they failed.

Now, on the day before the exhibition party, they'd come to the end. They had only one more night, and just a few moments ago, before returning to his room, Alistair had forbidden them to seize it. Mark too wanted to spare Elijah further harm, and he didn't trust himself to sneak out of the room later that night without Elijah noticing. But he couldn't imagine letting Alistair go with so much residual botheration.

Mark suspected Alistair might be right: maybe he and Elijah really did belong together. Indeed Mark had been surprised to feel a low boil in his loins when he and Elijah had embraced, after so many long weeks, on Friday. There it was, undiminished, at the ready: the old reaction of their pheromones. But he couldn't think about a future with Elijah until Alistair was in the past. Right now the prospect smacked of the sad moment in the dressing room when, after trying on an excellent new pair of jeans, you have to get back into your old ones. He wanted to fix Elijah in place, put him on ice, until such time as he could give him the consideration he deserved. He was being selfish, he realized, he was being cruel. He might have sworn off his father but in matters of love he himself was running a dirty business: hoarding a surplus, exploiting resources, dangling an offer with no guarantee that he'd honor it. He didn't know what he'd say to Elijah when he arrived later that evening. Part of him believed the kindest thing would be to say nothing at all. But he knew that silence, on their first night alone together in two months, would be impossible. And so he waited.

———

Over the past week Elijah had watched the preparations for the exhibition party come together piece by piece. By the time he emerged from his bedroom on Wednesday morning, after whisperingly calling the movers and confirming the time of their arrival, almost everything was in place. Five more TV screens had been mounted on the walls of Howie's living room, caterers had set up several food tables and bars, emissaries from an event-planning service had installed a DJ booth and LED lights, and now a small army of cleaners was at work scrubbing and vacuuming. Elijah wondered what all these various helpers made of Jay's videos, of the bunches of MAGA hats lying here and there like nightmare poinsettias. As far as he could tell they kept their heads down and focused on the innocent objects of their labor: screws, extension cords, dusters, platters. Howie tipped them all in $100s.

He went downstairs and found Jay in the studio. At some point soon, he imagined, it would reclaim its purpose as Howie's bedroom. Jay was sitting on the floor under a tripod, like a boy under a tree, typing furiously on his laptop. The screen bathed his face in an alien blue. He paid Elijah no mind.

"There's something I need to tell you," Elijah said.

Jay continued hacking. "I'm a little busy."

"It'll only take a minute."

"I don't have a minute," Jay said. "I'm doing your job."

Elijah had given up any pretense of being a helpful assistant. But in truth there was little left to do. Jay had brought his project to life, he'd secured a splashy profile in the *Grift*, and his nightly barnstorming of gay bars had borne fruit: he was expecting two hundred guests tomorrow evening. And yet for all this he seemed to have fallen mysteriously into low spirits.

"I hired movers," Elijah said. "They're coming in an hour."

Jay shut the laptop but remained bent over it. He fished his vape from his pocket and blew a cloud toward the floor. "Am I supposed to be surprised?"

"I wanted to tell you earlier," Elijah said. "I could never find the right time."

"Don't think I didn't notice you drifting away," Jay said. "I'm surprised you stayed this long."

"I'm grateful for everything," Elijah said. "You gave me a place to go. You gave me a job. You certainly gave me an experience."

Jay smiled grimly. His braces shone in the dim light from Howie's shaded windows. With his laptop cradled protectively in his lap, with his shoulders slumped and his mouth aglint, he'd never looked so much like the fifteen-year-old that, deep down, Elijah knew him to be. "He's back," he said to Elijah. "Isn't he."

For a paranoid moment Elijah thought he was referring to Alistair and blanched.

"Mark," Jay said. "That's where you've been going every day. To see him."

Elijah breathed. "He's back," he said. "But this doesn't have anything to do with him. I found my own place. I made my own decision. I need to start figuring out my life."

"Elijah grows up."

"Something like that," Elijah said. "And I'm still coming to the party." He swallowed. "I'm looking forward to it."

"That makes one of us," Jay said.

Elijah had little space in his mind to devote to Jay's sudden melancholy. Yet the odd desolation in his friend's voice tugged at him. "That can't be right," he said. "You've been looking forward to this all summer."

"And after this it's over," Jay said. "Who'll care about my videos after November?"

"Maybe he'll win," Elijah said. He swallowed again. "And then you can keep making them."

Jay looked at him defensively.

"You don't want that?"

"Do you think I'm insane?"

"Of course," Elijah said.

Jay sucked on his vape. "He's fun for now," he said. "If he wins, not so much. It would be like the whole country coming. And then everything would get very ugly, very fast. No beauty in that. No fun at all."

"Except maybe for his supporters."

"That would be the ugliest part of it," Jay said. "That man has no idea what he's whipping up. His supporters are horny, and if he wins they won't know when to stop. They'll descend on Washington. They'll storm the Capitol. They'll find him in the White House. They'll eat him alive."

Elijah felt a chill pass down his spine.

"And then my videos won't be much fun either."

"You can do something else," Elijah said. "You have talent."

"Please," Jay said. "Contrarianism is the easiest thing in the world. Read the room, do the opposite, and have the courage of your nonconviction."

Elijah was taken aback by Jay's deflation, by how much the prospect of his project coming to an end had sunk him. For a moment he worried he would call the party off. "Then be contrarian about something else," he said. "You don't have to be the gay Trump guy forever."

Jay stood, wiped his hands on his jeans, and smiled dapperly. "Little late for that," he said, "don't you think?"

It took the movers all of forty-five minutes to cart away Elijah's few possessions. He followed them in an Uber to Washington Heights, let them into his new apartment, and stood in the hallway until they'd finished. He'd face the facts of his downward mobility—the tiny kitchen with its laminate floor, the black canopy of mildew on the bathroom ceiling—later.

When he arrived at the Millennium Hilton he found Mark sitting in bed, waiting for him with a stiff expression on his face, a forced warmth. Elijah could hardly bear to look at him. The bruises on Mark's face pained him, and the mixed feelings in his eyes, his yearning for Alistair and all but indifference toward Elijah, pained him even more. He was certain that Mark and Alistair spent every night together, that this business of the separate rooms, this Hays Code sleeping arrangement, was a ruse. The hope he'd felt five days before, sitting with Alistair on the bench by the river, had returned in flickers here and there, but he'd lost his energy for deluding himself: he knew Mark's love for him was fading. "Let's go," he said and they walked to Alistair's room.

Alistair had already set up his workstation at the desk: the laptop on which he'd listen to the recording, the open documents containing his testimony and the contact information for the FBI and media tip lines, the little black phone on which, if need be, he'd call Mark. Now he dug in a bag from H&M and extracted a three-pack of black briefs. This was the last puzzle piece: where on Elijah's body to hide the recorder.

"When Herve frisks," Alistair said, "there's one spot where he won't put his hands."

Elijah stared at the briefs. "You want me to put the recorder on my dick."

"Not quite on it," Alistair said. He held up a pair in each hand. "I'm worried about what the heat might do to it. The heat and the moisture."

Mark couldn't help smiling.

"You'll wear two pairs," Alistair said. "We'll put it between them. But we should try it now."

Elijah took the briefs, considered going into the bathroom, then shrugged. There was not one inch of him Mark and Alistair hadn't seen, touched, or tasted. He took off his pants and underwear. He took off his shirt just because. He turned his body so as to present the crescent of his ass. Mark and Alistair tipped their heads forward and tried to affect tact, but they were helpless, Elijah noted with pleasure, not to marvel. He pulled on one pair of briefs and then the other. He put up his hands.

"Do you mind?" Alistair said, approaching with the recorder.

"Have I ever?" Elijah said.

Alistair slipped the recorder, a silver thing about the size of a toy car with a screen and two small speakers, between the briefs. His knuckles grazed Elijah's dick. "Walk over there," he said.

Elijah stepped to the far side of the room. Alistair sat before his laptop, pulled up the window of the recorder's corresponding program, and put in his headphones. He'd connected the recorder to the hotel's Wi-Fi by placing Elijah's phone next to it and OKing the automatic permission request; at the party Elijah would need to do the same before confronting Herve. "Say something in a low voice," he told Elijah.

"I can't believe my life has led here," Elijah said.

"Crystal clear," Alistair said.

Elijah began walking back but paused. "I think it's slipping," he said. "It's this cheap fabric. It has no tread. H&M is terrible."

Alistair and Mark looked studiously at his crotch.

"Just be careful," Alistair said. "Before you talk to Herve, pretend to scratch yourself. Make sure it's in place." He picked Elijah's jeans off the floor and held them out. "Put these on. Let's make sure it's not visible."

Elijah's jeans, they discovered when he slid them on, were much too tight in the groin. The oblong protrusion of the recorder was apparent and in no way confusable with a phallus.

"You need to wear looser pants," Mark said.

"I don't *have* looser pants," Elijah said.

Alistair walked to his duffel and pulled out a pair of relaxed-fit chinos. When Elijah put these on he looked in the mirror, frowning at the dumpy, sexless hang of the legs. "I look straight."

"Do you think Herve will notice you're dressed unusually?" Mark asked.

"Herve has seen me have a cocaine nosebleed at dinner," Elijah said. "I think he knows I'm out of sorts."

"That's it," Alistair said. "That's everything. We're ready."

The words resounded off the room's cheaply papered walls. There was nothing standing between him and his moment now, Elijah realized: no more planning, no more questions, no unfinalized details. Only twenty-four hours in this strange hotel with his men. Only a brief, eternal, anxiety-racked wait.

They ordered dinner. They drank. They ran through the script a few more times, Alistair playing Herve, Mark playing Herve, Elijah playing Herve and Alistair playing Elijah. At ten they finally called it a night.

When Mark and Elijah returned to their room they undressed, pulled back the bedcovers, and sat against the pillows at a chaste distance. Mark turned to Elijah and took in his bare torso, his underwear, his wary, expectant eyes. "I'm not sure it's a good idea for us to—"

"It's OK," Elijah said. He flapped his hand over his crotch. "I should probably get tested."

Mark gave a swollen, misshapen smile. When he reached to shut off his lamp Elijah spoke. A great rattling had overtaken his body, the beginnings of a great sob. He feared he would never find himself in bed with Mark again. "Are you coming back to New York?" he asked.

Mark eyed him carefully. "I'm certainly not going back home."

There seemed no way for Elijah to bring forth words without bringing forth tears. He spoke through a closed throat. "Do you think we'll see each other after tomorrow?"

Mark took Elijah's hand and, tentatively, pressed it. "I'd like that," he said.

Elijah waited for his imminent sob to abate. But when he spoke a moment later it came. "I thought maybe," he said, and then began his choking and clenching.

"We'll talk," Mark said gently. "We'll see—"

"I thought maybe you'd be proud of me," Elijah said in a burst.

Mark waited respectfully for the worst of Elijah's crying to pass. "I'm extremely proud of you," he said.

"Thank you," Elijah blubbered.

"But that's not why you should be doing this," Mark said. "That wouldn't be fair to you. I absolutely don't want you to do this for me."

As suddenly as they'd come, Elijah's tears petered out, and he answered. What he said sounded like a lie, and if he'd said it at the beginning of the week it would have been. But somehow, in the intervening days, it had become the truth, and his eyes were wonderfully dry with this knowledge. "I'm not," he said.

They turned out the lights and faced their respective walls, and very quickly Elijah felt himself drifting toward sleep. But his paranoia was insistent, and after an hour it was vindicated. He heard the slide of Mark's legs against the sheets, light footsteps crossing the room, the careful opening and closing of the door. Elijah wasn't surprised, and in a feat of mind control he abstained from imagining the things that would soon transpire in Alistair's room. The only vengeful thought he had he quickly dismissed. Yes he had the whip hand, yes he could leave now, in his wounded pride, and wreck the plan all by himself. No one who knew him, who knew his selfishness, would be shocked. But he stayed where he was, in his empty bed. He didn't know why. He only knew it wasn't for Mark. He only knew it wasn't for any reward at all. Add up everything you're willing to give, subtract what you might get back, and whatever's left over is the measure of your soul. He shut his eyes in peace.

———

Alistair sat up in bed, dreading Mark's knock, waiting for it keenly all the same. When inevitably it came he went to the door and made a show of anger.

"You shouldn't be here," he said. "What did I tell you?" But he gave Mark no chance to reply. As soon as the door had fallen shut Alistair's arms were around him. Mark shouldn't have come, he shouldn't have let him in, they shouldn't be doing this. But Alistair couldn't imagine going on with his life, resigning himself to the certain loneliness that awaited him, without doing this—and he felt he might be ready, at long last, to do it.

He led Mark to the bed. In the stray moments when his mouth wasn't fixed on Mark's he took deep breaths, trying to relax his body. A feat of hitherto unimaginable effort, if not of will, lay before him. He pulled Mark onto him, opened his legs, breathed and breathed. He met Mark's eyes only glancingly. He was being unfair to him, he knew, giving him one night of something only to deprive him of a lifetime of it. But in the same way Mark was being no less unfair, and they were being no more unfair to each other than they were to themselves. He'd learned this lesson with Mark and Elijah well. In fucking there was only ever unfairness.

He put his hand to the floor. He found the bottle of lube that he'd bought days earlier and that he and Mark had already fruitlessly half emptied. When Mark peeled off his briefs Alistair whimpered.

"We don't have to," Mark said.

"That's just not what I'd call a starter dick."

"I'll go slowly."

"Very slowly."

And slowly Mark went. Alistair stiffened, he clammed up, he dug his fingernails into his thighs. He told Mark to relubricate and try again, try again. He summoned the erstwhile drill sergeant in his head, the one he'd called upon whenever he'd had to stay up one more hour studying, complete one more problem set, write one more page of an essay. This was the same, he told himself, as any short-term suffering that was sure to bring lasting rewards. And yet, when at last he submitted, when at last he felt Mark pass through the first line of defense and advance toward the second, he understood that this struggle required a novel kind of determination. All his past strivings, in school and work, in his chasing of As and his chasing of money, had amounted to one great thrusting out and forth, one great convexity. This was different, this was a collapsing: not a triumph but a failure, not an acquisition but a renunciation, not a gain but a transcendent loss. After a while, even as Mark went harder and faster, Alistair stopped feeling any pain, stopped moving except to adjust his grip on Mark's back. He felt defenseless, he felt soft, he felt inert. His heart radiated not so much with desire as with a kind of astonished need. He felt defeated, after however many exhilarating punishing years he felt defeated, and that was what love was, he saw: it was defeat.

Afterward Mark asked for a report from, as it were, the interior.

"Not too bad," Alistair said. He didn't want to say what he really felt, because what he really felt was pity. He felt bad that Mark had never had the experience he'd just had, and he felt bad that he'd denied himself the experience for so long. "You?"

"No words."

They weren't so careless, so unmindful of Elijah, as to spend the night together. Mark returned to his room, and in the morning, when he and Elijah showed up with breakfast, he avoided looking at Alistair too ponderously. But Alistair saw it in his face, and he knew it showed in his own: their happiness, their looming grief. Once and never again.

The three of them passed the day in awful stillness. The hours were cruel in their insistence on passing. Noon became one, one became three, five became eight, and then there was nothing left to do but for Elijah to put on his two pairs of black briefs and Alistair's heterosexually loose chinos. He slipped the recorder into his pocket. He took a surreptitious-seeming photograph of Alistair sitting on the hotel bed. All day both men had edged around the fact that they would never see Alistair again. But now Elijah put his hands on Alistair's shoulders and looked him in the face.

"I don't see why I should," he said, "but I'm going to miss you very much." He kissed Alistair's forehead and walked out.

Mark lingered, but his parting from Alistair wasn't any more momentous. They kissed once, briefly. They collected each other's scents and the sight of each other's faces. The more Alistair looked into Mark's eyes the more he understood that Mark refused, deep down, to accept that this was the end. He refused, as he backed out of the doorway, to say goodbye at all. And though Alistair himself accepted that this really was the end he couldn't bring himself to say goodbye either.

He listened as the elevator dinged in the hallway and its doors opened and shut. He sat at the desk, brought up his windows, put in his headphones, and waited.

———————

In all the frenzy of the preceding days Mark hadn't stopped to imagine what Jay's party would look like, and now, entering Howie's penthouse a little after nine, he was glad he hadn't. Elijah, next to him, registered his shock and avoided his gaze. This was the madness he'd spent all summer bringing to life.

The overhead lights were dim, and along the floor strings of red LED bulbs shone strangely, spreading their glow upward, as if the room were bounded on all sides by a low fire. The music, incomprehensible electropop, thundered.

Covering almost every inch of wall were screens playing Jay's videos, an overwhelming assemblage of delicate faces and limber bodies, all hauntingly beautiful, falling and swaying, kneeling and crawling, following Mark's eyes with their own.

Then there were the flesh-and-blood guests themselves. So far there appeared to be about a hundred of them, spread throughout the room, bunched in small groups, queuing haphazardly at the food tables and bars, moving their heads to the music, many topped by red hats. They ranged wildly, just as Elijah had told him, in age and attractiveness. Most were men whom, if Mark had passed them on the street, he would hardly have deigned to notice. He saw few freaks, few bizarros or eccentrics, only members of the unremarkable anonymous middle, an accountant here and a lawyer there, an IT specialist here and a grad student there, which fact only quickened his dread. He'd assumed the kinds of people who'd come to such a party, who'd wear such a hat, were radically other, easily discernible and largely absent from the world he moved in. But they'd been there the whole time, assimilated and invisible. They were his people.

He and Elijah edged along the room, toward the nearest bar, keeping their heads down. Elijah pointed out a hatless man angling to penetrate a cluster and identified him as the writer from the *Grift*. They spotted Howie across the room, posing for a photograph with a slender boy in white briefs, his hand around the boy's shoulders, his fingers stroking his collarbone. But they saw no sign of Jay, and they saw no sign of the man they'd come for, until at last Elijah elbowed Mark and nodded. "There," he said, "by the windows."

The strange thing about Herve, Mark saw when he located him, was that he seemed like nothing if not a kindred spirit. He stood by the door to the terrace, staring out at the city ruefully, apparently as disdainful of the crowd and lights and music as Mark himself was. In his square tan blazer and shapeless light jeans he looked like an earlier, clumsier draft of his brother: larger, rougher, uglier, with buzzed gray hair and abraded dry skin. He glanced back at the party, his eyes alert. Every movement of his head was slow and cumbersome, as if his body were made of something extraordinarily heavy, or as if he were simply, improbably, shy.

Elijah caught Mark's attention and patted his pocket. "I'll go connect this," he said.

Mark watched him slink away. He remained shocked by Elijah's courage, and he was sorry to be shocked. He was sorry he'd never seen these reserves of strength in Elijah before, and he was sorry for whatever he'd done, in their years together, to keep them from surfacing. He followed him until he disappeared into the crowd.

He stayed by the bar, standing stiffly, avoiding the sometimes lecherous and more often stunned gazes of the men around him—he kept forgetting what he looked like. After a minute he sensed someone approaching.

"Christ," Jay said. He wore a MAGA hat and held his vape in the air. He gestured at Mark's face. "I love it. What happened? Did Elijah finally stand up for himself?"

"Leave me alone," Mark said.

Jay looked around. "Where is he? Or did you come by yourself? Your curiosity got the best of you."

"I hate you and everything you stand for," Mark said.

Jay sucked on his vape and shook his head reproachfully. "I don't stand for anything."

"Fuck you."

"Thank you for coming."

The minutes passed, outside the night grew darker, along the floor the red lights shone more brightly. The guests were getting drunker, their clusters tighter, their stares hungrier. Given what Elijah had told him about Jay's previous gatherings Mark had a sense of where this one might be headed. Herve remained stationed by the terrace door, turning occasionally, ever alert.

Elijah reappeared. "If I don't do it now," he said, "I never will."

Mark stared at him. He had a sudden instinct to call the whole thing off and spirit Elijah away. But Elijah turned and Mark let him go. He watched him weave through the crowd, toward the terrace door. He watched him approach Herve and speak into his ear, and he watched as they stepped along the perimeter of the room and down the hallway, toward the guest bathroom.

He darted through the crowd, snapped his photo of Elijah and Herve, and assumed his position by the bathroom door. Now that he'd moved farther into the room he smelled more distinctly the ambient sweat, sensed more fully the multiplying lust, felt more deeply the music in his chest: a rapacious rhythm pulsing, rising and quickening, climbing toward a hideous pinnacle. As he stood against the wall and readied his hand on his phone he felt certain they'd made a terrible mistake.

———

Like every room in Howie's penthouse the guest bathroom was capacious, large enough for Elijah and Herve to stand a good six feet apart. But as soon as Elijah entered and put his back to the sink Herve came toward him and stood close enough for Elijah to smell his rank breath. He tried to scatter his fear by telling himself this was an advantage: the audio on the recorder would be crisp. But his fear was instantaneous. It was complete.

"Here we are again," he managed to say. "Another interrogation."

"I have no questions," Herve said. "You're the one who has something to say. You tell me you have news."

Herve spoke as measuredly as he always did, but Elijah could see in his gaze the frustration, the desperation, the near insanity that had been building in him for weeks. After two useless months this useless person had thrown him a bone, and he was hungry.

Elijah began speaking his lines. He was surprised by the equanimity of his voice, the steadiness of his breathing. Everything about his actions over the past six days astonished him. He told Herve he'd seen Alistair. He took out his phone and showed him the photographic proof. He told him about his three conditions, and he stated the first.

"Hurt him?" Herve said expressionlessly. "I only want to talk."

Elijah nodded and swallowed.

"So," Herve said. "Talk."

Elijah told him his second condition, and here he really astonished himself. He played his monstrous role winningly. He was able to speak conspiratorially, even flirtatiously. He was able to pretend to find Herve's evil electrifying and to be in any case too desperate to care. Everything he hated about himself— his hollowness, his perversity—came to his aid. "Tell me everything," he said to Herve. "Tell me what they did. Tell me what you're doing. I'll lead you to him, but first I want to know."

Herve moved a step backward. He seemed confused by Elijah's words, and perhaps newly curious about him, newly impressed. But after a moment his frustration returned. "Why do you care?" he said. "What do you want, money? Name a number. Go as high as you want."

"I don't want just money," Elijah said. "I want a new life."

Herve became visibly more confused, and more frustrated. His face reddened and his jaw tensed.

"You told me to want something bigger," Elijah said. "You told me to do something that'll really shake the world. You've seen me flailing all summer, you've seen my hopelessness. You told me hopeless people make the best workers. So here I am. Put me to work." He smiled. "Make me your vessel."

"What did he tell you?" Herve said.

"Nothing," Elijah said. "And not for lack of my asking. But I get the sense he saw something he didn't like. Something that disagreed with his morals. He thinks he's ambitious, he thinks he'll do whatever it takes. But he's weak."

"And you're not?"

Elijah shrugged. "I have no morals to disagree with," he said. "I'd say that's a kind of strength."

Herve narrowed his eyes. "What use could I possibly put you to?"

"You said there's always work in making things look appealing," Elijah said. "I can certainly do that. I can do anything you want me to. What use did you see in Nikolai? He's a drunk. What use did you see in Alistair? He's a kid. You said it yourself. You like hopeless people. You like to take them under your wing and you like to own them. I'm just as hopeless as they are, but the difference is I don't mind being owned. I crave it."

Herve shook his head. "You don't know what you're saying. Let's make this much simpler. Name a number, show me to the boy. If you name a high enough number, you'll never have to work at all."

"I tried that for a while," Elijah said. "I'm ready for something else. All I'm asking is that you let me in. Tell me everything, and I'll take you to him. That sounds pretty simple to me."

Herve had moved closer again, and his breathing had quickened. If he'd been impressed by Elijah before, even aroused, he was now only angry. That this gnat of a person had any leverage over him seemed to strike him as a great injustice. "Bring me to Mr. McCabe now, and I'll tell you whatever you want."

"Other way around," Elijah said. "Or I can just leave."

Herve stared at him for what seemed like a full minute, and in the intervening silence the music from the party drifted into the room. The only thought for Elijah to hold on to was the image of Mark standing on the other side of the wall, waiting for any sign, ready to protect him.

Finally Herve's face fell, and his mouth gathered into a contemptuous pout. Maybe he saw that bringing Elijah into his fold was a small price to pay for Alistair. Maybe he simply looked forward to spoiling this gnat's innocence. "You're leaving me little choice here," he said, "and you're going to regret it."

"I can deal with regret," Elijah said. "It's all I've ever felt."

"I don't think you understand," Herve said. "Once I tell you even the smallest thing, you're done. You're with me. Whatever your life was before, it's over."

For a moment Elijah's performance collided with his reality, and he answered in perfect truthfulness. "That day can't come soon enough."

Herve fell silent again, moving his eyes over Elijah's face. In his anger were flickers of mistrust, paranoia, maybe even anticipation of hurt. "Phone," he said.

Elijah handed it over and Herve promptly chucked it in the toilet.

"Arms up," Herve said. He ran his hands roughly over Elijah's torso, down his arms, along his sides. He knelt and felt his thighs, his calves, his shins—everywhere but the spot Alistair had said he'd avoid. Elijah bent forward ever so slightly to keep his groin away from Herve's hands, but he held still enough to keep the recorder in place.

When Herve was finished he stood straight and looked at Elijah with strange relief. Alistair had told Elijah that at bottom Herve was a little boy, lonely and scared, that he lived in a world of many enemies and few friends, and now Elijah saw that he was right. Herve had procured himself a new friend, he'd bought himself a new toy, he was greatly looking forward to playing with it. "You really sure?" he said.

"I'm sure," Elijah said. And now his fear, curiously in abeyance during his performance, returned.

"Let's make sure you're really sure," Herve said.

Elijah felt his body go cold.

"You'll see things," Herve said. "You'll do things. And if you ever betray me, if you ever run your mouth, you'll end up just like them."

Elijah's lips parted. "Them?"

Herve stared at Elijah with brightening eyes and gave a final, terrible shrug. "That's when Alistair decided to run," he said. "Someone tried to blackmail me. I don't like threats. No one does, and I did what any self-respecting person would do. If you ever try to take advantage of me, you'll end up exactly where he did."

The cold was spreading through Elijah's chest, down his limbs. "And where is that?"

"In the woods," Herve said. "In a very deep sleep."

All Elijah could do was keep his face still. He was sure Alistair had enough now, but he remained pinned against the sink, behind a locked door. He shifted his body and shuffled his feet, desperate to escape.

"It would have ended there," Herve said, "and I would have been happy to end it there. But Nikolai and Alistair made a mistake. They'd made a mess, I'd cleaned it up for them, and then they made another mess. They got scared, and they abandoned me. As if I could let that happen. As if I could let them rat me out for cleaning up a mess they'd made. As if I could let them destroy everything because of some little blackmailer nobody. I'm sorry to say it, Elijah, but the truth is I don't just want to talk to Alistair. Talking is exactly what I can't let him do."

It occurred to Elijah, incredibly, amid his terror, that he could record Herve not only confessing to a murder but premeditating another one. "Will you take him to the woods too?" he said.

"Oh no," Herve said. "He'd pose too much of an inconvenience, even asleep in the woods. For him we'll have to do what we did for Nikolai. We'll have to go to the farm."

Elijah shifted, leaning as far back as he could. "Farm?"

Herve nodded, and as he began to explain about Nikolai an unmistakable sadness came into his voice. "We had a tail on Alistair's mother's house," he said. "Watched her every move. Even went in once. Nothing. My men said there was no point in sticking around. But I had a sense. I knew Nikolai loved that boy. We switched out the car and set up on the street behind the house. Night of the Fourth, my men see who else but Nikolai scampering across the backyard. Probably scared the kid's mother half to death. He comes out of the house an hour later, empty-handed, just like us. My men followed him for a while, let him drive for a bit, enjoy the night. They forced him off the road somewhere in the country. Brought him down to Pennsylvania. An associate of mine has a farm there. Cows, chickens, pigs. You know the really interesting thing about pigs?"

Elijah's voice, thin and high-pitched, seemed to come from far away. "Pigs?"

"They eat everything," Herve said. "Even the bones."

Elijah could only stare.

"Still sure?" Herve said. "I hope you're sure."

Elijah felt the edge of the sink digging into his back. He shifted and the pain increased. For a moment the only sound was the music from the party. The script had vanished from his mind. "I'll bring you to him," he said. "Tomorrow."

Herve shook his head calmly. "Now."

Elijah tried to remember the next part of the script, the third condition. But his mind was a void. He shifted again. "There's something else," he said.

"There's nothing else," Herve said. "You don't make demands anymore. You wanted in, you got what you wanted. Now bring me to him."

In his panic Elijah relented. "OK," he said. He knew Alistair was listening, he knew he had what he needed, he only hoped he had time enough to flee. "Let's go."

Herve edged backward, and Elijah pushed himself off the sink. As soon as he took his first step he felt it. Amid his fruitless, desperate shifting the recorder had slipped out of place. Before he could even reach for his groin he felt it fall, and Alistair's loose chinos left it a wide path. He heard it clatter, horribly, on the floor.

Herve looked down. There was no mistaking this object. There were the little speakers, there was the screen, with sliver-wide volume bars waiting for sound. Very slowly Herve crouched down, took the recorder from the floor, and, after fumbling for a moment, turned it off. Very slowly he laid it next to Elijah on the sink. Very slowly he raised his eyes to Elijah's face. And then very quickly he was upon him. He put his hand around Elijah's neck.

"What is this, what is this, what is this," he said.

Elijah, unable to breathe, emitted useless wet sounds. At the bathroom door came a pounding. "Open up!" he heard Mark say. "Open up!"

Herve glanced at the door, turned back to Elijah, and spoke in a hiss. "Who put you up to this? Who? Tell me and I'll let you go."

Elijah squirmed. He bent his leg, braced his foot against the sink, and thrust his knee into Herve's groin. Herve shot backward, releasing his grip, and then launched forward again. He seized Elijah by the shoulders, spun him around, pushed him against the sink, and wrapped him in his arms. His strength was so great that the mere fact of it incapacitated Elijah. He spoke into Elijah's ear. "Tell me and I'll let you go. Did he put you up to this? Did he? Where is he?" When Elijah didn't answer, only sputtered and writhed, Herve returned his hand to his neck. "Where is he. Where. Tell me."

At the door Mark cried, "Open up! Open up!" He heaved three times against the wood, and the hallway stirred with muffled commotion.

Herve took his hand from Elijah's throat and clamped it onto his mouth. "You tell me where he is, I let you go. You don't tell me, I snap your fucking neck."

"Open up!" Mark yelled. "Open up! Open up!" The door handle shook wildly, and there came another heave.

Elijah tried to wriggle his arms free. He tried to push backward. But he was under a boulder. He stared into the mirror, at Herve's face and his own. His skin was turning purple. He looked down at the sink, searching the world of objects, the tiny universe of the bathroom, for anything to grab, anything to hold on to. And then he saw it. At the far edge of the counter, behind a vase, was Howie's whalebone knife. Jay had been in here, picking at his braces. Elijah could see a speck of food on the knife's point.

"You have five seconds," Herve said. "Four. Three."

"Open up!" Mark screamed, jangling the door handle and heaving. "Open up! Open up! Open up!"

At last Elijah managed to free his arm. He lunged for the knife and got it securely in hand, and in his momentary confusion Herve failed to stop him. Elijah delayed for only half a second, in a mad search for available flesh, but this was all the delay Herve needed. He grabbed Elijah's hand in his.

Herve tried to shake the knife from Elijah's fingers. He tried to get purchase on the handle. He pushed Elijah's arm away from their bodies, and every time Elijah pulled it back. They kept at this for a while, grunting and grimacing, pushing and pulling, ever more forcefully. After a few moments, as Elijah yanked the knife back again, Herve, either in error or cynical resignation, let it land where, however unintentionally, it was aimed. With his hand around Elijah's hand he guided the blade into Elijah's stomach. And then he relented.

"That was stupid of you," Herve said, backing away. "That was very stupid."

At first Elijah felt nothing, or nothing bodily, nothing beyond a dawning horror. His hand was still on the whalebone handle, his pinky finger flush against his stomach. When he tried to stand straight the pain hit. He turned around, staggered for a moment, and then collapsed to the floor against the sink. The pain was coming now, in quicker and quicker waves that seemed oddly to originate from two places, as if there were two wounds, one very small, concentrated around a few cubic inches of his abdomen, and the other very large, body-wide and free-floating.

Herve looked at his hands. They were clean but he wiped them on his shirt anyway. "You did this to yourself," he said. "You did this to yourself."

The only thought Elijah was capable of was a banal one: he knew it was a mistake to take out the knife. After that he had few more. His vision narrowed. The sounds around him retreated. Time dilated and dilated until it lost any dimensional value. The small pain and the large pain were now merging inside him. Stomach was now body, stomach was now world, and world was getting very small.

Among the last things he saw was Herve, hilariously, gauging the escape potential of the terrace-facing window.

There came a great sound, from many miles away. This was the door being forced open. It was happening in a film, the kind Elijah had always liked: no narrative, little dialogue, all images.

The motion of many bodies brought him briefly to alertness. He observed men in red hats approaching Herve and tackling him. He saw, with amusement, that Jay's acolytes were not so consumed in their pleasures, so committed to their perversities, as not to meet a great human moment. And then he descended again.

Time stretched and warped. All became past. Every second already a history as it happened.

Someone was shouting his name. It sounded like Jay, but it couldn't be him. He hadn't seen Jay in years.

There was something hard against his head. The floor had come up to meet him. There was something wet on his hands and arm.

People around him were saying things, in a language he'd once understood, a very long time ago.

The pain was now without edges, without beginning, without end. He had no body. He was only a particulate of the pain.

Something was close to him. It was saying something to him. It was touching the part of the pain that was him.

He wanted to leave this room. But there was only this room. He'd been born in it, and there was no outside.

The thing close to him was lovely, warm and soft. Even as all else retreated it remained near.

More voices, more shuffling, more echoes of the long time ago.

The thing close to him was insisting on something. It was bringing him back, across the years, to the present. He didn't want to go. He had the strength only for one more moment of clarity, and he was reluctant to squander it. But the thing insisted, and so he journeyed back, and, oh, was it worth it. What a miracle that face was. His favorite miracle, in a world full of them.

But why, he wanted to ask Mark, are you crying?

PART SIX

LOST OBJECT

MAURA ARRIVED AT the restaurant an hour early. She told herself she was only scouting for a good table, and perhaps gathering her energy for the meal ahead, but she'd never been very good at lying to herself. The real reason was that she could think of nothing else to do. Her trip to New York City had been a wash. She'd come with ambitions of being a good tourist, of treating herself, of crisscrossing the city and stopping in at stores and museums, unencumbered at last by the pinched frugality she'd known all her life. But she had little interest in sightseeing, in shopping, in pleasure-seeking, in enjoying her new money and free time. Even now that she was a millionaire, even now that she'd quit her job, her desires remained terribly narrow. There was one thing she wanted, but she couldn't have it, not in a way that felt workable, and she could think of nothing else to want. She was even beginning to wonder, a year into her new life, if *that* was something she wanted, or should want, anymore.

She found a seat at the bar. The restaurant was a cavernous self-described New American place near Columbus Circle, and at so early an hour it was almost empty. She scanned the drinks menu, looking instinctively at the prices. Decades before, Sean had told her his strategy for ordering wine on the cheap. Always go with the second-least expensive, he'd said. That was the best way to respect your budget and yourself at the same time. When the bartender approached she cheated and ordered the rosé, the only one listed.

At the far end of the bar was a handsome man who looked to be her age. He wore a white dress shirt with a lavender tie and Oxford shoes with wooden soles. He held a drink in one hand and his phone in the other, consumed by whatever he was reading. Maura tried to imagine his life, the office he'd just left, the home he'd soon return to. She stumbled; she had few referents, few points of comparison. Yet she tried to imagine it nonetheless. That was one definite change she'd undergone over the past year. In Binghamton she knew only her former coworkers and her few friends, and she hardly ever left the city. In all her life she'd seen maybe ten thousand faces and come to know maybe a few hundred of them. But she was ever more curious about the people outside the sixty square miles that made up her world: people like this man, whoever he was, people like the person she was soon to meet for the first time. And yet she couldn't help feeling, however wrongly, that her curiosity constituted a betrayal.

She checked the time. Tomorrow morning she would leave New York and return to Binghamton, to Carey Street. But her relief at this thought only worsened her mood. As if going home would solve her dilemma. As if home offered her anything that this alien city withheld. She wasn't young—she was painfully aware of this—but she was too young to have nothing to live for.

She sipped her wine. What to do? What to do with her love?

After a while she felt a presence behind her and a hand on her shoulder. She swiveled on her stool and, in her loneliness, hugged him tightly.

"It's good to see you," Mark said.

And it was good to see him. Over the past year, the longest Maura had ever lived through, Mark had come to Carey Street semiregularly. He'd spent Thanksgiving with her, he'd come for Christmas, he'd come for Easter. But it had been a while since his last visit, which in truth Maura was grateful for. Four months earlier, at the end of April, she'd gone somewhere, done a little thing, and she'd made a promise not to tell Mark about it, and she wouldn't have wanted to tell him about it anyway. It was on this trip that she'd gotten a long-deferred taste of what she wanted, and it was on this trip that she'd seen its unworkability.

Mark led her into the dining area. "He'll be here soon," he said.

They found a spot by the windows facing Broadway and collected menus from the waiter. They said little, and they didn't have to. The reason for Maura's visit was practically sitting at the table with them. Officially she'd come to New York to mark the start of Herve Gallion's trial. The full proceedings would take years, but it wasn't looking good for him, and he was almost certain to spend the rest of his life in prison. Trials were also underway or in the offing for some three dozen other individuals: the men Herve had hired to organize his army; some, though not very many, of the foot soldiers they'd brought on; a few lackeys in the vein of the ones who'd surveilled Maura's house and whom Herve had sicced on Andy McCurdy and Nikolai Daskalov. Herve's project had imploded, and the worst of his people had been brought to justice: at long last that story was over. But in November it had become subsumed under another story, a larger one of which it was only one ugly part, and no one could be sure when that other story would end. Every time Maura read the news she felt it would go on forever.

"Enjoying your trip?" Mark asked.

"I'm not sure this city is for me," Maura said.

"Are you still thinking of moving somewhere?"

She reached for her glass. "I think that might be one of those things that you think about and think about and that never ends up happening."

"I'm familiar," Mark said.

He looked no different than he had the last time he'd visited. Maybe a little thinner, maybe a little tanner, but still lost behind the eyes, still wondering, still hoping against all hope. He wouldn't let himself be happy, wouldn't let himself settle into his new life, wouldn't—as Maura feared she herself might—commit that betrayal. She found it harder and harder to watch him suffer, and now, as she stared at him, she felt the renegade thought, the one she'd been working to keep at bay, asserting itself. She glanced at her purse. She sipped her wine.

A minute later Mark glanced up. "He's here," he said.

Maura had seen pictures of this person, she knew him to be handsome, but in her mind he'd accrued a kind of celebrity, and as he entered the restaurant she struggled to take him in all at once. He had marvelous dark hair, lovely brown eyes, and a radiant smile. He was wearing svelte black jeans and a burgundy polo on whose hem Maura noticed smudges of chalk.

"Finally," he said to her. His handshake was affectingly girlish.

"Hello, Elijah," Mark said.

"Hello, Mark."

As he sat Elijah noticed the chalk on his shirt and brushed at it. "They put me in this ancient, *ancient* classroom," he said.

"How are the students?" Mark asked.

"Summer session is for slackers and overachievers," Elijah said. "I'll let you guess which ones I relate to." He turned to Maura. "I feel like I should introduce myself, but I also feel like Mark has told you everything."

Maura smiled. "You're a fascinating topic."

"Oh no," Elijah said. "My old favorite word."

Maura did know a fair amount about Elijah, though Mark's updates on him had grown progressively sparser and lighter on details. Following the events of the previous summer, they'd made a second attempt at coupledom, but after two months they'd run into their old problems. Mark loved Elijah, but he still loved someone else, even if he couldn't have him, and Elijah, though he understood this and respected it, had lost some of his interest in pleading for Mark's affection, and in the end he'd been the one to break it off. Something had happened to him, he'd explained to Mark, though he found it hard to say exactly what. At some point between being nearly killed and leaving the hospital weeks later—the knife had penetrated his intestines and he'd developed severe sepsis—he'd stopped feeling that he needed others to give him his worth. He'd discovered that he could care about Mark without being the object of his devotion. He loved Mark, always had and always would, but he didn't need to be his boyfriend. And with that each man had gone his way, and they talked, Maura gathered, only occasionally.

The events of that night had turned out to have a small upside. The ensuing media coverage had briefly put Elijah, and to a lesser extent Mark, in the spotlight. They'd soon found themselves besieged by messages from old high school and college friends, and these renewed contacts turned out to be helpful when, come fall, the men had to contend with their dwindling finances.

Through a former Hamilton classmate Mark had found a job as a copy editor at an investment research firm with offices in Midtown. By his own description the work was numbing and ethically dubious: he wasn't sure how he felt about spell-checking prospectuses about drilling opportunities in the warming Arctic. But the position paid decently, surprisingly so, and it kept him in a comfortable studio in Prospect Heights, and since he was able to work from home, and since he could easily pretend that twenty hours of work had taken him forty, he had many mornings and sometimes whole weekdays free to make progress on the novel that he was writing and that he refused to tell Maura anything about. He also liked that the job brought him into contact, even glancingly, with Alistair's world, though he could see why Alistair had decided that world wasn't for him. And yet when it came to the occasional unsavoriness of the work Mark put up little resistance: he had no interest in perpetuating the fiction of his purity. He'd come to believe that there was no way to earn or spend money without somehow partaking of harm. As long as money remained the currency of human relations, and as long as it was able to pool in few hands and drain from many others, it would always implicate anyone who touched it in its cruelty. He had his family to thank for this lesson.

Mark could count on one hand the number of times he'd spoken to his family since last July. He'd learned, he'd told Maura, that his father had eventually sold his company for $30 million (Maura struggled to wrap her mind around the fact that this was perceived as a "humiliating" figure), and he'd learned that his brother, Eddie, had done ninety days in rehab. But beyond collecting these few updates he made no effort to talk to them. He loved them, he'd told them, always had and always would, but, to adapt Elijah's logic, he didn't need to be part of their lives.

Elijah had found a job substitute-teaching studio art at a magnet high school in Queens. He had no credentials, and his administrative observers didn't love his freewheeling pedagogic approach, but the students liked him so much that the school had been all but forced to bring him on full-time. He had no desire to make it a career, he claimed, though it was preferable to graphic design— he wouldn't be making anything even resembling art ever again. Eventually, though, he'd have to find something else. The kids, he explained now, after the three of them had ordered, drove him up a wall.

"Summer session has become the boob session," he said. "Lot of boobs, lot of butts, altogether just a lot of *down there*. They've discovered that you can paint porn and call it a nude and be 'classical.'"

"Are they wrong?" Mark asked.

"I try to make it a lesson in proportion," Elijah said. "Why is the man's penis longer than his leg? Why is the woman's breast three times the size of her head? But they've also learned about expressionism, so they have an answer to that." He sighed. The more he tried to force his students' hands, he told Mark and Maura, the more he felt it was futile, even counterproductive. If he'd learned anything in his life—and he'd learned almost nothing—it was that you had to let people make their mistakes. All you could do was hope they learned from them and be there for them whether they did or not. He'd teach one more year at the most, he said. If he had to critique another "nude" with a four-foot-long phallus he didn't know what he'd do. But the more he talked about his students the more it became obvious to Maura that he loved them, loved teaching, was possibly never more at home than in a room of sixteen-year-olds, had found his calling.

"Isaac doesn't do summer session," Elijah said, "so he's living vicariously through me."

"Isaac is Elijah's new boyfriend," Mark explained.

Elijah looked at Mark and smiled carefully. "Six months may not be eight years," he said, "but I wouldn't call him new."

"He teaches history at the same school."

"And he's teaching *me*," Elijah said. "He has me *reading*. I'll give that to you, Mark. You took me as I was. Never tried to change me."

"What's there to change?"

"Well, Isaac is continually amazed by the amount of things I don't know," Elijah said. "Which admittedly is a lot. And he doesn't buy my defense, which is that I lived history. I had a front-row seat to it."

Maura turned her gaze out the window. While she was ostensibly here in recognition of Herve's trial she'd been hoping to avoid mention of that topic, and she'd been hoping to avoid politics in general. But in the summer of 2017 that was tantamount to avoiding the weather. Last August, after details about Herve's project had become public, Maura had hoped that the news would be a nail in the coffin for Trump's campaign. No sane person could read about what Herve had been planning and not conclude that under Trump there would be more Herves, more foot soldiers, and that they would grow more numerous and more emboldened. But Trump, in his moronic genius, had weathered the controversy capably. He'd disavowed Herve and his operation. He'd said that he, unlike his opponent, couldn't be bought by "special-interest billionaires." And though the investigation into Herve and his project continued to generate headlines it very soon had to compete with other headlines, other campaign controversies, other Trumpian shocks. The man's genius, Maura felt, lay in the calculated chaos with which he buried one bad news day under another. And the sorry fact was that while there were many sane people there seemed, every day, to be more and more who were not. When Election Day rolled around, in November, Maura was less surprised by the result than most. And the only person who could have comforted her was gone, and all he'd left her was a pile of money.

Maura had mixed feelings about the million Alistair had set aside for her, just as he had mixed feelings about the million he'd set aside for himself. But Maura suspected that the recipient of the third million Nikolai had given Alistair was altogether content with her good fortune. Last summer, after Alistair had left, Maura had followed the instructions he'd laid out. She'd called the offshore bank, transferred the money to a domestic account, hired a lawyer to put half of her two million into a trust, and then asked the lawyer to notify its beneficiary: the girlfriend of Andy McCurdy, one Amber Osgood, of Whitney Point, New York. Maura knew nothing about this woman or how she was spending her money, and she didn't care to. All she knew, because Alistair had told her, was that she had a baby son. And over the past year it had brought her small and occasional comfort to imagine Amber and her newly broadened horizons. Amber didn't have Andy anymore, but she had her son, and she had a whole lifetime of that romance ahead of her.

For Maura that romance was now over. Alistair was never coming back, even if, as she'd told him when she'd visited him in late April, he risked nothing by returning. The FBI agent Maura had met with at the Bureau's outpost in Binghamton had stated the case plainly enough. *If he materializes, we'll have to question him*, he'd said. *But he helped us greatly. He did his country a service. We're certainly not going to go looking for him.* But Alistair wasn't staying away for fear of arrest. He'd made a mess of his life, he'd told Maura in April, he felt he'd ruined it before it had even started—he remained her melodramatic son. The things he'd been fixated on repulsed him now, and until he figured out what to make of himself next he wanted to remove himself from reminders of the person he no longer wanted to be, from the rapacity and ambition he no longer wanted to be prisoner to, and from the country that fostered these things with special insistence. And he was tired of burdening her. She'd lived her whole life for him and it was time she started living it for herself. He loved her too much to love her in the consuming way he always had, and to let her love him in the consuming way she'd always loved him. It wasn't until Maura boarded the plane home that she realized she'd been effectively broken up with.

When their meals arrived Mark returned to the subject of Elijah's teaching. "I see why the kids love you," he said.

"Because I let them paint erotica?"

"Because you don't make judgments. You're open-minded. That's the great thing about you."

Elijah raised his eyebrows. "Based on my experiences last summer," he said, "I think I can be a little *too* open-minded."

"The opposite is no better."

Elijah smiled impishly. "On that note, though," he said, "there is some news. If you're interested."

Mark looked at him warily. "What has he done now?"

Elijah's smile widened. "An article about him came out last week. In the *Grift*, by that same guy. 'The MAGA Maverick, One Year Later.' I couldn't bring myself to read it, but Isaac gave me the gist. Apparently Jay has done a one-eighty. He's posing as this die-hard anti-Trump crusader now. I checked his Twitter, and it's true. He has a 'resist' hashtag in his bio. And a Venmo link: 'Help me stop Trump!' I guess maybe he's trying to make a career out of it, though as far as I know he's still back in Richmond, working at the cidery."

Mark's face had paled. "He'll do anything."

"Is it possible he's sincere?" Maura asked.

"Literally neurologically impossible," Elijah said. And yet his expression shone with kindness. "I hope I never hear from him again, truly. But I can't help it. It makes me laugh. He's still himself, always will be. He's right back at it, the old chameleon. He's so sick, so sad, so hollow, but I love him. I just do."

"What about Howie?" Mark asked.

"Last I heard he moved to Miami," Elijah said. "Now that Herve's assets are frozen I think he had to sell the penthouse."

"How terrible," Mark said.

When the waiter collected their plates and returned with the bill Maura took it from him. She enjoyed the little fight she had with Mark and Elijah about the check, she enjoyed signing her name and treating them, her boys, and she felt again the shade of betrayal in her enjoyment.

Afterward they stood on the sidewalk, shielding their eyes from the sun. Elijah hugged Maura and Mark goodbye.

"I hope Alistair doesn't feel too bad about me getting stabbed," he said to Maura.

"I'm sure he does," Maura said. "And I'm sure he knows you're not mad."

"And I do appreciate that he came to the hospital that night, even if I wasn't conscious."

"In his hat and sunglasses and everything," Mark said. "Interrogating the doctors, making sure you'd live." He looked at the ground. "And then off again."

"Please let me know when you're in the city again," Elijah said.

"That could be a while," Maura said. "But you're always welcome in Binghamton."

"You know," Elijah said, "the way Alistair talked about Binghamton sometimes reminded me of the way I talked about Mark. This thing you hate because you can't stop loving it, no matter how hard you try."

Mark stared at Elijah and gave him a smile—a private smile—and then they parted ways.

Maura and Mark walked south for a while before turning west toward the river. From behind her sunglasses Maura studied her fellow pedestrians. Every block added another hundred faces to her repository, fed in great big spoonfuls her building curiosity. After tomorrow she didn't know when she'd see Mark again, and her renegade thought persisted. What was the point anymore? What was the harm in breaking her promise? She could see only one way of easing Mark's loneliness, only one way of easing Alistair's, only one way of forcing herself to move on. Alistair longed for Mark, as much as he tried to forget about him. He'd made Maura promise not to tell Mark where he was because he refused to let him give up his life for him, just as he refused to let Maura do the same. But Alistair's longing for Mark, Maura felt, was deeper than his longing for her. He was a man now, and he wanted his man, not his mother. Their romance had ended, and she could think of only one way to make its conclusion definite.

As they crossed Eleventh Avenue Mark pointed to a tower with a facade of brick red and cream. "That's where Nikolai lived," he said. "I actually thought about going to Bulgaria for the funeral. But I couldn't face it. Not even a body to bury."

"Understandable," Maura said.

"I bet Alistair misses him."

"I'm sure," Maura said. She knew, in fact, that he did, very much.

When they reached the river they sat on a bench, a few blocks south of the *Intrepid*.

"Apparently this is where Alistair and Elijah hashed out their plan," Mark said. He gestured back in the direction of Nikolai's building. "I've been scouting settings."

"For what?"

Mark turned up one corner of his mouth. "You must know what my book is about," he said. He opened his hands. "I'm writing this."

Maura looked toward the river. She had other things on her mind. It was getting late, the sun was setting, she was running out of time. She reached into her purse and took out the photograph she carried with her always. She'd gone through the trouble of having it printed; she liked to touch its surface. And now she handed it to Mark.

"There he is," she said.

Alistair, insistent that no one find out where he was, had let her photograph him only from afar. But he was easily distinguishable, the only blond boy on the beach. There he was: in a white T-shirt and blue shorts, facing the water, hands on his waist. Maura knew the landscape beyond him was unmistakable. She knew this was mostly all Mark would need, and she knew it was mostly all she would give him.

"You can keep it," she said. "I have copies."

Mark stared at the photograph dumbfoundedly.

"I went in April," she said. "We broached the idea of my moving there. But we knew it wouldn't work. I figure I'll go once a year."

Mark turned her way and searched her eyes. "Does he know you're showing this to me?"

"No," Maura said. "And he'd be very angry. And I don't care."

"He doesn't want me to come," Mark said. "If he did he would have contacted me."

"He doesn't know what he wants," Maura said. "None of us do." She put her hands in her lap. "I'll tell you two more things. I'll go only so far in breaking my promise."

Mark listened.

"He goes to the beach almost every day at sunset," Maura said. "And he takes the same street there every time, the one he lives off of, Rua Teresa d'Ávila. He walks directly onto the beach, and then he sits."

"Almost every day," Mark said. "Rua Teresa d'Ávila."

Maura nodded.

"Are you sure you want to tell me this?"

"No," Maura said. "But I had to."

Mark walked her back to her hotel. That night she slept soundly, more deeply, somehow, than she had in many months. In the morning she picked up her car from the garage and, after surviving the scariest traffic she'd ever experienced, left the city. For a while, as she coasted through the greenery of New Jersey, she felt buoyant, newly energetic, oddly liberated. Maybe she was only happy to be out of New York. But she suspected something else, something larger and a little frightening, had begun working through her. It had begun working through her the moment she'd handed Mark the photograph.

Her mood plummeted when she saw the first sign for Binghamton. And so, with the lightest, easiest, sublimest turn of her steering wheel she decided simply not to follow it. Instead, after Stroudsburg, she stayed on route 80. According to the map on her phone this would take her west, toward Cleveland. At any point she could turn onto another road and go wherever—wherever. What else did she have to do?

For forty-seven years she'd lived in this country and had never seen it. For half her life she'd grieved for her husband and worried obsessively for her son. For decades she'd forced the vastness of her love into the pinhole of his blond face. She'd kept her house in good order, fed Alistair and taught him, tried to protect him and failed, waited for him and sheltered him, forgiven him for everything, absolutely everything, pressed every fiber of her being into her devotion to him. And now he was gone, her little boy was gone, and she had two choices. She could either let her love shrivel or she could cast it around, spread it, let it travel as far and wide as it would.

She was now on roads she'd never driven before. The cross-beamed telephone poles to her right looked like crucifixes. She had few clothes but she could buy some; she had no destinations in mind but she could pick some.

She'd do this for a few weeks, maybe a few months, maybe a year. Pay every corner of her troubled, magnificent, still very young country a visit. She wasn't worried, and she'd made her decision already.

Renounce, renounce! It was the hardest and simplest thing to do. Renounce your object, abandon your singular infatuation, give up whatever yearning blinds you to everything but its endpoint, diverts your energy away from everything but your pursuit, justifies whatever harm, whatever waste, your quest entails. Renounce, renounce, and see how your love flourishes.

She stared ahead. She was an ordinary middle-aged woman, and her possibilities were limited. But right now, as she sped west under glorious high clouds, she felt as young and naive, as hopeful and terrified, as free and foolhardy as a girl.

Mark flew to Rio de Janeiro two days later. He told his job he was sick; he packed most of his clothes. He'd stay as long as it took.

His flight landed at night—too late for scouting. He got himself a room at a hotel in Leblon. He spent most of the next day on his little balcony, in slow-burn amazement at the city's landscape. Blink and it was still there, improbable in its majesty.

In the evening he waited for four hours on the beach, just off Rua Teresa d'Ávila, and didn't see him. The next evening he had no luck either. He understood why Maura had declined to give him a phone number: she wanted to break her promise as minimally as possible, and if Mark had called beforehand Alistair might well have retreated into the shadows, as he was so good at doing. The people Alistair loved had already done so much for him, and he didn't want to cause them any more hardship. But after the second evening Mark wished he had a number. He wished Alistair understood how much of a hardship life without him had become.

He saw him the third evening. Instinctively he shuffled away on the sand and turned his body. He watched Alistair walk to the shoreline, put his feet in the water, and then retreat to the middle of the beach and sit, knees up and arms around his shins. Occasionally he looked down the beach, briefly and aimlessly. Mostly he stared at the horizon, and Mark stared with him. There was no hard place for Mark to rest his gaze, no concrete point on which to fix his attention, and he felt frustrated at first and then, eventually, serene. He didn't need to wonder what exactly Alistair was looking at. He was looking inexactly, at everything and nothing at all.

After a while he got up his courage and sauntered over. Alistair turned, stared up blankly for a moment, and then in panic looked all around.

"It's just me," Mark said.

Alistair's eyes were as blue as ever, if less radiant. He moved his mouth with mute questions.

Mark sat down next to him. "Don't be mad at her," he said. "She didn't tell me to do this. She just gave me a few hints."

Alistair looked at the water, shook his head, and looked back. "You shouldn't have come," he said.

"Let's skip all that," Mark said. "I'm here. If you don't want me to stay, I'll leave. But I'm here."

Alistair sat in silence. He watched locals and sunburnt tourists parade up and down the beach. Finally, with a slump of his shoulders, he put his cheek to his knee and peered at Mark.

"What do you do here?" Mark asked.

"I'm learning Portuguese," Alistair said. "I figure eventually I can tutor English."

"That sounds like it'll take some time."

"Good," Alistair said. "I have a lot of it."

"What should I do here?"

Alistair continued to peer at him with his cheek against his knee. "What do you want?" he said. "Why did you come?"

"I don't want anything," Mark said. "This is the only place for me to be." He saw, looking into Alistair's eyes, how lonely he was, and how needlessly.

"I guess you can come closer," Alistair said after a moment. "If you insist on being here."

Mark slid toward him, until their arms were nearly touching. "Maybe we don't have to want each other," he said. "Maybe we can just need each other."

"I'm not going back," Alistair said.

"That's fine with me."

"And I have a new name. You'll have to use it."

"You never did tell me what it was."

Alistair reached into his pocket, slid out his ID, and handed it to him.

"Sean Miller," Mark said. "Not bad."

Alistair looked toward the mountains, then back at the water. "Sean was my father's name," he said. "Nikolai picked it totally at random." He shook his head in disbelief. "That's why I chose this place. My father always wanted to come. And I guess now, in a way, he finally has."

Mark put his arm around Alistair's shoulders. "I'll call you Sean," he said. "You can be whoever you want to be and do whatever you want to do, and I will love you."

"You'll need to get a visa," Alistair said.

"I'll let you walk me through that."

"I have money but it won't last forever."

"It has a way of not doing that."

"And I'm still doing the religion stuff."

"We can have separate hobbies."

Ever so gradually the sky was darkening, taking on a deep blue that didn't so much fascinate the eye as greet it.

"It's been a long time," Alistair said.

For a moment Mark was confused, and then he laughed. "Same here."

"Maybe we should do something about that."

"Lead the way, please."

Alistair led. He took Mark by the hand and walked him inland, down Rua Teresa d'Ávila and onto a side street. In the far distance, on the other side of a lagoon, steep mountains rose. Atop one of them a brightly lit man spread his arms out over the city. But these heights held no interest for Mark right now. All he cared about was the person next to him, and all he felt was the warm refuge of his hand.

ACKNOWLEDGMENTS

THANK YOU TO my agent, Chris Clemans, and my editor, Zack Knoll, the two most perceptive readers and most supportive colleagues I could have asked for—a dream team, truly. Thank you also to Roma Panganiban at Janklow & Nesbit and to everyone at Abrams/Overlook.

I would not have written this or any book without the guidance of my teachers and advisers. Thank you especially to Joshua Furst, Kristopher Jansma, Sam Lipsyte, Ben Metcalf, Gary Shteyngart, and Darin Strauss.

Many friends offered instrumental feedback and encouragement during the writing of this book. I'm grateful to Sam Carpenter, Miles Coleman, Dana Hammer, Heather Radke, Jessi Jezewska Stevens, Jen Wellington, and, in particular, Elina Alter. Thank you also to Michael Baruch and Travis Sharp for their insights into the business-student experience.

Thank you to my family for their love and support, and for teaching me how to tell a story.

Ian Forster, my love, forever and always—thank you.

ABOUT THE AUTHOR

DANIEL LEFFERTS was born in upstate New York. He holds an MFA from Columbia University and has taught writing at Columbia and Rutgers. *Ways and Means* is his first novel.